NUECES LEGEND

ALSO BY MARK GREATHOUSE

The Frontier Chronicles

Perilous Trails

Wyoming Calls

Longhorns North

Warpath

Hunter Vs. Hunted

Freedom Drovers

The Tumbleweed Sagas

Nueces Justice

Nueces Reprise

Nueces Deceit

Nueces Blood

Nueces Grit

Nueces Truth

NUECES LEGEND

THE FINAL MISSION

THE TUMBLEWEED SAGAS
BOOK 7

MARK GREATHOUSE

WOLFPACK
PUBLISHING
— EST 2013 —

Nueces Legend: The Final Mission
Paperback Edition
Copyright © 2025 by Mark Greathouse

Wolfpack Publishing
1707 E. Diana Street
Tampa, Florida 33610

www.wolfpackpublishing.com

Paperback ISBN 979-8-89567-099-6
Ebook ISBN 979-8-89567-098-9
LCCN 2025933458

Dedicated with love to my wife, Carolyn, and to our two sons, Mike and Matt.

COMMEMORATION

August 10, 2023, marked the 200th anniversary of the founding of the Texas Rangers by Stephen F. Austin.

I created Luke Dunn, the fictional protagonist in my Tumbleweed Sagas, as the prototypical Texas Ranger. I tip my hat to the likes of my Texas Ranger ancestors: grandfather Horace Charles Greathouse, cousin Rut Evans, and cousins John Beamond "Red John" Dunn and his brother Matthew Dunn. It has been an honor to learn the stories of and incorporate in my fiction the adventures of real-life Texas Rangers like John Coffee "Jack" Hayes, Samuel H. Walker, John Salmon "RIP" Ford, Ben McCulloch, William "Bigfoot" Wallace, Leander Harvey McNelly, and so many more who fought for justice on the vast and varied landscapes that are at the very heart and soul of Texas.

There's something to be said for the old story of the mayor of a town experiencing a riot and complaining to the Texas Ranger that showed up, "They only sent one Ranger?" And the famous response, "Well, pardner, thar's only one riot ain't ther'?" One riot, one Ranger about sums them up. Courage, determination, dedication, respect, and integrity comprise the bond that has held the Texas Rangers together through thick and thin.

I do invite readers to check out Texas Ranger museums in places like Waco, Fredericksburg, San Antonio, Falfurrias, and Austin, as they bring the exploits of the famed lawmen to life.

THE NUECES STRIP

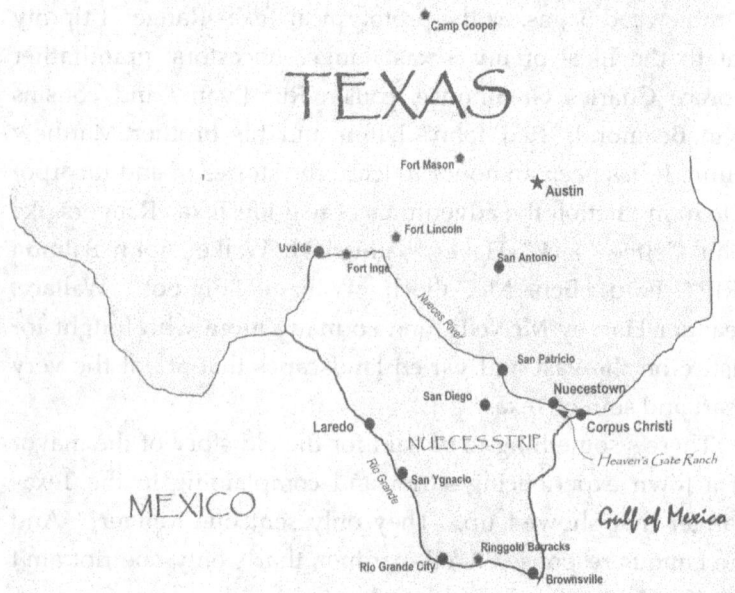

The vast Nueces Strip serves as the primary setting for the
Tumbleweed Sagas. The Strip was also called Wild Horse Desert,
owing to the millions of Mustangs that roamed its prairies. *(Sketch by
Mark Greathouse)*

NUECESTOWN

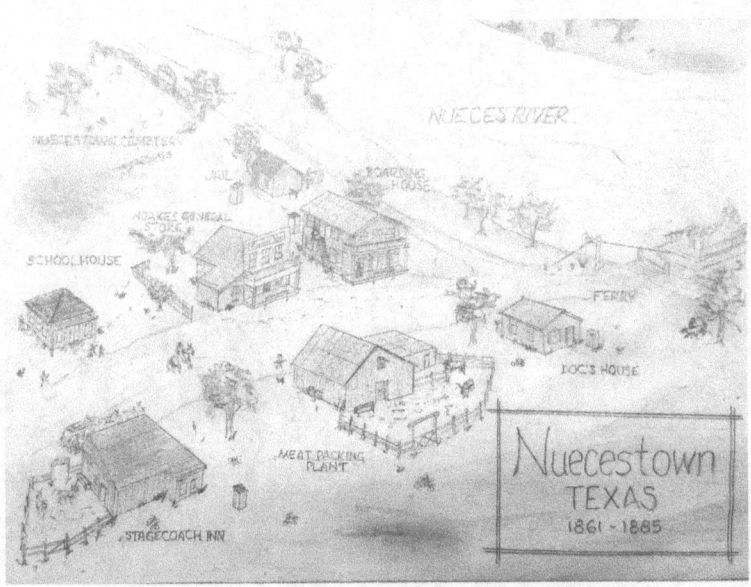

Nuecestown, Texas, established in 1852 by English and German settlers, was developed by Corpus Christi founder Colonel Henry Kinney along the Nueces River as a ferry crossing. Mostly thanks to the railroad passing it by, it's now a "ghost town" marked only by historical markers. All that remains is a preserved schoolhouse and the old Nuecestown Cemetery. *(Sketch by Mark Greathouse)*

THE CAST

Lucas "Long Luke" Dunn – *Gained notoriety as one of the greatest Texas Ranger Captains ever. Escaped Great Famine in Ireland to seek his fortune on Texas' Nueces Strip. Gained repute as Indian fighter and respected lawman. Conflicted between being lawman and rancher. Comanche called him Ghost-Who-Rides. He and Elisa are raising a large family on Heaven's Gate Ranch.*

Elisa Corrigan Dunn – *Luke Dunn's wife. Lost her family to frontier rigors, including fighting off Comanche. She and Luke build the Heaven's Gate Ranch and a life on the frontier.*

Lucas Dunn, Junior – *Junior is Luke and Elisa's youngest son, but the teen is growing up fast. He's destined to follow Luke's path.*

Sean Dunn – *Older brother to Junior and partner in his brother's schemes.*

Scarlett Rose – *Red-headed prostitute from Laredo who sought to overcome her past, including bad choices of men. Has married Walker Carson, as she begins a new life.*

William Meaney – *Former sheriff of Corpus Christi and now deputy sheriff of Nuecestown.*

Jaime Sanchez – *Works as vaquero at Luke Dunn's Heaven's Gate Ranch. Becomes valuable asset to Luke. His wife, Julia, helps Elisa with ranch chores.*

Walker Carson – *Cowboy and bungling bank robber. Became Texas Ranger and then Rebel soldier, before settling down with Scarlett Rose to run the Cacti & Boots haberdashery business.*

Edward Thorpe – *Wealthy Horatio Thorpe's heir to Magnolia Plantation. Freed his slaves during war. Rebuilds Magnolia and International shipping business after the war. Is beholden to Luke.*

Jubal Strong – *Widower cousin to the outlaw "Bad Bart" Strong whom Luke had brought to justice back in 1856 near Laredo. Jubal builds a ranch of his own.*

Jake Barber – *Earned keep helping Luke keep the peace on the Nueces Strip. Marries Cheyenne woman named Ameone and builds a business after the war.*

One Arrow – *Young Penateka Comanche Chief, protégé of Chief Three Toes and friend of Luke. Tries to understand White man ways.*

Coy Witmer – *Cutthroat who preyed on the Texas countryside during the post-reconstruction chaos and managed to avoid the long arm of the law. Said to have personally killed at least three dozen people, mostly from ambush.*

Bones Hollingsworth – *Deputy sheriff of Alice, TX, a burgeoning railhead in the heart of cattle country.*

Jesús Santos – *Mexican outlaw who schemes against Luke Dunn.*

Bull Samuels – *With his wife Martha he serves as innkeeper at the old stagecoach inn in Nuecestown.*

Randall O'Connell – *Corporal from Queen Victoria's 8th King's Royal Irish Hussars who fought in Crimean War. He knew Luke from rebellions in Ireland.*

Cassie McCully – *Lucas Jr.'s love interest. Her father owns a nearby ranch.*

Jim Bob Whitely – *Sheriff of Corpus Christi after Bill Meaney retired.*

Grant McCully – *Owns ranch near Corpus Christi. He's father to Lucas Jr.'s love interest and has business dealings with Luke Dunn.*

Judge Louis Crockett – *Eastern judge brought in by post-war Texas reconstruction government.*

HISTORICAL CHARACTERS

Governor John Ireland – *Lawyer and statesman from Seguin, Texas. He was the 18th governor of Texas from 1883 to 1887. Famous for the Fence Cutting War in which Texas Rangers would intervene to prevent folks from cutting barbed wire string across the range.*

Governor John B. Jones – *Confederate army officer, Texas Ranger Captain, and Adjutant General of Texas. As head of the Frontier Battalion, successfully fought Comanche, Kiowa, and Apache.*

Captain Sam McMurray – *Last of the notable Texas Ranger Captains of the late 1800s. Juan Nepomuceno "Cheno" Cortina Goseacochea – Mexican rancher, politician, military leader, outlaw, and folk hero who did not accept the terms of the Treaty of Guadalupe-Hidalgo and regularly fought against settlers, US soldiers, and Texas Rangers on the Nueces Strip.*

Sam Bass – *Outlaw who specialized in robbing trains and preying on stage-coaches. Killed in gunfight in 1878.*

John Wesley Hardin – *Outlaw gunfighter who killed his first man at age 15. Credited with killing between 27 and 45 people.*

John King Fisher – *Notorious rancher, murderer, rustler, and lawman who terrorized mostly South Texas up until his death by ambush in 1884.*

John Michel – *Famed as an Irish nationalist activist, author, and political journalist. He leveraged the famines to foment rebellion.*

John Beamond "Red John" Dunn – *Texas Ranger, vigilante, rancher, and museum curator involved in famous Good Friday Raid in 1875. Committed to delivering justice by any means deemed necessary.*

THEME

LEGEND

An extremely famous or notorious person, especially in a particular field or endeavor; a person who inspires legends

NUECES LEGEND

PROLOGUE

BLACKNESS. The rider, a shadowy silhouette against a pre-dawn sky, drew his coal-black horse to a halt before the entrance to Heaven's Gate Ranch. His dark beard, broad mustache, aquiline nose, and snakelike eyes gave him a sinister appearance featuring a jagged scar running from his left ear to the grim set of his mouth with its soul-shivering smile. It might be how some folks might conjure an image of the devil. Surely easy enough to visualize him slithering into his saddle. The serpent in the Garden of Eden could never hope to measure up to the poisonous blackness of Coy Witmer's eyes.

He'd traveled a long way. His mount fidgeted a bit at the interruption of their journey. "Easy," he growled. Witmer looked up at the wrought iron arch emblazoned with "Heaven's Gate." How delightfully ironic, he thought. He drew a sterling silver snuffbox from his coat pocket and took a snort. Those dark squinty eyes lit momentarily, as he stifled a sneeze and felt nearly bold enough to ride up the trail to Luke Dunn's very own house and confront the aging Texas Ranger. But that wouldn't do at all. And it couldn't be a bushwhacking. That'd count as a kill, but this was special—the crown jewel of his reputation. This demanded a mano-a-mano confrontation before an audience. He stuffed the box back into the pocket of his black leather coat. He reached into a vest pocket and reassuringly rubbed his fingers over the twenty-five grooves carved into the surface of a gold watch. He smiled ever-so-slightly. Witmer touched his spurs just enough to the horse's flanks, as he turned the steed westward toward the little railroad town of Alice. The brief stop at Heaven's Gate had been a necessary diversion for the man intent on burnishing his murderous record by taking down the legend of the Nueces Strip. He'd have to tend to a bit of business in the town named for famed rancher Richard King's daughter before he could bring his full energies to bear on killing Mr. Dunn.

ONE
A NEW MISSION

LUKE SAT on the gallery across the front of the two-story ranch house that served as the family and business centerpiece of Heaven's Gate Ranch. He gazed deep in thought as the pink-hued sky of the sunrise had begun to give way to a mostly deep azure that stretched about as far as humanly possible to see. There'd be no clouds this day to offer relief from the baking rays of the sun. He'd pretty much become one with the ranch in the years since mostly ending his lawman days gallivanting across the wide prairies of the Nueces Strip. The challenges of ranching in post-war reconstruction and the failure in Austin to adequately fund Texas Rangers had hastened his decision. In the twenty years since he'd hung up his badge, he'd covered just about every nook and cranny of his and Elisa's vast spread from where veldts of bluebonnet and Indian blanket wildflowers could be found for the occasional bouquet that he'd bring her and to the places that especially ornery longhorns might hide out. It was a good…no, a great life.

Luke's thoughts wandered back to his trials and tribulations during the War of Northern Aggression or War Between the States that had left a very heavy impact on Texas. Such was the dynamic of war and its aftermath. Luke chuckled to himself at how Texans preferred not to refer to the conflict as the Civil War. There was nothing civil about it. In any case, the frontier of Texas had become ever-more-vulnerable to predators of the human variety in the war's aftermath, and Luke Dunn had briefly assumed a key role in delivering justice until the economics of running a ranch and raising a family forced him to ease away from his lawman duties. The war hadn't faded into any sunset, as it lingered on folks' minds mentally and often physically. Now, two decades after the war, the Texas that Spanish conquistador Cabeza de Vaca had explored back from 1527 to 1536 was just beginning to truly manifest its destiny as an economic giant. The frontier was on the verge of being conquered.

It wasn't so long ago that Comanche, Caddo, and Kiowa roamed the rolling hills of Heaven's Gate. They'd all-too-briefly left their footprints on the earth, and their hands had fashioned objects that were their lifeblood but had long since been swallowed in the dust and grasses of the Nueces Strip. The breezes that blew across their lives now gently eased a tumbleweed or two past Luke's thoughtful gaze. The spaces occupied by the red man were ever more-empty of their souls. Only rudimentary pictures on buffalo hides and the White man's history books would offer remembrances.

Like the Comanche, Luke knew that he'd have to adapt to the inevitable march of civilization, of the taming of the Texas frontier. With the relentless advance of telegraph and railroads, it was little wonder that towns, ranches, and farms spread ever westward. The very heart of Texas was fast becoming an economic juggernaut, and the nascent Nueces Strip was no exception. Oil had not yet been discovered on Texas soil, and the economy was mostly based on growing cotton and raising longhorns and horses. Cotton was bundled and hauled to port for transport to markets in Louisiana and points east. Cattle were still mostly driven to Kansas and Missouri railheads to be shipped to the packing houses of the Midwest, though Corpus Christi was fast becoming a hub for the beef industry. This was all happening despite periods of drought that occasionally impacted large swaths of South Texas. During such droughts, the economic effect on those areas became quite serious, as livestock perished and settlers were often forced by economics to abandon their spreads.

Dunn recognized that despite the roughness of the frontier, the predations of savages and bandits, and a deeply divisive war with the resultant enmity of reconstruction, the factor that would ultimately win Texas would be the family; the larger the better as children struggled to grow up in the face of all manner of lurking dangers. He and Elisa had certainly contributed, as they'd brought ten children into the world. Families established the ranches and farms popping up not only throughout the eastern portions of the Nueces Strip but across Texas as a whole. Family, community, faith, and dogged determination were indeed the primary factors contributing to overcoming reconstruction and settling the Texas frontier, though romantics might be tempted to attribute the winning of the west to a gun or simply a spirit of adventure. Luke shook his head ruefully at the thought that along with settlement came the darker side of human nature: lawbreakers. Lawmen were relied upon to bring justice to the Strip with its hostile gangs and marauding savages. These threats demanded formation of larger organizations like the Texas Rangers to keep the peace.

While civilization cast its net well beyond the reaches of the Nueces Strip and measured progress in establishing ranches and towns and despite cotton and cattle, South Texas remained mostly a seemingly endless prairie of tall grasses and loamy-sands or rough brush that stretched far as the eye could see and beyond. The grasses were certainly high, often growing high enough to reach a horse's withers. Some called the Nueces Strip "Wild Horse Desert," as millions of wild horses roamed free. It reached south and west from Corpus Christi and the Nueces River all the way to the Rio Grande, its eastern boundary being the Gulf of Mexico. At its northern extreme was the little town of Uvalde near Fort Inge at the southern tip of what's called the Hill Country today. Laredo with its nearby Fort McIntosh was generally regarded as the main outpost of the western boundary of the Nueces Strip. Roads had begun to appear and the telegraph and railroads were spreading their tentacles. Roads were rough but serviceable. Bridges were mostly absent.

Mottes or small clusters of live oak or mesquite offered occasional shade relief on the sunbaked prairies of the Strip. Heaven's Gate was no exception to the roughness, the tenacity, the grit demanded by this land of promise and reward. Weather was pretty much whatever you wanted, if you cared to wait long enough. The often-dry creek beds or arroyos eventually would fill with rainwater and empty into the Nueces River and on into Nueces Bay and…farther to the east… Corpus Christi Bay. Flash flooding was an ongoing fear. Summers tended to be so hot and humid that folks simply got used to damp clingy clothes.

In his travels across southern Texas, Luke had come to appreciate the abundant flora and fauna on the Nueces Strip. Texas ash, cedar elm, persimmon, and live oak offered shade to flowers like bluebonnets, Indian blanket, primrose, and daisies. Much of that bounty of nature graced Heaven's Gate. And there was so much more. In addition to longhorns, horses, and buffalo, the Strip housed the likes of mountain lions, lynx, wolves, deer, javelinas, coyotes, prairie dogs, and armadillos. If you were on foot, it was advisable to keep an eye and ear peeled for rattlesnakes. They tended to blend in fairly-well with their surroundings, so their rattle was often folks first and only warning of an impending attack.

Luke had long ago learned of Texas' history of being forced to use violent means to gain safe footholds in the boundless wilds of its frontier. Prior to his arrival in 1855, Texas had already become a battle-hardened country though near destitute in terms of government monetary resources. Most significant fighting of the Texas War for Independence was fought on and just north of the Nueces Strip back in 1835 and 1836, and the Strip was scene to the first fighting of the Mexican American War of 1846. The region had been officially ceded to the United States by the Treaty of Guadalupe Hidalgo in 1848, though Texas had already laid claim essentially by squatter rights and having kicked Mexican General Santa Anna's sorry posterior back in 1836. Battle-hardened soil indeed. It's generally accepted that the only significant battles of the War of Northern Aggression fought on Texas soil were at Galveston Harbor and Sabine Pass, though it's notable that the final battle of the war was a short-lived Confederate victory at Palmito Ranch near Brownsville. An important Texas contribution to the war was in providing highly effective cavalry to support the Confederate cause. If there was further blessing to be found, it was that Texas was spared the sort of scorched-earth policies wreaked by Union General Philip Sheridan on the Shenandoah Valley of Virginia.

Before settling into his rancher role after the War of Northern Aggression, Luke Dunn had remained ever-conflicted over his roles of rancher and Texas Ranger. Danger lurked whichever choice Luke might make. Prairie fires, blizzards, floods, stampedes, desperate killers, rustlers, and savages were part and parcel to life on the frontier whether lawman or rancher. Just about anywhere he rode, death could be reaching for his reins. To complicate matters, Luke had built considerable notoriety and created enemies by virtue of his success in bringing lawbreakers to justice. Notches on gunfighter pistols were mostly dime-store novel creations, but there were ego-driven ne'er do wells like Coy Witmer that craved earning the sobriquet king of the fast draw by gunning down a lawman legend Luke Dunn. The dastardly murder of

Wild Bill Hickock in Deadwood, South Dakota and more recent shootout involving the Earps in Tombstone, Arizona were well-known, but there were plenty more—mostly ambushes—that never made the news headlines. While vigilante justice and lynchings or necktie parties abounded throughout the 1870s, Luke laid low and stuck with ranching and family matters. While he had established reliable allies over the years, many had by now grown long of tooth. When called to continue his role as a Texas Ranger on a special assignment, Luke found himself hard-pressed to deliver justice while raising his family. Now, in a world two decades after the War of Northern Aggression, Luke's dilemma took on new dimensions. Older? Wiser? Dedicated to justice?

Two decades ago, Luke had made significant headway in bringing justice to the Nueces Strip. Events often beyond his control had required a strong resolve and a major dose of grit. Sitting on the gallery, he stroked his mustache and thought back on how with the Texas Rangers disbanded during and after the war he had mostly settled into ranching. He and Elisa managed to grow Heaven's Gate Ranch both in terms of land holdings and livestock. In early 1870, Texas had been readmitted to the Union despite not having fully met conditions set by the federal government. In the fifteen years following readmission, political and economic conditions were rough at best. Outlaws and Indians, as well as charlatans of every stripe, were quick to take advantage. So-called carpetbaggers abounded. During Reconstruction, a Federally controlled force known loosely as the Texas State Police had briefly been responsible for enforcing unpopular new laws that came with reintegration. The police were so unpopular that they were disbanded in 1873. The election of Governor Richard Coke that year effectively marked the end of reconstruction, and he vigorously went about restoring order to boost the economy and reestablish the rule of law. The legislature recommissioned the Texas Rangers, and a special force called the Frontier

Battalion comprised of two companies of 75-men each was created under the command of Major John B. Jones.

Luke smiled knowingly, as he thought upon how the Frontier Battalion had soon been strengthened by the addition of the Special Force, a second military-style force of forty men under young Captain Leander H. McNelly. Luke had met the captain, but gut instinct led him to not hold the man as of the same stature as Rip Ford or Jack Coffee Hays. The controversial but beloved McNelly had the task of bringing order to the Nueces Strip, and he did so with a certain flair inclusive of a "capture and hang" policy and a tendency to stretch the bounds of border polity. McNelly died from tuberculosis in 1881, causing a shake-up in Texas Ranger leadership. It was the dynamic created in the aftermath of the Frontier Battalion Special Force that now tempted Luke from his "retirement" to once again pin on the Texas Ranger badge. Despite numerous near-death encounters, Luke Dunn had reached the ripe old age of fifty. He'd made mostly good choices and listened to wise advice, as he built his ranch holdings to more than twenty-five thousand acres comprised of three separate spreads between Nuecestown and Alice.

Luke's musings on the gallery were interrupted as a rooster crowed and strutted his stuff while he led his brood of chickens clucking their way around the yard. Luke could just about hear the grunting and squealing of the pigs in the new pen he'd built near the barn. The oinkers would be another stream of income for Heaven's Gate as well as make for good eating. While city slickers might think the place was noisy, Luke found a certain soothing peacefulness in the sounds of livestock. When the livestock had settled down for the night, ranch sounds were replaced with a cacophony of crickets, hoot owls, frogs, an occasional big cat scream, and coyote howls. He recalled evenings out on the Strip when it was so quiet, you'd swear you could hear the stars twinkling. It all made for a far cry from the flash and the explosive sound of bullets leaving the muzzle of a Colt revolver or the cannon-like blast of a Sharps buffalo rifle.

A few hints of gray were beginning to speckle their way among the fiery-red hairs of Luke's mustache, as he sat occasionally stroking it on the galley of the ranch house. A look under his hat likely would have revealed a few more gray hairs. He lovingly caressed the long blue steel barrel of his brand-spanking new Winchester Model 1885 falling-block-action rifle. He recalled seeing a Winchester advertisement a few years back featuring William "Buffalo Bill" Cody. With its 26-inch barrel, the Model 1885 was said to be the finest long-range rifle in production, better even than the Sharps and Remington rifles. He raised it and peered through the telescopic sight at the distant ranchland. He'd test-fired one of these masterpieces in Corpus Christi and came away totally impressed. The telescopic sight was his idea, as he rightly figured it would improve accuracy over long distances. Elisa had wondered to herself at why he needed such a rifle, as it seemed as though he hadn't done any Texas Ranger missions in ages and there was plenty of firepower already around the Heaven's Gate Ranch. Then again, she was confident he had his reasons. After all, he was a man, and men on the Texas frontier carried guns even as the endless reaches of prairie were tamed.

Luke had indeed pretty much settled into the ranching life. He was committed enough that he'd managed to resist the call to join the Texas Ranger Frontier Battalion. He hadn't wanted to steal any of Captain Leander McNelly's thunder, especially as he was elderly by lawman standards. He had added a large addition to the big house since the end of the war to accommodate his and Elisa's burgeoning family that had grown to ten children. They'd even managed to replace Elisa's beloved picket fence. Their lives had already been blessed with a couple of grandchildren.

The family of Luke's lead vaquero and ranch manager

Jaime Sanchez had grown such that he had a house built for them and even sectioned a piece of land they could call their very own. Heaven's Gate Ranch had become quite an enterprise. A bunkhouse had been built for the seasonal cowboys they'd hire, and the barn had been added on to as well. Luke sectioned off a couple of pastures, one aimed at breeding quarter horses and another for raising sheep. It was a far cry from the empire that was the King Ranch, but it was enough to be respectfully considered an economically feasible working ranch.

All this titillation of the senses lay displayed before him on this warm spring morning. He placed the scope to his eye as he swept the rifle across his field of view, magnifying the awe-inspiring landscape. Flowers were beginning to bloom, the dogs set to yapping at most anything that moved, and his breeder bull was down at the corral bellowing for action. He'd also obtained some of that new-fangled barbed wire. He wasn't a big fan of the spiked wire strands, but it was effective at protecting his water access from stray cattle herds. There was an old adage about trusting your neighbor but brand your cattle and protect your water. Luke looked out at the horses romping in the pasture closest to the house. He thought on Big Horse. Old age had finally caught up with the loyal cayuse just a couple of years back. The big gray stallion had gone a tad lame and was finishing his days at pasture. Luke had auditioned a couple of mounts, but none as yet fully suited him. His beloved gray stallion Big Horse had set a high standard.

As he slowly swept the rifle one final time across the horizon, something caught his eye. A rider was off in the distance and appeared to be moving steadily toward him. Luke thought it rather curious for someone to approach from the southwest rather than the ranch entrance located off the road to Corpus Christi to the east. He got up and poked his head into the front door to alert Elisa. "Lisa, sweetheart, there's a lone rider approaching. Too far off to tell whether or not it's trouble."

Folks couldn't be too careful these days, so Luke tended to opt for caution.

Elisa did a quick scan of the kitchen and sitting room to be sure all the children were accounted for, and then calmly walked to the gun rack by the front door and selected one of the Henry rifles. She slipped a round into the chamber and took a seat by one of the front windows.

Luke double-checked that his Colt revolver was ready and inserted a round into the new Winchester. He raised the rifle and peered through the sight as the rider crew closer. Whoever it was, Luke didn't recognize him. Besides, the heated air at any long distance tended to warp images as the air danced in waves. The telescopic sight overcame that just a bit. The rider had picked up his ride to an easy lope and was now roughly a third of a mile out. Luke could barely make out the strap of some sort of satchel slung across the rider's shoulder. He wasn't able to see whether the rider was armed, at least, no weapons were at the ready. "Looks like a courier," he mumbled under his breath.

A shot boomed out across the grasses, and the courier was quite literally lifted from his saddle. There was no mistaking the sound of a Sharps buffalo gun, nor its devastating impact. Even as far away as the rider was, the sound reverberated noisily off the surrounding hills.

Luke saw two men emerge from a live oak motte and scurry with horses in tow to where the rider fell. Luke aimed the Winchester and squeezed off a round. At 700 or so yards, it was more designed to scare the bushwhackers than hit anything. He could only watch helplessly as they lifted the satchel, mounted, and quickly rode off. Luke uttered a curse under his breath. What could have been so valuable?

Elisa had heard the rifle report but not seen what had happened. She'd fired a Sharps before, so readily recognized the distant sound. Shooting so close to a house wasn't something that was especially encouraged. If they were hunters, they'd likely have asked permission. She heard Luke's rifle fire and then his footsteps coming to the front door.

He strode purposefully through the door. He was calm, acting as though he'd not witnessed anything especially out of the ordinary. He matter-of-factly let Elisa know what had happened. "Somebody shot that rider approaching our house and robbed him of some sort of satchel. I'm going to saddle up the Appaloosa and see what happened." He traded the Winchester for a Henry. He didn't expect to be needing a telescopic sight, as the shooter and his accomplice would surely be long gone with whatever was in the courier's satchel.

Elisa wasn't about to stand in Luke's way. The lawman in him had kicked in.

"I don't expect to be long, Lisa. Keep lunch warm." He smiled and gave her a kiss as he headed for the corral beside the barn. Lisa was Luke's affectionate name for Elisa, just as she called him Lucas. It was part of the bond between husband and wife.

The Appaloosa stallion was the first horse that Luke had begun to think of as being in a league with Big Horse. He happened to have been bred from the old stallion having been paired with an Appaloosa mare. It'd been Big Horse's final hurrah at stud. This could be the spirited young stallion's baptism so to speak. The children had named him Twister for his swirling dark gray coat crowned by the random gray spots on his hindquarters, all highlighted by a dark gray mane and tail. They'd learned about tornadoes, or twisters as they were often called, so the horse's name seemed appropriate to them. Twister was nearly the size of Big Horse but perhaps a bit stockier of build. While Luke appreciated the children's thoughtful naming process, he found himself simply referring to the stallion as the Appaloosa. He felt pretty certain that Twister shared the bloodlines bred into the horses by the proud and capable Nez Percé people. Worthy mount for sure.

Luke led the Appaloosa from the corral into the stable and

saddled up quickly. He double-checked his Colt revolver and saw to it that he had a few rounds for the Henry rifle. Twister for his part seemed to sense the excitement, as his ears perked up and he took to snorting and pawing at the ground until Luke finished cinching the saddle, climbed aboard, and headed out to where the unknown rider had fallen.

The courier's horse had remained close by the fallen man, so the body was fairly-easy to find in the tall prairie grasses. Upon reaching the spot, Luke dismounted and looked the man over. The Sharps had done its job, as the man's chest featured a dark gaping wound that had bled out quickly. By the look of it, he'd likely died nearly instantaneously. The apparent courier likely hadn't suffered any. Quickly realizing there was nothing he could do for him, Luke checked for identification. Lodged in the pocket of the man's bullet-mangled vest was a Texas Ranger badge. Luke made an involuntary gasp at the discovery. It was then that Luke realized the man had in fact been well-armed. He had a Colt in his holster beside a large sheath containing a Bowie knife with ornately carved bone hilt. Another Colt resided in his belt. Luke noted the Winchester in the scabbard alongside the saddle of the man's horse. None of the weapons had done him much good in the ambush. The Nueces Strip had taken another victim, yet this was different. This had taken place on Heaven's Gate land. That made it personal.

Luke pulled a wallet from the other side of the courier's vest and pulled out a bloodied and tattered piece of paper. "Clyde Simpson," Luke half whispered. "From Victoria." The whispering was more out of respect.

He walked over to the courier's horse. The animal was calm, though still sweating from its apparent long ride. Saddlebags were slung behind the saddle, so Luke unfastened the flaps on each side in turn to see whether there was anything of note. A photograph fell out. Luke picked it up and took a long look. It was of a man and a couple of children.

Luke's eyes flitted between the courier's face and the man in the photograph. Looked as though Clyde had a family. Luke prayed they'd be cared for. He dug a bit deeper and came upon an envelope with "Lucas Dunn" emblazoned on it. Apparently, the courier's satchel had been a decoy. Luke absentmindedly stuffed the envelope into his pocket.

He walked over to the motte from where the ambushers had lain in wait. It didn't take Luke long to find the exact spot from which the shooter had fired. He looked around for any clues. Other than one of their horses having a broken shoe, the only pieces of evidence were a 50-caliber cartridge casing carelessly dropped along with an empty tobacco pouch.

Luke had observed the bushwhackers' tracks heading west, so he suspected he might pick up their trail in Alice. His shot from the gallery had likely scared them half to death, so they'd be long gone by now. Luke decided it really wasn't going to be productive to give chase just yet. Besides, he wasn't up to dealing with a possible bushwhacking where he'd be the target. Ambushes were all-too-common in the rough and tumble Texas frontier. No point in tempting fate.

By the time he'd wrapped Clyde's body in a blanket, tied him over the saddle, and led the horse back to the ranch house, it was well after midday. He hitched the horses in front of the house, bounded up the steps, and strode through the front door. "Lisa! Lisa, sweetheart, I've got to take this man's body on to Nuecestown. I'll be back in…"

She interrupted with hands on hips. "Slow down, Lucas Dunn. You do have a minute to eat afore you head off."

Luke realized he was hurrying unnecessarily. "I smell cornbread." He gave Elisa a playful squeeze. "Yes, I surely do have time to eat."

As he sat, he was swarmed by his remaining brood of children. Time had flown, or so it seemed. The twins Peter and John were twenty-eight years old and Andrea Anne was but a year behind and the spitting image of her mother. All three had found spouses and born grandchildren. Three more of their brood were sparking potential spouses and had begun to find their paths in life. The four who remained home at Heaven's Gate were still of an age to clamor competitively for Luke's attention. "Junior, you want to ride up to Nuecestown with me? I have some business you could help with."

Elisa quickly conjured a vision of the teenage Luke, Junior helping his father deposit a dead Texas Ranger. "You sure, Lucas?"

"The boy has to grow up, Lisa. It's not the toughest thing he's likely to face." Luke thought back to the arrows their first-born had collected after Comanche raids.

Grace offered up a pout that said, "What about me?" She'd already become a solid horsewoman and could hold her own with a rifle.

"Gracie, we have work to be doing here." Elisa's rejoinder ended that.

"Sean has some barn repairs to get done," Luke added. "Oh, I almost forgot." Luke fished out the folded-up envelope he'd stuffed in his pocket, smoothed it out, took out his knife, and slit it open. He pulled out the letter inside and held it thoughtfully for a moment before unfolding it. He had a suspicion as to what it might be about, as he read it first to himself. He gave an involuntary, "humph." He thoughtfully looked around at the children and decided not to read it aloud but rather handed it to Elisa. "It's from Texas Ranger Captain Sam McMurray. You can guess what he's looking for." McMurray was one of the Rangers that had hung around after the death of Texas Ranger Major Jones. Decent leaders had become few and far between, and McMurray was well respected.

Elisa's shoulders heaved ever-so-slightly with a barely audible sigh, as she took the letter from Luke and read McMurray's invitation. "What do you think, Lucas? Looks like he's trying to lure you back into the Rangers." It was more than a luring. McMurray knew what made Luke Dunn tick, and that the idea of pursuing a wanted outlaw like Coy Witmer might bring him out of retirement. Elisa thought back on what had amounted to Luke's final effort at delivering justice nearly twenty years back when a distant neighbor named Bent Evans and his family were to be unjustly evicted from their homestead. There'd been hell to pay in persuading the reconstructionist Judge Crockett to change his ill-conceived ways. Evans had been ever grateful, though Luke nearly was shot by the colored men who'd been hired as police to do the judge's dirty work. Crockett was still around but managed to hide any ill will toward Luke.

As Elisa considered this latest violence a full two decades after the war, she couldn't help but be tentative in her support.

Luke looked again on the now inquisitive faces of the children and circled his gaze back to Elisa. A space deep in his heart was always with the Texas Rangers. "Seems I have a few days to think on it, Lisa." Swimming around in his head was the question of what those two bushwhackers had seen as so all-fired important enough to kill the courier. He wondered, too, what they might do when they discovered that the satchel had been a decoy? More importantly, who had sent them?

"Here ya go, Mistuh Witmuh." The man thrust the satchel at the now fashionably dressed character sitting in the corner of the saloon. Aside from the barkeep, they were the only ones taking up space in the room at this hour.

Coy Witmer's fancy duds couldn't camouflage the evil that yet oozed from every pore. Bigger men having heard of his reputation had been known to physically cower to his smug over-confident manner. His ego drove him to presume the mantle of the top gunslinger in Texas upon the death of John King Fisher in 1884. Fisher? Well. he'd been credited with killing thirty-eight men. Witmer wore the crown proudly, though he was still about a dozen killings shy of Fisher's record. He saw as exaggerated the murderous exploits of the infamous John Wesley Hardin and viewed the likes of the Younger and James brothers as mostly dime-store-novel creations. More importantly and unlike Hardin, he'd managed to avoid the long arm of the law. He'd even run into Texas Ranger Captain McNelly a few years back and evaded capture, much less a bullet. He'd managed to steer a wide berth from Luke Dunn, and he wasn't especially anxious to have the supposedly retired Texas Ranger be lured into putting full energy into pursuing him. Like most of his kind, Witmer preferred ambush to confrontation, and Luke Dunn wouldn't be easy to bushwhack. Besides, that mano-a-mano dream yet danced in his head. A lot of lawbreakers had tried to get the Texas Ranger, and all had failed.

"Did you open it?"

"No...no suh. Ya said not to." The man shuffled his feet uneasily.

Witmer unlatched the still dusty leather satchel, opened it, and peered inside. He reached in. His expression turned to concern and then apprehension as he pulled out blank scraps of paper. He looked suspiciously at the two men who'd brought him the satchel.

The men's eyes darted nervously about the saloon. There was no escape from Witmer's all-too-obvious anger.

Witmer turned the saddle upside down and shook it. He laid it on the table, took out his knife, and slit the fabric lining in search of a secret compartment. He finally pushed away the now-mangled satchel, sat back, and began to calmly clean his fingernails with the knife. He pulled a cigar from his coat pocket, snipped the end, lit it, and took a couple of long drags. He sent a couple of smoke rings skyward. "Where is it?"

"Where is what?" The men were now extremely uneasy.

"The envelope."

"Honest, Mistuh Witmer, suh...we...we didn't open the bag. Don't know 'bout no envelope."

Witmer's eyes drilled straight through the men. On the one hand, he knew they were far too stupid to know the mission of the courier much less what the contents concerned, while on the other hand they'd of a sudden become inconvenient. They did know too much. He placed the burning cigar on the edge of the table with its glowing tip hanging clear.

One of the men placed a hand on the table and leaned forward. "Do we still get paid, Mr. Witmuh?" His hand brushed the lit stogie, and it fell to the floor. "Uh, sorry, Mr. Witmuh." Everyone's attention was drawn to the cigar.

Witmer wrapped his fingers around the hilt of the knife. His eyes locked full on with the man who'd knocked his cigar to the floor. He brought the knife back behind his ear and in a single motion his knife-laden hand carved an arc through the air, releasing the knife at just the precise moment to let it fly with unerring accuracy and brute force dead-center into the man's chest.

As the first man crumpled to the floor, the second man began to step away, turned hurriedly, and tripped over his own feet. Too late. There was a deafening report and bright flash as the bullet exploded from the muzzle of Witmer's Colt. The lead missile tore into the man's butt severing his spine and leaving him desperately clawing through the sawdust with only his hands in a vain attempt to escape from the saloon.

Witmer looked over at the barkeeper. The smell of gunsmoke lingered in the air.

The barkeep shrugged and made busy wiping the bar.

Witmer got up from the table, yanked the knife from the first man's chest, and tossed a gold piece at the barkeep. "That should cover these two," he half sneered. He wiped the knife on the dead man's shirt to clean off the blood and slipped it back into its sheath.

He strode over to the man he'd shot and used his foot to

flip him onto his back. The man grimaced in terrible pain. Sawdust and blood covered his face, and there was a gaping hole where the bullet had exited his chest. As Witmer stood over him, anyone watching would have sworn they'd heard a rattlesnake's rattle. Witmer smiled wryly, as he casually thought to put a mercy bullet into the man's head. He released the hammer and holstered the gun. He stared briefly into the dying man's pleading eyes and walked on out of the saloon. "That's twenty-six and twenty-seven," he murmured under his breath. He figured he'd best get out of Alice. No time to etch two more grooves in his watch. It was a close-knit community and word of the cold-blooded murder of the two men would get out right quickly. It wouldn't do for Witmer to literally be hanging around.

"Have a deposit for you, Bill." Luke remarked to himself how age had been kind to Bill Meaney. He and Clara had moved to Nuecestown a couple of years back, as Corpus Christi sought a younger man to be sheriff. These days he mostly complained about aches and pains, told anyone who'd listen about his exploits at San Jacinto back in 1836, and occasionally got to play with his grandchildren.

Meaney squinted into the mid-morning sun. "Good to see you, too, Luke. See you brung Junior with you." He nodded to Luke Junior. "Who's the deceased?"

"Texas Ranger named Clyde Simpson. He's got family up Victoria way. He was bringing me a message from Captain Sam McMurray and got himself ambushed only a short way from our house." Luke passed Simpson's personal effects to Meaney.

"Dang. Must've been an important message." Meaney looked over the courier's body slung across the saddle. He looked over deferentially at Junior. "We'll get the body home, Luke. Likely box it and send it up by wagon."

"Appreciate it, Bill. I reckon the horse will compensate for the box and sending Clyde home. I've got a message for Captain McMurray, if you'd be so kind as to ensure that it gets posted." He handed an envelope to Meaney.

"Any idea as to the bushwhackers, Luke?"

Luke dismounted and motioned to his son to do the same. "Don't know, Bill. Could be connected with what Captain McMurray wants me to look into."

"Heard that some fellow up in Alice named Coy Witmer killed a pair of ne'er-do-wells. Knifed one and put a couple slug into the other. It's said he's killed better than two dozen."

Luke stroked his mustache. Only his raised eyebrows gave away any concern. "I've heard that name. Quite a reputation." He thought a bit more. "Interesting that he's nearby." He didn't mention to Meaney that Witmer was the subject of McMurray's request. Luke sought to change the subject. "How's Doc getting on?" He knew Doc Andrews was at least eighty years old and had retired from his medical practice.

"He hangs here and there, Luke. I expect the boozing he did years ago hasn't made it any easier on him." He absent-mindedly looked over at the boarding house. "Bernice and Agatha look after Doc. Bless their hearts, but they're not getting any younger either."

"Heard anything lately from Jake and Ameone?" Luke tried to keep up with his old friend Jake Barber and his farming. The fact that the big man had settled with a Cheyenne woman rather tended to please Luke. He'd been curious how mixed-race marriage worked out ever since he'd heard about Sam Houston having been married to a Cherokee woman named Tiana many years back.

"Old Jake's bringing in cotton these days, Luke. I think he's got four youngsters now."

Junior had been listening quietly. "Who's Witmer? You going after him, Pa?"

The question grabbed Luke's attention. "We'll talk about it on the way home, son."

As he turned to mount Twister, he paused and turned back to Meaney. "You heard anything about fence cutters, Bill?" It was almost a rhetorical question. With the ever-wider use of barbed wire, there'd been a growing problem with frustrated cowboys who'd go around cutting the fences. It was growing into a war, and legislators in Austin were increasingly concerned. "I don't use much of the wire myself, but I've heard of some nasty fighting over it."

"Nothing to speak of Luke, though more folks around here have begun to use it to protect their crops and lay claim to their water rights."

"I hear tell folks in Austin are going to make it illegal to carry fence cutters. I know they're looking out for the big ranchers that are protecting their property, but it bothers me more every day that the government gets in our pants. I guess I'm for less government and more personal responsibility, Bill."

Meaney nodded. "Seems they love to make new laws up in Austin, Luke. They listen to where the money comes from."

Luke climbed into the saddle. "I try to send them as little money as I can." He smiled wryly. "The new sheriff in Corpus staying in touch?"

"Whitely? Yeah, he tolerates me some, Luke. Hell, it takes me an hour to just get up from bed these days." Meaney laughed as Luke began to turn Twister to head back to Heaven's Gate. He called out to Junior. "Son, you watch after your pa."

As they rode off, Luke turned to Junior. "Reckon I'll be going after that Witmer fellow, son. That okay with you?"

Junior nodded thoughtfully. "Gonna be dangerous, Pa?" He released the buckboard brake and chucked at the horses.

"Going to be dangerous." Luke corrected his son's language. "Yes. I expect your ma won't be any too happy about it."

"Can I come?"

Luke smiled. The boy was fifteen years old. "You're nearly of age, Junior...but...well, this will take an experienced hand."

"I suppose I'd be a distraction, right Pa?"

"I appreciate you wanting to come along, son. You've likely got Texas Ranger blood running in your veins. You're a fine marksman and have a savvy head, too. But this is indeed a one-man job." He saw Junior's spirits lift just a tad from the compliment. "Won't be long, and you'll be ready." Luke gave Twister a little kick with his spurs and father and son trotted off on their way back to Heaven's Gate.

As Luke and Junior pulled up to the barn at Heaven's Gate, they couldn't miss the carriage standing in front of the house. A man was sitting on one of the chairs on the gallery relaxing with a cup of coffee that Elisa had apparently given him out of her sense of Texas hospitality. Luke recognized the man and was none too pleased. He turned to Junior, "Son, see to the horses. Looks like I've got some business to tend to." With that, he handed the Appaloosa's reins to Junior and headed toward the house.

"What you doing here, Crockett?" Luke wasn't up to slinging niceties. Crockett was a judge installed by the powers that be during the post-war Texas Reconstruction era. To have ever recognized Crockett as a judge stretched the bounds of credulity. He fancied himself a power broker, sitting like a spider having woven a web of treachery and deceit from which he captured and enslaved folks' lives. Had he not tangled with the up-and-coming challenger Archie Parr, he might not have ever considered getting out of Nueces County.

Crockett took a sip of coffee. "Came to apologize, Mr. Dunn."

Luke laid a steely-eyed gaze on his former tormentor. The judge seemed but a shadow of his former self. A nasty divorce, dalliances with whores, too much booze and cigar smoking, and sleazy business deals tended to tear at the fabric of the man. "Apologize?"

"I did you wrong way back, and I'm sorry." Crockett's wrinkled face gave off a deep sadness. "I'm leaving. Be heading back to Boston."

Coursing through Luke's mind was the beating he took twenty years ago from Crockett's contingent of black Texas State Police upon falsely accusing him of the bushwhack murder of their sergeant. Crockett had parked Luke in the Corpus Christi jail for nearly a month before the actual murderer had been discovered. Worse, he'd allowed his black State Police thugs to deliver a beating or two. They'd even lashed Luke's back a time or two, and he still bore the faint welt-like scars. Since Crockett had figured he had the man who'd done the crime, he hadn't undertaken any further investigation. He had it in for Luke ever since the Ranger had discovered the then-married judge having his way with a local whore. Crockett's dalliance with the prostitute that Luke had held as a weapon over him didn't matter anymore, as his wife had long ago discovered his indiscretions. It was by dumb luck that retired Sheriff Meaney happened to be in a saloon in Victoria and had overheard the bushwhacker talking about killing the black man on the road to Corpus Christi and was aiming to kill more. Upon dragging the grizzled rebel veteran back to Corpus Christi, Crockett had taken his sweet time releasing Luke. Ever since, the two men had operated under a truce of sorts. With the end of reconstruction upon Texas's rejoining the Union in 1873, Luke had been none too pleased that Crockett had lingered on the bench for another dozen years. "You came all the way out here to Heaven's Gate figuring to lessen your guilty conscience?" Luke's mind journeyed back to the beatings he'd taken at Crockett's jail.

"I did you wrong Mr. Dunn."

About this time, Elisa appeared in the doorway holding a coffee pot and cup. She ignored Luke's disapproving glare, refilled Crockett's cup, and poured a cup for Luke. "Here you go, Lucas." She smiled winsomely, then whispered, "Justice and redemption, cowboy."

Luke watched her go back into the house.

"Mr. Dunn, I'm not here to beg for your forgiveness, though Lord knows I likely should. Despite my long-held and unfounded prejudice against you, it's hard not to notice that you've always proven to be a man of character. You managed to see beyond my terrible treatment of you in the State Police murder case. My pride wouldn't permit me to feel the guilt that should have racked my soul. It's weighed ever heavier upon me."

Luke stroked his mustache as he sat and sipped his coffee. He tried to gauge what Crockett was up to. His mind flashed back to that intimate conversation with Elisa at the creek about his tendency to apply redemptive values. He had long ago realized that redemption was the act of working toward forgiving someone, and, when both forgiveness and redemption are working to heal souls, the journey to being able to accept someone's wrongdoing becomes more easily supported. Nevertheless, Luke was all too aware that redemption did not replace punishment. It's where justice came to bear.

"I didn't come out here to simply apologize and make myself feel better. Lord knows, I've had twenty years to do that." Crockett reached into his coat pocket and pulled out a sheaf of official-looking papers. "These are deeds to properties I've legitimately acquired during my time here. They represent roughly 150,000 acres." His eyes locked on Luke's as though searching for some sense of compassion. "I've signed them over to you to do with as you see fit."

Luke's jaw dropped. He gathered his wits as best he could and took a deep breath. "I'm much obliged, Judge Crockett, but I can't accept them."

"If you're concerned as to whether they were acquired illegally, be assured they were not. I own them fair and square."

"That's not the reason, Judge. There are folks around these parts that would benefit greatly from your largesse, regardless of your motivation." Luke took another sip of coffee. "I can and have forgiven you for how you treated me, but I will not dispose of these properties on your behalf." Luke was actually saying that he didn't want to be a component of Crockett's assuaging of guilt. "You've been around Nueces County long enough to know who'd benefit from these properties."

Crockett placed his empty coffee cup on the side table and stood. "You remain an honorable man, Luke Dunn. I admire that in you. It's humbling to a prideful man like myself." He extended his hand. "I deeply appreciate your forgiveness and promise to duly dispose of these properties as you've suggested."

Luke stood and shook Crockett's hand.

Crockett nodded to Elisa who now stood in the doorway. "You've got a fine husband, Mrs. Dunn. Texas could use more men like him." He bowed slightly, stuffed the packet of deeds in his coat, and ambled slowly toward his carriage.

Elisa moved to Luke's side as Crockett climbed into his carriage, turned the team, and drove away. "I'm proud of you, Lucas."

As Luke was about to give her an especially passionate kiss, an inquiring voice interrupted. "Ma? Pa? Any eatings left?"

TWO
THE NUECES STRIP BECKONS

WITMER RIGHTLY FIGURED he'd been hornswoggled and that Luke must have received the message from McMurray. The bungled attempt to stop the delivery had cost four lives, three of them by his own hand. But who was counting? Well, he was. He'd added three grooves to the old watch. Before disposing of his two hired bushwhackers, he'd first tortured a Texas Ranger to death to learn that McMurray was going to call Luke Dunn from retirement to hunt him down. At best, he'd likely only delayed the inevitable manhunt, and he didn't especially cotton to being prey to a lawman of Dunn's reputation. He might have simply left Texas, but he'd found himself haunted by the possibility of being stalked by the accursed Texas Ranger. Pursuing Luke Dunn had become an obsession, as specters clawed and nagged at him in his very dreams. Mano-a-mano or ambush mattered none. He desperately wanted to send the Ranger to the grave.

Uvalde didn't seem like a half bad place to lay sort of low until he could learn for certain whether Luke was coming after him. The hilly countryside offered plenty of cover for escape or, better still, ambush. It wasn't so much that he appreciated the natural beauty of the landscape so much as it offering so many opportunities for foul play.

The room where he'd spent the night wasn't exactly palatial, but it wasn't a pigsty either. Homely would best describe it. The bed was clean save for being soiled by his own exploits the previous night with one of the local whores. She wasn't beautiful, but she compensated with eagerness to please.

Witmer just needed to stay out of trouble. One of the first things he did upon entering Uvalde last evening was to tear down the wanted poster that was nailed to the front wall of the jail. He thought it offered an inadequate description in any case. He learned that the town had a new sheriff with a reputation for not tolerating violence or disruptive behavior. In fact, Sheriff Conner was known to mostly shoot first and ask questions later. The good news was that the sheriff hadn't been required to do any such shooting lately.

The fracture meandering across the middle of the mirror didn't keep him from admiring himself. He allowed a pencil-thin smile to crease his chin as he cinched up the fashionable string necktie and slipped on a black leather coat that was ample enough to hide his pearl-handled Colt revolver nestled on his hip from view. Witmer only carried one, as he figured to never need more firepower. He steadfastly avoided situations where he'd be outnumbered by more than two to one. In his experience he'd found that it only took a single, well-aimed bullet to kill a man. Given that he was prone to bushwhacking rather than direct confrontation, he really had plenty of bullets to do his job. He'd actually appreciated not using two bullets on the second bushwhacker back in Alice. Better in his own evil mind to simply leave the man to die in his agony. He guarded against growing soft on his victims. Mercy killing wasn't exactly in Witmer's repertoire. He had a reputation to protect.

He took a final look in the mirror, hitched his gun belt, opened the door, and went on downstairs to the dining room.

Breakfast was still being served. "Y'all got something left for a hungry patron," he said to no one in particular. He found an empty table. On the other side of the room, he caught the eye of the whore he'd had the night before. From the way she was sitting and talking, the man she was with was more likely husband or friend than client or boss man. As she noticed Witmer enter, she leaned forward and whispered something to her companion who shifted uncomfortably. He glanced furtively over his shoulder at the gunman, whispered something to the whore, and walked from the dining room. Witmer chortled to himself and nodded patronizingly in her direction.

His idyll with the prostitute was interrupted as a pretty young woman approached. "We're serving up eggs and ham today, sir." She had a sweet voice, pleasant to the ear yet just a tad tentative, given the darkness surrounding this guest.

"Great. Y'all have any coffee?" It was a rhetorical question. No self-respecting eating establishment in Texas would not serve coffee.

"I'm sorry, sir. I meant to bring it from the kitchen." She force-smiled as sweetly as she could and ran off to fetch the coffee. Likely as not, she managed to suppress a feeling of fear that sent a chill up her spine.

Witmer allowed himself a self-satisfied smile. Uvalde might be a good place to hang out for a short time. If that Texas Ranger was to come after him, he'd surely hear of it in time to escape. He figured to toy with the Ranger's mind... tease him a bit...at least until he could set up the perfect opportunity to add the best groove of all to his watch. Watch? Not a gun? The gunman wasn't inclined to soil the surface of a beautiful revolver with notches. His signature was to carve a deep groove into the surface of a gold watch he carried in the left pocket of his vest. There was one groove for each man he'd killed, though he figured the first to have been most important.

He got to thinking, as he was wont to do from time to time, on the life events that had shaped him. He'd grown up in the northern reaches of Wyoming. He vaguely knew his mother who died pitiably at the heavy hand of his drunken father. Mountain Jack Witmer had been a trapper turned outlaw who gotten so drunk one night that he had been sucked into marrying Coy's mother who was carrying the boy at the time. Old Mountain Jack couldn't even be sure the child was his, and the mere thought of that possibility would rile him up into rages occasionally exacerbated by whiskey. Coy recalled his mother being a pretty woman, even beneath the frequent bruises she bore. After his mother passed, Mountain Jack would take out his resentments on young Coy. One night when Coy was about fifteen years old, he laid in wait for Mountain Jack to return from an evening of boozing and whoring. The inevitable drunken rage was sure to follow. Coy had reached his limit, just about had enough. Physically, he'd grown to an inch or so taller than his father though was no match in girth or muscle mass. As his father staggered through the door, Coy tripped him. As Mountain Jack planted his face into the floor, Coy whacked him across the back of the head with a shovel. Incredibly, Mountain Jack got up and shook it off. He turned menacingly to face his son. But he was still dazed from the shovel blow. The man's final words were unintelligible as Coy's knife found his throat. Blood gushed from the gaping cut across his neck and quickly spread down his front and puddled on the floor. Coy Witmer stood motionless as he watched his father drop to his knees, fall forward on his face, and die.

In Coy's mind, Mountain Jack Witmer had been too evil to waste a bullet on. This was personal and only a knife would do. He recalled reaching down and removing his father's gun belt and old Colt 1851 Navy revolver. He wiped some blood from it before strapping it on. Mountain Jack sure wouldn't be needing it anymore. He took the dead man's wallet and a sack with a few gold coins, but his final act would have the greatest significance to the teen. He lifted his father's old railroad watch from his breast pocket. He couldn't recall what made him do it, but he used the knife he'd killed his father with to carve a small groove on the back of the casing. What had gone through his mind at that moment always served to trouble him...he murmured "number one" under his breath. He'd taken a final look at his father's now ashen face, as he lay in a pool of blood and urine. He grabbed a sack of victuals gathered while planning the grisly murder and his escape. He stepped through the front door, leaving it open to whatever varmints chose to come make a meal of the old man. Then he climbed onto his father's horse, checked the load in his rifle, and rode off to make whatever fortune awaited him.

That was then, this is now. This was a long way from Wyoming and the sonofabitch excuse for a father. Even in death, the old man haunted him. Another night with the whore would be a sort of salve for whatever ailed him.

Luke and Elisa stood on the gallery looking out onto Heaven's Gate Ranch. The quiet of early morning enveloped them. None of the children had as yet stirred.

"You're accepting Captain McMurray's offer?"

Luke nodded. If he were to look in a mirror, he'd see it was written all over his face. There was no hiding these sorts of things from Elisa. He was still steadfastly driven toward delivering justice. The spark had remained burning within him for the past twenty years. It showed in corrections of even the smallest injustices from a naughty prank by his children to a neighbor's longhorn sporting the wrong brand. He made for a doggoned fine rancher, but he was especially good at being a lawman. He thought back just ten years earlier to his cousin Red John Dunn's gathering a posse and running off a gang of Mexican marauders near Nuecestown that had kidnapped members of the Dunn family, stolen valuable Noakes saddles, and killed a few folks. Deep in his heart, it gnawed at Luke that he hadn't been called to lead that posse on what had been labeled forever in history as the Good Friday Raid. Had his absence from the Texas Rangers and commitment to building Heaven's Gate been seen as some sort of lack of resolve toward delivering justice? It mattered not that Red John's ego likely couldn't handle Luke's reputation and lawman skills. Red John was pretty much viewed as the black sheep of the Dunn family and as a Texas Ranger had reportedly been acquitted twice of murder. It was likely just as well, that Luke had been snubbed that day.

Elisa had begun to grow comfortable with Luke's Texas Ranger days having been left behind. She now found herself grappling with readjusting her thinking. She gazed deeply into his eyes. Yes, the embers of his days traipsing over the Nueces Strip bringing lawbreakers to justice still smoldered. "It's still in your soul, Lucas," she said more compassionately and lovingly than resignedly.

Luke swept her into his arms and held her tightly. "I love you, Lisa Dunn."

She knew that. "The Strip seems to have a hold on you, Lucas." She knew that, too.

Luke smiled. She was right. He led her over to the bench. "I've heard talk about this Witmer fellow, but I've got to learn more about him beyond his reputation. Bill Meaney says he heard that Witmer killed a couple of men at the saloon in Alice. Expect I'll take a ride out there and see what I can dig up. It's a tight community and an even tighter saloon crowd." Luke was already mapping out his approach to tracking down Witmer and bringing him to justice. "Someone might be able to tell me where he was headed."

Elisa had begun to warm up to Luke's new mission. "You think Witmer might leave some clues?"

"If he's like most of his breed, his ego will eventually overcome any common sense. If he's behind the ambush of that courier, and I think he was, he knows that I'll be coming after him."

Elisa smiled. "I think that should make him nervous." She was justly proud of her man.

"I hope so." Luke turned his eyes lovingly upon her. Since they'd first met, she'd adulated him. Her unbridled support, her love, fueled him like nothing else could through all their years together. Now, the Nueces Strip beckoned once again. Theirs was a love story written for the ages...Elisa...the Nueces Strip. It had long since eclipsed the memories of his days back in Ireland fighting against the British oppressors. Justice had become one with Luke Dunn's soul.

"Ma, we eating breakfast?" Junior's head popped from the doorway.

Their musings were ended for the moment. Elisa squeezed Luke's hand and started to get up to tend to breakfast and begin the day.

Luke pulled her back, gave her a light kiss as she fell into his lap, and smiled mischievously. "Let's see if Gracie and Heather can rustle up some grub."

Pots and pans were heard rattling around the kitchen soon enough.

Luke gave Elisa a wink. "There'll be a full moon at the water hole tonight."

Elisa glanced over at the kitchen to be sure the children weren't looking before giving Luke a decidedly fetching smile.

The days were mixed for One Arrow. He'd moved what was left of his band close to Cache, Oklahoma not far from the famous Quahadi Comanche war chief Quanah Parker. Parker had finally surrendered to the reservation life back in 1875 and was well respected among the various Comanche tribes. There was a certain security in locating close to the Quahadi chief, but there was also a palpable mourning in the loss of the old ways of One Arrow's Penateka Comanche band.

One Arrow had weathered the cultural predations of the whites better than most largely as a result of his exposure to the wisdom of his old mentor and adoptive father Three Toes as well as to the ways of Ghost-Who-Rides. He still wore the bone necklace with its silver cross during tribal ceremonies, though he mostly wore the carved one Three Toes had gifted him. The Penateka Comanche chief's relationship with Luke was one of mutual respect. He'd only recently figured out upon deep reflection that the bond between Three Toes and Luke had evolved from the chief's initial instinctive sense hunting him down to respect for and obligation to the Texas Ranger. They had saved each other's lives more than once. It was an intimate part of their brotherhood that thus far eluded One Arrow.

Thanks to Luke's influence, Cactus Flower was still looked upon as his primary wife. She'd borne him two sons and a daughter and was the most creative of his wives so far as spicing up their sexual life. Cactus Flower had retained a fresh beauty even as she'd matured. Bird Woman had passed on a couple of years back, and One Arrow found himself missing her sage advice. Blue Feather was no longer young and inexperienced but had the misfortune to have had a dalliance with a warrior of the Quahadi Comanche. One Arrow sought fifty horses from the warrior as compensation, and eventually settled for twenty-five. With Bird Woman and Blue Feather out of his life and Cactus Flower still favored, One Arrow nevertheless felt that he had a reputation to uphold. He took on a petite and alluring young woman named Blue Eyes as a new second wife. Blue Eyes's beauty was of course enhanced by her crystal-blue eyes, no doubt a genetic trait handed down from her ancestry. One might be led to believe that the chief's life was pretty good.

If one word could describe One Arrow's life, it was routine.

Yes, routine fully characterized the young chief's existence. Other than sex, tending horses, and an occasional tribal council meeting, life was routine. He longed for the old ways. Longed for adventure, hunting buffalo, counting coup, and routing rival tribes. He still couldn't quite grasp why the White man saw this as savagery.

The sun had risen high enough to begin to warm the landscape. Cactus Flower found him standing on a bluff not far from their house. One Arrow had his arms folded and his chin held high, as if looking off into some imaginary distant world. She sidled alongside and ran her hand along the contour of his butt. If he was up for sex, this was the signal that usually aroused him. No reaction. She shrugged and looked off in the direction he was looking. "What thoughts?"

One Arrow appreciated that she understood him almost better than he understood himself. "Hunt buffalo."

She nodded. "Buffalo gone." She knew that he knew that. This time she sensed a spirit of sadness that accompanied his wish.

One Arrow sighed. He felt the beginnings of a tear well up in the corner of one eye, but he wouldn't let it fall. "Miss Ghost-Who-Rides."

"Go find him, husband."

The chief looked lovingly at her. "Cactus Flower wise woman." How could he not marvel at how well she understood him? Cactus Flower had been Three Toes's youthful second wife, but had quickly bound herself to One Arrow upon the chief's all-too-sudden demise.

Cactus Flower acknowledged the chief's compliment by turning her gaze knowingly off into the distance.

It had been nearly twenty years since One Arrow had last seen his Anglo friend, and yet it seemed like only yesterday. He'd almost left the reservation to search for Ghost-Who-Rides about ten years back, but the arrival of Quanah Parker squelched that endeavor. It took him several years to acclimate to the convergence of the various Comanche tribes. The Quahadi and the Penateka had a long history of being at odds. He'd given considerable thought to whom he'd leave in charge during his absence. "I leave Running Bull in charge." The young warrior was his oldest son, and was showing wisdom beyond his years.

"Cactus Flower keep home warm for One Arrow." She once again stroked his backside. This time, she wasn't to be disappointed.

The cool waters of the creek with its gentle current had a soothing effect. Soon enough, Luke and Elisa climbed to the rock promontory just above the wading pool. A cooling breeze wafted over and around them. His arm wrapped around her nakedness and drew her close beneath the warm folds of a blanket and warding off the chill, as they stared up at the full moon.

It was at this very spot, this full moon, this rock set above the cool waters and offering its view of the vast prairie stretching to infinity and beyond that Elisa had fallen in love with her Texas Ranger. Their wet naked bodies still glistened in the moonlight. Now, here and now, better than twenty-five years later, she wanted her man to drown her in the passions she'd come to expect. She nuzzled closer.

"Have I done well, Lisa?"

The spell was broken. She'd lost him at least for the moment. She knew her man well enough. Whatever was weighing heavily on his mind had to be resolved. She'd sensed it while they frolicked in the swirling waters of the creek, but his distraction came on strong now.

"What do you mean, Lucas?"

Luke's arm pulled her closer, and he pulled the big blanket around them to ward off the slight nip in the air. He looked off at the moon, then down at her. "Have I made a difference?"

Elisa struggled to keep her jaw from dropping with wonderment. How could Luke have any doubt of having made a difference? Anyone who'd ever crossed paths with Luke Dunn as lawman, rancher, or family man knew exactly what he stood for. There was never a doubt as to what to expect from Luke Dunn. Thoughts raced through her mind of his having fought off lawbreakers and Indians, but perhaps more importantly, redeemed the lives of folks like Scarlet Rose, Walker Carson, Gordon Belknap, Horace Rucker, and the Comanche chiefs Three Toes and One Arrow. "Lucas, what do you do when you're riding alone?"

Luke blinked. "What's that got to do with making a difference?"

She smiled. She knew what he did out on the Nueces Strip, when he was away weeks at a time tracking human prey. Her question was almost rhetorical. "Humor me, Lucas. What do you do?"

"Well...I'm always on guard for unexpected threats."

"Lucas...what else?"

He realized that so much of his time on the prairies was a sort of second nature. "I guess...I sing ballads...quietly, of course." Luke looked back up at the moon. "I do enjoy the rough beauty and vastness of the prairies and the sky...the grandeur of the sky. Not much prettier than a prairie sunset." Luke turned his gaze back to Elisa. "I do pray...to be doing the right things...to be brought home safely to you and the children." He glanced at her. "Yes, I do pray a lot."

A warm smile radiated across Elisa's upturned face. Her man was an enigma on the rough vastness of South Texas. There was a godliness of soul, an affection and love that pervaded Luke's spirit and enabled him to make wise choices between justice and redemption or both. It was this deeply embedded part of her man's character that made him legendary in the minds of so many but especially to her. It freed Luke to achieve his full potential as lawman, rancher, and husband, yet he was so humble as to be blithely and genuinely unaware of the scope of the positive impact he had on the lives of so many. For Elisa, Luke's most attractive characteristic was how he steadfastly followed the path God had laid before him. He'd turned the trials of his years being persecuted back in his native County Kildare into this true manly man with whom she'd bonded for life. Her thoughts paused, as she watched him look back up at the moon.

Luke's face softened. "As I ride? I dream of you, Lisa. I look for flowers to bring to you upon my safe return." The many colorful bouquets were an unspoken love pledge to Elisa from the depths of her big Texas Ranger's heart. She unfailingly stood by him, nursed his wounds, birthed their children, ran their ranch, been an anchor to his soul.

Her hand raised up to his chin and turned his face toward her. Their eyes met ever so gently. "I think God would say 'well done, good and faithful servant,' Lucas."

Indeed, for all the dangers he'd faced, it was as though there was some sort of mantle of protection that saved him time again from certain death. "I love you, Lisa Dunn." His lips softened as they met hers. They fell back onto the blanket.

Luke stood tall as Elisa pinned his old Texas Ranger badge onto his shirt. She burnished it a bit with her sleeve. He stood before her—all six-foot-three-inches of well-muscled lawman. From the spurs on his boots to the gun belt strapped around his waist, the deep-blue shirt, and red bandana to the well-manicured fiery-red mustache and tan Stetson, Luke Dunn was every inch a Texas Ranger. The few flecks of gray in his red hair failed to diminish his imposing presence. Aging was being kind to him. While the children stood in rapt awe, the impromptu ceremony of badge pinning held a far deeper meaning for Elisa. It was her way of accepting the inevitability of her husband's choice. She held her emotions together right well until she turned to the children. The lump stuck in her throat. "Everyone." She had their attention. "Raise your right hand." She surveyed the children. "Right hand, Junior." She smiled at his contrariness.

Luke dutifully raided his hand and winked at Junior who had nervously switched hands.

Elisa turned to Luke. "Repeat after me. I promise to uphold the laws of Texas and the United States."

The children echoed her words.

"So help me God."

The children repeated her words and dropped their hands. Luke began to drop his.

"I'm not done with you, Mr. Texas Ranger."

Luke's hand went back up.

"Repeat after me. I promise to return safe and sound to my loving wife and family. So help me God."

Luke nodded. "I do."

"The words, Ranger."

Luke dutifully repeated the promise, dropped his hand, swept her into a bear hug, and planted a kiss full on her lips. The children all blushed. He winked at his brood. "That's how the promise of a husband and wife is sealed. Y'all be mindful of that."

"Lucas, do be careful." She walked arm-in-arm with him until they stood beside Twister. The big Appaloosa stallion seemed to sense that this was something special, as he pawed the ground, whickered a bit, and turned his head to nuzzle Luke.

"I'll be back tomorrow. I don't plan to linger in Alice, Lisa." She nodded apprehensively.

"I've got plenty of time to catch up to this Coy Witmer fellow. I don't expect he'll have hung around." He saw that she was beginning to feel more assured. "After I return, we'll have to get me packed for a longer journey. It might take a few days to track him down. In the end, I expect this man will be no different than so many others."

"I love you, Lucas."

"Love you too, Lisa." He planted a goodbye kiss and swung into the saddle.

As he began to ride off, Elisa couldn't help but watch her man admiringly. What a beautifully handsome figure he cut as he rode off sitting tall in the saddle.

Luke paused a bit down the trail. Elisa was still watching him, and the children had lined up on the gallery. He waved, turned Twister, set off at an easy loping stride up the trail, and was soon gone from sight. He looked off into the pasture where Big Horse had spent his final days. "Your daddy's watching us Twister." The Appaloosa seemed to sense his sire's spirit, as he snorted and broke into a gallop that Luke had to quickly rein in.

THREE
FENCE CUTTERS

LUKE HAD NEARLY REACHED Alice when three shots rang out. No shooting appeared to be aimed at him, but it sure grabbed his attention. Gunfire always demanded an investigation, especially out on the prairies of Texas. He instinctively turned Twister toward the sound and moved cautiously forward.

A lone rider approached at a gallop with two behind him giving chase. One of the pursuers had a lasso and seemed intent on lassoing the man they were pursuing. In but a couple of minutes, the first rider had passed Luke so closely that he was nearly struck by the sweat and froth the beast was throwing off. The rider was hell-bent on outdistancing his pursuers, even if it cost him his mount.

Luke pulled out his Henry rifle and quickly moved Twister into position to confront the two men who were giving chase. "Halt!" His booming voice of command was reinforced by the muzzle of the rifle leveled at the lead pursuer.

The two men pulled up in a cloud of dust. It became quickly obvious that they were angered and frustrated by the interruption. "Who the hell...?" The man with the lasso began to recoil his rope in frustration, as he spat into the ground. His partner's hand began to reach for a revolver, but the man quickly had second thoughts as Luke cocked the Henry.

"I'm Texas Ranger Captain Luke Dunn. What's your business chasing that man?"

"Fence cutter! He's a damned fence cutter!"

Luke recalled his conversation with Bill Meaney about the fence cutting that had been plaguing the region, but this was the first time Luke had encountered any of the apparent vigilante-style violence connected with it. Luke hadn't strung much barbed wire, but could relate to the men's plight. "You promise me you'll bring him to me in Alice alive, and I'll let you chase after him."

The men looked at each other in consternation. "He deserves hanging!"

"You hang him, and you'll answer to me." The dark muzzle of the Henry looked ever more ominous.

"We'll bring him in…we promise."

"See y'all in Alice." Luke lifted the rifle and motioned them to continue their pursuit. The fence cutter had become a speck on the horizon by now. Luke figured it was an even chance they wouldn't catch the man, as the fence cutter's horse likely wouldn't last much longer.

Jubal Strong arose lazily from the comfort of the bed. His joints weren't getting any younger, but there were chores to tend to. JD had fallen back asleep after their morning tryst. He smiled at her, as he pulled on his boots. She was still but a slip of a woman. After a tough start with miscarriages, she'd found some frontier spirit deep within and borne him three children. One of their two girls, Priscilla died at age eight from a rattlesnake bite. Daughter Amelia and son Sam were now both teens and already exhibiting the sort of spirit that would sustain them in a booming Texas world. JD's mothering instincts belied her history of having pretended to be a man so as to serve as a Texas Ranger with Luke Dunn. She'd managed to shoot a lawbreaker or two before meeting Strong and settling down. Doggone, but he loved her. She made his move to Texas from the North Platte River country the best decision he'd ever made.

He poured a cup of coffee from the pot young Amelia had prepared and sauntered on out the front door of the cabin he'd finished just a couple of years back. His boss and Luke's cousin, Nick Dunn had deeded a piece of property to him as reward for years of faithfully helping run the ranch. He'd be digging fenceposts and stringing barbed wire this day on his own small spread. Strong had bought a Hereford bull and cow and was intent on building a small herd of his own. Strong's land bordered a creek that eventually fed into the Nueces River, so it became logical to ensure that his livestock had access to water. The last thing he needed was some land baron stringing barbed wire ahead of him and cutting off his access to the stream.

He soon had the mule hitched up, had Sam seated beside him, and was heading the creaking old wagon full of posts and coils of wire out to where they'd stopped work the day before.

In but an hour, he was at the work site. "Damn!" He cussed loudly at what lay before him. "Sons of bitches!" Not only was barbed wire cut, but a dozen fenceposts had been yanked. He looked around. Nobody was to be seen. Other than a few hoof-prints, there was no evidence of the skunks who'd undone his labors.

"What are we gonna do, Pa?" Sam was rattled to say the least. The boy was only fourteen, though he'd been growing up fast. You had to grow up right quick on the Nueces Strip.

"Come stand next to the wagon, son. Keep your head down." Strong's first instinct was to protect his son. No point in the boy being a sitting duck for some crazed bushwhacker. Now, he strapped on the gun he'd brought along. It was extra weight he really didn't cotton to in the heat of the Nueces Strip summer, but it made him feel more secure.

"I'm going to look around." He walked a circle around the work site. Nothing much to see. The land was mostly flat, and there didn't seem to be anyone around.

"Okay, Sam, let's repair the damage." Digging fencepost holes and stringing wire was tough in the best of circumstances. With a heavy gun now strapped on his hip and warming temperature, it was a tad more difficult. Father and son stripped off their shirts in hopes of better catching any breezes.

They began to reinsert the posts. It was a blessing that they hadn't been broken. It was time-consuming, but Strong was determined to get the job done. As he picked up the last of the fallen fenceposts, he noticed a folded piece of paper that had been slipped under it.

He opened it and read slowly aloud. "String wire. You die." That was pretty straightforward. Now, what was he to do? He cautiously scanned the area again. There didn't seem to be anyone watching, but then, if anyone was surveilling him, they'd likely not intend to be seen. It was reassuring that whoever it was hadn't acted by now. The stubborn streak in him wanted to string more wire, but the sensible part was nagging him to call it a day. He was disinclined to go it alone and tempt fate against whoever was threatening him. "Sam, this isn't good. Let's call it a day. After we get this rig home, I'm riding into Alice to talk to the sheriff and see what I can dig up."

Luke rode easy-like into Alice. The evening air was warm and dry, and he could hear the faint creak of the leather of his saddle as the Appaloosa ambled along. The town had been growing by leaps and bounds thanks to the intersection of the railroads. The local saloon wasn't hard to find. From the look of the five horses hitched out front, some cowboys were likely drinking away the dust of a tough day. Luke paused before he passed on by and continued on to the jail.

The law in Alice these days was a fellow named Bones Hollingsworth. Technically, Hollingsworth was a deputy sheriff. Alice was still part of Nueces County, so fell under the jurisdiction of Sheriff Whitely in Corpus Christi. There was a suspicion going around that Bones was a breed, a bit of Cherokee being somewhere in his bloodline. His high cheekbones, hooked nose, and ruddy complexion were the evidence folks said pointed to his lineage. His apparent heritage didn't especially seem to affect his lawman duties. Bones was sitting out front of the jail chewing tobacco and half-heartedly whittling away on a stick, as Luke approached. He looked to be just about half asleep, though awake just enough to handle the sharp blade in his hand.

Luke rode up to within maybe half a dozen feet from the deputy. He could hear the first hints of snoring, as the lawman flirted with a nap. With that, Luke decided to call out louder than usual. "You Bones Hollingsworth?"

At the sound of Luke's voice, Hollingsworth nearly fell from his chair and did manage to blow his chaw out into the street. Bones gathered himself and looked up at the source of the booming voice. He couldn't miss the Texas Ranger badge, though he'd never met Luke. He looked forlornly at the chaw sitting in the dusty street, but quickly gathered his wits. "That be me. Who have I got the pleasure of talkin' with?"

"I'm Texas Ranger Luke Dunn." Luke had decided to stop using his captain rank, as he really wasn't heading a company of Rangers these days. "You have a couple of minutes to answer some questions?" He slid out of the saddle and extended a hand to Bones.

Bones had by now gotten up from his chair but still found himself looking up at Luke. "Dang, but yer a big fella," he muttered. He made an appraising head-to-toe scan of Luke. "Questions? I 'spect so, Ranger. Gotta believe yer lookin' fer that Witmer fella."

"You'd be partly right, Sheriff."

"Witmer lit outta here yesterday headin' west. Likely as not, goin' up toward Uvalde by my reckonin'." He focused his view on the Colt parked in Luke's holster. "Nice piece there, Ranger. Looks like it's been coddled."

Luke smiled friendly-like. "It'd likely be offended by the word coddled. Well cared for would be more like it." He winked. "It's been put to good use." He brought the conversation back to his intended purpose. "So, did Witmer behave himself?" Luke knew the answer, but figured to hear it straight from the sheriff.

Bones wiped away a residual drool of tobacco juice with his shirt sleeve. He glanced again longingly at the chaw remains that lay in the street. "He added a couple ne'er-do-wells to our cemetery. Knifed one an' shot the other. Barkeep says twas pure murder."

"You didn't arrest him?"

Bones gave Luke a you've-got-to-be-crazy look. "I'm forty years old, Ranger. Like to live a couple more."

That told Luke what he needed to know about the sheriff's character while confirming the killings. "Anything else to add?"

"Witmer gave the barkeep a gold piece to pay fer burials."

Luke nodded. "Paid for burials?" He repeated the deputy's words. "Curious of him."

"Nothin' curious about him from what the barkeep had to say, Mr. Dunn." Bones wiped his mouth on his sleeve again. "Witmer didn't even deliver a mercy shot to one of the men. Just let the pitiful soul die in his agony."

"You certain he headed in the direction of Uvalde?"

"That'd be my guess." The sheriff paused and delivered an afterthought. "One of the men Witmer killed was sporting a

Sharps rifle. Dang nice piece. I woulda thought Witmer would take it, but he left it behind along with the remains of some sort of satchel."

"Well, that answers at least one thing. The two men were likely hired by Witmer to ambush a courier sent to deliver a message to me." Luke had quickly deduced that Witmer was somehow connected to the bushwhackers that killed the courier. "Thanks, Sheriff."

"Pleased to help, Mr. Dunn."

"Something else around these parts got my attention the past few days, Sheriff. You been hearing about fence cutters?"

"Hey, Luke! Luke Dunn!" Strong had spotted Luke from afar as he walked up the street toward the sheriff's office. He shouted out at just the moment Luke was posing the question to Bones.

Luke turned at the familiar voice and broke into a big grin at Strong's approach. "Jubal, great to see you."

"What brings you to Alice, Luke?"

"Getting some information on a murdering lawbreaker named Coy Witmer, though I was just asking the sheriff here about some fence cutting."

"Well, that's what I'm here about." Strong nodded to Bones to indicate what he was saying was intended for the sheriff, too. "My son Sam and I went out to put up some fence only to find part of what we'd worked on yesterday had been torn up. Whoever did it left behind this here threatening note that we'd be killed if we put up more fence. From the horse tracks, it wasn't likely more than two men." He handed the note over to Luke.

Luke thoughtfully stroked his mustache as he read the note and took in what Strong was describing. "Ran into a couple of cowboys chasing a fence cutter this morning. They're supposed to bring the cutter here to Alice if they catch him." He handed the note back to Strong. "Could be connected, but likely not."

Hollingsworth began to look just a tad overwhelmed. He'd let a murderer escape town, and now he was dealing with what had the early markings of a fence war. "I'll be lookin' out fer fence cutters, Mr. Strong."

Luke restrained himself, as he absorbed Bones's weak-kneed response. "You do that, Deputy." He turned to Strong. "Let's go over to the saloon and grab a drink, Jubal. Maybe we'll learn something from the cowboys before they get too drunk."

Luke and Strong had just about sat down and begun enjoying their beer, when they heard a whole lot of shouting from the street. The cowboys in the saloon had already begun heading out the door and were intent on joining the commotion. Luke pretty much figured what he'd be seeing, as he followed Strong out to the street.

Sure enough, there they were. The two cowboys who'd been chasing the fence cutter had apparently caught their prize.

The prize? Well, he was looking a bit haggard and forlorn. He'd been roughed up, set backward in the saddle, hands tied behind his back, and a poorly tied noose dangled from his neck. He looked as though a lynching might be a relief from what he'd been through.

"There he is!" One of the captors pointed to Luke. "We got 'em, Mr. Ranger. Can we hang him?"

The small crowd turned its attention Luke's way. This was the first they realized a Texas Ranger was in their midst.

Luke nudged Strong and whispered, "Watch my back." He strode over to the captive.

"We caught up to him just a few minutes after you stopped us, Ranger Dunn."

Luke chewed on that fact a minute, indulging his habit of

stroking his mustache to think as much as measure his response. He made a point of looking over the captors' horses. "I'm amazed, boys. Looking at those horses, I can't believe they could run that fast for that long."

"What you sayin'?" The second of the captors dismounted as he challenged Luke's observation. Like most men, he found himself in the awkward position of looking up at Luke.

"Just a couple of things, boys. In the first place, your cayuses were well-lathered when I stopped you. Second, your fence cutter was at least a half mile off and moving away from you. Third, your cayuses wouldn't have had it in them to close that ground much less catch up to your prey. And fourth... well, the man you were chasing had brown trousers." No one in the gathering crowd could miss the fact that the captive was wearing blue pants. "Looks to me like you got the wrong man."

"We found these in his saddlebag, Ranger Dunn." The first man wasn't totally backing off, as he dangled a pair of wire cutters at Luke. "What do you make of these?"

Luke nodded. "First, let's get this man dismounted."

The two cowboys grudgingly obliged Luke's request.

Luke had a hunch. He walked over to the captive's horse and unfastened the saddlebag flap. He peered inside, then looked over at Strong. "Jubal, come check this out." Luke pulled out a wire cutter but proceeded to drop it on the ground as though disinterested.

About this time, Hollingsworth made his appearance. Bones wisely didn't get in Luke's way.

"Where's that note you had, Jubal?"

Strong handed Luke the note.

Luke fished a torn piece of paper from the saddlebag. He held it up so all could see, and sure enough the torn edge of the blank paper matched the torn edge of the warning note that had been left for Strong. Luke smiled. "Seems y'all got yourselves a fence cutter...just not the one y'all had been chasing."

"Can we hang him now?"

Luke shook his head. "Somebody hired this man to do the fence cutting. If y'all hang him, we won't know who it was, will we?"

The cowboys were decidedly disappointed but nodded agreement.

The captive, who'd likely thought he was on the cusp of a reprieve, now had a new threat to face. He was pretty banged up and ached to be away from Alice, Texas.

Luke unfastened the noose from their captive and turned to face the crowd. "If y'all don't mind, we're going to take a walk down to visit Deputy Hollingsworth's little jail and have a talk with the prisoner." Luke smiled at Bones. "Sheriff, please do place this man under arrest."

Bones fully appreciated Luke deferring to him, especially after he'd permitted Witmer to leave town. It was what they called face saving. By now, he'd availed himself of a fresh tobacco chaw, so was feeling like a full-fledged lawman again.

Luke turned to the cowboys who'd captured the fence cutter. "Your fence cutter is still out there, boys. But we very much appreciate your work capturing this man." Luke fished a couple of coins from his pocket. "Have a round on me. If you do get your man, I ask that you once again do the honorable thing.

"Come on, Jubal. We'll finish those beers later." Luke followed Bones and the fence cutter to the jail, while the cowboys milled around the street for a couple of minutes congratulating the two fence cutter captors. They quickly enough worked up a thirst and headed back into the saloon.

★★

Uvalde wasn't the most exciting place to be laying low on this particular day. The game was boring. One of the players had drunk too much and had leaned over and barfed beside his chair. Blessedly, he'd mostly missed the table, but the barkeep was slow in coming over to mop up the mess. Witmer had won a few pots, but was barely staying solvent. He was convinced that the man to his left was cheating, but was reluctant to risk his peaceful stay in Uvalde by calling him out. It would have been easy to add the man to the list of his previous twenty-seven victims.

"I think I'll call it a night, gentlemen." Witmer began to push away from the table.

"What you in such an all-fired hurry to leave for, mister?" The man Witmer thought was cheating was itching for one more crack at the outlaw's money.

Witmer eyes turned to slits as he began to lay one of his evil glares on the cheater, but then he eased back. It didn't seem worth it to start any trouble for now. "You've got enough of my hide for one night."

"You implying I'm cheatin'?

"Nope. If you hang around town a couple more days, I'll give you another chance at my wallet." Witmer forced a smile through his thin, serpent-like lips. "I'm tired."

The cheat flashed him a suspicious look. "Ain't I seen you before?"

Witmer sighed resignedly. "I doubt it." This exchange was beginning to get on his nerves. It was all he could do to contain his urge to accuse the man of cheating and be done with it. "As I said, I'm calling it a night." As he got up, he made certain the cheat had a clear view of the blue-gray steel of the revolver poking from the black leather of his holster.

The move wasn't missed by the others at the table. They simply nodded and wished Witmer a good night. They'd likely decided not to be sitting in on Witmer's next game with the card cheat. Cowboys tended to be risk averse with these sorts of things.

As he strode from the saloon, Witmer began to think on where he might head if he was forced to eliminate the card cheat. He much preferred sticking around until he'd gotten word of Luke's latest whereabouts. The Texas Ranger had surely been to Alice by now. Maybe putting a good, old-fashioned whupping on the cheat would do for now.

"What's your name?" Bones had the fence cutter manacled to the chair near his desk.

"Ozzy Smith." The man wasn't sure of his fate at this point. Could be his hanging was simply being delayed. "And I never been in trouble with the law before."

Bones gave him an apprehensive look. "This is Alice, Texas, Mr. Smith. As best we can, we follow the law. Men are considered innocent until proven guilty in a court of law." Bones looked from Luke to Strong. "Y'all have an interest in this man. You have any questions?"

Luke worked up an angry tone. "Nope. Hell, let's just hang him and get it over with." His eyes drilled menacingly into the captive.

They noticed a wet blotch begin to spread itself at Smith's crotch. It added a certain pungency to the aromas of sweat and tobacco already lingering in Bone's office.

Strong had picked up on what Luke was up to. "Hold on, Luke. Maybe we can show some leniency if he tells us who hired him to threaten me?"

"You'd let him off?"

Bones enjoyed watching the dynamic between Luke and Strong and the expression of hope that suddenly spread across the still-bloodied face of Smith.

"Couple years in Huntsville might set Mr. Smith straight, Luke...if he tells us the truth."

Luke shrugged. "We'll see." He brought his face to within inches of Smith's. The prisoner reeled a bit at the heat of Luke's breath. "Who hired you?"

"Ott. George Ott. He hired me and Clem Haskins." In his nervousness, Smith right quickly gave up the name of the other fence cutter he'd worked with.

Luke stood back. "I know Ott. He's an irascible old-timer who hates fences. I expect we can find Haskins right easy, if he's still around." Luke turned to Bones. "How about locking this man up, Sheriff. I think you have all you need to put him in front of a judge. Jubal and I are going to go enjoy a beer. I'll go have a chat with George Ott tomorrow." He shook Bones hand and led Strong out of the jail and up the street to the saloon. "You done good in there, Jubal. I was hoping you'd pick up on my strategy."

The prisoner watched the two men leave, as the deputy led him to a cell. He shuffled along as though he could delay what seemed inevitable. "Am I gonna hang?"

"Up to the judge, Mr. Smith. It's up to the judge."

Smith's facial expression transformed from reluctant captive hopeless resignation to his fate. He had the crestfallen demeanor of a doomed man.

"I'll say that you cooperated." Bones offered a ray of hope.

Smith seemed relieved as he sat on the bed in the cell. Maybe, just maybe, life would give him a second chance.

"We'll get the doc to have a look at you."

FOUR
THE HUNT BEGINS

THE RIDE back to Heaven's Gate would take a bit longer than usual, since Luke was obliged to pay a visit to old man Ott's ranch. He didn't exactly look forward to this duty, especially as he himself had begun to string barbed wire at Heaven's Gate. As the saying goes, he had a horse in this race. Nevertheless, Luke was lawman through and through, and he wasn't going to truck the sort of threats Ott was spewing. Now that he wore the badge again, he had no choice.

Luke thought back on enjoying those beers with Jubal Strong at the saloon back in Alice. It was always good to catch up with old friends. What with all the work of running ranches and raising families coupled with often long distances between spreads, the occasion to tip a brew or two with friends was all-too-infrequent.

He glanced up at the archway spanning the entrance to Ott's ranch. It'd seen better days. So had the weather-worn sign hanging off kilter on the post, though it was certainly ominous. It read "KEEP OUT. TRESPASSERS WILL BE SHOT." Luke figured that sounded mighty un-Texan. He checked that his .44 caliber Colt Frontier was loaded just in case, swallowed hard, and ventured up the trail toward Ott's ranch house. He knew Ott had experienced rough times, losing his wife to yellow fever and having been swindled out of most of his live-stock. Still, the old man clung doggedly to the old ways.

Luke was perhaps two hundred yards from Ott's house, when a bullet whizzed past.

"Get off my land!"

"Yep," Luke thought to himself. "That's George Ott." Thankfully, the man's reputation for less-than-skilled marks-manship was well-earned. Luke didn't want to take a chance on him getting off a lucky shot. "Luke Dunn here, George! We need to talk!" He knew Ott's hearing was failing, so yelled as loudly as he could.

"You comin' as rancher or lawman?"

"Coming as a friend," Luke shouted!

"Ain't got no friends." Ott was being as cantankerous as ever.

Luke nudged Twister forward.

"I'll shoot yer butt oughta that saddle, Dunn."

"You better aim better, George!"

"Dammit, Dunn!" Frustration tempered the old man's curse. He might be an old crank, but he knew better than to shoot a lawman.

By now, Luke had ridden to within twenty feet of the front door. He'd already noticed that the old bunkhouse about fifty yards behind the house was in disrepair and empty by all indi-cations. "Come on out and talk with me, George." Luke was still talking loudly so Ott would hear him clearly. He put both his hands out palms up to show that he wasn't a threat.

The door creaked open, and grizzled old George Ott limped on out. "Whatta you want, Dunn?" His voice sounded like he appeared: gruff and rough. He smelled to high heaven even from that all too close twenty feet away. His clothes were ragged and hung loosely on his gangly frame. Likely, he hadn't bathed in weeks.

Luke resisted the temptation to cover his nose with his

bandana. "I'm here in my duty as a Texas Ranger, George." Luke made sure his badge was visible. "Lean that rifle against the door real gentle like."

Ott rolled his eyes, gave a half-snarling so-what look, and obediently leaned the rifle beside the door jam.

"Folks around here don't cotton to threats, George. I'll get right to it. Did you send men to threaten Jubal Strong for stringing barbed wire?" Luke didn't figure to mess around with niceties, as neither he nor Ott were in the mood.

Ott took a more defiant stance. "Yer damn right I did!" He spoke the words loudly, as many folks going deaf do.

"Well, you damn near got one of them lynched. He's sitting in the Alice jail. I'll be arresting the other one soon enough." Luke laid his most penetrating gaze on Ott. "If I don't arrest you, George, can you promise me you won't threaten any more folks?"

"Damned bob wire. It's killing the range, Luke."

"Well, it's here to stay, George. The folks up in Austin are making it a crime to cut wire fence, so you're going to have to get used to the barbed wire. Fact is, cowboys with fence cutters in their bag can be arrested." Luke paused to let that sink in. "You going to stop cutting fences and threatening folks?"

Ott tried to stare Luke down to no avail, then hung his head sheepishly. "Yeah, I promise."

Luke repeated emphatically, "Can't hear you, George!"

"I promise I won't cut fences or threaten anybody."

Luke pretty much knew that Ott had barely a penny remaining to his name, so wasn't going to ask the rancher to pay restitution to Strong. The old codger had likely used what little he had to pay the two he'd hired as fence cutters. "Here's what I'm going to do to make this right, George. I'm not going to put you in jail and not going to make you pay damages to Jubal Strong."

Ott looked up quizzically.

"Here's a piece of paper. You write an apology to Jubal Strong. I'll see that he gets it." Luke handed Ott the paper and a barely serviceable pencil.

Ott sat on the bench next to the front door and scribbled out an apology as best he could. He folded it and handed it up to Luke. "Thanks, Luke. Sorry fer the trouble." He had begun to appreciate the break Luke was giving him. Breaks hadn't been coming his way.

Luke took the note, then had a thought. "George, you ever think of selling this place and moving into town?" He knew the old man was lonely and not physically up to ranching. He just might benefit from social contact. "I know someone who might buy this place."

"Appreciate the thought, Luke. I'll think on it." It was clear that Ott stubbornly hung onto his memories of this place in its heyday.

Luke smiled. "You do that, George." He was relieved at no longer shouting to be heard, as he turned Twister eastward toward Heaven's Gate. He'd be sure to let Sheriff Whitely worry about catching the fence cutter's partner, Haskins. The man was likely long gone anyway. Luke's mind was again free to do some serious thinking as to pursuing Coy Witmer.

"Deal." Witmer had newfound energy. He'd won a couple of hands and was feeling lucky. A new deck of cards had appeared, and the players were working at getting them roughed up a bit. Wouldn't do to have the cards be too slippery. The man whom he'd suspected of cheating hadn't arrived just yet, but Witmer likely wouldn't have to wait long. He had a prime seat with his back to the wall. He'd heard what happened to Wild Bill Hickok up in Deadwood nearly a decade ago. Hickok failed to secure his favored seat with his back to the wall and was shot in the back of the head by disgruntled rival Jack McCall. Witmer wouldn't truck with that fate. He'd pass on any game before leaving himself so vulnerable. There'd be no so-called dead man's hand this day or any day.

The dealer had just checked his hand when he heard the familiar voice. "Can I join y'all?"

Witmer barely looked up and smiled. Had he been the snake his features so closely resembled his tongue would have darted out between a pair of fangs. "Sure, have a seat."

The cards had already been dealt, and the dealer called for anteing up. As Witmer's turn came around, he upped the ante and took one card. He had a straight, king high. He glanced at the new player. "You have a name?" He preferred to know the names of folks he might wind up having to kill.

"Jake Collins."

Witmer paused before responding. He turned to the dealer and laid out his hand. He'd won. As he scooped the pot his way, he spoke softly in Collins's direction. "My name's Witmer...Coy Witmer."

Collins shifted uncomfortably. "The Coy Witmer?"

Witmer's dark eyes darted about in mock surprise. "Seems like." It was all he could do to suppress a grin. There was something gratifying about having built a reputation.

"I assure you, Mr. Collins. I don't cheat none...nope... never."

"That's good to hear. So, relax, and we'll deal you in." Witmer nodded friendly-like to Collins who sat directly opposite him. If there was to be any cheating, he'd have a clear line of sight.

Collins nervously joined the game. It didn't appear there'd be any gunplay in Uvalde this night. The dealer glanced around the table, as though assuring himself that everyone was into the game. If he'd done any cheating before, he decided not to do any this day.

★★

Luke leaned back in his chair. He'd thoroughly enjoyed the breakfast feast Elisa had prepared. He pondered which would most likely be Witmer's destination of choice. Uvalde or Laredo? The folks in Alice hadn't been that much help other than Deputy Sheriff Hollingsworth's vague notion that the outlaw was heading northwest. Far as he could figure, that would take the man to Uvalde. He'd heard that the outlaw had an aversion to Mexicans, despite the hint of Hispanic and even Kiowa blood that apparently ran in his veins. Given the greater Mexican population of Laredo, Luke believed he'd most likely head to Uvalde. It was a bit further away, but that likely made sense for the fugitive. Word had it that Witmer also liked to pass his time playing poker, so he just might stick around so long as he'd managed to not kill some card cheat. Luke cogitated on how so many men that made a life on the wrong side of the law wiled away their hours gambling. Cards...cockfights...horse races...plenty to bet money on. Funny how they'd talk about their winnings but never their losses. Go figure.

Elisa refilled his coffee.

Luke arose and slipped quietly out onto the gallery. He was so deep in thought he hadn't heard her follow him out. He snapped out of his trance. "Thanks, sweetheart." He looked up from his cup to watch her walk back toward the door. She was sure worth watching. Hard to believe she'd borne ten children. Her slim petite figure was likely the envy of plenty of women around Corpus Christi. It sure was Luke's envy. As she grabbed the door latch, he couldn't resist. "Just coffee? No fringe benefits?"

She stopped in her tracks and smiled to herself. The spark seemed always to be there. She didn't turn just yet. "What do you have in mind, Mr. Texas Ranger?"

Luke put his coffee cup down, got up from the bench and

eased on over behind her. He kissed the nape of her neck. "Thanks again for the coffee…and that fine breakfast."

She turned, holding the hot coffee carafe away from her, and gave him a kiss. "That better?"

He nodded. "Seemed like some sort of deposit on a future benefit." He chuckled at his own humor.

"Deposit? Why, you're just going to have to wait until later to collect the balance due." Now, it was her turn to laugh. She smiled winsomely and stepped inside only to be brought up short.

Luke had begun to follow but came to an abrupt halt right behind her. His eyes quickly adjusted from the daylight and he could see past her shoulder.

Facing them just a few feet away was an angry diamondback rattling its fool tail off.

Ever quick to gather her wits, Elisa threw the remaining hot coffee at the snake. The scalding brew hit the rattler square in its fanged mouth and threw it into paroxysms of pain and even greater anger. It writhed about shaking its rattles madly.

Luke's hand had filled in but a heartbeat with his Colt Frontier revolver. A writhing snake didn't make for an easy target. Three blasts echoed through the house as the Colt belched flame and smoke. Two of the .44 caliber slugs actually hit the snake, one of them nearly slicing it in two and pretty much making a mess of the reptile.

For a moment, Luke and Elisa stood motionless in the doorway.

Grace appeared first on the stairway, followed by Junior, Sean, and Heather. "Momma! What the…?"

"Just a snake, Gracie. No bother. Your father took care of it." She didn't mention throwing hot coffee at the now dead reptile.

Junior walked cautiously over and picked up what was left of the snake that had been riddled by Luke's shooting. "Dang, the skin's ruined, Pa."

Junior's nonplussed reaction broke the shock-induced trauma of the situation. Luke and Elisa began to laugh.

"Watch those fangs, son. The danged thing still has his poison juices." Luke now began his detective work. How on earth did the rattlesnake manage to find its way inside the house? "Let's get that thing outside and look around for how it might have found its way to our kitchen."

"Gracie, Heather, let's make some more coffee. Looks like we'll be needing some fresh brew."

Luke and Junior dropped the snake outside on the gallery and began snooping around the foundation of the house.

"Pa, look here." Junior pointed to a crack in the foundation wall at the place where the addition met the house.

"That could be it, Junior. The addition settled enough to create a gap big enough to lure that rattler's curiosity. Guess we have a chore ahead of us." He sensed that Junior was anxious to fix the problem. "Remember how we mixed up some of that mud for the cistern?"

Junior nodded. "I'll get to it, Pa."

Luke smiled approvingly. Of his six boys, Junior seemed to be the one most like him. He felt confident in letting his son patch the gap, so lightheartedly vaulted up the stairs and into the house. "Lisa, is fresh coffee ready?" It was pretty much a rhetorical question. He poured himself a cup and sat at the kitchen table. It was sort of a signal that they needed to discuss something.

Elisa rolled her eyes in a what-now sort of way and plunked herself in a chair opposite Luke. "You're going to tell me about this mission?"

Dang, but she knew every time. Luke simply nodded and took a sip of coffee. "Might be gone a couple of weeks. Recall that McMurray's asked me to hunt down that Coy Witmer fellow." He let that sink in. "I understand he's up in Uvalde." He didn't have to tell Elisa that the northern reaches of the

Nueces Strip were characterized by wooded, hilly country ripe for ambush.

"Did you figure how the rattlesnake got into our home?"

"Junior found a gap in the foundation where we added the new bedrooms. It's likely the spot. He's going to throw some of that concrete into it." Luke smiled. "You up to fixing what's left of it for dinner? Maybe mix it in the chili?" He grinned broadly. "It's meat likely has a coffee flavor."

Luke's good-humored suggestion hadn't yet registered with Elisa. She ignored her husband's lighthearted humor. "Thank the Lord the snake never found its way to one of the children's rooms."

"Likely as not it was looking for a way out, but got side-tracked smelling your great cooking."

Luke wasn't letting up. "Guess he's destined to become part of tonight's chili." Elisa smiled at the thought. Turned out rattlesnake was pretty tasty when fixed right. Sort of a cross between chicken and sea scallops. "Just need to skin and bone the thing." She turned her full attention to Luke. "Final mission?" Interjecting about the rattlesnake had given her a momentary chance to think on Luke's upcoming adventure. She'd known since his exploratory trip up to Alice, that accepting the mission was a fait accompli. She simply wished it wasn't against so dangerous a man.

"I expect so. I'm not getting any younger." Luke knew he'd lost a step or two, but he was every bit the marksman and could ride with the best. "Where's Blue?" Blue was the puppy Luke had brought home a couple of weeks back. At the mention of his name, the pup came bounding down the stairs. It was a Blue Lacy, the same breed as the wounded pup they'd nursed back to health nearly twenty years ago. El Gato had been a loyal dog, helped with annual roundups, and loved the children. The Lacy was a blue-colored mix of English shepherd purportedly mixed with greyhound and wolf. They'd been bred by some fellow named Lacy, ergo the moniker. El Gato had earned his name by besting a lynx in a nasty fight. El Gato, of course, was Spanish for "the cat." He'd become so beloved by the family that it only made sense that they'd find another Blue Lacy to replace him after old age had finally caught up with the old foundling. Blue was nearly a year old and full of energy.

Elisa stroked him. "Wonder where he was when that rattler came calling? And he didn't even come downstairs at the sound of gunfire."

"He's not deaf, Lisa. I expect he was…"

"He was shut in our room, Pa," Gracie admitted as to how she and Heather had taken in Blue for the night. "We let him in last night."

Luke sighed. "You know he's supposed to sleep on the gallery. We made a nice bed for him out there."

Elisa added, "It's so he can warn us of trouble, girls."

"But…he…" Gracie quickly realized there was no point in arguing.

"He's got a job to do, girls. Everyone has a job to do, and Blue's is very important. He can't do his work snuggled up with you." Luke smiled as he appreciated their close relationship with the dog.

Elisa hesitated. "Your father's right, girls." She glanced at Luke who anticipated what she was going to say and nodded. "But just maybe, we can find another dog for your very own."

Luke signaled his approval. "Y'all can be thinking about a dog. I'm heading a bit north of here and do a bit of target practice. I'm thinking I'll be bringing that new Winchester with me." He tipped his hat to his young girls and turned but then hesitated. "If you young ladies would like to plink a target or two, you're welcome to come join me." Luke thought for a second on using the word plink. It sounded in retrospect to be inadequate to describe what a slug from the Winchester would do to a target.

"I'm coming." Gracie was ever her mother's daughter.

★★

Coy Witmer was growing uncharacteristically bored. He'd enjoyed a few nights of winning at the poker table, but the tedium of the game was fast overtaking him. Cards, whores, and whiskey couldn't compensate for a sense of purposelessness. He craved some sort of action beyond this routine that had begun to seem depravedly monotonous even with his skillful card playing. There were no players to challenge him. He didn't even have to deal with any card cheats, as his reputation had pretty much discouraged anyone so inclined. He sat in his room looking at the four walls. The view from the one small window of his room offered naught but the drab cream-colored siding of the building next door. He'd even caught himself counting the ceiling tiles. To relieve the ever-more-tiresome routine, he wended his way down to the gallery along the front of the hotel and kicked back on a bench. Now, he could count horses, or women, or whatever grabbed his attention and just might relieve that sickening sameness.

What to do? What stuck in Witmer's craw as much as anything was not having heard news about the famous Texas Ranger that was supposedly being sent to bring him in dead or alive. He was tempted to throw caution to the winds and ease back on down to Alice and maybe even tempt fate by going to Nuecestown to see what he might stir up.

His idyll was interrupted.

"Mr. Witmer?"

Witmer looked up from his seat on the gallery of the hotel. A young boy was holding a package out to him.

"The postman said to deliver this to you straight away, Mr. Witmer."

The outlaw smiled and took the package.

The boy remained standing before him.

Witmer's grin turned to one of resignation as he reached

into his pocket and fished out a coin. "Here you go, young man."

"Thank you, sir." And he ran off.

Apparently, there were some feelings left in the deep inner recesses of Witmer's soul. He looked at the address label. It was from New York City. He'd been expecting this. He began to open the package and drew out a fine brocaded black vest. He felt for the special pocket nestled in the lining. Yes, it would be perfect for the Colt Derringer he'd recently acquired. It was a single-shot weapon, but the 41-caliber slug it delivered was very effective at close range. He would no longer have to rely on reaching for one of his Colt revolvers in the event of trouble at the poker table.

He went to his room to try on his new acquisition. Perhaps he'd even wear it to the evening's games. Better still, he might get to use the Derringer hidden within its fancy fabric. Another night at the tables would be just fine, but tomorrow he figured to see what he might stir up.

Elisa had sent Luke down to the barn to prepare his equipment for the mission. She wanted him out of her hair while she whipped up a breakfast befitting her man who was about to ride off into danger.

Luke could smell the cooking aromas wafting down from the house. He lovingly finished cleaning his saddle. He examined each bullet hole and cut in its supple leather. Each told a story of near-death experiences and mayhem in his quest to deliver Texas justice. After many years strapped onto the back of Big Horse, the saddle had found its new home on the back of Twister, the big Appaloosa stallion. It was like a mystical connection from one loyal mount to the next. Luke would be leaving later that morning. He'd sit tall in the saddle, every inch the Texas Ranger that was his heart and soul. He looked forward to Elisa once again pinning the silver badge onto his blue shirt. It was a tradition begun a few years back and while Luke didn't believe in luck, he wasn't going to be changing the routine…especially as it seemed to comfort Elisa.

He'd given serious thought to recruiting Jake Barber or one of the other posse members that he'd led to put a Texas whipping on the Younger gang. Luke looked forward to returning to Uvalde and the scene of that victory from two decades ago. He was pretty sure that Coy Witmer was there.

Twister looked over from his stall and let out a snort or two in anticipation of being saddled. Horses had a way of sensing that something is about to happen. Luke went over and stroked the Appaloosa's forehead before heading back to the house.

Luke sat at the table flanked by four young Dunn children.

Elisa placed pancakes on a platter onto the table before untying her apron and sitting opposite her husband.

It was all Luke could do to get through a brief blessing before lathering his stack of pancakes with butter and honey and seeming to try to clear his plate in but a single bite. Dang, but Elisa sure could cook. He smiled lovingly at her, as his eyes then went from child to child. As with their six older children grown and leading their own lives, he saw the future of his family and of Texas before him. He was bust-a-button proud.

"What's on your mind, Lucas?" Elisa could see that Luke was experiencing an emotional moment.

"Just thinking on how lucky I am. God's plan sure has worked for us, Lisa." He sighed. All-too-soon, he'd be leaving the peaceful confines of Heaven's Gate Ranch and heading out to track down a depraved killer. He'd be putting himself at considerable risk, but that was part and parcel to the life path he'd chosen.

"I pray God's plan is to bring you back safe and sound, Lucas."

Luke gave final instructions to each of the children. Junior and Sean would share duties as men of the house. Heather would help her older sister. Luke left Grace for last. "That was some fine shooting yesterday with the Winchester, Gracie. Now, you be sure to be a help to your mother, but you might help Sean and Junior if the need arises."

Grace blushed. She had indeed obliterated several targets at respectable distances. She was her mother's daughter in more than appearance.

Soon enough, he led the Appaloosa up from the barn. At fifty years old, Luke didn't cotton to sleeping out in the elements so wrapped a large oilskin coat with his bedroll to use as a sort of tent. He'd thought about bringing a packhorse, but decided to travel light and be less of a target should Witmer decide on an ambush.

Luke held Elisa in his arms. He'd hugged each of the children, but this was by far the most difficult goodbye. He looked deeply into her near-tear-filled crystal-blue eyes. "I love you, Lisa. I'll be back."

He'd always returned. Seemed no reason to think he wouldn't this time. "I love you, too, Lucas."

They kissed a long, deep, love-filled kiss. The children blushed and covered their eyes.

Luke mounted the big Appaloosa. He sat tall in the saddle, once again every inch a Texas Ranger. He loved the scent of pursuit in the name of justice. The freshly oiled saddle squeaked as he leaned down, way down, and gave Elisa another goodbye kiss. "I love you, Lisa." He was soon riding off, turning once to give a wave to Elisa and the children before he was out of sight.

His thinking was to take the road from Nuecestown to Alice and San Diego, then head northwest, cross the Nueces River, and follow the Frio River to Uvalde. It would take about a week if he pushed hard. The upside was plenty of access to precious water, while the downside was...well...the all-too-real possibility of his prey setting an ambush. The countryside afforded plenty of ideal places to bushwhack an unsuspecting soul. Luke didn't feature Witmer becoming the hunter rather than the hunted.

FIVE
RUMORS AND FACTS

UNBEKNOWNST TO LUKE as he headed northwest from Heaven's Gate, the cauldron of trouble along the southern Texas border continued to seethe and boil. Mexican bandits were alive and well, and the Lipan Apache had not yet given up. Luke heard about the trouble, but couldn't be in two places at the same time. Depending on how his hunt for Coy Witmer turned out...but no, his days of hopscotching across the far reaches of the Nueces Strip were pretty much over. Deep in his gut, he knew that Witmer represented his final mission. The answer was that Texas Ranger Captain Sam McMurray would have to handle the border.

Riding the grassy prairies of southern Texas as Luke had done over roughly three decades, left such solitary riders quite alone with their thoughts. As he plodded along aboard Twister, Luke's thoughts turned to how Texas had changed since that memorable day when he'd landed on the pier at Corpus Christi and bumped into James Callahan. From Irish rebel to Texas Ranger turned out not to have been so great a leap. He right quickly came to the realization that Texas was far different from his native Ireland. County Kildare and Nueces County were far apart as to landscape, weather, and culture. He'd come to the realization that Texas...nay, America...was more than just a country with defining borders. It was an idea, likely one of the greatest ideas ever concocted by mortal man. He stroked his mustache. Dang, but he was part of this unique creation that a bunch of visionary folks a century earlier had come up with. Luke gently shook his head in wonder at how the land had evolved, as wave after wave of folks sought to better themselves, to carve livelihoods, to raise families. He was in a manner of speaking living the dream.

Luke brought the big Appaloosa to a halt and scanned the horizon. He took a deep breath. He couldn't afford daydreaming. Soon enough he'd be reaching scenery that might not be so friendly at least so far as his mission. The American idea had not stopped the lawbreakers or the hostile Indians. Humans, after all, were a frail lot, as virtues like prudence, temperance, justice, faith, hope, charity and fortitude weren't always ascribed to. Greed, vengeance, selfish pride, and more spawned the need for men like Luke to keep order and to bring justice to the victims. It wasn't always a pleasant task and as with this mission to capture or kill Coy Witmer, it could be downright dangerous.

He gently nudged Twister with his knees, sighed, and reminded himself to be extra vigilant. Soon enough this harsh, unforgiving countryside would be offering cover for bushwhackers or even Indians.

The ride to Alice went easy. It was late afternoon, so Luke went directly to the jail and hailed Bones Hollingsworth. "Bones! Get your sorry butt out here."

Bones staggered out onto the step and half stumbled into the street. He scrunched up his face, chewed a moment, spat into the dirt, and retorted, "Damn! Your hollerin' could wake the dead, Luke Dunn!" At least, this time he hadn't lost his chaw.

"Looks like I have." Luke grinned broadly. "Come on, Bones. I'll buy you dinner."

Bones squinted and paused as though deep in thought. "Yer bein' awful nice, Mr. Ranger. You lookin' fer somethin'?"

"Just company. From what I've heard, I've got a long ride ahead."

"Stow yer gear up at the Becham Place boarding house, and I'll meet you at the saloon."

"See you there, Bones." Luke turned the Appaloosa and rode up the street to Becham Place. It was a new establishment and represented a chance to get a final night's sleep in an actual bed before heading cross country in the morning.

Soon enough, Luke and Bones were seated in a back corner of the dining area of the saloon enjoying steak and beer. The aroma coming off that steak and fixings was just about enough to drown out the pervasive odors of sawdust, sweat, and booze that emanated from the bar. Luke relished the opportunity to sink his teeth into a thick slab of beef, especially given the likelihood that it might be a few days before he'd be sitting down to feast on another.

"What became of that fence cutter you had stuck away in your jail?"

Bones nodded. "Oh yeah. Doin' five years in Huntsville. Never did find his partner, though."

"I had a few words with George Ott. He apologized to Jubal and said he'd think on my suggestion to give up his ranch and move to Alice."

"Ain't seen him here, Luke. Let you know if he shows up."

"You might check on him, Bones. The man's a dying breed of sorts. Stubborn old cuss for sure." Luke paused thoughtfully. "Guess I'm going to be heading up to..."

Bones interrupted. He was well aware of Luke's mission so

strove to turn the conversation to other subjects. "You been followin' the crazy lawlessness down on the Rio Grande?"

A couple of cowboys at a nearby table perked up at mention of the Rio Grande.

Luke chewed thoughtfully on a piece of that mouthwatering steak. "From what I hear, Bones, Cheno Cortina's days raiding the lands along the Rio Grande are long gone. The old Red Robber earned the ire of his former friend President Porfirio Diaz." He took another bite of steak and savored a bit of cornbread. Not nearly so good as Elisa's, but worthy as cornbread went. He glanced up and saw that Bones was waiting for him to continue. "Ironically, Cheno's old enemy Rip Ford lobbied to save Cortina from execution. That having been said, it was the considerable money given to Diaz from ranchers in South Texas that led to the bandit's arrest. Pity that many loyal Cortina followers had been with him during his days of banditry in support of President Benito Juarez a mere dozen years ago. He's left high and dry on his own now."

"So, who's doin' the rustlin' and killin' on the border these days?"

"There's an old friend of Cortina named Tonto Lightfeather stirring things up. Lightfeather is a half breed of Mexican and Kickapoo blood and actually bares a slight resemblance to Cortina. He's managed to gain a following owing to his achieving some success mostly rustling beeves. He's making those South Texas ranchers rue the day they gave money to Diaz, as Lightfeather has rapidly become the bane of every Texas rancher. Hear tell there's a fellow named Catarino Garza waiting in the wings to take his place." Luke laughed and took another bite of steak. "Hey, you've got me doing all the talking. Anything exciting in Alice?"

"Usual." Bones squirmed a little.

"Something bothering you? What's on your mind?"

"Heard a rumor that Coy Witmer might be comin' back this way."

Luke raised his eyebrows.

The cowboys at the table next to them were now all ears.

"How'd this come to you, Bones? Uvalde's a long ride off yet."

"See that gentleman over at the far table?"

Luke nodded.

"Says he played cards with Witmer up in Uvalde. Almost got shot 'cause Witmer thought he'd cheated." Bones lowered his voice. "Says Witmer carries one of them Derringers in a pocket inside his vest these days."

"But he can't say for sure that Witmer's leaving Uvalde?"

"That evil sonofabitch likely doesn't know hisself whether he's leavin' Uvalde. The man's likely off his feed. If'n I knew that a Texas Ranger named Luke Dunn was chasin' me, I'd be right edgy too."

Luke glanced at the two cowboys who were now pushing back from their table. When they'd heard who he was, they decided to get acquainted.

"Pardon sir, did we just hear that you're Luke Dunn?"

Luke was pretty much resigned to his notoriety by now. "Yes. I'm Luke Dunn. May I help you?"

"Just wanted to make your acquaintance, sir. We'd heard stories back on the ranch of you keepin' law and order out on the Nueces Strip. Seems you've saved many a life fightin' outlaws an' such. From what we been told, yer sort of a legend."

Luke couldn't help but blush. Being referred to as a legend made him major uncomfortable. "Don't know about being any sort of legend, gentlemen. Just been doing my job." Being called "sir" stuck in his craw just a tad, as it made him feel old. "Of course, it's been a while since I last gallivanted across the Strip."

"Well, we're all grateful."

Luke took a last bite of cornbread. "Thanks...thanks kindly." Sure felt good to be appreciated.

The cowboys took turns shaking Luke's hand and departed. He was left chewing on a last bite of steak while Bones fought to contain his laughter at the Texas Ranger's discomfort with fame.

"Legend, huh?" Bones was still laughing.

Luke sought to change the subject. After all, he was buying dinner. "Did you hear about that Apache Chief Costalites?"

"Ain't seen no Apache in ages."

"Well, I heard he met his end gnawing on a dead rabbit while trying to stave off the effects of starvation. That Indian fighter Colonel Ranald MacKenzie stuck him in prison after the chief took a beating from black Seminole scouts at Coahuila, Mexico. Sad end. Costalites went on a hunger strike and managed to escape but met his end with that dang rabbit in the hills west of San Antonio."

Even Bones was affected. "Terrible end, Luke. I know lots of folks believe the only good Injun' is a dead Injun', but no human bein' should die in such misery." Bones quaffed the last of his beer.

"Well, the Apache haven't given up. Chief Magoosh stepped up. He's allied with the Mescalero Apache and is moving the Lipan band toward New Mexico. Likely good riddance so far as the Texas ranchers along the Rio Grande."

"Thank the Lord, it's all a long way from Alice, Luke."

Luke rightly figured Bones wouldn't cotton to fighting Apache. "If you'll excuse me, Bones, I think maybe I'll have a word with that fellow that played cards with Witmer. Be back in a couple of minutes I expect."

By now, the card player had attracted a couple of men interested in doing a bit of gambling.

Luke ambled over to the game.

"Care to join us?"

"Thanks, I don't play." Luke let his Texas Ranger badge show. "Mind if I ask you a couple of questions?"

The gambler's expression became quizzical. "Have I done something wrong?"

Luke smiled. "No. Heard you'd had a run-in with Coy Witmer."

"He seemed to think I was cheating. Witmer acted like he was itching to plug me, but then backed off. Guess it wasn't my day to die."

"Did he seem like he was going to stay in Uvalde for a while?"

"Seemed more like he was waiting for something. In my profession, I read folks, Mr. Dunn. I sensed that the man was seriously troubled, though he never revealed what it was. Given his reputation, maybe he was worried about you." The gambler shuffled the deck and began to deal. "As to him staying in Uvalde...hard to tell. He had an itch. That was clear as day." The gambler glanced up at Luke, smiled wryly, and then went back to the game. "Ante up, gentlemen."

Luke nodded. "Thanks." He watched the gambler deftly slip a card up his sleeve.

Bones sidled up to Luke. "You 'bout ready to go?"

"Just about. Let's go over to the bar for a few minutes."

Once at the bar, Bones whispered, "why the sudden interest in the card game?"

"You see the dealer slip that card up his sleeve? I wonder how long before someone notices?" Luke leaned against the bar and watched the action at the table. "Figure it shouldn't take long, Bones." Luke smiled knowingly.

Didn't take all that long, as it turned out. Bones leaned over toward Luke. "See that?" The deputy motioned to the barkeep. "Johnny, keep yer scattergun handy."

One of the players began to push back from the table. His hand slipped over the butt of the pistol at his side. "Yer a damned cheat!" rang out in the saloon.

The gambler had just begun to move his hand toward his gun.

Luke was at the table in just a couple of strides. His hand grasped the accuser's gun hand in an iron grip. Almost too late, the gun fired, the sound echoing in the confines of the saloon and the bullet plowing harmlessly through the floorboards. Time froze for a moment that seemed to last forever, as smoke from the gun hung in the air.

Bones held his own Colt on the gambler. "Mister, you can drop that gun to the floor real easy like. You got five minutes to be on yer horse an' ridin' outta here."

The gambler dropped his gun and then moved to grab the pot.

Bones fired into the ceiling. "Damn! Don't you dare touch that, mister! Just get yer lily-livered butt outta Alice." He swung the muzzle of his Colt to about a foot from the gambler's chest. "You want to test me?"

The gambler swallowed hard, stood, and began to briskly walk toward the door. As he passed Luke, his hand dug inside his coat. Before he could draw the hidden pistol, Luke's Colt arced through the air like lightning as the butt creased the back of the man's head. The gambler crumpled to the floor. Luke smiled and looked over at the men at the card table. "You boys go ahead and enjoy your game. Bones, looks like we've got a tenant for your jail." Luke picked the gambler up by the collar and dragged him out the front door. He paused and looked back at the twin boot toe marks through the sawdust that were left in the unconscious man's wake. "Come on, Bones, help me with this load."

A shaft of sunlight found its way to Witmer's face. He pulled the blanket over his head none too gently.

"Hey, I'm cold." The whore didn't appreciate his yanking most of the blanket from her. She pulled herself closer to his body. Her hands playfully sought his manhood beneath the folds of the blanket. "Warm me up, baby," she cooed.

Witmer groused. "Get your ass ought of here, bitch. I've got work to do." He pushed her away roughly and sat up.

"You owe me." She lay back, her nakedness half draped with the blanket, and pouted.

The outlaw grabbed a roll of bills and threw a couple on her ample chest. "We're even. Now, be gone."

She collected her things, forced a smile out of professional courtesy, and grudgingly slipped out.

Witmer watched her leave, thinking she hadn't been half bad in bed. Hard to look at, but good at her line of work. He'd already decided he was done with Uvalde. Gambling, booze, and sex were getting old as a steady daily diet. Time to move on. He intuitively knew that damnable Texas Ranger was coming after him. Maybe it was time to take care of that business once and for all. He pulled on his pants and boots, then strapped on his gun belt. Yes, it was time to take care of business. He fondled the gold watch with its two fresh grooves. He had a long way to go before he caught up with King Fisher's tally, but that damnable Texas Ranger sure would add luster to his credentials. Before leaving the room, Witmer gave a final glance at himself in the mirror. His smile likely as not should have put another crack in the glass. It was time to be the hunter, not the hunted.

He had a mission that now fully dominated his thoughts. It had risen to being an obsession. He had become the biblical evil one sent to steal life, to kill and destroy.

SIX
AMBUSH

LUKE HAD PRETTY MUCH FORGOTTEN what it was like to sleep on hard ground. Lonely, too. Years of coming home to a soft bed and loving wife had been kind to his aging body. The scars of battles past had long since healed, but his aching joints called out for his attention.

He stirred the coals and got a small fire stoked. A little coffee would be great about now. He'd appreciated the comfortable bed the night before at the boarding house back in Alice, and it had been good to get further acquainted with the deputy sheriff. The incident with the gambler managed to stoke the old memories of keeping the law. It was encouraging that he hadn't lost his lawman instincts.

Luke sipped a bit of coffee. Nice and hot. Chasing after Coy Witmer wasn't an easy task. The man obviously knew Luke was coming after him. He'd managed to evade the law for several years while leaving a trail of bodies. Twenty…thirty… forty…didn't matter much. Lives had been taken, loved ones grieved. Murder was an ugly business made so by ugly people. While shame was surely the legacy of fools, Witmer was surely a fool without shame. As his deeds went unpunished, his ego-driven taste for more as enhanced by his apparent obsession with Luke made him ever more likely to make a fatal mistake. In all his years of tracking outlaws and savages, Luke had learned to be ready, when the prey made that last mistake.

He chewed on some jerky and finished his coffee. His senses of impending trouble were heightened. His intuition laced with experience told him that the ride to Uvalde might not go so smoothly. He kicked dirt on the fire. He'd have to be doubly alert, as he rode closer to the town. No telling where Witmer might be lurking. Worse, he'd be traveling in territory that lent itself to bushwhacking opportunities. Witmer might very well lie in wait for him. Ambush was the method of cowards, and Witmer was ever the craven, gutless, lily-livered, shameless epitome of that role.

Luke stretched his aching muscles, saddled the big Appaloosa, and once again heading straight across the prairie toward his destination. He figured to follow the Nueces River to where it met up with the Frio River which he'd then trace to Uvalde. Twister for his part seemed a bit feisty, as though he sensed that this was no ordinary ride.

A lone Comanche riding a dun-colored pony with a packhorse in tow was not exactly an attention-getter given the path One Arrow had chosen to follow to find his friend Ghost-Who-Rides. From the outset, he'd decided to stay well to the west of the growing cities of northern and central Texas. Wherever possible, he followed less-traveled trails through dense forest and underbrush. The last thing he sought was to draw attention to himself. His buckskin shirt and leggings combined with the color of his horse served as fairly effective camouflage. The Henry rifle was hidden in a buckskin scabbard but easily accessible, while his lance and bow and arrow were tied to the pack horse close behind. One Arrow had become ever more reliant on the rifle with its firepower and ease of use. At his waist, his knife was easy to reach be it for hunting or scalping.

The Comanche chief's western route eventually took him to Uvalde. One Arrow knew that the Frio River would lead him toward Nuecestown and the Dunn's Heaven's Gate Ranch. Perhaps it was a coincidence or perhaps some sort of divine providence that found Indian, gunman, and lawman converging in the same area. That none knew of the others' presence made it highly unlikely that they'd cross paths. The chief now became extra cautious, as he knew that his journey was increasingly taking him through ranchlands, small towns, and military outposts. With the dense forest cover and escarpments along the Frio, it was reminiscent of his days with his adopted Penateka father and Chief Three Toes as the tribe hid fsrther north along the Guadalupe River. He recalled how the landscape afforded great opportunities for hunting both animal and human prey.

It was a great location at the top of an escarpment overlooking the dancing waters of the Frio. It made sense to Witmer that anyone traveling to Uvalde would track along the Frio. His field of view was mostly unobstructed, but for a few bald cypress growing along the river bank. Eventually, he'd see just about every traveler that journeyed past. He was sheltered from view by some Texas madrone and a few lofty oaks. He was high enough that he could even build a small fire and it'd be tough to spot from the river.

Witmer had eschewed the black jacket and vest he'd mostly worn in Uvalde. From his gambling winnings, he'd acquired a fringed buckskin coat. It helped him blend in rather well with his forested surroundings high on the escarpment. Sitting high on the rocky escarpment, he resembled a cold-blooded rattlesnake absorbing the warm rays of the sun.

Despite his mano-a-mano preference, he'd decided that there was no way he was going to confront the Texas Ranger. The grooves in his watch didn't distinguish how he killed folks. Bushwhacking was Witmer's modus operandi anyway. From what he'd heard, he dared not miss his opportunity. Luke Dunn had seemingly come back from the dead more than once to vanquish a foe that mistakenly thought they'd killed him. The outlaw was actually intrigued by the mystical treatment given the Texas Ranger by the Comanche who called him Ghost-Who-Rides.

He figured it might take a day or two yet, but he had plenty of provisions. He'd even managed to pack a couple of bottles of whiskey, though felt incentivized to not touch them until after he'd killed his prey. The weather was cooperating with cool breezes and a cloudless sky. It gave him a chance to look through the pamphlets he'd found at the general store in Uvalde. He couldn't read very well but his imagination was caught up with the drawings of the desperadoes profiled within the pages. He was especially taken with John King Fisher and Sam Bass, though Billy the Kid had captured his fancy as well. He was confident that his likeness and stories would soon grace the pages of one of these dime-store rags, assuming he could gain penultimate notoriety by adding Luke Dunn to his list of victims.

To catch such a big prize would take patience. He had time on his side, but he had to guard against his patience wearing thin.

As the hilly terrain became rougher, Luke became ever more alert to his surroundings. He had long since left the Nueces River and found himself tracing a pathway alongside the Frio. The big Appaloosa was proving to be a great traveler. The steed seemed to have no complaints. Luke could even direct him using his knees and an occasional heel. Not using vocal commands might be important to the task at hand.

Luke figured he could bet even money that Witmer would try to bushwhack him. He was concerned lest the hunter become the hunted. The terrain along the Frio afforded plentiful ambush vantage points. From what he'd heard, Witmer wasn't the sort of killer to confront his prey. It was highly unlikely that the outlaw would try to stalk him, so the common tricks for tracking prey would be pretty much useless. Heading off double backs and false trails wouldn't likely be coming into play. He tried to put himself inside the mind of a cowardly ambush artist like Witmer. Seemed likely that the outlaw would seek a high vantage point with a sweeping view of the river. Of course, it was assumed that folks traveling to Uvalde from the southeast would pretty much follow the river. In a sense, Luke was falling into Witmer's trap by continuing his track along the riverbank. He pulled up and pondered that a moment. He looked at the tangled underbrush of cypress roots and vines. They weren't especially inviting. He decided to adjust his travel further east of the Frio itself, though eventually he might be forced by the rough hilly terrain to track back along the river.

Boredom was inadequate to describe Witmer's state of mind. He felt like a circling buzzard waiting for its prey to die, only he'd have to kill it first. On the other hand, he held a perfect position if…a huge if…his prey wandered along the banks of the river. It had only been two days.

A lone rider with a pack horse appeared in his field of view. Witmer's mind raced with possibilities. It was a tall man. Hard to make out details at a distance. Was it Luke Dunn? If it wasn't, might a gunshot spook his prey?

The outlaw shrugged reflexively. A little practice might not hurt. It'd sure relieve the sheer tedium of waiting. He took a prone position and sighted on the rider. He was perhaps 200 yards off. With no wind, this would be easy. The outlaw aimed, let his breath out easy like, held it, and squeezed off a shot. The rider jerked involuntarily and fell from his saddle. Witmer watched cautiously. He could just about make out the form of the man lying face down in the Frio. He wasn't moving. Now, he had to get rid of the evidence in case his actual prey happened along. No sense raising suspicions.

He wended his way down to the river and waded the shallow waters until he reached the body. No question the man was dead. Number 28 for Witmer. The horses simply stood nearby. Witmer fetched the saddle horse. The outlaw managed to lift the dead man and hoist the body over the saddle. It took a bit more effort, as the man's clothes had absorbed water and made the body considerably heavier. Witmer tied him to the saddle and led the horses upstream past his own vantage point up on the escarpment. He gave the lead horse a swat on the rump and it ambled off with the pack horse in tow.

Witmer became annoyed with himself if only because he risked exposing himself and now was soaking wet and needed to dry off. He had become uncharacteristically vulnerable. He cursed his impatience.

One Arrow's ears perked up at the sound of the gunshot. Hunter? His curiosity was aroused. Despite the echoes reverberating from the hills, he had a general idea of where the sound had come from. He'd figured to trace the river the White man called Frio anyway.

Luke's journey up the Frio took him to a point where he was finally forced to turn back into the river itself. The banks no longer featured trees and underbrush, but had given way to cliffs and escarpments. He realized he'd become vulnerable but had little choice. He took out his telescope and scanned the upper reaches of the surrounding terrain. If there was anyone lurking, they'd be well hidden. He too had heard the gunshot, and it served to heighten his sensibilities.

He eased the Appaloosa forward. Something didn't feel quite right. Perhaps, it was the gunshot. It could have been a hunter, but...perhaps not. He clung to the north bank where the water happened to be shallower. A branch snagged his shirt and caused him to glance down. What was a hat doing floating on the water? He dismounted to investigate. On closer inspection, there were spots of what appeared to be blood on the brim. His intuition of looming danger was being validated. His practiced eyes surveyed the area. A small splattering of blood was on a nearby rock.

Coy Witmer's attention had been diverted reading one of his pamphlets for what seemed like the hundredth time. He glanced down at the river below. "Damn!" he muttered under his breath. Luke Dunn was standing just about where that unfortunate traveler had been the day before. He hurried to get into position. He fancied himself having nerves of steel, but such was not the case today. At a mere 200 yards, he felt confident—maybe a bit over confident. Excitement coursed through his veins. Jitters of any kind were not what he needed at this crucial moment.

He peered over the edge of the escarpment. He was deciding whether to let the Texas Ranger come just a bit closer, when he realized that Dunn was examining the hat that belonged to the stranger Witmer had killed earlier in the day. Alerted prey was especially undesirable to a cowardly killer intent on bushwhacking.

Luke had begun to scan the escarpment for any sign of a

threat. He was thinking that whoever had separated the hat from its owner might very well be long gone. It was no hunter. He grabbed Twister's lead and began to wade up the river. He stopped every few steps to scan the heights. He'd gone perhaps another twenty yards when he paused. The hairs were standing on the back of his neck. Danger was the loud and clear signal coursing through him.

Witmer took careful aim. This was a larger target than the day before. Damned well looked to be that Texas Ranger. Big man...red hair...yes, it was his prey. He took what most folks would consider perverse pleasure at how easy this was to be. His nerves steadied. He exhaled a bit and held his breath. His finger caressed and began to squeeze the trigger. Two near simultaneous explosions sent their echoes careening off the surrounding cliffs. The outlaw's eyes popped wide as he looked incredulously at his suddenly shredded hand and the splintered forestock of his rifle. He dropped the still-smoking weapon, fought off the urge to double over with the excruciating pain, and half ran and half tumbled toward his horse. He untied the hobbles with his good hand, threw the saddle onto the steed's back. He looked around in a panic. Where had that shot come from? Was he still in danger? He cinched the saddle with utmost difficulty, as his useless left hand throbbed terribly with pain. Wherever the shot had come from, the shooter must not have a full line of sight to his hiding place. Witmer caught his breath as best he could, as he wrapped his shredded hand tightly with his bandana to staunch the bleeding. He needed to get away from this place and fast. The pain was fast becoming excruciating, forcing him to double over the saddle horn and clutch the reins tightly, desperately.

Luke scrunched over reflexively with initial shock and pain. A bullet had creased his shoulder and whizzed past the Appaloosa. He instinctively drew his Colt revolver, though he knew it likely wouldn't be effective unless the threat was close at hand. Despite the cacophony of echoes that had reverberated through the river canyon and the pain from his wound, he was convinced there'd been more than one shot. He'd briefly seen a puff of gun smoke high on the escarpment above. Given that he'd heard two shots fired, his instincts suggested that whoever had fired at him was likely escaping. He took cover behind a pair of large boulders at the river's edge. Now, the question was where had the second shot come from?

He grabbed his bandana and pressed it against the shoulder wound to staunch the blood, as he scanned the surrounding cliffs for whoever else was out there. The danged wound hurt like hell. He'd been shot before, even wounded seriously by a Sharps rifle. But the kicking in of his adrenaline did little to assuage this pain. Maybe it was age. In any case, Luke was exposed and could only pray that the second gunman was no enemy.

"Ghost-Who-Rides." It was a near whisper.

Luke looked around trying to deduce where the voice had come from.

From the rocks upriver, One Arrow now appeared with two ponies in tow. He carried his prized Henry rifle. "Man gone. One Arrow shoot." He smiled broadly. It'd been a tough shot for the chief looking up at the bushwhacker high on the escarpment.

"One Arrow? What the..." To say Luke was surprised at the appearance of the Comanche chief would be a considerable understatement.

"You okay, Ghost-Who-Rides?"

"Just a nick to my shoulder." Luke's attempt at manfully downplaying the impact of his wound was lame at best.

They looked at each other in curious wonder. More than the sheer luck at meeting there in the middle of the Texas frontier on the Frio River, they were confronted with physical change. It had been twenty long years. Luke was fifty, and One Arrow barely a half dozen years younger. Both had flecks of gray in their hair though had stayed physically trim. Hard work would tend to do that.

To Luke, the chief remained every inch the image of the fierce Comanche warrior locked away in his memory. "It is good to see you, One Arrow."

The chief appreciated the understatement. Had he not appeared on the Frio when he did and seen the bushwhacker, Luke likely would have been breathing his last. "Hungry?" One Arrow motioned toward a level rocky area sheltered from any line-of-sight from the escarpment above and suitable for building a small fire. "Have medicine for wound."

They led their mounts over to the spot. The chief gathered some wood and built a fire. One Arrow drew some materials from his pouch and was soon making a poultice to apply to Luke's wound.

"How did you find me?"

The Comanche shrugged, as he applied the poultice. A chance encounter wasn't easy to explain in English, but an ambush was. "One Arrow leave Penateka to visit Ghost-Who-Rides. Travel long way." He gave an enigmatic smile. "One Arrow hear gun. Wonder if hunter. Follow river. See man up high, then see Ghost-Who-Rides. Think fast."

Upon realizing that it was indeed pure chance that the chief had arrived at exactly the right time and place, Luke sank to his knees and muttered a short prayer. He was incredulous. "I thought you were with your people. You say you come to visit me?"

"Great Spirit call me to find Ghost-Who-Rides." One Arrow was equally caught up with the sheer chance of the moment. "Three Toes right. Ghost-Who-Rides have strong medicine." He reflexively toughed the cross dangling from the bone necklace.

Luke sat back, stroked his mustache, and smiled. "Seems like." The poultice was already having its soothing effect, and he began heating up some coffee while One Arrow produced some venison jerky.

"Why you travel this way?"

"I'm hunting an evil man. Likely the one that tried to bushwhack me."

"Bushwhack?" One Arrow looked questioningly.

Luke had forgotten that the chief was still learning English. "Ambush. The man kills people from hiding."

One Arrow shook his head. At least, Comanche killed people for a purpose as in acquiring a rival tribe's horses or proving a warrior's manhood. "Why he kill?"

"He's sick in his head. Loco." Luke looked up at the top of the escarpment. "Let's ride up there and see what we can find."

One Arrow had anticipated Luke's next move. He too was curious as to what they'd find.

They finished up the coffee and jerky. Luke ignored the dull pain in his shoulder and mounted up. They were soon seeking a way to the top of the escarpment.

The terrain didn't exactly make for a fast escape, but Witmer was doing his best. His left hand hurt like blazes. Where had that shot come from? Bad enough he might have failed to kill the Texas Ranger, but there was apparently someone out there who was protecting the damned lawman. This added an entirely new dimension to his situation.

He headed back toward Uvalde. He had no idea what had happened to whomever had shot him. It had been stupid to warn his prey and whoever else was out there by killing the traveler. He desperately wanted to get back down to the chilled waters of the Frio and clean up his hand. The bullet had surely broken some bones and would likely cost him a finger that hung by a mere thread of skin. He finally made his way ever-so-carefully down to the river. He was at least a couple of miles from the ambush site, so didn't figure they'd be chasing him in broad daylight.

He dismounted and plunged his hand into the water. It hurt like hell, but the chilled waters ultimately soothed the pain. He removed his hat and became aware that the bullet that had torn through his hand and ruined his rifle had put a clean hole through the crown of his hat. He'd nearly been killed.

It gave him pause to think a bit more on his own shot at the Ranger. He had no idea whether his bullet had found its target. Here he was running from whoever had fired at him and possibly a wounded Texas Ranger. Fear of the unknown was working its havoc on his cowardly evil mind.

Witmer decided to continue his ride on to Uvalde and have his hand tended to. He wouldn't be doing any lingering, not with one or more people hunting him. Maybe after he got his hand dealt with, he might double back and see if he could see who was on his trail. But that might not be too wise given the condition of his wounds. Shooting a rifle was not likely to be in the cards for a while. He needed a new rifle for certain, as the bullet that hit his hand had splintered the rifle's wooden forestock that he'd been holding and seriously damaged the barrel. Thus, armed only with his revolver and Derringer, discretion was in order. There'd be time for regrets, for adding number 29 to his list. Better to move on. Laredo started to work its way into his thinking.

"This good place for bushwhack." One Arrow pronounced the last word slowly.

Luke had already begun to investigate the site. He kicked dirt onto the remaining embers of a fire. His eyes caught the glint of sun on blue steel over near the edge of the cliff. "Dang,

Chief. You made a mess of the man's rifle." Luke couldn't contain a smile of approval. "I expect your bullet hit just as the shooter squeezed the trigger. A split second later, and you might have been burying me."

One Arrow nodded grimly.

Luke kneeled to examine the splintered wood from the rifle and the spray of blood droplets around where the man had lain and his wound had bled. "I'd say you hit his hand, Chief. Likely hurt him seriously." Luke shook his head in wonder as he arose to continue his search of the site. "Looks as though he was up here for a couple of days." A bedroll and saddlebags remained, as the man had run off in a desperately big hurry. Luke dug into the saddlebags. He pulled out two bottles of whiskey, opened one, and took a whiff. "Whew, this is rotgut whiskey, Chief." He poured out the contents, then reached back into the saddlebag. "What's this?" It was a rhetorical comment. Luke had come up with a wanted flyer. "Look here, One Arrow. This flyer has Coy Witmer's name and picture on it." Luke read the copy at the bottom of the flyer. "Says he's dangerous and has killed twenty-four people. Only twenty-four? Must be an old poster. Seems like there's a pretty big reward dead or alive."

One Arrow looked quizzically at Luke. "What is reward?"

"Comanche take scalps, maybe horses. That is Comanche reward. White folks pay money to capture or kill lawbreakers. That's called a reward."

"Not same. Comanche brave. Count coup first. Warrior count coup, kill, and get scalp as reward." One Arrow folded his arms as if to say that was his final position on the matter.

Luke stroked his mustache thoughtfully. The Comanche chief actually made sense...at least for the tribal culture. He threw Witmer's saddlebags over the back of the Appaloosa. "Let's head to Uvalde, my friend."

They made their way down from the escarpment and were soon slowly tracing the Frio toward the town.

✷✷

By the time he reached Uvalde, Witmer's hand was throbbing enough to make him nauseous. Loss of blood combined with hunger were clouding his thinking. He desperately needed to get medical attention.

A full moon lit the last mile of Witmer's ride into Uvalde. It was all he could do to stay in the saddle. He stopped in front of the hotel and half slipped, half fell from his horse. He staggered toward the front door, opened it, staggered, and finally fell into the foyer.

The hotel clerk had been closing up for the night and was startled by the door being flung open and the sudden thud of Witmer's fall. "What the?" He rushed over to the fallen man's side.

Witmer face was white as a ghost. He could do naught but mumble, "Doc...doctor."

The clerk dragged him over to a nearby settee and lifted him onto it as best he could. He couldn't help but see that Witmer's hand was in bad shape despite it being wrapped in the blood-soaked cloth. "Damn, that looks bad. You stay here, mister. I'll fetch the doc." Witmer wasn't going anywhere.

SEVEN
THE HUNT RESUMES

"ELISA'S GOING to be none too happy with me ruining this new shirt." Luke was making small talk with One Arrow, as they waded through shallow waters and occasionally mounted up and rode along the banks of the Frio River on their way to Uvalde. They were soaked to the skin from the waist down. The fragrant aroma of wet leather and denim was a not so heavy price to pay, as they dodged rocks and overhanging branches. After all, the route up the Frio was the most efficient path.

"She be happy you safe, Ghost-Who-Rides."

Luke couldn't argue that point. "No question you shot the man. Wonder how bad he's wounded."

"Saw red cloud. Heard yell. You saw blood on ground."

Luke chewed on that. He was still trying to figure out how serious Witmer's wound might be. The red cloud was likely a mix of dust and blood. He hadn't heard any shout, but then he was rather distracted at the time. He'd long since gathered his wits, as he had a mission to complete. A little extra help might not hurt. "You want to join my hunt?"

One Arrow smiled broadly. He recalled Three Toes's tales of hunting Mexican bandits with Luke. He'd dreamed of such an opportunity. He stopped smiling and gazed intently at Luke. "We hunt."

They hadn't ridden but another hundred yards or so, when Luke pulled up. "What's that on those rocks over there?" He rode over for a closer inspection. "Dang, but we were right, Chief. The man is seriously wounded." Luke wished he could confirm that this was indeed sign that it was Coy Witmer who'd been wounded. The blood spots were a dark reddish brown, having been there long enough to have already dried.

"I think he's not going to stay in Uvalde long, Chief. He'll get his wound tended to and continue his escape."

"He no food, Ghost-Who-Rides."

Luke nodded. "There was money in the saddlebag. He might have a little on him. He'll need to find food and get another rifle. Likely have to pay some doctor something, too." Luke would prefer to catch the outlaw while he was most vulnerable, but their prey had at least four hours head start from the scene of the ambush. It was the price the Texas Ranger had to pay for having his own wound tended to and investigating the site of the ambush.

"Where you think he go, Ghost-Who-Rides?"

Luke stared at One Arrow. "My friend, please call me Luke."

The chief was quick to oblige. "Where you think he go, Luke?"

"If he's got the strength, he'll likely head to Laredo. The weather is getting to be right changeable to the north." Luke knew Witmer wouldn't be fool enough to chance that. He'd know how the Texas Panhandle could be hot and bone dry one day and blow a raging blizzard at unsuspecting travelers the next. "Maybe we could try to intercept him." Luke realized One Arrow likely wouldn't understand intercept. "We could cut him off from where he's headed."

"How Luke's shoulder feel?" It was a gentle reminder that Luke just might want a White man's doctor look at his wound.

Luke sighed. He knew One Arrow was right. The wound throbbed just a tad in spite of the soothing effect of the poultice the chief had applied. "I'd sure like to get ahead of Witmer... but you're right. Let's head to Uvalde. Maybe he'll have passed out somewhere."

★★

"That's about the best I can do, mister." The doc had stitched up Witmer's hand, though try as he might he couldn't save the little finger. "I'm afraid you're going to have one less finger." The doc finished bandaging and began to pack up his bag. "We should change that bandage in the morning. It'd wouldn't do to have the wound get infected."

Witmer was still groggy. He turned to the hotel clerk. "I need to eat something. You have any food?"

"I'll see what I can do, mister...?"

"You don't need to know my name."

The clerk wasn't going to argue. He shrugged and ran back to the kitchen to see what grub he could rustle up.

The doc looked at the outlaw with concern. The wound was clearly the result of a bullet. "How'd you manage to get this wound?"

"Shot with my own rifle, doc. Stupid of me."

Doc knew right away that the wound wasn't self-inflicted. There was no gunpowder residue. He'd pulled a couple of wood splinters from the outlaw's hand, so that served as evidence of something more than an accident. "Well, you'd better get some rest. I'll leave my bill with the clerk in the morning. You can pay me when I stop by to change that dressing." Not said was his plan to pay the sheriff a brief visit on his way home.

Witmer was already thinking on his escape from Uvalde. Between that and his growling empty stomach, he was beginning to get desperate again.

The hotel clerk reemerged with some victuals.

The outlaw wolfed down the meal as though he'd never eaten before. Between bites, he stared up at the still startled clerk. "Know where I can get a rifle at this hour?"

The clerk wanted to ask why, as the man obviously wouldn't be shooting a rifle for a while. There was something familiar about the wounded interloper, and he sensed it wasn't a good feeling he was having. He looked at the Colt revolver nestled in the man's holster. Maybe it was best to not challenge the stranger. "I'll see what I can do."

"Do make it fast. I won't be staying here tonight. I'll pay you whatever the rifle costs." Witmer struggled but managed to sit upright on the settee. "Just find me one that can shoot."

The clerk disappeared into the night.

Witmer sat rubbing his forehead. This was not turning out well at all. Botching the ambush seemed to be the least of his worries. He was certain the doctor recognized him. His heavy thinking was interrupted by the return of the hotel clerk.

"I found an old Winchester 1873, mister."

Witmer nodded. "Thanks." The rifle was a lever-action piece that didn't exactly lend itself to a one-armed shooter, but it would have to do. "You have ammunition?"

The clerk handed the outlaw a bag of bullets.

"What do I owe you?"

"Five dollars, mister."

Something clicked inside Witmer. "Show me how this works." He knew full well how the Winchester worked. He'd owned one.

The clerk dutifully loaded the rifle.

"And the lever?"

The clerk cocked his head inquisitively. "If you're gonna shoot, you might want to go outside, mister."

"Well, let's go outside." Witmer was still feeling a tad weak from loss of blood, but he was nevertheless in command of his faculties. The food had served to reenergize him a little. He got up as gingerly as he could from the settee, paused to find his balance, and followed the clerk out the door. They stood in the street near Witmer's horse. The cool evening air further revived him. "Cock that thing and hand it to me."

The clerk did as he was told.

With his good hand Witmer pointed the Winchester at the clerk.

The clerk's eyes bulged. What was happening?

The outlaw swung the muzzle to the left of the clerk. He squeezed the trigger, and an explosion ripped through the still night air as fire and smoke belched from the muzzle of the Winchester.

"Ugh!" A grunt emanated from behind the clerk. The doc had indeed fetched the sheriff who now lay bleeding out in the dirt of Uvalde's main street.

Witmer tossed a coin at the fear-quivering clerk. "My name is Coy Witmer. In case anyone's counting, that was number 29." An evil smile swept across his face. He hesitated before slipping the rifle into the empty scabbard and climbing into the saddle. "If anyone's looking for Coy Witmer, you tell them he headed north." He looked down at the dead sheriff, kicked his heels into the sides of his mount, and galloped off.

The clerk was left in a dazed stupor. He'd totally voided his bowels at the sound of the rifle. As he turned to check on the sheriff, two riders appeared at a gallop. First a murder before his very eyes and now a big White man with an Indian appeared before him. He fainted.

Luke pulled up and dismounted. He and One Arrow had spurred their horses at the sound of the rifle. The sheriff was obviously quite dead. The other man was breathing but stunk to high heaven.

A small group of citizens began to gather around. The saloon emptied onto the street.

"What'd that Injun do?" An accusatory growl got Luke's attention.

"Who said that?" Luke turned to face the crowd. His Texas Ranger badge was on full display and one of his Colts had found its way into his hand.

A grizzled half-drunken cowboy stepped up. "Me. I said it."

"Well, the chief here is with me. You want to make that accusation again?"

"Who the hell are…"

"He's Texas Ranger Captain Luke Dunn, George. Don't you go messin' with him." Another voice had joined the conversation.

Luke ignored the men, holstered his revolver, and motioned to a couple of bystanders. "You men take care of the sheriff's body. If he has any family, you better let them know. Is there a deputy?"

"No, sir. Guess we'll have to find another."

Luke turned his attention back to the hotel clerk who was now on his knees and had managed to come out of his faint. He looked down and was embarrassed at the large dark dampness around his crotch, not to mention a worsening stench.

One Arrow sat astride his pony taking it all in. He admired the way Luke took charge. He looked very chief-like and stared down a couple of the bystanders that were likely thinking like the old drunken cowboy.

The hotel clerk finally stood. He was desperately uncomfortable. "What happened?"

Luke shook his head resignedly. "I expect you met Coy Witmer." Luke pitied the young man. "Go clean yourself up and get yourself back here pronto."

The clerk wasted no time running wide-legged into the hotel while avoiding eye contact with the bystanders.

Luke recognized the judgmental looks on the bystanders' faces. With his practiced lawman eyes, he surveyed the small crowd. "Give the young man a break. He just had a man fire a bullet past him at point-blank range." He couldn't contain a smile, as he stroked his mustache. "The shooter was Coy Witmer. He's wanted for murder. Anyone see which way he rode out?"

Blank looks.

"Was he in Uvalde before today?"

The old cowboy was sobering a little and managed to sound less grumpy. "He played cards at yonder saloon for a few days. Thought he was gonna kill a card cheat first day." The cowboy shook his head at the thought. "Lit outta here a couple days ago. Said he had some sort of appointment."

The hotel clerk reappeared. He was cleaned up and not so embarrassed. He still carried some residual odor with him. "Mr. Ranger, the man did say he was Coy Witmer and if anyone was lookin' for him to say he was headin' north."

Now Luke had a dilemma. Did Witmer say north to get Luke to head south? Did the man think Luke would fall for that old ruse? "Which way did he ride?"

The clerk pointed north. "That way, sir."

"Thanks. Was he wounded?"

"The doc tended to him. Mr. Witmer's left hand was messed up pretty bad. Lost a finger, too."

"Did you see his horse?"

The clerk pondered that a moment. "The horse looked to be in good shape, Captain." The clerk thought a minute. "He didn't have no food or water with him. No saddlebags or bedroll either. But for saddle and bridle, the horse was pretty much naked."

One Arrow pushed his pony closer to Luke and the clerk much to the consternation of the crowd. "Was rifle Henry?"

The clerk wasn't used to being questioned by a Comanche chief.

Luke didn't hesitate. "Answer the chief."

"I gave him a lever-action Winchester." The clerk shook his head. "Damn. I loaded and worked the lever for him. He could've killed me."

"Not likely, son. He needed someone to pass along his message."

"Are you hunting him?"

"Afraid so. But I have a great hunter with me." Luke nodded toward One Arrow who proudly suppressed a smile.

"After he shot the sheriff, Witmer said 'that was number 29.' That's when he mounted up and told me who he was."

A twittering of concern ran through the bystanders at the outlaw's boast of having killed his twenty-ninth victim. "You think you can get him, Mr. Ranger?"

Luke gave an aw-shucks sort of smile, then got serious. "We're sure going to try." He looked around. "You have a livery stable around here?"

The clerk stepped up. "Up the street. Happy to give you a room, Captain, but we don't allow them kind." He nodded toward One Arrow.

"We'll sack out at the stable. No point in chasing Witmer in the dark. That full moon doesn't offer enough light except to make bushwhacking too easy. Looks like it's clouding up, too. Tougher to track a man." Luke took the reins of the big Appaloosa and walked up the street toward the stable.

One Arrow dismounted and came up beside him. "You good man, Luke. Maybe you make good Comanche." He gave an uncharacteristic chuckle. "White men look at me like I take dead man's scalp." He laughed again.

Luke could do naught but smile at the chief's attempt at humor. "We'll head toward Laredo in the morning. Let's get some shuteye."

Soon enough they'd tended to their horses and were sacked out on thick beds of straw.

Unsure as to whether he'd hit Luke, Witmer wasn't wasting any time heading away from Uvalde. He rode about a mile out of town before turning south toward Laredo. He figured he'd likely find a ranch or two along the way and get some grub. Once in Laredo, he'd head across the Rio Grande into Mexico and hole up there to let his hand heal a bit. Likely as not, there'd be a sawbones who could change the bandages on his hand. He knew just enough Spanish to get by so far as being able to communicate with the locals. As to being safe in Nuevo Laredo, he was well aware that Texas Rangers had been known to cross into Mexico to get their man.

Meanwhile, the trail was rough enough in daylight. He had little choice but to stop for the night. Lack of a bedroll and no food became the least of his worries, as a misty rain set in. The rain didn't last long, but it was just enough to make him more miserable than uncomfortable.

He didn't even know who had shot him, and the facts that he didn't know whether he'd hit his target and he'd been wounded himself weighed heavily on him. Fear of the unknown was always a scary partner, even for someone like Witmer who was a coward of the first order.

EIGHT
ROAD TO NUEVO LAREDO

THE SUN HAD JUST CRESTED the eastern horizon, its rays casting the lingering mist in a phosphorescent glow. Luke lay for a few moments with his head propped against the saddle. He looked at the nearby bluebonnets waving in the gentle morning breeze. With a bit of a grunt, he managed to stand.

The coals were still smoldering, so he stoked the fire a bit. No sense tracking Witmer on an empty stomach. He looked over at One Arrow. The Comanche was just beginning to stir. "Beautiful day, Chief." Luke had by now begun heating up some coffee. He broke out a small fry pan.

A sizzling sound grabbed the chief's attention. He wasted no time shaking the straw from his blanket and ambling over to the fire. "Eggs? Where you get eggs?"

"Farmer dropped by at sunup and shared a few." Luke smiled at his good fortune. "No ham or bacon though."

One Arrow peeked outside the stable and sniffed the air. "Rain last night."

"Yep, and Witmer likely got a bit wet." Luke smiled at the sense of justice he found in that thought.

Anxious as they were to get on the trail, they barely

savored their feast. Luke offered to pay the stable boy, but having a Comanche chief sleeping in the stable had unnerved the young man such that he was relieved to simply have Luke and One Arrow be on their way.

"The hotel clerk said Witmer rode north. I expect he wouldn't go far before turning south. Despite the rain, we should be able to find his trail." Luke was nothing if not confident. The outlaw was wounded and hungry, and those two factors generally led to carelessness.

The chief agreed. "He wounded. No eat. Need help with rifle. No hunt."

Luke nodded. One Arrow had that right. Witmer would likely get ever-more desperate for food. They'd have to especially be on the lookout for any ranches that might cross the outlaw's trail. "Likely should do one more thing before we leave Uvalde. I must let Elisa know we're all right."

One Arrow looked inquisitively at Luke.

"Won't take long. I'll send her a telegram by those wires." Luke pointed up at the telegraph wire.

The chief could only shake his head with astonishment.

"My friend, you have learned many English words and know the letters of our alphabet. The telegraph has a code for each letter."

One Arrow looked puzzled.

"The code is made of long and short signals. Short signals are dots, and long ones are dashes." Luke grabbed a stick and scratched a dot and a dash in the dirt. "The code for an "S" is three short signals. For an "O" it's three long signals." As he etched dots and dashes in the dust, Luke tapped out the chief's name in the code that Samuel Morse had invented for the telegraph.

The chief repeated the code.

"That's pretty good. I'd be happy to teach you more. It might come in handy one day." Luke got to thinking that the code might even prove useful in the hunt for Coy Witmer.

Once Luke sent off his telegram to Elisa, he promptly refocused on the task at hand. They departed Uvalde and rode up the road slowly, as they kept an eye out for sign. Twister seemed to sense the excitement of the hunt but eased along quietly with an occasional nod of his head. They'd ridden not much more than a mile, when One Arrow was first to spot it. He pointed to a break in the brush. "He sleep there." The chief rode over to a depression beyond the gap in the undergrowth. "Plenty horse track."

Luke dismounted and examined the ground around the depression more closely. Despite the light rain, there was evidence that Witmer's wound was still bleeding slightly. Luke wondered whether the man might die from infection before they could catch up with him.

A narrow column of smoke could be seen off in the distance. With the warm rays of the rising sun and the prospect of resupplying, Witmer began to feel some renewed vigor. It was hard to tell from a distance, but it looked like a campfire. The all-important question was how many folks might be at the site?

Witmer turned the horse toward the smoke. He cursed that he'd slept over top of his wounded hand. He'd managed to keep it dry, but it had begun to bleed a bit and now it throbbed mercilessly. The desperado needed to get close enough such that his revolver would be effective. There was no way he was ready to work the lever on the rifle. Might even blow his head off trying.

At about 300 yards, he'd not yet been noticed. He dismounted. The rough brush was tall enough to just about hide him. He was downwind, which made his approach a bit stealthier. He kept his bearings by watching that telltale column of smoke. He finally drew close enough to hear voices.

From the sound of voices, it seemed to be no more than two men. Perhaps, number 30 and 31 were close at hand. He wasn't up to parlaying, especially since he had no money left to trade with. It'd save him time and effort to simply kill whoever was there.

The early evening air seemed to hang especially heavy, as Witmer managed to draw within a mere 75 feet or so of the two men. He made the men out to be cowboys. Likely, they were returning from a day of chasing down stray beeves. He had them dead to rights, totally unaware of his presence. He didn't give a second thought to approaching them peacefully. He didn't see any benefit in negotiating that would likely still wind up with him shooting them. Just as he'd pulled back the hammer on his Colt and was preparing to open fire, the unexpected happened. There were loud grunts and snorts and squeals, and a pair of wild hogs came crashing through the brush. Inexplicably, they ignored him and darted on past on a dead run. The sounds fully alerted the two cowboys.

Bullets began to fly in Witmer's direction, as the surprised men unloaded at the hogs. Witmer could almost feel the heat of at least a couple of bullets as they whizzed by. His horse wasn't so lucky, taking a mortal wound and falling with a panicky screeching death knell.

The outlaw remained amazingly cool, as he leveled his revolver and fired at the cowboys.

With their focus on the wild hogs, the men hadn't noticed Witmer or his horse. Return fire from hogs had been the least of their worries, as they emptied their guns at the beasts. First one and then the second cowboy ate Witmer's lead. Their final breaths came through facial expressions of surprise and disbelief followed by pain as the reality of their mortal wounds sunk in. They dropped to their knees before falling face forward into the Nueces Strip dust.

Witmer walked cautiously toward the scene of carnage.

Two cowboys and two wild hogs lay dead. He stood for a moment just staring at the scene, amazed at his good fortune.

Breakfast was still cooking in the pan and coffee had been brewed. He dispassionately ignored number 30 and 31 and set to gorging himself on the eggs and what appeared to be rabbit or prairie dog sizzling in the small skillet.

With his appetite sated, the outlaw took stock of his situation. He was concerned that the gunshots might have been heard by others. Witmer surely needed to get back on the trail as quickly as possible. The horses seemed to be prime stock, and the tack was better than his. He only had to fetch his rifle from under the carcass of his own dead mount and grab one of the cowboys' bedrolls to be pretty much fully equipped to continue his odyssey. He checked out the dead men for anything of value. Their boots were nothing special, so he'd keep his. One had a gold watch that he might be able to pawn. He did decide to take one of their guns, as it would save him from the awkward challenge of having to reload with only one hand. He emptied their saddlebags of the personal effects of the cowboys, keeping only necessities he felt might come in handy. They didn't have much money on them, so he figured to yet look for an opportunity to replenish his pocketbook.

Witmer kicked dirt on the fire. He didn't figure to take the time to do any burying of bodies. If the dead cowboys were part of some trail outfit or nearby ranch, they might eventually be found. Meanwhile, the dead wild hogs had begun to stink even worse than when they were alive. The outlaw took one final look around the scene, mounted up, and resumed his journey toward Nuevo Laredo.

But for Witmer's easy-to-follow trail, Luke and One Arrow might have ridden on past the scene totally unawares. As it was, the odor of dead wild hogs greeted them long before the macabre spectacle came into sight.

"Luke...One Arrow smell death." The chief covered his face. The dead hogs stunk to high heaven. He looked up and pointed to a couple of circling buzzards that had found whatever carrion was rotting below.

Luke didn't waste any time slipping a bandana over his own face.

Soon enough, they came upon the scene.

The stench was such that Luke tried to talk without breathing. "Dang, Chief. This is a mess." The Texas Ranger wasn't keen on hanging around, but he knew his duty. The Appaloosa stallion was none too pleased at the horrible odor either and snorted frequently to be sure his displeasure was noted. The flies didn't make it any easier, and Twister was casting a wary eye at the coyotes that had already been attracted to the scene. Luke searched the bodies of the cowboys for identification and knew he had to bury them as best he could. He was quick to discover that whoever killed them...likely Witmer...must have taken anything of value. Luke figured to drop what remained of the cowboys' personal effects off at La Pryor, a newly forming ranch town they'd pass through on their way to Laredo. It was the least he could do. He gripped his small trail shovel and began to dig.

One Arrow held back, as though going near the bodies was some sort of bad medicine. He had watched for a couple of minutes of Luke's digging before guilt overcame his reluctance. He dismounted, walked over with his nose covered, and helped his friend. "This bad medicine, Ghost-Who-Rides."

Luke realized full well that this was delaying their pursuit of Witmer. His practiced eye readily noticed that the outlaw had likely acquired a new mount, as there was a dead horse nearby and only one still-hobbled mount that was outfitted for riding the range. It meant that the killer was not only resupplied but was increasing the distance between them. Luke was grateful that the likelihood of Witmer trying to bushwhack him again was still slim thanks to the man's wound. But uncertainty on that account hung heavily in the air.

With the burial finished, Luke nodded gratefully to One Arrow. He unhobbled the remaining horse, slapped it on its haunches, and sent it on its way. He turned to the Appaloosa and mounted up. Both Luke and One Arrow were relieved to be back on the trail and once again breathing fresh air.

The young man accepted the tip from Elisa, as he handed the telegram to her. She examined the outside of the message, running her fingers gently over Luke's name. She was thrilled to receive word from her husband, as it meant that he must be all right. She opened it on her way over to the bench on the gallery and sat down to read it.

November 3, 1885

Mrs. Elisa Dunn, Nuecestown, Texas. Safe in Uvalde. One Arrow with me. Heading to Laredo.

Love you
Luke

Short, sweet, but thoughtful. It gave her the sense of security a woman has when she knows she's ever on her husband's mind. It was as though he'd sent a shield of protection. He'd likely had similar thoughts years back but no telegraph to send her messages.

"Is that from Dad?" Junior had strolled up from the barn. He'd heard the messenger gallop off.

"Just letting us know he's okay."

Junior smiled. He so wished he could be on the manhunt with his father.

The travel to Laredo was over especially rough country. Aside from the hilly terrain, the brush seemed to be of a mind to constantly tear at horse and rider. Occasionally, Witmer found trails that had been blazed over time by cattle or wound his way along semi-dry arroyos. It wasn't until the fourth day that he reached the road from Alice to Laredo. His hand was healing, but it was still a long way from being able to work the lever on the Winchester. He could have done it with one hand and the butt of the rifle jammed into his hip, but that would have been awkward and didn't exactly lend itself to bushwhacking. The outlaw had found it uncomfortable simply scratching the markings for victim numbers 30 and 31 on the rear casing of his pocket watch. He surely didn't want to lose track, as he might yet find some itinerant journalist that would write his story for one of those dime-store tracts and make him famous.

Traveling on an open road now presented its own set of risks. Being more vulnerable, he took to being extra cautious in the event that he encountered travelers that might take advantage or even bounty hunters that might recognize him. He'd sought to lessen that chance by shaving off his mustache and wearing his hat such that it tended to partially hide his face. An unanticipated downside of shaving off his mustache was that it left a whitish streak under his nose. He rubbed a bit of trail dirt on it, but he had no mirror and could only hope it helped disguise him.

Witmer was perhaps two days out of Laredo and beginning to look forward to getting across the Rio Grande to Mexico and the hiding places afforded by Nuevo Laredo, when he encountered a trio of cowboys heading eastward.

He nodded as he passed them by, but then it happened. He'd traveled but another few feet, when one of the cowboys pulled up.

The cowboy's sudden stop caused his companions to pull up as well. He whispered something to them and they nodded agreement before turning to face Witmer who was easing on down the road. The cowboy called out. "Pardon, traveler, but might I ask where you got that fine horse?"

Witmer froze even as his horse took a few more steps. He could feel the three cowboys' penetrating eyes on his back.

The cowboys began to move cautiously toward Witmer. The cowboy who'd called out spoke loudly enough to his friends that Witmer couldn't help but hear. "I'd swear that's Sam Fine's cayuse. Even has the Circle H brand on it." The cowboy rode up beside the outlaw. "How'd you come by that horse, friend?"

Witmer's good hand had by now found its way to the handle of the Colt nestled in his waistband. He gripped the revolver, pulled it out just enough to not shoot a hole through his coat, and fired just as the cowboy pulled alongside. The other two cowboys saw the flash from the muzzle and the gun smoke about the time they heard the bullet hit their companion with a sickening thud. The bullet went clean through the cowboy's chest with enough force to lift him out of the saddle and into the path of one of his companions. The cowboy's rearing horse kept him occupied such that he was unable to reach for his gun, as Witmer turned and got off two shots at the third cowboy.

Wounded, the third cowboy turned and dug his spurs hard into his horse's flanks, launching headlong into the dense brush alongside the road. He was quickly gone from sight.

Witmer couldn't know whether he'd delivered a mortal wound and wasn't up to finding out. He spurred his own mount to a gallop and escaped the scene as quickly as he could.

The remaining cowboy who'd nearly fallen from his saddle was left to look after his companions. The first was quite clearly near death, and the other was now hidden somewhere in the dense grasses and brush nearby. He dismounted and looked down at his friend as the cowboy took his final painful breaths. His other companion reemerged from the side of the road but was obviously also seriously hurt. "Damn, Kyle...you okay?"

Kyle replied in a weak but angry voice, "Who the hell was that sonofabitch?"

The second cowboy helped him dismount. "Looks like Pardee here is a goner."

"I'm hurting, but I'm thinking I'm gonna live." Kyle sat near Pardee. "Whoever that was is ridin' Sam Fine's horse fer sure. Pardee never saw it comin'." He shook his head in dismay. "Jack, grab that extra shirt outta my saddlebag. Gotta stop this damned bleedin'."

Jack tended to his friend's wounds. They were superficial but bled pretty well. He was lucky to be alive. "We owe it to Sam to mosey on up to the Circle H and let them know 'bout his horse bein' stolen."

"Ghost-Who-Rides." It was whispered. One Arrow put his hand to his ear to indicate his having heard something.

Luke still hadn't fully broken One Arrow from calling him by the mystical name the Comanche had bestowed on him. He'd heard the sounds, too. "Long ways off."

"Maybe...two...three gunshot."

They'd just reached the road to Laredo and were confident that they were closing the gap with Witmer. "Maybe Witmer has found trouble." He spurred the big Appaloosa to an easy trot.

They'd ridden nearly another hour, when they heard hoofbeats approaching ahead of them. What greeted them wasn't pleasant.

Three horses were slowly making their way along the road.

One horse's rider was unsteady in the saddle and clearly injured while a second horse had what looked to be a body draped over its saddle. The lead cowboy didn't even flinch at the sight of the big traveler with the savage for a companion. They pulled up upon seeing Luke and One Arrow, figuring that their lives couldn't get a whole lot worse.

Luke pulled up a few feet from the trio. "I'm Texas Ranger Captain Luke Dunn. This here's my friend One Arrow. You men seem to have run into some trouble."

The men felt a sense of relief that they were dealing with a lawman. "Name's Jack and my wounded friend here is Kyle. Ran into trouble back yonder with a sonofabitch on a stolen horse. He shot and killed our friend Pardee here."

Luke looked knowingly at One Arrow then turned his attention back to Jack. "Horse have a Circle H brand on it?"

"Yeah, how'd you know?"

"The man you tangled with is a fella named Coy Witmer." Luke let that sink in. "He killed the horse's owner and left him and his companion to rot in the sun. My friend and I buried them a couple of days ago. We dropped their personal effects at La Pryor. Witmer ambushed me up on the Frio near Uvalde a couple of days before that. I'm trying to bring him to justice."

"I'd help you out, Ranger, but I'd best get Kyle here to a doctor and let the boys at the Circle H know what happened. By the way, that horse he's ridin' belonged to Sam Fine."

"Well, you ought tell that to the folks at the Circle H. I don't know who his companion was. Do tell them that we're hunting down the killer."

"Much obliged Captain Dunn. I'll be sure to let them know." Jack looked suspiciously at One Arrow but said nothing. "Good luck with that damned Witmer fella."

Luke urged Twister forward.

One Arrow and the cowboys exchanged inquiring glances but nothing was said. The chief knew it wouldn't be the last time folks would be curious as to why a Comanche chief was riding with a White man. He wondered as to whether there ever truly would be an understanding between White man and Red man.

Coy Witmer figured he'd killed at least one of the cowboys. It distressed him immensely that he couldn't be sure of the other one he'd shot at. He was sure he'd hit the cowboy, but couldn't be certain that he'd delivered a mortal wound. He could honestly only add number 32 to his score.

As he saw Laredo off in the distance, he scrunched his hat lower around his face. With any luck he'd soon be crossing the Rio Grande and the relative safety of Nuevo Laredo.

His hand throbbed a bit, making him tempted to seek a bit of medical help while he was still on the Texas side. He wasn't confident in the doctoring skills of the Mexicans.

NINE
DOWN LAREDO WAY

"MAN BAD SPIRIT, LUKE."

Luke was momentarily taken aback yet pleased by the chief addressing him by name rather than the Comanche spirit name. "Er…yes. Evil." He smiled friendly-like at One Arrow. "We're close to Laredo. I think we should go slow and be very careful. We don't want to overtake him and scare him off."

One Arrow nodded agreement. "He wait for night."

"I expect you might be right. By now, he knows the law is getting close to him."

"Luke follow One Arrow." The chief abruptly plunged his pony into the tall grasses by the side of the road. He stopped behind a motte of trees.

Luke followed.

"Stay low." One Arrow hugged his pony's neck. He pointed ahead of them.

Luke's eyes nearly bugged out of his head. Not a hundred yards off was none other than Coy Witmer. Had it not been for one small problem, Luke could have delivered justice right then and there.

"We downwind. Talk quiet."

"Wonder who those folks are with him?" Luke whispered. "Looks like they have a wagon."

One Arrow shook his head. "Squaws."

Luke watched the outlaw talking with the two women. He began to stroke his mustache, as he thought on what best to do next. Gun play looked to be out of the question. Even at close quarters, innocent folks could get shot. Whatever Witmer was up to, he was having fun, assuming laughter was to be any indicator. He slipped down from the Appaloosa's saddle and took a seat under one of the trees. He motioned to One Arrow to join him. "We wait."

"Cora and Anne...what lovely names ladies. Since you're headed to Laredo, do you mind if I join you? My name is Coy." Dang, but he realized he'd used his real name.

The ladies were more accurately girls...very young girls, and their giggles revealed their youth. "Why Mr. Coy, we'd be pleased to enjoy your company." There was plenty of flashing of budding breasts and long lithesome legs. They might have been in the early blossoming of womanhood, but they'd already practiced their chosen profession.

Witmer surveilled the scene and, seeing no one, availed himself of the opportunities before him. "I hope you ladies enjoy fine dining and great wine." He was setting the stage for a long evening of pleasure.

"Why Mr. Coy, we especially enjoy fine manhood." Anne gave him a hug while her hand slid down toward his crotch but paused. "Why, Mr. Coy, what's this in your pocket?" She pulled out his pocket watch.

Witmer grabbed it from her. "Just an old pocket watch, ladies."

"How'd it get all those scratches?"

"I put them there. They help me keep count of some things." He stuffed it back into his pocket. He figured he needed to divert the ladies' thinking, so opened his trousers to their pleasure. They didn't disappoint.

They were thus involved until the sun had sunk below the horizon.

It took Luke about as much restraint as he could muster, as he endured Witmer's carrying on with the young women. Whoring went against his morals in a big way. It brought back memories of the Laredo whore Scarlett Rose and her dangerous journey through the evil shades of prostitution before finally finding a good life and happiness thanks to Luke and Elisa's largesse.

One Arrow was nonplussed at the antics occurring down trail, as he kicked back against a blanket and tried to take a nap.

Luke shook his head resignedly, slipped his Colt from its holster, laid it gently beside him, and put his head back. He too was soon asleep.

Noises from the direction of Witmer and the girls awakened Luke with a start. As Luke was digesting the sounds from Witmer and his ladies as they were preparing to head into Laredo, an unwelcome sound caught his attention. There was still enough light to make out the coiled body and menacing eyes of a stirred-up rattlesnake. It was about ten feet from the Comanche chief.

One Arrow began to stir. He squinted over at Luke who was pointing his Colt close to where the chief lay. He simultaneously heard the snake's rattle and the click as Luke pulled back the hammer of his Colt.

Luke hated to alert Witmer, but there wasn't really much

choice. The explosion from the revolver seemed to boom even louder in the stillness of early evening. Luke's bullet shattered the rattler's head. At the same time, he heard Witmer holler and whip the wagon horses into a gallop.

One Arrow had jumped to his feet upon the blast from Luke's Colt. He quickly composed himself and tried to put on a calm exterior, but his pulse was pounding like no tomorrow.

Luke smiled. He couldn't worry about Witmer. "Pretty fair shooting for an old man."

By now, One Arrow had fully collected himself. "Humph. Good to eat." He promptly strode over and cut what remained of the head off the rattlesnake. "Evil man and squaws gone. We stay. Eat here."

Luke had eaten rattler a couple of times, so the chief's offer was no surprise. "Let's cook it up." Luke smiled. "Maybe it's part of Witmer's family."

Even One Arrow chuckled at the humor.

Witmer wasn't hanging around to see what the gunshot was about. The ladies' giggles turned to screams, as the lurch forward of the buckboard thrust them head-over-heels back into the wagon bed. Witmer wouldn't be stopping much less slowing down until he'd reached the town limits of Laredo proper.

He was conflicted between seeing to his still throbbing hand and high-tailing it across the Rio Grande or spending the night in orgasmic frolicking with Cora and Anne. He rationalized that whoever fired the gun didn't appear to have been shooting at him, so he was likely safe at least until morning. The gunman was haunted nevertheless by the prospect that the damned Texas Ranger might be hot on his trail.

The quick ride into Laredo did turn exciting as measured by the delight the young ladies took in the jouncing and bouncing. It seemed they found most anything Witmer did to be amusing enough to illicit laughter and giggles. He'd have been amused himself save that grabbing the reins even with both hands did no favors to his still-healing hand.

He pulled the rig to a stop in front of the hotel. The place was pretty much as he remembered it from a couple of years back. A boardwalk had been built across the front with the purpose of keeping ladies' skirts out of the mud on the infrequent occasions that it rained in the town. "Wait here, ladies. I'll get us a room and some victuals." But for his injured hand, he was feeling right good, even showed a bit of a bounce in his step.

Being that it was still early, Witmer figured he wouldn't have any particular difficulty renting a room. He wasn't to be disappointed. He sidled up to the check-in counter in the lobby and rang the bell.

"Kin I help yuh, mistuh?" A young man with disheveled hair and rumpled clothes appeared. To look upon, he was the antithesis of what hotel clerks might be expected to look like. "Yuh needin' a room?"

"Your best." Witmer wasn't quite certain how to react to the clerk, as the fellow didn't seem bright enough to light up a room. "I'll be needing a bath...oh, and can you send up some wine and three glasses? What sort of victuals do you offer?" These were questions that would be determining just how good a night he was to enjoy.

"Ain't got but biscuits an' gravy o'er beans right now... Mistuh." He looked down at the register. "Mistuh Smith. I kin getcha the wine easy nuf though."

"With three glasses."

"Lemme show yuh the room, Mistuh Smith." The clerk led him up the hall a short way. He turned, unlocked the door, and swung it open. He covered his mouth with surprise, glanced at the couple fornicating on the bed, and slammed the door shut.

"Whoops...wrong room! Sorry, Mistuh Smith." He crossed the hall. "Here yuh go."

Witmer gazed inside. The bed was large and looked soft. It'd be perfect for an all-night frolic.

"Yuh gonna have a guest?"

"Yes, two."

The clerk raised his eyebrows and scanned Witmer from head to toe. He gave a lecherously broad smile. "Damn, but ain't yuh the man." He was impressed.

Witmer waved his hand in front of the clerk. "You have a doctor in Laredo."

"Yep."

"Where does he hang out?"

"Gotta sign out front of his house. Be up the street a bit."

"Send the doc to my room in the morning." He slipped the clerk some extra coin, and then headed back to the street to fetch the girls. "Come on, ladies. Let's have some fun." He jingled a bag of coins before their eyes. The young ladies' eyes grew wide, and they laughed with greater enthusiasm. It seemed they'd be enjoying their first customer in Laredo, and they hadn't even officially settled in yet. Witmer tipped the clerk to see to the wagon and horses. As he looked up, the outlaw saw a pair of riders entering Laredo at the far end of the main street. He couldn't make out who they were but something told him he should eventually find out. Fortunately, or not, the girls didn't seem to want their fun delayed any longer than necessary.

Luke watched the wagon being driven from the hotel toward the livery stable. By his reckoning, he now pretty much had Witmer where he wanted him. He looked over at One Arrow. "Let's let our friend get comfortable, then we'll pay him a visit." He was also trying to calculate how to best make use of his Comanche friend without alienating the good citizens of Laredo. It was 1885 Texas after all, and folks were still not exactly welcoming to savages.

They sized up the hotel as they rode past. It wasn't much of a building. The deteriorating establishment featured one of those false two-story fronts on a single-story building that made it look bigger than it was. The wooden slat boardwalk across the front completed the illusion of a reasonably civilized hotel. He rode around to the rear of the hotel with One Arrow following. Luke was pleased to see only one exit. "Let's give him an hour or so to get comfortable, then I'll pay him a visit. Let's go take a walk up to the jail."

One Arrow followed Luke up the street toward the jail.

Witmer was none too happy. The image of the two riders at the end of the main street stuck in his head like glue. They looked like trouble to his ever-alert senses. It was seriously affecting his performance with Cora and Anne. After a couple of glasses of wine and a bit of light carrying on, he barely managed to service Cora. It was quick.

Anne looked at his privates. "Don't look likely you're gonna be ready for a bit." She giggled, but it was laced with disappointment.

"Sorry ladies. I'm just a tad distracted. I've got to tend to some business, then I'll be back." He strapped on his gun belt and grabbed his saddlebags and the Winchester. "Leave a few swallows of wine for me." He winked and forced a laugh as he exited the room.

The outlaw used the rear entrance, so the clerk wouldn't see him leave. He had three things to do: confirm that the damned Texas Ranger was for certain following him, rouse the town doctor to examine his hand, and hightail it across the Rio Grande to Nuevo Laredo.

Witmer stealthily walked behind the establishments facing onto the main street until he arrived at the jail. Sure enough, the Ranger's Appaloosa was hitched behind the hoosegow. The horse's ears twitched, as he caught the outlaw's scent. Witmer thought the Indian pony and packhorse nearby made for an odd combination. He had no idea what tribe the savage was part of, but he rightly didn't cotton to the possibility of losing his scalp if he ran afoul of Luke's companion.

As he walked toward the doc's office, he mumbled a string of curses at his terrible luck. He'd be missing a great evening with those wild young ladies he'd chanced upon. He found the doc's sign and walked up to the door. He knocked. No answer. He knocked louder.

"Dang, but who's raising that racket?" Came the voice from within.

"Come on back to bed, Darryl." A woman's voice called out.

"Got to see who it is, darlin'." He opened the door and looked directly into the muzzle of Witmer's Winchester.

"I need your help, doc. Now."

"Don't need the rifle, my friend. What you needin'?"

Witmer lowered the rifle. "Doc in Uvalde said the bandages need to be changed." He thrust his hand up in front of the doctor.

Doc scrunched his nose. He could see the dried blood that had oozed through the bandage and smelled dying tissue. "Come on in and let me see. You got a name?"

"Smith. Name's Smith." He stepped inside. "My hand got shot accident-like when I was cleanin' my gun."

"Well, let's have us a look." The doctor showed Witmer into his office and began gently cutting away the bandage. He raised his eyebrows. "You don't take better care of this, Mr. Smith, you're going to lose your hand. All of it. You got some serious infection happening."

"Can you save it?"

"Do the best I can. This is going to hurt like blazes."

Witmer sunk his teeth into a twisted bandana, as the doc began to cut away dead tissue. The whole procedure took the better part of an hour. The outlaw was in a cold sweat by the time the doc finished the surgery and had him bandaged up.

"If you're hanging around Laredo, come back and see me in a day or so. I'll give you a fresh bandage." The doc gave him a hard look, as he reminded him, "Remember…if you don't take care, you're going to lose that hand."

"Thanks, doc." Witmer felt a bit light-headed but knew he had to get to the livery stable and ride out of town. He paid the doc, steadied himself, and eased on out the door.

Sheriff Toady Jones leaned back in his chair. His heavy jowls and long scraggly hair laid atop a massive chest and even more massive stomach. It was said that Jones never met a scrap of food that he didn't like. Add beer to his impressive culinary intake, and you had likely as not the fattest lawman in all of Texas. It was said that if he couldn't kill a man with his gun, he'd sit on his chest and suffocate him to death.

Jones kept nervously glancing at One Arrow as though not knowing quite what to make of him. Likely as not, he felt a combination of fear, in-built prejudice, and maybe a twinge of guilt at having slain a few Indians at various times in his life.

One Arrow appeared as nonplussed as possible in returning the sheriff's stare. He didn't know quite what to make of the sheriff, and allowed an aura of mystery to settle on himself by remaining stoically silent. The chief was fascinated at a man of such girth and worked at suppressing a laugh as he thought on how a horse might feel with Jones in the saddle.

For his part, Luke was looking to simply wile away an hour with small talk before heading back up to the hotel. In sizing up the sheriff, he'd already decided Jones to likely be more liability than asset in arresting Witmer. To wit, Luke never mentioned the outlaw. "Been great chatting with you, Toady. Just wanted to get a bit acquainted. We'd best get on with our evening." Luke had concocted a story about scouting bivouac sites for a company of Texas Rangers, and Jones seemed to have bought it.

As Luke followed One Arrow out the back door, Jones pulled him back. "Say, Captain...how'd you get to be friends with a Comanche savage?"

Luke smiled and gave Jones a confidential look. "Threatened to scalp him, if he got out of line."

The sheriff was left with his mouth agape.

Luke and the chief led their horses back up to the hotel. He positioned One Arrow at the back door. "If Witmer comes out, stop him best you can. Just don't get yourself shot." Luke walked around to the front and entered the hotel lobby.

The hotel clerk was working hard on a chaw and didn't see Luke come in.

Luke rapped on the counter. "You sleeping or running a hotel here."

The clerk choked on his tobacco and nearly fell from his chair. He coughed, managed a spat in the spittoon, gathered his wits, and staggered to the counter. "Sorry, suh. Can I help yuh?" He looked up at the imposing figure before him.

"I'm Texas Ranger Captain Luke Dunn." Luke let that sink in, as he'd already judged the clerk to be a bit slow of mind. "I'm looking for a man who came in here earlier with two young ladies."

"Shall I fetch him, suh?"

Luke shook his head as much to say no as to express his dismay. "No. Just let me know which room he's in."

"320 jus' down the hall."

"You have a third floor?"

"No suh. Owner thinks it sounds like the place is bigguh.

Don't even have no second floor." He gave an apologetic look. "Just go on up the hall there. First door to yur right. Ain't heard any noise since early on, except them girls carrying on."

Luke walked cautiously up the hall, stood back facing the door, pulled out one of his Colts, and kicked it open.

The screams were enough to shake the very foundations of the decrepit old hotel which was just about falling apart anyway.

Luke's eyes darted around the room in an attempt to find Witmer. He hadn't featured having to include a pair of naked young ladies in his line-of-sight. Worse still after their initial screams, the girls started giggling and made no attempt to cover their nakedness in the face of a handsome, six-foot-three-inch, well-muscled, hunk of a man. Luke stepped back and pulled the door shut. "Damn!" He wasn't one to swear, but he couldn't hold back.

One Arrow heard the screams and the door slam shut, so he peeked in from the back door.

Luke caught his eyes and shook his head in dismay. "He's not here. I'll meet you out front."

As the chief rounded the front corner of the hotel, he looked past Luke and pointed at a lone figure riding out hard.

Luke turned to look where the One Arrow was pointing. "He's headed to Mexico. We'll never catch him at night." He shook his head disappointedly.

For Coy Witmer, riding onto Mexican soil never felt so good. He pulled up on the Mexican side of the Rio Grande, looked back at Texas, and took a deep breath. He still felt a bit light-headed, but was confident that the damnable Texas Ranger wouldn't be following him this night. Now, he needed to find himself a place to spend the night. If he had any immediate regret, it would be not spending the night in lascivious lustful pleasure with those two young whores. What a terrible waste of bad wine!

He rode toward what appeared to be a cantina, figuring they'd point him to a place where he could catch up on some much-needed sleep. Pulling up in front, he hailed the first vaquero he encountered. His Spanish was haltingly inadequate, but he gave it his best shot. "*Perdóneme...¿dónde* hotel?"

The vaquero blinked, then laughed. "*Esta aquí, gringo.*" He pointed to the ramshackle hotel located next door to the cantina.

Witmer missed the snub and didn't especially appreciate the laugh, but wasn't about to take issue. To his way of thinking, Mexicans wouldn't count on his list of victims. Like many Texans, he held built-in prejudices against Mexicans and Indians especially so far as considering them full-fledged humans. He wasn't in fighting shape in any case. He sighed and chose to be as gracious as possible. "Gracias." He eased on over to the ramshackle building that apparently passed for a hotel in Nuevo Laredo. Feeling as he was, he had no room for looking down his nose at the place. It reeked of sweat, booze, and urine and was likely a breeding heaven for bedbugs, roaches, and all manner of creepy critters.

He looked at the old man at the desk. "*¿Tienes un...*er...room?"

"*Yo hablo inglés, señor.* I speak English." The old man flashed a toothless grin. "Ten pesos...in advance."

Witmer dropped a silver dollar on the counter. "Keep the change."

The old man pursed his lips and bit the coin with his gums as though to confirm it was silver. "*Muchas gracias.*" He handed over a key and pointed to the stairway. "You have caballo?"

"Um...yes...*si.*"

"I take to stable in back."

"Thanks." Witmer picked up his saddlebags and the

Winchester and headed up the stairs. He unlocked the door to the room. He was too tired to notice the whoring sounds from the room next door through the paper-thin walls. When he did, it made him think of those two young whores he'd had to leave behind. "Damn," he murmured under his breath. His head hit the pillow, and he was out.

TEN
DEADLY ESCAPE

THE SCORPION DIDN'T ESPECIALLY APPRECIATE
BEING shaken from Witmer's boot and sat for a moment as
though itching to fight its tormentor. It paused and curled its
tail threateningly before scurrying off. Likely as not it was
professional courtesy.

Witmer scratched at a couple of bedbug bites. This fleabag
hotel wasn't exactly his idea of a worthy hangout. Nor did he
cotton to being on the run. He much preferred being the
hunter to being the hunted. Worse yet, there was no assurance
that the damned Texas Ranger wouldn't come after him in
Mexico. Unlike the US Army, the Rangers never considered
themselves restricted from following lawbreakers into Mexico.
Witmer knew full well that he needed to put some distance
between himself and the law until he'd healed up properly.
Given his preference for bushwhacking, being able to have full
use of his hand was essential. In any case, he needed to find
better lodgings. Dared he go deeper into Mexico or make a run
eastward across the Nueces Strip? Perhaps head to Monterrey
or Camargo in Mexico? Maybe ride to San Ygnacio or Rio
Grande City in Texas?

Putting on his hat and slinging the saddlebags over his

shoulder, he grabbed the Winchester and headed to the front desk. A different clerk from the night before, a smarmy-looking character, sat behind the counter. Witmer assumed this one would also understand English. "Where can I eat, pardner?" Blank look from the clerk. Witmer sighed. "¿Dónde comer?"

The clerk's expression still remained pretty much blank, but at least he responded. "Cantina por allá, señor."

"And my horse? ¿Mi caballo?"

The clerk finally moved, pointing to the back of the hotel.

Witmer recalled the night clerk mentioning a stable behind the place. He figured to grab some victuals before taking an exploratory ride around Nuevo Laredo. He nodded respectfully to the clerk and stepped out onto the street. The sun had risen and the warm dry air gave promise of a decent day.

He strode through the front door of the cantina and scanned the place. It wreaked of sawdust, piss, booze, sweat, and about every bodily odor imaginable. A couple of men were engaged in animated conversation, but the place was otherwise empty. He wondered whether that was testament to the quality of the food. The two men had barely touched whatever it was on their plates. One wore a brown leather bandolier filled with rifle bullets across his chest. Wide Mexican sombreros hung on the back of their chairs. Both wore gun belts with old revolvers, and there was at least one knife that he could see. He couldn't make out what they were talking about in their rapid-fire Mexican lingo. The men paused, as he entered. He thought he heard the word *gringo* hissed through gritted teeth, as they continued their conversation. Witmer sat at a nearby table and nodded to the barkeeper. "Huevos, por favor."

"Simone...por ahí." The barkeep simultaneously called a server, pointed to Witmer, sneezed, and wiped his nose in his sleeve.

The server shook out her dark curls and adjusted her

bodice before slinking over to the outlaw. *"Bienvenido, señor. ¿Puedo ayudarte?"* Her deep sexy voice wasn't quite what Witmer expected. She leaned forward to display her ample cleavage.

He smiled, not at her but at the thought of the pair of young nubiles he'd missed out on last night. He looked up from the table to her breasts to her eyes and sighed. *"Huevos, por favor."*

"Si...gracias." She quickly realized he wasn't interested in anything other than breakfast.

A third man sat by himself at the remaining table. A curious feeling ran through Witmer. It was as though evil was meeting evil. The man was watching. It was very clear that he didn't want to engage. He was effectively an observer.

As Witmer waited, he glanced at the two men as they continued their animated conversation.

One finally pivoted in his chair and looked directly at Witmer. His smile revealed two blackened teeth half hidden by a large mustache. The large gun, possibly a Colt, still dangled menacingly from his holster. He absentmindedly took a long drink of coffee. *"¿Señor, eres Coy Witmer?"*

The desperado didn't know how to react. Should he be flattered at having been identified? Was he being threatened? "Who wants to know?"

The man turned back to his tablemate. *"Es verdad."* Clearly, they'd been talking about him since he'd entered the cantina.

The server cautiously walked over and laid a plateful of eggs with biscuits before the outlaw. *"Disfruta, señor.* Enjoy." She slowly backed away. There was a hint of fear in her eyes.

The way she was behaving left Witmer to wonder what had caused her to be cautious of a sudden. Running through his mind was that it was far too early for trouble. He took a deep breath and took in a forkful of eggs while keeping an eye on the two men.

The man dressed in black continued to watch. He seemed

to smile at the machinations of the two men who seemed to be mustering the courage to confront Witmer.

The first man arose from his chair and eased on over to the bar. He was doing his level best to be nonchalant.

Witmer's eyes followed him across the room while his peripheral vision caught the second man shifting his revolver from his holster to his lap. The Winchester leaned against the wall next to the outlaw's chair and wouldn't be in play here in any case. He took another bite of eggs.

The man now at the bar stood facing the outlaw's table. *"Señor...¿matas a mucha gente?"* Strange to be making small talk about Witmer having killed a lot of people.

Witmer stared intently into the man's eyes. What was new? Yes, he'd killed many people. *"No cuento mexicanos."* He didn't count Mexicans. The insult floated like a lead balloon across the room. He placed his fork beside his plate.

"Soy Tejano, no Mexicano." The man was quick to note that he was Texan, not Mexican.

Perhaps Witmer would add him to his count after all. *"¿Estás listo para morir?"* Are you ready to die? Sometimes, this would dissuade a full-of-himself young buck like the man standing at the bar. The simple question as to readiness to die occasionally worked. *"¿Quieres el número 33?"* Did the man indeed wish to become number 33?

The man at the table and his friend at the bar exchanged glances. It was two to one, and one of them already had his gun at the ready.

Witmer vastly preferred ambush but figured to be quick enough and sufficiently accurate to handle these two.

The man in black leaned began to straighten a bit as though preparing to duck for cover if necessary. He looked over at the man at the bar. *"No deberías hacer esto."* The man didn't have to do this at all.

Witmer was curious that the man had stuck himself into whatever dynamic was at play.

The man at the bar was more curious. *"¿Por qué?"*

"Me llamo Jesús Santos. Este hombre te matará."

The young buck knew who Jesús Santos was—a killer with a big reputation of his own. Standing at a bar with two gunmen of considerable reputation in the same room was a bit more than unnerving, it was downright intimidating. Foolish bravado had no place here. Blotches of sweat appeared on his shirt, and he was forced to wipe his brow. His vulnerability was showing for all to see. He had understandably become embarrassed and none too happy with his predicament.

Witmer also recognized the name. Given that Santos was Mexican, the outlaw had already discounted him. He couldn't imagine Santos could match him in a fight, but then again, he wasn't aiming to put his thesis to a test. Not this day at least.

Santos smiled patronizingly and nodded at Witmer, then turned back to the man at the bar. *"Un Texas Ranger lo está siguiendo."* He meant it to warn the young man that he was messing with serious enough trouble that a Texas Ranger was tracking Witmer.

The barkeeper had been watching the scene unfold. He bent down and pretended to tend to something. He poked his head up from whatever he was doing behind the bar and eased a large-gauge shotgun onto the bar top. *"Amigos, esta no es una buena idea."*

The young man at the bar sighed deeply, looked at the barkeep's shotgun, motioned his friend toward the front door, and followed him out.

Witmer never outwardly appeared concerned. He picked up his fork and took another bite of eggs and a hunk of biscuit. He guardedly looked over at the barkeep and nodded. *"Gracias."* He couldn't blame the man for not wanting his place shot up. Seemed like it was always left to the barkeeps to pick up broken furnishings and wash the blood off the floor. The outlaw finished eating and tossed a couple of coins on the table.

Witmer looked over at Santos and nodded. It was professional courtesy.

The server stood fetchingly at the end of the bar and smiled.

Witmer smiled at her. *"Otro momento, señorita."* Another time indeed. He grabbed his saddlebags and rifle and headed out the front door. He saw no sign of the two men he'd encountered, as he walked down the alley toward the stable.

"Gonna be hotter than hell, Chief."

"Hell?"

It was this sort of moment that reminded Luke of One Arrow's lack of familiarity with Christian beliefs like heaven and hell. He stroked his mustache, as the chief awaited his explanation. "It's the place evil folks go when they die."

"Evil?"

"Evil...like a Comanche who steals his chief's woman."

Now, One Arrow nodded that he understood. "Evil go to hell." He pondered that a moment. "What hell like?"

"Hot. Plenty of fire, my friend. Folks in hell burn for all time."

"Good end for Comanche who steals chief's woman." The chief chuckled, as he recalled having dealt with such a circumstance not so long ago. "Where we go on hotter than hell day?"

"Across the Rio Grande. Nuevo Laredo."

"Mexico not good for Comanche."

"You're with me." It was as though Luke was casting some sort of symbolic protective shield around One Arrow. He knew of course that there'd be no love lost for the chief by the Mexicans.

They headed up Laredo's main street, riding past the hotel that Witmer had attempted to use. The two young whores sat outside on a bench flirting with passersby. They'd likely be okay until one of the local madams caught up with them and demanded her share of their takings.

One Arrow cast a disapproving look on them. "Need clothes, Luke."

The Texas Ranger nodded and chuckled. "Lotta cowboys don't share your opinion, Chief." He kicked the big Appaloosa into a loping stride, and One Arrow followed. The chief rode close behind as they crossed over into Nuevo Laredo. One Arrow was a fearsome sight with his long black hair in a braid down his back, his well-muscled chest covered in a bone vest, buckskin breeches, and beaded moccasins. It was more likely the combination of the Henry rifle, bow and arrow, and the war lance with its scalp trophies that instilled fear. A few women and old men hanging around were aghast at the appearance of the Comanche. Small children were fearfully pulled to shelter while older children looked on with curiosity.

Luke pulled up at the cantina. He and the chief dismounted and entered. The place was empty save for the barkeep and the ever-sexy Simone the server. They caste wary eyes on One Arrow.

Luke flashed his badge, hopeful that the barkeep wasn't so old as to recall the bloody James Callahan led Texas Ranger raid of 1855. "You see a man with a bandaged hand?" He pointed to his hand. "*¿Mano herida?*"

The barkeeper knew just enough English to understand. He looked again at the Comanche. "*¿Quien...?*"

"Comanche chief. I'll let him scalp you if you don't talk."

That got the barkeep's attention. "*Señor, hombre, acaba de partir*...he just left."

The desperado had walked briskly from the cantina. He was about to hail the stable boy, when the two men who'd troubled him in the cantina stepped from the barn. Their guns were drawn, and there was no questioning their intentions. One of them had Witmer's horse saddled and ready to ride.

"We like your choice of horseflesh, Witmer. Ain't no shotgun backing you up here."

The outlaw didn't say a word. Three shots belched their orange fire from his gun. The two men crumpled in a heap. Witmer wasted no time stepping over the bodies, stuffed the Winchester in its scabbard, took a quick look around, and mounted up.

The three gunshots had caught everyone's attention.

He nearly bowled Luke and One Arrow over, as he came careening from the alley at a full gallop.

Luke reacted like the lawman he was. There was no fighting any urge to investigate the shooting scene. He remembered he was in Mexico. Wasn't his jurisdiction. He nudged One Arrow, and they ran for their mounts.

The escaping outlaw saw that he'd nearly been able to reach out and touch Luke and One Arrow as he bolted past on his way toward the Rio Grande. Thinking quickly, he took a hard turn to his left just before the river by way of shaking off any followers. He knew he had a lead of several hundred yards, so was likely out of sight.

Between the dust and scattering onlookers, Luke didn't see Witmer turn. He and One Arrow had quickly remounted and headed toward the border, but sensed right quickly that they'd lost their man.

They soon found themselves back in Texas with nary a clue as to where the fugitive had gone. It was as though he'd vanished into thin air. Luke turned Twister in a circle, staring hard at the ground and then up into the distance. There were far too many hoofprints in the sandy soil and no way to identify them as belonging to Witmer. Finally, he looked back across the Rio Grande.

One Arrow pulled up alongside. "Evil one disappear."

Luke nodded. "Seems like, my friend." He felt a chill, sort

of like the feeling of some sort of premonition. He had the
feeling that the desperado was watching them.

One Arrow scanned the Mexican shoreline. "Evil one out
there, Luke."

Witmer watched Luke and One Arrow from his hidden
vantage point on the southern shore of the Rio Grande. He'd
begun to breathe easy after the short frenetic escape. He pulled
out his pocket watch and scratched two marks into the casing.
Number 33 and number 34. He figured they'd said they were
Texans, so he wasn't going to argue the point. He put the
watch back into his pocket and slipped the Winchester from its
scabbard. Ever so purposefully, the outlaw stuck the butt hard
against his hip and with his good hand levered a bullet into
the chamber.

Now, it was a question of the Texas Ranger or the
Comanche. He'd only get one shot. Like Mexicans, the savage
wouldn't count as a kill, but it might be good sport. He still
wanted to have some fun taunting the lawman. Killing the
Comanche would mess with the Ranger's mind.

He sat tight and erect in the saddle trying to keep his horse
steady, raised his arm across his body at shoulder level, and
rested the muzzle of the Winchester across his forearm. The
chief was sitting his pony as still as stone for the moment.
Witmer aimed, exhaled partly, held his breath, and squeezed
the trigger.

One Arrow had just raised the Henry rifle to a position
over his chest. He'd felt the same feeling as Luke. The sense
that they were being watched. The .45-caliber slug smashed
into rifle's forestock just ahead of the trigger, driving it with
crushing force back into the chief's chest. Much of his beaded
bone breast plate shattered as the impact lifted the Comanche
clean off his pony. He landed on his back. What air the

crushing force of the bullet took from his lungs, landing full on his back knocked out the rest. He lay stunned and gasping for breath. A couple of ricocheting bullet fragments had cut his flesh but merely added superficially to the damage.

Luke saw where the shot had come from. He fought the urge to pursue but had no choice but to see to One Arrow.

Witmer controlled his horse, calmly slipped the rifle back into its scabbard, waved boldly at Luke, and rode off. He figured he'd eliminated the Comanche.

Blood seemed to be everywhere, as Luke kneeled beside his friend.

A passerby ran over. "Damn, mister…you kilt an injun!"

Luke resisted the urge to hit the man. "Fetch the doc."

"He don't need no doc, mister."

Luke gave the man his toughest don't-mess-with-me glare. "Dammit, I'm Texas Ranger Captain Luke Dunn and I'm ordering you to fetch a doctor…now!"

The man headed at a run up the street to fetch the doctor.

One Arrow was finally beginning to get some air into his lungs but was unable to speak. He tapped Luke's arm.

It took a moment or two before Luke realized that the chief was signaling him with the Morse code Luke had been teaching him. The tapping translated to "Chest hurts."

"Your chest hurts?" Luke nodded. "Lie still, my friend. Help is coming." Luke looked around. The Henry rifle lay nearby. Its forestock was a mangled mess. It finally struck him just how lucky One Arrow had been.

The chief tried to rise to a sitting position but to no avail.

The doc arrived but a moment later. "What's happened here?"

"My friend's been bushwhacked, doc. Slug hit his rifle full on and knocked him from his pony."

The doc paused a moment upon realizing that he was about to help a Comanche savage. He looked at Luke. Compassion and his Hippocratic oath took over. He looked the chief over.

"How'd this happen?"

"I'm Texas Ranger Captain Luke Dunn. One Arrow here is helping me pursue an outlaw named Coy Witmer. Seems Witmer tried to kill my friend."

Doc now noticed Luke's Texas Ranger badge. "Let's get him out of the street. My office isn't far, Captain. Amazingly, I don't think your friend is hurt so badly as it appears."

Luke and the doc helped One Arrow to the doc's office. A couple of passersby brought the horses behind them, though the big Appaloosa was none too happy.

They sat the chief on a bench on the gallery of the doctor's house. "We'll clean up the cuts from the bullet fragments, but he's not going anywhere for a while. His sternum...er...breastbone is bruised pretty bad, and he's got cracked ribs."

Luke watched the doctor treat the wounds, knowing full well that One Arrow would soon enough replace any bandages with one of his poultices as soon as he was able. The chief was breathing, but each breath was obviously a struggle.

"Does your friend know English?"

One Arrow stared at the doc and responded before Luke could answer. He let out a barely audible, "yes. Me talk."

The doc had trouble containing his surprise that the Comanche savage could speak much less understand any English. "You rest. Maybe ten days." The doc held up ten fingers for emphasis.

Luke shook his head slightly at the quite apparent prejudice. "Thanks, doc. He's strong. One Arrow here is a great leader of his people. He has many wives, horses...and... scalps." Luke felt that he needed to establish the chief's bona fides.

The doc raised one eyebrow at the mention of scalps. "Lost my grandfather to Kiowa a while back. They took his scalp."

"Sorry, doc."

"Get him the hell out of here."

"What do I owe you?"

"No charge. Just go." The doctor was already heading inside.

One Arrow struggled to his feet and took a couple of unsteady steps toward Luke. "Need water. We make camp."

Luke knew they wouldn't be pursuing Witmer until the chief was ready to travel, so there was no hurry. "There's a shady motte of trees up near the edge of town. Let's make camp up there."

ELEVEN
FUMBLING GAMBLER

WITMER HAD WISELY DECIDED to stick to the Mexican side of the river and cross back into Texas near San Ygnacio. From there, he could get supplies and head eastward across the Nueces Strip. He had no idea who might now be pursuing him, as the Mexicans would surely be joining in the hunt. He figured to have better chances dealing with Mexican soldiers and the red-coated dragoons or even Apache than to run into that Texas Ranger and his seemingly charmed life. He thought back on those whores outside Laredo and rued how Luke Dunn's pursuit had robbed him of their pleasure. There was no relaxing to be had, despite his feeling confident that the damnable Texas Ranger was likely burying the Comanche and wouldn't be tracking him any time soon. In Witmer's mind, funerals for Indians were a waste. Better to let coyotes and buzzards do their job. His hand was beginning to throb again, so he figured he could get the bandages changed once back in Texas.

He was confident that Cheno Cortina, the Red Robber of the Rio Grande, was still under house arrest and wouldn't be causing him any concern so far as bandit threats. All in all, the outlook for the immediate future was not particularly daunting. He felt guardedly optimistic that he could reverse roles with Dunn and once again be the hunter. First, he had to learn where the Texas Ranger was and then where he was headed. With that, he could set another ambush. Facing Dunn mano-a-mano was no longer a consideration.

Luke got to figuring that Witmer's trail would be pretty cold by the time One Arrow was healed enough to ride. He sat deep in thought, staring at the small kettle on the fire.

"Coffee ready?" The chief had acquired the White man's taste for coffee. He realized that Luke was engaged in some deep thinking. "We lose evil one?"

Luke snapped from his trance. "Likely. I'm going to send a telegram." He walked over to the kettle and poured a cup of coffee for One Arrow. "Figure to let Elisa know that I'm heading home."

"You giving up?"

"No."

"You have a plan?"

Luke smiled. "Been thinking. He knows we're after him. Or at least, that I'm hunting him. He likely thinks you're dead. I'm figuring to break it off for a while. Let Witmer think we've stopped tracking him." He looked over at One Arrow. "My shoulder's still sore. We could both use a rest."

"Maybe, me go back to my people."

"That's up to you, my friend. Happy to have you stay."

"One Arrow talk to Great Spirit."

Luke poured a cup of coffee for himself. "Let's go into Laredo and eat. It's time White folks treated you like a human."

"Human?"

"A living man...no matter the color of your skin."

One Arrow smiled. He'd have laughed, but his chest still hurt. "One Arrow leave scalps here."

Luke nodded vigorously and laughed at the chief's sense of humor. "Yep, folks wouldn't be too happy about them."

The patrol of red-coated Mexican dragoons rode along lazily. They were decked out in their fancy uniforms festooned with gold buttons, plumed hats, black boots, rattling sabers, and lances. They looked capable enough if spit and polish was to be the measure, though appearances could be deceiving. Boredom was a constant companion, as they found themselves on the lookout for cattle thieves and hostile Apache. They strove to be alert for pretty much anything else that came along. A lone rider, especially a gringo, with a bandaged hand fell into the anything else that came along category.

The point rider came to an abrupt halt and shouted back to the patrol, "¡Mira capitán! ¡Gringo!"

The dragoons wasted no time reacting, as they spurred their mounts into action. "¡Ataque! ¡Ahora! ¡Avance!"

Flashing sabers, shouting, galloping horses all served to quickly grab Witmer's attention. His black eyes darted around seeking the best escape. The choice wasn't difficult, as the low spot along the Rio Grande shoreline suddenly looked like the place to cross the Rio Grande into Texas. He figured he wasn't that far from San Ygnacio, and there was no point in risking action with the Mexicans. He was about two-thirds of the way across the river, when the patrol reached the spot on the south bank of the river where he'd plunged in. He had too great a head start to be run down with their sabers and lances, so the dragoons resorted to their carbines. Blessedly for Witmer, the Mexicans' carbines weren't especially accurate at longer distances. By the time the dragoons had unlimbered their guns, the best they could do was scatter a few bullets near Witmer but not close enough to threaten the escaping outlaw.

Water dripped plentifully from man and horse, as Witmer slipped, slid, and desperately struggled to climb the steep riverbank on the Texas side. He reached dry land, turned his horse southward, smiled, and waved to the dragoons. He was ever so happy to be back on Texas soil and especially happy to not be in the clutches of the Mexicans. Had they captured him, they'd surely have quickly learned of his killings in Nuevo Laredo.

As the dragoons shook their fists, shouted insults, and reluctantly rode off, Witmer took stock of his situation. He figured that he'd be pretty much dried out by the time he reached San Ygnacio. Otherwise, he was pleased to have escaped unscathed. Now, he could refocus on that Texas Ranger.

One Arrow followed Luke into the restaurant and sat across from him at the only available table. The chief was still plenty sore from Witmer's bullet and wouldn't have chanced a meal at a White man's restaurant had Luke not insisted. The Comanche was not up for any trouble. He could feel the penetratingly judgmental eyes of the patrons as their mealtime was interrupted by the appearance of a savage hostile. One Arrow looked uncomfortably at Luke. "Why you do this, Luke?"

"Relax. We're going to enjoy a fine meal."

A young woman walked hesitatingly over to Luke's table, casting furtive glances back at the owner who'd sent her. The owner, an overweight matron, kept urging her on. Finally, she reached the table. She couldn't quite look Luke in the eyes and certainly wasn't going to look at the Comanche. "I'm sorry, sir, but your friend must leave."

Luke looked at her, then at One Arrow. He stood up and

scanned the room full of diners, locking eyes with each one of them. He unexpectedly broke into a broad grin. "Howdy, folks. My name is Luke Dunn. I'm a Texas Ranger captain on a special mission to arrest the notorious killer Coy Witmer. My friend here is helping me track the outlaw." He had their undivided attention. The server girl had meekly backed away. "I've been Rangering for nigh unto twenty-five years across the Nueces Strip from here to Corpus Christi and Uvalde to Brownsville. I've brought dozens of men and women to justice whether by bullet or the end of a rope. Likely as not, I saved some of your lives or the lives of folks you know." The diners were beginning to grasp Luke's message. "My friend has come a long way. He comes in peace. We intend to enjoy a meal here at this fine establishment." He took a final scan of the dining room. "Does anyone have an objection?"

A silence had settled over the room. Luke sat down and turned to look at the young server girl. He smiled gently. "Are you ready to take our order?"

"I'm sorry, sir, it's our restaurant policy."

Luke thought a moment. "Well, I'm hungry. I'll have a steak cooked rare and a baked potato."

The server nodded and even ventured a little smile. "Yes, sir." She glanced over at the now scowling owner.

"Oh, and a beer would be nice. In fact, I'd like two."

"Yes, sir."

Luke and One Arrow stared at each other in silence for the next couple of minutes, at least until the two beers were placed in front of Luke. He smiled and passed one over to One Arrow. As he did, he glanced over at the matronly woman who was still fuming over a Comanche being in her establishment. He smiled and raised the beer to salute her.

Soon enough, the steak and baked potato were placed on the table before him. Luke promptly turned to the server girl. "You know, this won't be nearly enough for a big hungry Texas Ranger. Please bring me another order of the same."

"Yes sir."

As she walked away, Luke shoved the dinner over toward One Arrow. "Enjoy dinner, my friend."

The owner was fuming but could see that she had no support from the restaurant patrons. Certainly, no one was objecting to the Texas Ranger and the Comanche.

Luke heard the clopping sound of boots enter the room and looked up to see Sheriff Toady Jones looking at him with consternation. "Dang it, Captain Dunn. The owner sent for me 'bout yer friend."

Luke could see the owner standing triumphantly near the restaurant entrance with her arms folded. "Have a seat, Toady, and we'll discuss our options."

At the commanding tenor of Luke's voice, the sheriff pulled up a chair and sat. The chair creaked as though it might fall apart, but it ultimately held.

"Can I get you something, Sheriff? A beer?"

The proprietor was beside herself and headed to the kitchen in a huff.

Luke and Toady engaged in a bit of small talk and it wasn't long before Luke and One Arrow had eaten their fill. Luke excused himself, said his goodbyes to the sheriff, and left some extra money on the table as he got up. He looked around, but most of the patrons had finished their meals and departed. Luke looked over at the owner and smiled. "Thanks for the fine dinner, ma'am. My friend and I will leave now. He gets restless after a good meal and tends to want to scalp everyone in sight."

An expression of horror swept across the owner's face. She didn't get the joke.

Luke smiled broadly at his own attempt at humor.

One Arrow looked quizzically at Luke, as it went over his head as well. "No scalp, Luke. One Arrow no scalp."

Seems little is worse than having to explain a joke. "We know that, my friend. I was teasing."

The Comanche shook his head resignedly. Would he ever understand the White man's ways?

Luke tossed a couple of coins on the table and smiled at the poor young lady who'd been tossed into the middle of the controversy instigated by the prejudice of the proprietor. He smiled inwardly, as he shifted his thoughts to Coy Witmer and how the outlaw's patience would likely wear thin and his self-doubt would build over whether he was actually capable of hunting down this Texas Ranger.

The table was old with a couple of deep cracks running through its time-roughened surface not to mention the stains of plenty of spilled booze and even some blood. It'd likely seen many a card game, many not necessarily on the up-and-up. Four men crowded around seated in rickety cane-back chairs. There was barely enough room for a deck of cards, much less hands dealt to the pretty much bored players betting and carrying on because there was little else for them to do. The two other tables in the room were equally diminutive and well worn. There were only a couple of other patrons, and they seemed content to sip whiskey or coffee or both and watch the card game. The intent of the layout seemed to be to not crowd the bar behind which an obese Mexican-heritage barkeep ruled the comings and goings. He seemed a reasonably jovial character, but there was the sense that no one messed with him.

It was early in the day, so there were no señoritas hanging around. The whores of San Ygnacio could best be described as Laredo rejects. They'd been used up to one degree or another servicing the sexual needs of the frontier-toughened men, the cowboys and drifters, that found their way to and through the slightly larger town to the north. Best that could be said for these ladies? They were experienced. Very experienced.

Little San Ygnacio wasn't much to look at so far as towns

go, but for now it served Coy Witmer's purposes. He judged that it would take a while for that damnable Texas Ranger to relocate his trail. He might relax for a couple of days, and it'd buy him time for his hand to heal. The doctor in Laredo had effectively enabled the restarting of the healing process by cutting away the infected dead tissue. Witmer took the doc's words to heart about taking care of the hand or he'd lose it altogether.

About the only thing that might throw water on his plans would be if those Mexican dragoons happened to run into the Texas Ranger. Unless Captain Dunn chose to trace a path down the Mexican side of the Rio Grande that eventuality seemed highly unlikely. Plus, he couldn't imagine the dragoons admitting that a wounded man outnumbered eight to one got away so easily.

He found a room for the night in a dilapidated house that was as sorry an excuse for a boarding house as might be found. The good news was that the bed was soft, the roof didn't leak, and the bugs seemed minimal. By late afternoon, Witmer was ready to find some entertainment. He strapped on his holster, checked the load in his Colt revolver, and slipped the cold iron-gray muzzle into its waiting sheath. He didn't figure to use the gun given that he planned to spend a couple of days in town. For now, it was more a decoration that in his often-demented mind defined his manhood. The holster nestled on his right side a bit lower than his hip, more on his upper thigh. He didn't take to a technique some supposed gunslingers were purported to do by facing the gun butt to the front and drawing by reaching across their body. Since he preferred ambush, he wasn't about to engage in any one-on-one confrontations that involved getting the Colt from his holster quickly.

As he walked into the saloon, one of the men was just leaving the poker game. Witmer paused and looked around, sizing up each of the patrons as to potential threat.

One of the players looked up from the table. "Hey stranger. You a player? Come join us." The man looked friendly enough. He sported long hair and a few wisps under his nose that could be considered a mustache. His most distinguishing feature was his large hands that comfortably cradled a poker hand. The old Colt 1851 Navy in his holster was a throwback weapon. As old as it was, the man would be lucky if the cylinder didn't explode when the gun was fired. They were known for metal fatigue.

Witmer was in a momentary trance as he focused on the revolver, but he quickly came around. "Sure." He walked toward the table waving his bandaged hand. "Might be a bit awkward, but I'm happy to join you." As he pulled up the recently vacated chair, he called to the barkeep, "You have any beer...¿cerveza?"

The barkeep was put off. "We speak English around these parts, mister." He acted as though having to leave the sheltered confines behind the bar to deliver a beer was a huge inconvenience.

The man next to Witmer leaned toward him. "*Estas loco. Hablamos inglés aqui.*" He laughed. "The barkeep is from Camargo...crazy and as Mexican as they come." It was a friendly enough welcome to the game.

The man who'd hailed Witmer turned out to be a young itinerant cowboy named Hayes. He was nearly done healing from a busted-up leg suffered when a horse fell and rolled on top of him.

The outlaw managed to awkwardly make it through a couple of hands, but it was a test of patience...his and the other players. Fumbling hands at serious card games was fully undesirable. As though that weren't enough, in his peripheral vision he noticed one of the patrons at a table to his left that seemed to be growing uncomfortable. Witmer finally looked directly at him. He got the sense that the man sort of recognized him but wasn't coming up with a name. Witmer nodded, and the man quickly looked away.

After several more hands, Witmer found that his good hand was beginning to cramp up a bit from clumsily manipulating the cards. That and several beers were clouding his card-playing judgment. "Gentlemen, I've appreciated your hospitality, but I've had enough for today. Hope to be here tomorrow."

The other players had about played themselves out as well. Everyone pushed back from the cramped table, exchanged smiles, and otherwise prepared to go their separate ways.

"Excuse me." The words floated out from Witmer's left.

The desperado looked over at the now drunk man at the other side of the room and teetering back in a rickety old chair that had surely seen better days.

"Ain't you Coy Witmer?" He waved a dime-store novel. "You the feller in this here book?"

The words darted through the stale air of the saloon like a lightning strike. The couple of men still there froze in place. Witmer looked over at the man while his right hand eased gently over the butt of his gun. "What's it to you, friend?"

"Yep, yur him!" The drunk smiled. "Pleasure to make yur acquaintance."

Witmer was a bit foggy with alcohol himself, so had begun to feel relieved that this encounter wasn't looking to involve gunplay. Trying to aim a gun would be chancy at best, and he had enough of his faculties to fear shooting himself accidentally. "Likewise," he offered and nodded to the man. The outlaw vaguely thought of heading toward the door, but changed his mind and eased unsteadily-like over to the drunk's table. He looked at the novel the man had waved about. "Hmmm. Cowboy Tales?" He half gagged through a belch then shook his head. "Damn, can't even spell my name right." There in the title was a reasonably accurate sketch of Witmer with a title reading "Coy Whitmer: Murder & Mayhem on the Frontier."

"That…that's you, ain't it?" The drunk's words trailed off just a bit. "Gonna get yuh, Mr. Witmer…I gonna…" His voice fell silent as he wobbled a moment in his seat. The man's head dropped onto the table as he collapsed in a drunken stupor. An old Remington Model 1858 revolver slipped from his lap to the floor, landing with a decided thud.

Witmer steadied himself against the table as he kicked the chair enough for the drunk to topple to the floor in a heap. He smiled as he looked down at the man, gathering that it might be a good idea to keep an eye on the man were he to show up the next evening sober. The man's intentions had been crystal clear, though his judgment was surely clouded by the rotgut whiskey. Booze could tend to make a weak man get crazy ideas. With that wise thinking, Witmer reflected on his own condition. He picked the dime-store novel up from the floor, shook off the sawdust, and half-staggered from the cantina while stuffing the fictional tome in his hip pocket. Swirling in his mind were thoughts of straightening out the stupid editor.

"Imagine!" he mumbled, "spelled my name wrong!"

Junior didn't just go plinking. He'd borrowed his father's old gun belt and holster along with a .45 caliber Colt Single Action Army revolver with a barrel just over seven inches long. Whatever a bullet from the muzzle of the Colt struck was sure to be destroyed.

He'd snuck from the house early, saddled one of the roan geldings, grabbed some sticks for targets, and headed on out. With only about three dozen bullets, he wasn't going to be gone all that long. Drawing the heavy revolver and shooting a .45 caliber slug was not child's play and could test anyone's arm and hand strength. Hitting targets consistently was every bit as great a challenge.

He rode down into a slight depression, dismounted, and

tied off the roan to a nearby live oak. He paced off about thirty feet up a slightly elevated section and shoved the six sticks into the ground. From this distance, the tops of the targets would be at roughly shoulder level. They weren't all that big, so hitting them would be a challenge.

Junior slid the Colt from his holster and carefully inserted six rounds. He slipped the gun back into his holster and adjusted its position tight alongside his upper thigh. He took a couple of long breaths, crouched a little, and quickly pulled the gun from the holster. He fired six shots in rapid succession. The fifth hit a stick. It wasn't a target.

Junior shook his head in disgust and reloaded. He didn't have to erect any new targets, but that wasn't a sort of convenience he was looking for.

For Elisa's part, she didn't long wonder where her son had gone off to. Junior couldn't hide from the booming reports of the Colt as it echoed across the low-lying hills. She sighed resignedly. "Gracie, come with me. Sean, you and Heather keep doing your chores. We'll be back shortly." She grabbed an old Colt 1861 Army from the mantel and led Grace out the door and down to the barn. "Hurry. Let's saddle up and go show Junior a thing or two."

Junior had just completed his second round of practice, when he heard hoofbeats. He'd actually hit two targets. He quickly reloaded in case the incoming riders meant trouble. It was trouble but not what he expected. "What are you doing here?"

Elisa smiled. "We could ask you the same thing." She and Grace dismounted. Junior's mom smiled devilishly as she looked at the six stick targets, noting that two had been winged. "Did we hear twelve shots fired?"

Junior blushed at the implication. Twelve bullets and two hits on target was admittedly pretty sad. He took a deep breath. "You want to take a try?" It was a weak challenge if ever there was one.

Elisa walked over to the spot Junior was shooting from and drew out the old Colt. She made sure it was fully loaded. "Just say when, Junior." She hung the revolver by her side.

"Now!"

Elisa raised the Colt and began firing. One...two...three... missed target...five...six.

Junior raised his eyebrows. "Holy smoke, Ma!" He grabbed some more stick targets and set them out.

Elisa couldn't contain a huge grin. "Not bad for a little old woman, huh?" She looked over at Grace. "You give it a try, Gracie."

Grace watched a competitive grit sort of expression on her brother's face. "Let Junior try again."

Junior swaggered over and checked the load in his gun. Once again, he pulled quickly from the holster, though this time he didn't fire so quickly. He obliterated four targets. He turned to Grace and his mom. "That's better." He wasn't about to admit that his arm was getting a bit tired from the heavy gun combined with the .45 caliber recoil.

Grace smiled. "How many bullets do you have left, Junior?"

"Six."

"May I borrow the Colt you're using?"

Junior handed her the revolver butt end first and dropped six bullets in her free hand. She opened the cylinder and dropped in the six rounds. "Are you going to replace the four targets you destroyed?"

"You need them?" he teased, then went and replaced them.

Elisa enjoyed watching the competitive spirit at work. "Take your time, Gracie."

Grace nonchalantly lifted the heavy revolver and one by one wiped out all six targets.

Junior was aghast. "Dang, sis! That was some shooting!"

"I practice too, brother." Grace smiled. "Remember what Dad said. 'It's not about speed, it's about hitting the target.'"

She recalled Luke sharing that gunfights in the streets were the stuff of dime-store novels, and not so likely in real life. Outlaws vastly preferred bushwhacking to confrontation, and street challenges were mostly decided by the man who took the time to aim. It stuck in her craw just a bit that the stories of gunfights were invariably about men, as though women couldn't defend themselves. She's heard enough about her mom's encounters with savages and bandits to know that a woman could hold her own or at least needed to be prepared to.

The three cleaned up the shooting site then mounted up and headed back to the house. Junior yammered all the way home about Grace's prowess. Elisa could do naught but enjoy the moment.

Witmer opened one eye and stretched as a shaft of morning sun shot across his face. Half-blinded, he felt the warm soft skin of a woman's body alongside him. He shielded his eyes from the light and took a long appraising look at her. Not bad. Not bad at all.

She must have felt his stare as she opened her eyes. *"Buenos días,"* she whispered sexily. She gave him a fetching smile that said she was ready for encores.

For his part, Witmer appreciated insatiability up to a point. He was about to demur, when he felt her tongue exploring his body.

It all didn't take long. Witmer soon enough found himself sitting on the edge of the bed shaking any possible varmints from his boots. His thinking was that he could safely stay one more day in San Ygnacio. He looked over his shoulder at the now fully sated woman. *"Hasta la vista, señorita."* He left a silver coin on the chest of drawers.

She pouted. *"Luego seguro, señor."*

"*Si. Luego.*" He slipped the Derringer into his vest pocket and headed to the restaurant to enjoy a breakfast. He'd certainly built an appetite.

As he began to walk through the doorway to the restaurant, a man brushed past him and hurried to a seat beside a young lady. Witmer might have let it pass save that the man bumped his wounded hand enough to set it throbbing. He fought off the quick anger that welled up inside.

He walked over to the couple who were now sitting and whispering with their heads nearly touching and their hands where most folks might not prefer in public. "Pardon, but do you normally try to knock folks over?" Witmer had brushed back his coat just enough to reveal the cold blue steel of the Colt revolver.

The young man looked up from his tryst, clearly oblivious to his offense. "I...I'm sorry, sir."

"Just don't be in such an all-fired hurry, friend. Bumping the wrong person could get a man killed in this part of Texas."

The young man's lady friend smiled sweetly and grasped her lover's arm.

The outlaw shook his head at their cluelessness. "Have a nice day, folks. Just be careful." Likely, it was just as well that they didn't know who he was. They didn't seem worth another grove in his father's watch. He walked over and took a seat at a nearby table. He wasn't going to engage in an altercation that would ruin his breakfast. The aroma of gunsmoke could make food taste terrible. Besides, the spirit of a certain Texas Ranger was quite possibly haunting his mind and keeping him just a tad on edge.

One more night in San Ygnacio, and he'd be on his way.

TWELVE
MANHUNTING

LUKE'S MIND was working overtime. Knowing the tendencies of whom you were hunting was an essential skill for any successful lawman. He was trying to climb inside Coy Witmer's head. In the case of this prey, it was akin to hunting some wily prey like a mountain lion. Bushwhackers tended to blend into their surroundings so as to optimize their chances of a successful ambush. But for his premature shot on the Frio River that warned Luke and gave his position away to One Arrow, Witmer had thus far proven to be decidedly effective at ambush. He also led a charmed life, having escaped with the bushwhacking attempt with a shot up hand and avoided the trap Luke had set for him south of Laredo. Charmed life indeed. Luke figured that eventually luck would run out…his or Witmer's.

He was also troubled by One Arrow's injuries. The Comanche chief wasn't healing up so fast as they'd hoped. While Luke was of a mind to take a break from hunting the outlaw if for no other reason than to give Witmer a false sense of security and make him impatient, it was becoming apparent that the chief would likely be more liability than asset should he decide to resume the hunt.

"You not worry about One Arrow. You go, Luke." The chief was insistent that he could take care of himself. He too recognized that he wasn't up to doing any rough trail riding just yet, and their prey's trail was growing colder by the day.

"You're right, my friend. I'll leave you with plenty of supplies. Nobody around Laredo is going to bother a friend of Luke Dunn."

"I will find you, Ghost-Who-Rides."

Luke knew he would. He changed the subject. "Where do you think he went?"

"No stay in Mexico. They look for him."

"I think you're right. He knows Texas." Luke was rubbing his mustache, signaling that his brain was in overdrive.

One Arrow smiled. "You stroke hair under nose, when you using head."

Luke had never really thought about that. It was something he'd always done. "Well, you know when I'm going to come up with some hair-brained idea."

"What hair-brained?"

"Silly…crazy…not so well thought out."

One Arrow fought the urge to laugh, as his ribs couldn't handle it. "Luke have good ideas. You find Witmer."

"Maybe I'll ride across the river to Nuevo Laredo and see what I might learn."

"Keep touching hair under nose." The chief smiled.

Elisa and Junior stood in front of the stable, as he curried the stallion.

"When do you think Dad will get home?" Junior was itching to show off his ever-improving marksmanship. He'd also saddle-broke this newly acquired young stallion that he'd become partial to. "Think he'll let me keep Wildfire?"

Elisa was wondering how you keep a horse from a teen

that's already named it. "Your dad will have the final say, son. Maybe you can buy Wildfire. You might be thinking on what you might do to earn him." She watched admiringly as her youngest son lovingly stroked the horse's muzzle.

Junior stuck away in his fertile brain the idea of purchasing Wildfire. "I will, Mom. I'll come up with an offer."

"You might talk to your cousins Nick or Mike about what he might be worth saddle broken and all."

Junior knew that Mike bought and sold horses and Nick speculated in livestock. They'd sure as shooting come up with a fair value. "Thanks, Ma. Can I ride out in the morning and visit?"

"Lots to do around here, young man. Your dad's going to be away for a bit yet." As she said the words, a courier rode in bearing a telegram. He handed it to her and waited patiently for a hoped-for tip. She looked at the cover. "Looks like it's from your dad." She reached deep into her dress pocket and fished out a coin. "Thanks, Sam. You take care."

She and Junior walked on up toward the house.

"What's Dad got to say, Mom? Is he heading home?"

She gave him a just-be-patient look as she slowly unfolded the message. "My, but the telegraph is surely wonderful, isn't it, Junior?"

"Mom?" he whined impatiently. "What's he say?"

Elisa looked extra serious, then smiled. "He's still tracking the outlaw. One Arrow is injured but will be okay. Might be a few days yet."

"Doggone."

"He sends his love, Junior…to all of us." She appreciated the lesson to be found in forcing patience on her son. She looked lovingly at him. His earnestness reminded her of her younger brother from a couple of decades back, though it saddened her to remember his passing from a rattlesnake bite. She looked lovingly at Junior and sighed. "You can ride over to your cousin's spread day after tomorrow. It'll give you time to figure Wildfire's worth."

Luke rode easy-like into Nuevo Laredo and up to the cantina where he and One Arrow had briefly encountered Coy Witmer a couple of days before. A couple of smarmy-looking men leaned against the wall beside the front door. Luke slipped his jacket over his Texas Ranger badge. No point in possibly resurrecting old memories of Texas Rangers illegally roaming across the Rio Grande into Mexico under Captain James Callahan in pursuit of outlaws and savages. Luke had earned his badge that day, as he took on the Mexican dragoons that had been in cahoots with the Apache and set upon the Rangers. The Mexicans' redcoats had caused memories of his fighting the British back in Ireland to flash through his head and led him to perform like some savage barbarian. Several dragoons met their Maker at Luke's hands. It had impressed Callahan, scared Luke, and indelibly imprinted the incident in the minds of the Mexicans. Indeed, Luke was wise to hide the Texas Ranger badge.

One man spat on the ground, narrowly missing Luke's foot. Luke laid his steely-blue eyes on him. The man blinked. He'd be no threat.

Luke stepped through the front door and sidled up to the bar. "*Hola, tabernero.*"

The barkeeper looked up lazily from washing glasses.

"*¿Cómo estás?*" Luke was doing his best to be friendly.

"*¿Qué deseas, gringo?*"

Luke reached back into his lexicon of Spanish learned from his foreman Jaime Sanchez. "*Estoy buscando un hombre.*" He hoped it came out that he was looking for someone.

"*¿Quién?*"

"*Fella llamado Coy Witmer.*"

The barkeeper's brows came together, and he spoke in an angry growl, *"¡No esta aquí!"*

Luke figured that was pretty emphatic. *"¿Dónde?"*

The barkeep seemed to be an impatient sort. Height-wise he stood at chest level to Luke, but he sported ample girth and was none too happy at a gringo asking questions. *"Pregunta a los dragones."* He deferred further questions by directing Luke to the dragoons.

"Gracias." Luke didn't figure to bother the barkeep any longer than he had to. Apparently, the Mexican Army dragoons knew something about Witmer.

"Mató a dos hombres estúpidos y se dirigió al sur."

Luke stopped just as he'd reached the door. He knew enough to make out that the two men that had taken on Witmer were stupid and dead. "Who are you?"

"Jesús Santos."

Luke had vaguely heard of him, and what he'd heard wasn't good.

Santos waved friendly-like, as though sizing Luke up. *"Buena suerte, señor Dunn."* He'd heard about the successes of the aging Texas Ranger, especially that he had a successful ranching operation near Corpus Christi.

Good luck indeed. Luke was curious that Santos had poked his head into the matter at all. But he didn't figure to inquire as to why just now. He strode from the cantina, climbed back into the saddle, and began a tour of the town riding real easy like. With their bright-red uniforms, Luke pretty much figured the dragoons would be easy to find among the brownish hues of Nuevo Laredo. Maybe this little side trip to the town would pay off quicker than expected. Santos hung in his mind, but mostly as a curiosity. There was something in the air about the Mexican bandit, but Luke couldn't quite figure it. Besides, he had Witmer to worry about.

Nuevo Laredo lived up to its name as a sandy, rocky place. It had been carved away from Texas back in 1848 by the Treaty of Guadalupe Hidalgo. Its streets shot westward in parallels from the meandering thoroughfare that traced along the gentle bends of the Rio Grande. Luke headed along the river, and it wasn't long before he came upon the dragoon's bivouac. It wasn't hard to miss what with red coats and all sorts of brass-adorned weaponry hanging from tree limbs and posts. The men themselves were mostly enjoying siestas. Luke rode up real easy-like so as not to rile anyone up. He'd long since managed to keep at bay the old night terrors, the visions of battling British redcoats on the heather of County Kildare back in Ireland. The only other hitch might be if anyone recalled those raids thirty years ago. He yielded to discretion, unpinned his badge, and tucked it into his shirt pocket.

"Buenos *días, dragones.*"

A couple of dragoons leaped to their feet at the greeting. One, apparently an officer though it was hard to tell without his tunic, spoke out. "*¿Quien es?*"

"*Luke Dunn. ¿Habla inglés, por favor?*"

Turned out it was the dragoon commander who greeted Luke. "*Un poco, inglés.* I am Lieutenant Gonzales. You need help?"

An offer to help. Luke thought that was right neighborly. "I'm looking for a man wanted by the law."

The dragoon officer thought on that. They hadn't seen many people in their recent travels. It was mostly a boring trek along the Mexican side of the river. "How did he look?"

"He's a White man dressed in dark clothes. Has a bandaged hand. Nice horse."

The dragoon shook his head with a bit of regret. "We chased him day before yesterday." He sighed. "He escaped. Crossed the Rio Grande toward San Ygnacio."

Looking at the ancient rifles and unwieldy lances the dragoons carried, Luke wasn't surprised that Witmer might escape. "That's a big help. *Muchas gracias.*"

"You a lawman?" The lieutenant was getting extra curious.

"Bounty hunter." Luke wasn't about to open that knotty issue. A Texas lawman in Mexico was a dicey proposition.

"You hungry?" The dragoon was becoming very hospitable.

"*Gracias*, Lieutenant. *Muchas gracias.* Got to get on with my hunting." Luke saluted by way of gratitude and rode on past the bivouacked dragoons.

"*De nada.*" The lieutenant went back to his siesta. He didn't really want a *gringo* dinner guest anyway.

Luke picked up his pace a bit now that he had a reasonably solid idea as to where he was headed. He saw no point in aggravating any Mexican soldiers or tempting any Apache still running loose, so decided to cross back over into Texas and point Twister southeastward toward San Ygnacio. He could only hope that Witmer would become over-confident and hang around the town for a few days.

Witmer lucked out. He'd found a doctor passing through on his way to El Paso and managed to have him change the bandages on his hand. The good news was that the infection was gone, and the hand was healing. If there was bad news, it was that the recovery wasn't going so fast as the outlaw would have liked. On the plus side, the new bandage wasn't quite so ponderous and awkward as the one it replaced. He'd actually be able to hold cards with his wounded hand.

He'd found the well-worn copy of "Cowboy Tales" that the drunk in the cantina had been waving about and found himself laughing at the exaggerations of his gunplay that it described. He was still miffed that they misspelled his name and had him carving notches in his gun rather than grooves in the gold watch, but the story the editor had concocted was pretty good. His ego pumped, he decided to head to the cantina.

Witmer soon found himself at a table drinking and playing cards for his final night in San Ygnacio. Three men joined his game. They were not exactly what casual observers might call the scions of San Ygnacio society, or maybe they were? Two of the three were locals.

"Go easy on me this evening, gents. The doc just replaced my bandages." Witmer established his excuse for slow, deliberate play. He'd made a point of sitting with his back to the wall. He had dime-store-novel-stoked visions of Wild Bill Hickock a decade earlier being shot in the back of the head in a saloon in Deadwood. He wasn't inclined to repeat Wild Bill's mistake.

The outlaw looked across the table at an apparent newcomer to San Ygnacio. He wore a fancy black flat-brimmed hat and embroidered vest but was otherwise dressed like most any cowboy. Even his boots were well worn and the rowels on his spurs had seen better days. A long scar ran from his left ear to the corner of his mouth. It gave him a slightly sinister appearance. In a way, it reminded Witmer of himself. The newcomer's hands were not especially rough, as though he didn't partake of the outdoor life. Remington revolvers hung from holsters on each hip with butts facing forward—not a configuration a cowboy would use. Witmer opened the conversation looking directly at the newcomer. "Let's get acquainted before I deal. The gentlemen to my right and left are Jorge Gonzalez and Bill Wise. My name is Coy. All you need to know. You have a name, mister?"

The stranger looked directly into Witmer's eyes. "Sam Woods. Pleased to meet y'all."

"Curious…Sam for Samuel?"

Woods smiled. "Sam for Samson."

Appropriate name thought Witmer, as he realized that Woods was a quite well-muscled specimen of manhood. "Where you from?"

"You gonna play or ask questions all day?" Woods was getting just a bit testy.

Witmer began to deal the first hand. "Five-card draw, gents. Deuces wild. Ten cents ante."

The stranger won four of the first five hands and was amassing a pretty good amount of loot.

By now, Witmer was keeping a close eye on Woods. He could see nothing unusual. It didn't seem like the man was cheating. He held a stoic expression throughout play, seeming to focus on his opponents' facial expressions. "Damn, but you're good, Sam. How do you do it?"

"Folks tell me I'm lucky." Woods smiled sort of sheepishly. It belied the confidence he played the cards with. "It can be streaky though." At that, he lost the next three hands.

Witmer began to feel better, as he won the pot on two of those. He seemed on his way to recouping his losses. Jorge and Bill were not so fortunate but played on gamely.

Each man had consumed a few drinks, with the exception of Woods. Tongues were loosening up, bets were getting sloppy, and all but the newcomer were experiencing ever less enjoyment. Woods took the pot in seven of the next eight hands.

Witmer still had seen nothing unusual in Woods's play, but then the idea of cheating at cards was to not be caught. "You seem to have found your luck again, Sam. Thought I'd seen everything, but I still haven't figured out how you do it."

Woods's eyebrows furrowed. "You implying something, Coy?"

"You mean cheating? Far be it from me to judge. But you do seem incredibly lucky."

"Just lucky." He smiled friendly-like. "I think I'll call it a night." Woods began to gather his winnings, and he pushed away from the table.

Jorge and Bill were watching to see what Witmer might do. They had begun to pull away themselves. In fact, a general hush had fallen over the cantina, as patrons stared at the potentially volatile situation evolving between Witmer and the stranger.

Witmer slowly put his hands on the table palms down. "Come on back tomorrow night, Sam. Maybe your luck will have changed."

Woods smiled as he stuffed his takings into a small leather sack. He tossed a tip to the barkeeper, turned, and began to walk with an easy stride toward the exit.

A bright flash of orange and an ear-shattering explosion rocked the crowded saloon. Sam Woods froze, then crumpled face first to the floor. Blood gushed from his chest, quickly puddling amid spilled beer and sawdust. He was likely dead before he hit the floor.

Witmer stood with his still-smoking Colt in hand and scanned the room for any threat. "The sonofabitch was cheating." He boldly replaced the spent cartridge, pulled out his pocket watch, and scraped a 35th groove on its case.

Everything was still deathly quiet. "Anyone think he didn't deserve what he got?" Still silence. "If anybody comes asking, tell them Coy Witmer was here." He scooped up Woods coin bag, pocketed a handful, and then tossed it to Jorge and Bill. "Good night." And he strode from the saloon. He figured to leave San Ygnacio in his dust come morning.

With the very real prospect of reengaging with Witmer's trail, Luke felt a new wave of confidence. It would take a little more than a day to cover the distance from Laredo to San Ygnacio. He figured to take it easy, as it would go better for him and the Appaloosa. Witmer, after all, would have likely had a couple of days to rest up. His mount would be fresh regardless.

Luke saw Apache on the Mexican side of the Rio Grande a

couple of times. They were fragmentary bands of a half dozen warriors or so and were likely Lipan Apache and may have had a loose affiliation with Geronimo, the Chiricahua Apache leader and medicine man who'd become the bane of the US Army. Luke managed to stay well-enough camouflaged to avoid detection.

His thoughts strayed from Elisa to One Arrow to his family, as he rode the dusty trail. He stopped every hour or so to rest and let Twister avail himself of a drink from the Rio Grande. It wasn't brutally hot, and low humidity made the heat easier to handle. The trail to San Ignacio was easy enough to follow, especially as compared to pushing through tall grasses and brush that had characterized the travel from Uvalde to Laredo a few days earlier.

Luke wished One Arrow were along, if only for companionship. Neither of them was getting any younger, but together they were a formidable force. He'd taught the chief some Morse code and worked at improving the warrior's English. They hadn't talked about God versus the Great Spirit very much, but that seemed to await the right timing. The chief still wore the necklace with its cross, despite not yet appreciating its meaning.

The hunt had indeed resumed. Luke was ever more appreciative of Witmer's inclination to use ambush. Had One Arrow not intervened back at the Frio, Luke would have been pushing up flowers from six feet under. As the Texas Ranger drew closer to San Ygnacio, he paid ever-greater attention to his surroundings. There was the possibility that the outlaw would head back toward Laredo, and they'd encounter each other on the trail. Even worse, Witmer could try to bushwhack him again. Luke had to figure how to better anticipate the outlaw's moves, to climb inside the man's demented thoughts. He found himself veering off the trail now and then, as he came upon places suitable for ambush. He occasionally circled back just in case the outlaw had reversed roles and was now hunting him. The tactic was slowing him down, but he couldn't be too careful.

Witmer enjoyed one more night with the eager San Ygnacio whore. He couldn't help but occasionally think back to the what-could-have-been romps with Cora and Anne back in Laredo, but there was something to be said for an experienced woman.

The morning had brought a steady light rain with it. The landscape became a murky gray. The locals were pleased. From Witmer's perspective, the only meaningful benefit would be slowing down that damnable Texas Ranger and giving him time to plan another ambush.

"¿Una más, señor?"

There was the call of the insatiable pocketbook of an aging prostitute. One more roll in the blankets seemed a small price to pay. It might be a few days before he'd be humping another in whichever town he chose. In fact, that was foremost in his thinking, as he had to stay ahead of that confounded Texas Ranger. He'd seen the Comanche savage take a heavy hit and counted One Arrow as likely dead, which meant that his pursuer was alone again.

The whore looked winsomely at him, as he pulled on his boots, stood, and fastened his trousers. She was ready for another tumble, his mind was elsewhere.

He glanced out the window. It was still early. Seemed like nothing was stirring. After last night's incident in the saloon, he was glad there was no sheriff or marshal in San Ygnacio. That would surely have complicated his exit, though it might have led to number 36. He thought on how much closer he was getting to King Fisher's achievement.

He thought about changing the bandage on his hand once more, but figured it might be better to put that off and gain some distance between him and possible pursuit by the Texas Ranger. Witmer longed to change roles from prey to hunter. He grabbed his saddlebag and rifle and headed from the room, taking one final look back at the whore lying fetchingly on the bed. "*Adios, muchacha.*" He took pains not to call her a *puta*, a whore. She likely didn't care.

He stopped at the front desk. "If anyone asks for me, tell them I'm headed to Corpus Christi." He slipped a tip onto the counter.

Once on the street, Witmer paused. He was running from the Ranger and not so certain he really needed to run. He retrieved his horse from the livery stable and turned the cayuse toward Laredo. Maybe the hunted could become the hunter.

He was beginning to think that perhaps this Luke Dunn fellow wasn't so special after all. The Ranger had fallen into his ambush rather easily and only survived by dumb luck. Perhaps the lawman wasn't the legend folks were making him out to be. Dunn was nothing more than an aging Texas Ranger with an equally aging reputation.

Witmer took the road toward Laredo. As he left town, he saw a small gathering at the town cemetery as they buried Sam Woods. The outlaw smiled to himself, thinking on how he'd likely rid San Ygnacio of a card cheat. The funeral was a simple little affair, as nobody apparently knew the deceased. He watched as the witnesses dutifully diffed their hats and bowed their heads to wish farewell to the pine-boxed remains. Soon enough, flesh-eating critters would find their way into the box and take care of whatever was left of Sam Woods.

The rain had let up, as he spurred his horse lightly and continued up the road. He decided to be extra cautious, as he was no fool. Luke just might have learned of the outlaw's San Ygnacio visit and be headed his way.

Twister whickered a bit and directed his ears forward. The big Appaloosa was on full alert. Luke sensed it too. Danger was in the air. He pulled the telescope from his saddlebag, opened it, and scanned the horizon ahead. Sure enough a rider was ahead on the road. Better still, it wasn't just any rider. By the appearance and especially the bandaged hand, it had to be Coy Witmer.

Luke telescoped the spyglass and put it back in the bag. He surveyed his surroundings. What place afforded him the optimum chance to capture Witmer alive? The bank from the road to the Rio Grande dropped steeply. To his left was a steep stone outcropping with plenty of brush and a couple of stubby trees. He hadn't much choice. The road ahead took what appeared to be a sharp bend such that an approaching rider wouldn't see him until being nearly upon him. Luke pulled Twister off the road behind a cluster of trees and bushes. The coat of the Appaloosa conveniently blended well with the landscape. The Ranger drew out one of his Colt Frontier revolvers and waited. This would be a close-quarters encounter. He prayed this would go down easy like.

Witmer slowed down. He had the feeling that this was going a bit too easily. Up ahead he saw a sharp bend in the road. He thought to himself how that would be a right perfect place to ambush or be ambushed. Something in his evil mind told him to be extra cautious. The hairs on the back of his neck involuntarily stood on end.

He turned his mount into the brush to his right and soon found an arroyo that meandered in rough parallel to the road but was perhaps fifty yards apart from it.

Luke waited patiently. Witmer was taking far too long to reach the bend in the road. This was definitely not a good sign. He stroked his mustache thoughtfully, as he slipped the Colt back into his holster. Now on even higher alert, he began to surveille the scene.

The Appaloosa's head followed its ears turning slowly toward Luke's left and well behind their location. He'd sensed another horse. There was no sound from Twister this time. The stallion was on high alert.

This was fast becoming a dangerous game of cat and mouse for Luke. He edged Twister back onto the road and headed for the bend where a large motte of trees afforded a degree of shelter from prying eyes. He faced the Appaloosa back toward from whence they'd come and waited.

It wasn't but a couple of minutes before he saw a shadow moving along cautiously in the dense brush. Witmer came into view and was facing away from Luke not more than thirty feet off. He was so close as to seem surreal. Clearly, the outlaw was scanning the brush for what he figured to be a bushwhacking lawman, but he wasn't watching his backside. Luke quietly eased from his saddle and stood behind the Appaloosa. He would have liked to have pulled out his rifle, but he was so close to the outlaw that the sound of metal on leather might have given him away. Using the big horse as a shield, he ever-so-slowly and gently drew the Colt from his holster and pointed it at Witmer. "You looking for something, friend?" He then eased from behind the Appaloosa and took a couple of steps toward the fugitive.

Witmer froze. "Damn!" he thought.

Luke's commanding voice rolled out, "Coy Witmer, you are under arrest. Come down real easy off that bronc and keep your hands where I can see them."

Witmer had a decision to make. There was a break in the brush to his left. He could be on the trail and galloping back toward Laredo in a flash. How good a marksman was the aging Ranger?

"You deaf?" Luke could sense what was likely going through the outlaw's head. "Get down now!" Luke's voice thundered in the still air.

"The hell with you, you sonofabitch!" Witmer spurred his horse, crashed through the opening in the brush, and was near-instantly on the road to Laredo. He dropped low, clinging to his horse's neck.

Luke got off two shots. He was sure one bullet hit the fleeing outlaw, but it hadn't slowed him down. He dashed back to the big Appaloosa and vaulted into the saddle. Twister for his part was ready to ride. Luke turned him toward where he'd seen the outlaw escape but pulled up after galloping but a few yards. He could still hear the outlaw's departing hoof-beats. A chase was foolhardy. It would be too easy for Witmer to pull off the road and lay in wait to bushwhack him.

He rode a few feet with considerable caution, then looked down and saw a couple of droplets of blood on a rock along the road. He bemoaned the lost opportunity, but perhaps all was not lost. He wondered now just how badly Witmer was wounded. His hand stroked his mustache, as he thought on just what had driven this outlaw like so many before him to become a murderer. He recognized that Witmer offered no hope of being redeemed from his crimes, as evil and right-eousness simply could not coexist.

Despite being wounded, the outlaw now had the advan-tage of knowing that Luke was back on his trail. Having come so close to capture, Witmer would be extra cautious. If he had any doubts as to Luke's ability to track an outlaw, he'd gotten his answer. To his way of thinking, the Texas Ranger had climbed inside his head enough to figure what the outlaw was going to do. Despite his vileness, the thought of being prey to so skilled a hunter unnerved him.

For Luke, he only knew that his wounded prey was somewhere between him and Laredo. Would Witmer be so bold, so arrogantly confident as to return to the town? He tried to put himself into the desperado's mind. What might such a man do? Luke surely wasn't going to do anything so foolish as to stay on the road and be a target, so why would Witmer?

It occurred to him that San Ygnacio was no more than an hour's ride away. He had already recognized Witmer's overconfident, boastful nature. Just as he'd done back in Uvalde, the outlaw had likely announced his destination to someone. Luke took a long look up the road toward Laredo, then looked back down at the spot of blood. He sighed and turned the big Appaloosa toward San Ygnacio. He rather expected the logical place to begin would be the cantina. It was yet early enough in the day, that he might be able to resume his tracking of Witmer with plenty of daylight left. He wouldn't be traveling at night, partly to avoid giving the outlaw the advantage of darkness and partly in the event that Witmer left the trail altogether.

THIRTEEN
KISS AND TELL

THE SOFTLY ROLLING hills and byways of Heaven's Gate Ranch didn't make searching for stray beeves any easier. A person used to the peaks and gorges of the Rockies would rightly be justified in calling this region of the Nueces Strip tableland. Just try to convince someone trying to find a wandering longhorn cow and calf that it's all flat. Junior thus found himself meandering hither and yon mostly through tall grasses as punctuated by an occasional motte of live oak or mesquite. He'd saddle broken Wildfire, but was still working with the young stallion on the intricacies of subtle commands like responding to knee pressure so necessary in the grasses and brush.

His side mission was to ride on over to his cousin Mike Dunn's spread and get a feel for the value of this horse under him that he'd begun a cowboy love affair with. If he hoped to persuade his father to sell Wildfire to him, he needed to come up with a well thought out proposal as to the cayuse's worth and just how he proposed to pay for him.

Most of Heaven's Gate was free of fences, so Junior's travels met with no significant physical obstacles. At age fifteen, he sat a horse well as enhanced by his natural tendency to sit especially tall. He was already better than six feet tall, and likely to grow taller than his father. If there was much difference in appearance, it was that he had his mother's blond hair and wasn't yet able to grow a mustache like Luke's. He'd taken one of the old Henry rifles with him and, at his mother's insistence, one of the new Colt Frontier model revolvers the family had recently acquired.

As horse and rider ambled along, his cousin's relatively small ranch soon came into view. He eventually pulled up near the fence with the intention of following it to Mike's house. Junior was immediately struck by the condition of one section of the fence. It had a large gap and there were lots of cattle hoofprints, as though stock had been driven through onto his cousin's land. Junior guessed that maybe a dozen beeves were in the herd. Given that Mike raised horses rather than beeves, it quickly occurred to Junior that the cattle could be wearing the -HG brand. The next logical thought was who might be running Heaven's Gate cattle?

Part of Junior cautioned to hustle back home and get some help, but his father's blood raised his curiosity sufficiently to want to follow the tracks. He slipped through the gap in the fence and cautiously followed the clearly marked trail. The hoofprints and cowpies didn't seem particularly fresh, so Junior figured he was a goodly distance behind whoever was moving the small herd.

After about thirty minutes, he looked off into the western horizon and saw a bit of dust being kicked up. Something was moving out there, and it would take a lot more than a mere dozen beeves to raise so much powdery grit from the loamy sands of the Nueces Strip. Wasn't long before he'd ridden across Mike's ranch and was facing another fence where the barbed wire had been neatly cut to allow cattle to pass. Again, there were plenty of hoofprints. Now, he also made out the prints of shod horses.

He continued to trail what he decided by now must be

rustlers. He'd heard his father talk about fence cutters, but by now he figured he was on the trail of a greater crime. Rustling, after all, was a hanging offense. It had also occurred to Junior that he might be significantly outnumbered. That got him to thinking on what his father might do. Luke sure as shooting wouldn't be foolhardy. The terrain was flat and open enough that he'd likely have a serious challenge getting close to any cattle rustler sight unseen.

Junior took a long wistful final look at the dust cloud and turned for Mike's place. A dozen longhorns would be a terrible economic loss, but his mom might not so easily get over losing a son.

It had taken nearly two days. Witmer thought about passing up Laredo and making a beeline for Corpus Christi, but he had an itch to see Cora and Anne for one more roll in the hay. He rode into Laredo and up to the doctor's house. He took a long gander up and down the street, dismounted, and tied the reins to the hitching post. The outlaw looked down at the slight trace of blood that had run from just below his knee and down the side of his boot. It was what some folks called a flesh wound, uncomfortable but not life threatening.

The doctor answered his knock and greeted him with one of those not-you-again expressions. "What sort of trouble did you get into this time, mister?"

Witmer looked furtively. "Got into an accident." He took a long pause. "That Comanche hanging around?"

"Haven't seen the savage. Just as well. He scared the beejabbers out of most folks. Damned savage nearly got himself killed." The doc glanced down at the outlaw's leg and sighed resignedly. "Come on in and let's have a look." The doc missed the surprised look that swept the fugitive's face, as Witmer realized that One Arrow was alive.

The outlaw emerged about an hour later. He still found it hard to believe that he hadn't killed the Indian. He tried to shake it from his mind by washing most of the traces of blood from his pants and boot. He walked a bit stiffly, but it didn't stop him from easing on down to that fleabag hotel he'd deposited the young ladies in. He limped up the step and through the front door. He scanned the room before shouting to the barkeep, "Say, do you still have those two young ladies staying here?" Witmer wanted to be certain the ladies heard him.

"Damn right I do. They keep sayin' you're gonna pay for their room."

Witmer shook his head. "We'll see. Where they at?" His smile took on a sinister air.

"Down the hall to the left...room 301." He pointed down the hallway. "I think they have a gent in there with them." The clerk chuckled. It didn't make sense that this man was paying for the young ladies' room while they sold their private wares.

"Thanks." As Witmer moved toward room 301, he could hear carryings on emanating from the within. It was clear that the trio were enjoying some wild sexual adventures. Squeals, giggles, oohs, and ahhs gave him clear indication that they wouldn't be paying attention to the door. He slipped his revolver from its holster, turned the doorknob, pushed hard, and stepped boldly into the room. Three totally naked humans cavorted on the bed in full orgasmic lust. They were momentarily oblivious to his entrance. The man had his face down and planted into the ample chest of one of the lady's, while his butt rocked rhythmically above to the delight of the second lady.

The blast from the outlaw's gun shattered the orgy. A bullet went clean through the man's prodigious hind quarters and sped on into the bedpost.

Everything stopped.

"Damn! Damn that hurt!"

"Get your ass out of here pronto or I'll give you something that really hurts!" Witmer waved the gun about menacingly. The girls cowered back while trying to digest what was happening. The man gathered his clothes and staggered out the door, trailing drops of blood from his naked posterior along the way.

"Why Mr. Coy...you're back." The naked girls cluelessly giggled in unison despite the gunplay moments before. Cora smiled and puffed out her bodacious chest in Witmer's direction. "We've missed you." Anne smiled fetchingly as she stood atop the bed on her knees with her hands on her gyrating hips. They made no attempt at modesty.

The outlaw slammed the door shut and locked it. He turned to the young girls. "Do me, bitches." He dropped his pants and displayed his manhood.

The ladies were only too happy to oblige. They'd grown tired of their previous client in any case. It was time to pleasure the man paying the bills.

Luke noted the fresh earth piled over a gravesite as he rode past the San Ygnacio cemetery. He wasn't curious enough to dismount and inspect it, but filed the observation away in the back of his brain.

The decrepit old door to the only drinking hole in the town creaked loudly as Luke stepped on through and eased on over to the bar. Despite a bright late morning sun, the interior retained its dark, musty, acrid atmosphere. The dim kerosene lamps cast just enough light to reflect noticeably off the polish of his Texas Ranger badge. It was enough to catch the barkeeper's attention.

"You lookin' fer that Witmer fella?"

"Yes. I'm Texas Ranger Luke Dunn. I ran into Witmer back

up the road apiece. Winged him, but he got away. Did he say where he was headed?"

The barkeeper paused from wiping down the bar. His chubby jowls parted in a grin of sorts. "Said to tell anyone who asked that he was headed to Corpus...if you can believe a sonofabitch like him."

"He have anything to do with that fresh-turned ground back in the cemetery?"

"Yep...said somethin' 'bout number thirty-five."

Luke shook his head with regret. He was beginning to feel the pressure as though he was letting folks down. "Thanks for the information." As he turned to leave, a female voice brought him up short.

"Mister?"

He looked over his shoulder. It was the whore that had been servicing Witmer during his stay. But for her dark hair, she reminded Luke of what Scarlett Rose might have come to look like in old age as a used-up prostitute. Clearly, this whore hadn't been afforded the same sort of opportunity as Scarlett. He tried to avoid pity in his facial expression, paused, took a breath, and gave her a serious inquisitive look. "Can I help you?"

"The man you're looking for...he told me he thought he might see some ladies in Laredo before he headed east. From what he said, they're very young." She looked a bit crestfallen at the implied admission of her own getting on in years.

"Thanks." Luke laid a couple of coins on the counter, smiled at the barkeep and the whore, and walked on out. He'd thought to spend the night in San Ygnacio, but now he felt as though heading back to Laredo was important enough to get back on the trail. He poked his head back into the saloon. "Y'all got a telegraph here?"

"Brand spankin' new. Post office is up the street."

Before he departed, Luke sent a message to Laredo with the

hope that the postmaster there would not be so bigoted as to refuse to deliver it to One Arrow.

One Arrow had set a modest campsite a couple of hundred yards from the rear of the livery stable. He had recovered sufficiently to use his bow, so had managed to bring in a fine deer. One of the local citizens that harbored no particular ill will toward Comanche stopped by each day to gift the chief with a couple of eggs. Eggs and venison were a great combination to speed the healing process both physically and mentally. The shattered bone beads of his breastplate and the mangled forestock of the Henry rifle laid out on a nearby blanket were stark reminders of his brush with death. The incident had also served to strengthen his belief that Luke possessed some sort of strong spirit.

He'd just settled into gnawing on a roasted venison rib, when a young boy approached. The boy's timid steps made him want to laugh, but that still would have hurt. The chief smiled and raised his hand as a welcome sign.

"You the Comanche?"

The chief nodded.

"Postman said to give you this." The youngster handed the telegram to One Arrow, reaching out with enough fear that he almost dropped it.

One Arrow took the message and smiled again to put the boy at ease. "You like eat?"

The boy turned and ran off in a panic.

The chief smiled at the boy's fear and opened the telegram. He had a tougher time reading English than speaking it, but slowly sounded out the words of the message. Essentially, Luke was letting him know that Witmer might show up and that he would be riding back to Laredo as quickly as possible.

★★

Witmer was just about out of energy as he strove to keep the two insatiable teens satisfied. He looked at his now flaccid member. "Damn, ladies...lookee there. You've done worn that thing out."

The girls giggled and redoubled their efforts to get him aroused again. Cora finally pulled back. "What'd you do in San Ygnacio, Mr. Coy?"

"Ladies, I don't kiss and tell." He managed a wry grin.

"You shoot anyone?"

"Killed a man cheating at poker."

The girls offered mock expressions of surprise. "Do you ever miss, Mr. Coy?"

"Not supposed to miss. Missing can get a man killed."

The girls cooed, "You must be very brave." Their hands explored Witmer's body much to his enjoyment and their disappointment.

"Ladies, when a man's done, he's done." He grinned at their enthusiasm. "Give me a little more time, and we'll do another tumble." He knew full well that he was also beginning to feel the pressure of the growing possibility that the Texas Ranger might be on to him and heading his way.

★★

"Mike...Mike!" Junior had arrived at his cousin's house. His horse had barely stopped as he leaped from the saddle and dashed through the gate to the fence surrounding the house. "Mike!"

Mike emerged upon hearing Junior's hollering. "Junior... what the? Catch your breath, son. Calm down."

"R...R...Rustlers! Rustlers, Mike!"

"Ease up, Junior. What's this all about?"

Junior placed his hands on his hips and took a couple of

deep breaths. He finally felt as though he might be able to ease the story on out. "I was heading to your place when I found a gap cut in the fence." He took a breath and began to relax. "I saw a lot of hoofprints. I followed them to the other side of your spread and found another cut. There was lots of dust being kicked up off in the distance. My dad's away and Jaime's at home, so I figure they could be stolen -HG beeves."

"Any horses?"

"Yes...and they were shod."

"Well, whoever it is, they're long gone, Junior. By the time we get up a posse...well...it's unlikely we'll catch them."

Junior felt a little miffed but tried not to show it. He wanted to say, "If my dad were here, he'd be chasing after them." Instead, he gave a sort of a resigned nod.

"What were you coming to see me about, Junior?"

Junior sighed. "Coming to see you about this here horse. I want to buy him from my dad, but need to know what he's worth."

Mike appreciated his cousin's frustration over the likely rustling but was inclined to accept life's realities. Rustling was a hanging offense after all, but they could be tough to bring to justice. It wasn't a one-man job. Add the crime of fence cutting to rustling, and whoever was stealing beeves was in a heap of trouble. "Tell you what, Junior, let's ride up and see the deputy in Alice, and we can talk about your horse on the way."

That seemed to mollify Junior. "Great, Mike. Let's go."

"Hang tight a Texas minute, Junior. I still have to finish my lunch and saddle up a horse. Come on in and grab a bite. Catherine's got some warm cornbread."

An hour later, they were headed to Alice.

"Looks to be a good piece of horseflesh, Junior. He's nearly two years old I'd guess."

Junior was surprised but not surprised at his cousin pinning down Wildfire's age so closely. "Yes, nearly two years."

"A bit more than fifteen hands. Great musculature. Good hide. Well cared for. Yep, I'd say you have a mighty fine piece of horseflesh there, Junior. You saddle broke him yourself, right?"

"Yes. I just taught him to respond to knee pressure, too."

"Horse like Wildfire might be worth upwards of two hundred dollars, Junior. Being you're family, a fair price for your dad might be a hundred fifty."

Junior chewed on that a bit, then slowly spit out, "That's a lot of money, Mike."

Mike nodded agreement. "That's a lot of horse under you. I'm sure you and your dad will work it out."

★★

"Gotta hit the road, ladies. Your room is paid through the end of the week, then you're on your own."

"You're really leaving us, Mr. Coy?"

"Maybe I'll get back here afore too long. For now, I've got unfinished business to take care of." There was a sense of relief in his voice. For all the dreams he and other men might have entertained about sex with multiple women, he'd found that the reality simply didn't measure up. It had taken all the energy he could muster to get aroused for a final romp with Cora and Anne.

"Where you heading, Mr. Coy?"

The girls still didn't even know his last name. He couldn't be sure it would even have made a difference. They were only intelligent about one thing, and at that, they were geniuses. "Corpus. Heading to Corpus Christi." Witmer gathered his gear and bade a fond farewell, as he exited and headed toward the stable. It was a crisp clear day. His hand was feeling ever better and his leg was no bother. He had a sense of mission. Somewhere between Laredo and Corpus, he intended to kill Texas Ranger Luke Dunn.

As he neared the stable, his peripheral vision caught an image that caused him to do a double take. His brows knitted together in frustrated anger. "Damn," he thought. "It's true. The doc was right. I didn't kill the sonofabitch Indian after all."

The image of One Arrow alive and well weighed heavily. Witmer simply couldn't leave Laredo with what little conscience he had without taking care of the immediacy of this unfinished business. He decided to saddle up and then finish off the Comanche savage on his way out of town.

One Arrow had just looked up from a final bite of venison rib, seen Witmer, and recognized the facial expression that comes with surprise at discovering something unexpected. He was grateful to Luke for sending the telegram about the evil one heading for Laredo. The chief knew he had little time so gathered essential personal effects, quickly kicked dirt over the coals of his cooking fire, and mounted his pony. He knew full well that he had to be gone before the outlaw reappeared. Under normal circumstances, he'd have led a man like Witmer off into the brush and laid an ambush. His still-painful chest and ribs left him not quite up to firing arrows much less charging his foe with a lance. He wished he still had a working rifle. He eased his pony up the trail at a slow silent walk before picking up the pace. He decided that he'd ride in a wide arc, intending to eventually sweep back to intersect with Luke's path from San Ignacio.

Witmer emerged from the stable to find that the Comanche had disappeared. He cursed the air that he hadn't taken care of business before saddling up. If he'd had the Winchester loaded, cocked, and ready for action, he'd have already finished off the savage. Damned luck that the chief had somehow not been killed. The bullet that had left Witmer's rifle had instant death written all over it, but the fool Comanche was alive and apparently quite well. Now, the question was where did he go and was it a fool's errand to chase the savage? He sighed and shook his head. Out in the brush, the damned Comanche would have the upper hand. Better to head out the road toward Alice and keep his eyes peeled for the Indian...and the Texas Ranger.

★★

At the Alice jail, Junior painstakingly described the evidence of rustling he'd come across on his way to Mike's spread.

"Where's Luke?" Bones had looked up from carving a walking stick to ask the logical but mostly rhetorical question. He knew full well what Junior's father was up to.

"Chasing an outlaw across the Strip."

The deputy nodded.

Mike decided he'd better chime in sooner than later. "Deputy Hollingsworth, if what Junior here says is true, those thieves made off with maybe seven or eight hundred dollars-worth of prime Heaven's Gate beeves."

"Well, from what you're saying, they've got a long lead on us, Mike." Bones was pretty much ignoring young Junior.

The teen was not to be put off. "I'd have chased them..."

Mike cut him off. "But you had better sense than to tackle the job by yourself, Junior." It was a combination compliment and a way of respectfully including the youngster in the conversation. He nodded to Junior and turned back to Bones. "I think my cousin Nick was talking a couple of weeks back about some of his beeves disappearing." He turned up the pressure a notch. "What are you going to do about it, Bones?"

For his part, Bones Hollingsworth didn't especially like the danger associated with chasing likely well-armed rustlers. He was partial to cleaning things up after the fact. He sighed resignedly. "Okay. Lemme see if I can muster up some sort of posse."

"Can I go, Mike? I can identify the brands."

Mike looked at Bones who shook his head almost imperceptibly. "I don't know. You're still pretty young for this sort of thing, Junior." The pleading expression on the youngster's face was hard to resist. Mike finally gave out an exasperated sigh. "Luke's gonna kill me, and I don't want to deal with your mom. You ride in the rear. I'm not dealing with your folks, if something happens to you."

Bones shook his head and motioned them to follow him. "I know a couple of out-of-work cowboys who'll likely join us. They're loyal to me. Downside might be that they're prone to lynching rustlers."

Junior pulled Mike aside. "Mike…do they have a telegraph here?"

"Far as I know. You fixing to send one?"

"I'm thinking I'd better let my mother know I won't be home tonight."

Mike smiled and nodded. "Sounds right thoughtful, Junior. We'll go on over to the post office before Bones gets back here with our posse."

For his part, it was all Junior could do to suppress a broad grin. He was glad he could tell his mother what he was up to, though she'd likely be upset as all get out. He wouldn't be hanging around waiting for an answer. First and utmost in his mind was to make his dad proud.

Bones soon returned with two cattle-drive-hardened cowpokes, rough around the edges but with seemingly good natures. Shorty Smith and Neezer Tyler were well-armed and already talking about stringing up cattle thieves.

Their bold chattering took just a bit of the edge off the excitement for Junior. This had fast become all too real.

One Arrow had swept up his belongings hurriedly. Escaping the outlaw had been first and foremost on his mind. He now pulled up to gather his wits. He rerolled his blanket and made sure all he carried was in order. If the outlaw were to follow him, he'd receive a very unwelcome reception. The chief still regretted the loss of the Henry rifle, but he hadn't lost his touch with the bow and arrow and lance. The prospect of hand-to-hand combat would raise his spirits such that his still-healing chest would not be an issue.

He stayed on his plan to try to intersect with Luke's path. He surveilled the area around him carefully before riding out slowly, wary of the possibility of being followed. It was slow going through the thick brush, but he found a couple of dry creek beds that contorted around the landscape in the general direction he was heading. Arroyos tended to mostly hasten travel through thick flora and fauna but often attracted other critters both animal and human, so One Arrow had to be especially alert lest he meet with unexpected and possibly disastrous encounters.

FOURTEEN
THE LAREDO-ALICE ROAD

LUKE HAD BEEN RIDING ALONG easy-like, keeping a keen eye out for any place along the trail where Witmer might have decided to head east. He knew it was unlikely but wasn't about to take a chance. The country was so rough that a wounded man, even one as diabolically obsessive as Witmer, made it unlikely he'd leave the road. Luke strove to look ahead for places in the landscape that might offer an opportunity for ambush. Witmer might be the one hunted and nursing wounds, but he was nevertheless a dangerous animal. Cornered prey could get right nasty.

About the time Luke figured he was drawing close to Laredo, he heard the muffled sound of an unshod pony to his rear. He slid the Colt Frontier from its holster while simultaneously turning the big Appaloosa to face the challenge from behind. The revolver sat easy-like across his saddle pommel as he stared intently up the road. His concern turned to relief quickly enough.

One Arrow raised his hand as he rode toward Luke. He didn't have his horse at a gallop, as that would have jarred his still-healing and quite-painful ribs. He mustered enough air to call out. "Luke!"

Luke reholstered the revolver and waited for the chief to draw nearer. He smiled as One Arrow drew alongside. "You got my message?"

"Evil one you call Witmer. He almost get me," replied the Comanche grimly.

"How are you feeling?"

"Hurt when laugh." One Arrow offered a sheepish smile at his own humor.

Luke nodded his understanding. The chief was putting up a brave front. "Witmer's a bad one. I thought I had him trapped down near San Ygnacio. I wounded him, but he got away from me."

"I saw him take trail from Laredo. He go to rising sun." One Arrow made a motion eastward with his hand for emphasis.

"The folks in San Ygnacio said he was heading for Corpus Christi. I don't understand why he wants to go there." Luke's tone was decidedly facetious.

"Maybe he like warm weather." The chief smiled as he delivered his own bit of ironic perspective.

"I just don't see what he might be going after," Luke repeated. "Unless...of course!" He shook his head, guffawed, and stroked his mustache. "Guess he decided to come after me on my stomping grounds. Just a tad reckless, I'd say."

"One Arrow think he fool."

Luke offered a barely perceptible nod of agreement. "Well, we must travel through Laredo. I'll send a telegram to Elisa to be careful and another one to Captain McMurray to let him know what's happening. Then we can get on the road to Alice. From what you're saying, Witmer has maybe a four-hour lead on us." Luke looked at the watch Elisa had given him. "We'll have to be extra careful."

"One Arrow have idea."

Luke was all ears. "What are you thinking of?"

"Me go cross country…short path between two places. Maybe find evil one when he not looking."

Luke pondered that a moment. "How will I know when you've found him?"

"Me send signal. Tap code on tree."

Luke smiled with the satisfaction of having taught the Morse code to One Arrow. Witmer wouldn't have a clue. He'd likely think it was a woodpecker. "You sure you're up to it?"

"Healing good. One Arrow can do this."

"Go ahead, my brother. I'll listen for your signals. Likely be a day or so before you get close to him." Luke knew how the practice of being forewarned could be a tremendous advantage hunting an outlaw on the Nueces Strip, especially one with a proclivity to bushwhack.

★★

Elisa was beside herself, as she crumpled the telegram, straightened it out, and reread it.

"Mom…what's wrong?" Grace looked up from her butter churning.

"It's that brother of yours…the younger one. Sean's got enough sense to stay here and do his chores."

"Something hasn't happened to Junior, has it?"

"Not yet, Gracie. He's joined a posse with our cousin Mike to chase down rustlers. They apparently stole some of our longhorns." In a way, Elisa was proud of Junior for taking the initiative. "He'd better be careful." She was scared that his impetuosity might place him at risk.

"Should we send Sean and Jaime after them?"

Elisa smiled appreciatively. "I'd guess they're too far to be caught up with. Mike will look out for him." She tried to give Grace a sense that Junior would be at minimal risk. As she turned to return to her sewing, a rider could be heard approaching. She glanced out the window. "The courier is back. They ought to set up the telegraph here...it'd save a lot of trouble."

Elisa went out onto the gallery to greet the young man. "Golly, Pete, they're keeping you busy today."

"Yes ma'am. This one's from Mr. Dunn." He stood in his saddle and handed it up.

"Thanks, Pete. Say hello to Pastor Rucker for us when you get back to Nuecestown." Rucker had taken on post office and telegraph responsibilities. The retired Army colonel was looking forward to the upcoming visit of his son Rex who was now a general stationed in the nation's capital.

Elisa opened the telegram. Luke was just letting her know that he was safe and thinking of her. A surge of warmth came over her. She missed her man.

"Good news, Mom?" Grace noted the hint of moisture in her mother's eyes.

"Your dad's safe. Sends his love." She didn't share the last line that warned of Coy Witmer heading to Corpus Christi. Would the fugitive dare stop at Heaven's Gate and make trouble?

"See that dust o'er yonder, Mike?" Junior had been at the head of the posse up to now given that he knew where the fence had been breached and which way the rustlers had been heading.

Mike looked to where Junior was pointing. "Looks to be quite a way off."

"If we ride hard enough, we might get close by sundown." Bones figured to push on and not take any rest. He knew they'd outpace the thieves given that the rustlers were necessarily slowed down by the cattle.

Mike laid a commanding sort of look on his young cousin. "Junior, you've done a great job getting us this far. From now on, you ride behind me."

The implication of staying under Mike's protective wing wasn't lost. Junior knew this was coming. He'd played his role. He nodded to Mike and fell back to the rear, checking that his Colt revolver was fully loaded. He didn't know whether he'd be getting a chance to do any shooting, but he'd be ready.

There it was, about a hundred feet north of the road. The live oak motte screamed out to him as the perfect spot to bushwhack that damnable Texas Ranger. It afforded a wide field of vision to spot any rider approaching from the west or south. Better still, there was no place in sight where an interloper might hide and mess with his ambush as he'd experienced up on the Frio River. He wasn't up to being bushwhacked himself again.

He was maybe a day and a half out of Laredo, and it'd take him several more days to reach Alice. He had no idea as to when Luke might have arrived in Laredo and then departed to track him. The Comanche had put a hitch in things, but Witmer figured he might get a chance to take another crack at the savage.

It occurred to Witmer that he was lonely. He'd left the young prostitutes behind in Laredo, not that he'd established any deep social relationship with them. They had been decent company and been fun to cavort with. Their total naivete as to anything other than sex made for an invigorating experience. Like all of the women in his life had been, the two whores were simply objects for his sexual gratification. The only other thing he saw women as possibly good for was if they had something worth stealing.

With the sun easing down toward the western horizon dragging a golden wake in its path like some great blanket, the outlaw made camp. Naturally, he was totally oblivious to the grand beauty of the sunset. The air was still but not unbearably warm. His aim was to be up bright and early so as to keep an eye on the road. He might even grab a bit of shuteye after feasting on a little whiskey and some venison jerky to take the edge off his appetite. Other than birds, crickets, and an occasional coyote howl, all was silent as nightfall approached.

Witmer's hand was beginning to feel much better. He removed the bandages and decided that exposing his hand to the air and gently flexing his fingers might promote faster healing. There was an ugly scar forming where one of his fingers used to be. Given the infection he'd been afflicted with, he considered himself fortunate to have not lost his entire hand. He couldn't know for certain, but he had put the situation on the Frio River near Uvalde together in his mind and decided that it was the damned Comanche that had wounded him. Killing the savage would avenge that event.

Luke had decided to ride on through the night. The crescent moon and millions of stars didn't cast so much light, thus making him more or less difficult to see. He knew One Arrow would also travel under stars, so his senses were on high alert waiting for the Comanche's signal. He was confident that One Arrow would locate Witmer. Nevertheless, every sound from the night prairie seemed amplified and grabbed at his attention. Even the stars seemed to be making noises with their twinkling.

Twice the previous night, he'd seen coyotes silhouetted against the landscape and, while he couldn't be positive, was pretty sure a lynx had crossed his path. The big Appaloosa seemed at ease, as though nothing could fluster him.

As Luke looked off toward the eastern horizon where a pale pinkish glow was just beginning to ready the sun for its appearance, he heard a tapping sound. At first, he actually thought it was a woodpecker, but then he realized that there was a rhythm to the staccato of the sound. One Arrow was telling him that their prey was camped under a live oak in a wide-open area of the prairie.

Luke pulled the Winchester from its scabbard and began to tap a response on the wooden stock. The sound was like two woodpeckers looking to mate. Now, the Texas Ranger turned north and rode a wide arc that would put him far out of the outlaw's view. He aimed to approach from behind the desperado and with any luck thwart any bushwhacking plan.

Witmer awakened to the final night sound of a howling coyote and the annoying rapping of a couple of woodpeckers. He got up and stretched. Just for the hell of it, he rested the barrel of his Winchester 1873 on a low-lying branch of the live oak and sighted down the road to the west. Nothing in view. He backed up, eased the rifle down, and let it rest against the gnarled tree trunk. Then, intuition grabbed him. His senses were aroused. Had he been a rattlesnake, his tail likely would have been rattling. He scanned the area surrounding him. Nothing. Maybe he was being overly cautious. He stirred up the coals from last night's fire and began preparations for heating some coffee. To further relax, he took out some tobacco and rolled himself a smoke. He was hoping he wouldn't have to wait too long. The damned Ranger was surely on his trail. He pulled out his watch with its tally carved into the casing. Thirty-five grooves were etched into the back of the watch. He still needed three kills to catch up with King Fisher. After killing the Ranger, he'd need just three more to move ahead of his hero. He figured to get the Comanche chief, but was hard over on not counting Indians or Mexicans. As he stirred the coals of last night's fire, watched a couple of fresh pieces of wood catch fire, and prepared to pour himself a cup of coffee, he hardly expected to have his evil idyll interrupted.

"Coy Witmer, raise your hands high where I can see them. You are under arrest." Luke's commanding voice seemed to boom from a dark form made silhouette-like by the sun rising behind him.

The air around Witmer had been shattered. He froze at the apparition before him. Was this some sort of bad dream? The sonofabitch Texas Ranger wasn't supposed to appear from the east. "Who...who's there?"

"Texas Ranger Captain Luke Dunn. Don't you dare move a muscle." Luke took a couple of steps toward the outlaw revealing himself in the brightening glow of Witmer's campfire. The muzzle of his rifle was aimed straight on toward the outlaw's chest.

The fugitive's eyes darted from side to side as though desperately trying to find an escape. His peripheral vision caught sight of One Arrow with an arrow nocked.

Luke saw that Witmer had seen the Comanche chief. "Do you have any idea what an arrow feels like as it sinks into a human body? Because that's what's going to happen, if you make just one false move." Luke noted that Witmer hadn't put his gun belt on as yet. "Now, you back away about a half dozen steps from that tree."

Witmer glanced at the rifle leaning against the live oak. Even if he could reach it, he'd have a devil of a time chambering a round and getting off a shot.

Luke tossed manacles at the outlaw's feet. "Put these on with the chain running behind your back." He watched as Witmer did as he was instructed. "Chief, you can come out now."

One Arrow appeared from a few yards behind Luke. He was smiling broadly at their tracking success. In a way, the chief wished Three Toes was still alive, as this was likely the sort of adventure his mentor had enjoyed with Ghost-Who-Rides. "Can we scalp?"

An expression of horror spread across Witmer's face. "You...you can't do that!"

Luke grinned. "We'd have to kill you first." He collected

the outlaw's weapons. The Texas Ranger examined the old Winchester. "Dang, Witmer. It'd be amazing, if you could shoot someone with this antique. Did you see that the sight is bent?"

"It ain't bent."

Luke bashed the rifle against the live oak. "It is now." He proceeded to be sure Witmer's pistol was empty, then paused and stared at the desperado's vest. "Don't move a muscle, Witmer. A twitch could get you killed." Luke reached forward to divest the outlaw of the gun he had stuffed in the special vest pocket.

Luke was a lot bigger than Witmer, but it didn't stop the murderer from trying to lift a knee into Luke's crotch and driving a shoulder into him. He might as well have been trying to take down a stone wall. Luke reacted by doubling over slightly but quickly straightened up and landed a crushing blow with his fist straight on Witmer's nose. The crack could likely be heard for a goodly distance. The man didn't just fall face first into the Nueces Strip soil, his smashed nose was squished into some fresh horse droppings. So much for trying to escape. Luke rolled him onto his back and took the gun from his vest. It wasn't as though Witmer had a prayer of fighting back, as it was impossible to throw a punch with your arms chained behind your back.

One Arrow laughed. "You right, Luke. Lawbreakers not smart."

"He tries that again, I'm going to let you scalp him, chief... alive."

Witmer was just conscious enough to have heard Luke's threat. "K...K...Keep that redskin away from me." He sat up, wiping blood and horse droppings away as best he could with his shoulder.

Luke picked up the outlaw's hat. "Let's get you on your horse. We've got a long ride to Alice."

Despite his still bleeding and now decidedly crooked nose,

Witmer managed a sort of hangdog grunt of being resigned to his fate...at least for the present. He now suffered the ignominious fate of being pretty much lifted onto his horse. He kept glancing at One Arrow who stoked the outlaw's fear by teasingly running a finger across his own forehead in a scalping motion.

Luke poured he and One Arrow some of the outlaw's coffee before flashing a triumphant grin at Witmer and kicking dirt over the now dying embers of the fire. There was full satisfaction from having outfoxed another outlaw. The reward would be welcome, but it was more about justice being served.

"Looks like three men, Deputy." Mike pretty much had stated the obvious. They were perhaps four or five hundred yards from the rustlers.

"Yep. One of them looks a bit like Sonny Driscoll. Saw a flyer on him just last week. Dang if he isn't already wanted for stealing beeves."

Shorty and Neezer were mentally licking their chops at an opportunity to bring some rustlers to justice, though they'd prefer to deliver the justice quickly at the end of a rope. Shorty turned to the deputy, "Damned if we haven't got 'em outnumbered, Deputy Hollingsworth."

Bones leaned forward as if to get a better view of the rustlers. They were so focused on herding the beeves that they hadn't yet seen the posse. He was thinking on what might be the best approach. He much preferred not killing anybody. "Let's spread out about thirty feet apart and move forward. Have your rifles ready just in case. Junior, you stay close to Mike. When we get close, I'll do the talking."

The five men moved forward toward the small herd. They'd about cut the distance in half when one of the rustlers spotted them approaching. "We got company!" he shouted.

Bones didn't hesitate. "Hey! Y'all pull up in the name of the law!"

The topography didn't favor an escape for the three rustlers. They had moved the herd along a shallow gulch with steep enough sides that any attempt to climb out on horseback would be ill-fated. The one Bones had identified as Driscoll went to pull out his rifle.

Neezer didn't hesitate. "Stupid sonofabitch." He leveled his rifle and squeezed off a shot that caught Driscoll in the shoulder.

"Hold off, dammit!" Bones hollered out. He yelled out again at the rustlers, "Get yer hands high where we can see 'em!"

Driscoll was doubled over in pain, but raised his unwounded arm. "Don't shoot! We surrender."

"Dismount and drop yer hardware." The posse kept their rifles aimed at the men. "Shorty...Neezer...if any of them try anything, you shoot to kill." The idea was to instill a sense of fear in the rustlers.

It had almost been too easy. Bones led the posse on in. "Junior, what brands you see on those beeves?"

Junior rode forward cautiously. He looked carefully. "It's a mix, Deputy. There are maybe three -HG beeves and even a couple of Santa Gertrudis beeves with the King Ranch brand." He was proud that he'd been asked to investigate.

Bones addressed the rustlers. "Y'all have bills of sale fer them beeves?"

The men shrugged and shook their heads.

"Then you are under arrest for stealing cattle and cutting fences. Mike, would you do the honors?" He grabbed two sets of manacles from his saddlebag. "Driscoll there is wounded. He's bleedin' pretty good, so let's tie his arm tight to his chest to put pressure on the wound. Wouldn't do to have him bleed out afore we get to Alice."

"What about the beeves, Deputy?" Junior had found his voice.

"I think Shorty, Neezer, and I can handle escorting these men to Alice. You and Mike are free to herd the beeves back toward your place. Y'all can telegraph the other owners 'bout where to retrieve their cattle." Bones watched patiently, as Junior and Mike went to work rounding up the herd and had begun turning it back toward Heaven's Gate. Once the duo was out of sight, the deputy led the prisoners off in the direction of Alice.

The remaining posse with its prisoners hadn't gone very far, when they passed a stand of reasonably sturdy oaks. Neezer looked at Shorty. "Shame them trees be goin' to waste."

Bones heard the comment and was none too pleased as to what Neezer was implying. "Don't you fellas be gettin' any ideas 'bout takin' the law in yer own hands." He realized too late that Shorty had moved in behind him.

The butt of Shorty's rifle across the back of Bones's head pretty much answered the deputy's warning. He fell from his horse and hit the ground hard. He was out cold. "Sorry, Deputy. Hope you'll thank us later."

The rustlers' eyes grew wide with fear, as they quickly realized what fate lay in store. They thought to run, but the manacles on their wrists combined with the horses being tied together, made that impossible. They looked at each other with panic coupled with resignation to their fates.

Neezer went to work fashioning the nooses. "This is gonna save the county the cost of a trial, Shorty." He smiled wryly and turned to the rustlers. "You yellow-bellied sonsofbitches done stole yer last beeves."

It didn't take long before the three rustlers were sitting their final saddles beneath the oak tree with nooses around their necks and ropes wrapped high around sturdy branches.

Together, Shorty and Neezer slapped the rumps of the horses, unsaddling the horse thieves and leaving them

gagging and finally twitching in their final throes of stran-
gulation.

"Bones is gonna be plenty unhappy when he wakes up
Neezer. We better get long gone from here." And the two
headed out at a gallop to get as far away as possible from the
scene of their crime.

"Mike, hold up. I have a bad feeling."

Mike looked at his cousin quizzically. Was the son
equipped with the same sort of intuition as the father? "What's
that, Junior?"

"Something isn't right with those two cowboys the deputy
recruited. We have to be sure they get to Alice."

Going through Mike's head was the inconvenience of
herding a dozen longhorns an extra few miles, especially as
the late afternoon sun would mean they'd be out on the prairie
through the night. "You want to do this on a feeling?"

Junior looked back from whence they'd come. If he'd had a
mustache, he'd likely have been stroking it like his father.
"Trust me on this, cousin."

FIFTEEN
GUILT

JUNIOR IGNORED the clouds of trail dust kicked up by the herd. He was lost in his thoughts, wishing the beeves would hustle just a bit more. A feeling of foreboding deep in his gut wouldn't go away. It seemed as though he'd of a sudden grown far more mature than his mere fifteen years would evidence.

Mike was figuring to humor his cousin. He was a lot older than Junior but didn't have an inordinate need for control that many men might exhibit. Fact was, Mike was one of the most charitable souls in Nueces County. Likely as not he inherited his giving heart from his own father, John, who gave land and money generously to the local church. What there was of Mike's adventurous spirit lived vicariously through Junior. The boy was hell-bent on answering whatever call now had them backtracking, and Mike wasn't going to hamper the young man's as yet unresolved curiosity.

Junior moved to the lead as the little cattle drive crested the top of one of the low rolling hills near the Nueces River. It was more anxiousness than eating dust. He looked off toward a cluster of trees off on the far horizon. "Mike!" He spurred his horse into a full gallop.

Taken by surprise at Junior's action, Mike found himself momentarily held up among a half dozen longhorns. "Dammit, Junior!" Soon enough, he was following on his young cousin's heels.

Both pulled up to the trees, bearing witness to the grizzly sight of three limp bodies dangling in the late afternoon sun and a groggy deputy sheriff as yet unable to stand.

Junior was getting a firsthand education as to the violence still resident on the expanses of the Nueces Strip. First, it was the bushwhacked Texas Ranger courier back at Heaven's Gate, then rustling, and now three lynched rustlers. "Mike...how could they? They're no better than the rustlers!"

"You're right about that, Junior. It's the sort of injustice your father's been fighting against all these years." He paused to let Junior calm a tad, then coolly set the youngster to action. "You see to the deputy. I'll cut these men down."

Junior dutifully dismounted. It was hard to keep his eyes from those bodies swinging gently in the breeze with their ghastly facial expressions and tongues hanging out. They hadn't died easily. He took a canteen over to Bones and kneeled beside the deputy while watching Mike cut the rustlers down. He finally looked down at still the groggy deputy. "You okay, Deputy Hollingsworth? Looks like you've got a nasty cut on the back of your head...isn't hardly bleeding much though."

Bones took a couple of swallows of water. "Sonsofbitches caught me unawares. I had a feeling they might try to do something like this." He winced as he rubbed the back of his head. "Shorty and Neezer are long gone by now."

"Are you okay?" Junior helped Hollingsworth to his feet.

Bones stood unsteadily but was quickly gathering his wits. "Could y'all gather up these poor soul's horses, and I'll take the bodies back to Alice for burial. I'm pretty sure Sonny Driscoll had a price on his head."

Mike, who'd spent his life raising and selling horses, was

ever up for an opportunity to make money even though he tended to give most of it away. "You going to share that reward, Deputy."

If Bones hadn't intended to, he was for damn sure going to share it now. "Um...I'll see that you and Junior here each get a third."

Junior perked up out of his guilt-ridden funk over the lynching. A reward could contribute to buying Wildfire. "Much obliged, Deputy Hollingsworth. Much obliged."

Mike sensed what was going through Junior's head. "Tell you what, Bones, send my share to young Mr. Dunn here. He's got an itch to buy that fine piece of horseflesh he's riding from his father."

"You needn't do that, Mike."

"Oh, but I must, cousin. You've earned it fair and square."

Within the hour, Bones was leading three horses with bodies draped over their saddles back to Alice and Junior and Mike had returned to driving the beeves back to Heaven's Gate Ranch.

"You're never going to get me to jail, Dunn. You and your savage friend here ain't enough to hold me."

Luke just looked at Witmer. Why were these types always so arrogant? What led them to kill for the sake of killing? Why did they invariably make the same mistakes and get caught or killed? As he stroked his mustache, he realized the questions ruminating through his head were pretty much rhetorical. He watched a couple of tumbleweeds bounce by. "If you think you can escape, you're welcome to try, Mr. Witmer. Keep in mind that if you did escape, I'd be hunting you down again." Luke looked away nonchalantly. "And...well, there's always that scalping thing." This was to be the first night after the capture, and Luke reckoned that they'd best rest up. One

Arrow was already showing the physical effects of the exertion it had taken to track Witmer.

"Maybe you wouldn't be able to hunt for me. Dead men can't hunt."

"You'd best rest up for our travels, Mr. Witmer." With that, Luke double-checked the outlaw's manacles before laying down nearby with his head resting against his saddle. He'd cuffed the outlaw to a tree. Luke looked over at the chief. "One Arrow, you take second watch." He figured the chief could relax and sip coffee while he watched Witmer for a couple of hours. "Wake me for my turn, when the moon is high."

Witmer muttered profanities under his breath as he glared past his mangled and bloodied nose and sized up how to escape from his captors. This Texas Ranger had become the bane of his existence and had to be eliminated.

Mike looked off and saw Jubal Strong riding the fence line. He was soon in hailing distance. "Hey Jubal!"

"Mike? Junior? What's up with those beeves?" Upon riding closer, he noted a couple of brands very familiar to him. His brands. "Where'd you find those mavericks?"

"Junior here found where some men were rustling a small number of mostly longhorns and sought my help. Deputy Hollingsworth put together a small posse, and we caught the rustlers." Mike wasn't long-winded. "That was about it. There are about four different brands, two of them Heaven's Gate. You're welcome to cut out your beeves."

"Shoot, I was riding up to Alice. How about I pick them up at Junior's place on my way back?" Strong thought a moment. "What happened to the rustlers?"

Junior knitted his eyebrows with just a touch of frustration tinged with anger. "Posse overpowered the deputy and lynched the three rustlers." He didn't need to elaborate.

Strong shook his head. "Lynchin' ain't right, Junior. But you should be proud about finding those rustlers. Your dad sure will be."

"Thanks, Mr. Strong. We'll hold those beeves for you."

Strong and Mike exchanged glances. They both recognized the rapid maturing of Junior and how much as Luke was deeply embedded in the values and character of his son. You had to grow up fast on what was still Texas frontier.

Jubal Strong tipped his hat and was on his way.

The coffee One Arrow brewed was so strong it seemed likely to be able to dissolve most anything put in it.

"Dang, chief. Did you use all of the coffee grounds?" Luke's eyes snapped open wide as he took a sip.

"Make great coffee. Strong." The chief smiled and took a big swig. He coughed and spit it out. "Humph. Maybe too strong. Could kill pony."

Luke could do naught but offer up an infectious laugh that soon enough had the chief laughing.

Witmer took this all in. He wasn't laughing. He couldn't breathe through his nose, his hand was still very tender, the manacles chaffed, and the flesh wound in his leg hurt just enough to be annoying. He was a sorry sight to say the least, not what aficionados of dime-store-novel gunfighters might imagine.

One Arrow grew serious. He grasped Luke's shoulder and looked dead-on into his eyes. "One Arrow enjoy hunt with Ghost-Who-Rides. Understand why Three Toes your friend. One Arrow your friend, too." He took a deep breath and stepped back. "Now, it is time to return to my people."

Luke was taken aback by the Comanche chief's unexpected announcement. "I've enjoyed your help, my friend." He sensed that this was an irrevocable decision. "I wish you safe travels." He reached into his saddlebag and handed Witmer's Colt revolver to One Arrow. "Take this. It might come in handy. He won't be needing it, and you lost your rifle."

One Arrow brandished the gun about, causing Luke and Witmer to reflexively duck a couple of times. The chief smiled. "It is good. Thank you."

It wasn't a long goodbye. They finished breakfast, got Witmer back in the saddle for the final couple of hours ride into Alice, and One Arrow turned his pony northward. Luke watched his proud Comanche friend ride off sitting tall.

"Now it's one to one, Mr. Texas Ranger."

Luke looked at Witmer like he had to be crazy. "Considering your situation, it wouldn't be much of a fight. You'll be parked in the Alice jail soon enough and likely swinging from the gallows not long after." Luke grabbed the halter lead and turned Twister toward Alice.

A cloud of Nueces Strip dirt preceded the longhorns into the large corral near the barn. Lost somewhere in the snorting and bellowing and dust, Junior and Mike emerged. The teen was relieved that Mike had stayed with him and the herd, as it would be a lot easier to explain their impromptu adventure to Elisa.

As they rode up from the barn, Elisa stood on the gallery with hands on hips and a stern glare that could have melted a glacier.

This was not the welcome home pose a fifteen-year-old wants to see upon his return from a risky outing. "Hi, Mom! We're back..." His words trailed off.

Elisa's glowering turned grudgingly to just a hint of a smile. She was relieved to have Junior home and safe.

Mike had ridden up behind the teenager. "Elisa, how good to see you again. My but you've got to be rightly proud of this young man. He near single-handedly captured a dozen rustlers." He could barely hold back his laughter.

Junior shot him a squinty-eyed look at the gross exaggeration.

"Rustlers?!" Elisa shot him a penetrating look. "Michael Dunn, how could you?" When a woman uses a man's full name in a scolding tone, it signals the utmost caution. The time for any levity had ended rather abruptly.

"Junior here found a couple of breaks in our fences, saw unusual livestock tracks, and fetched me. We got Deputy Hollingsworth in Alice to form up a posse. Junior guided us back to where he'd seen the tracks." Mike watched Elisa's frown begin to soften. "Junior hung back as he was told while we captured the rustlers. He identified the beeves as a mix from several ranches, and we herded them back here. Hollingsworth took the cattle thieves back for justice. That's about the whole story. Like I said, you ought to be proud of Junior." He let that sink all sink in. "Oh, and there was a price on one of the rustler's heads, so Junior gets part of the reward."

Elisa smiled. "What's a mother to do? Come on in and have some coffee and fresh-baked cornbread, you two."

Junior's grin broadened. "And Mike here set a fair value on Wildfire."

Grace and Heather had been listening at the door. As soon as Junior and Mike walked through the threshold, they had to repeat the story but in greater detail for the girls. Sean soon came up from his chores, and the ever-more-embellished story was told again.

A few citizens interrupted their walks along the main street to gawk at the tall Texas Ranger riding easy as he led his prisoner into town. Most had no idea who the manacled outlaw was.

The gaping mouths and pointing fingers of a handful of passersby gave evidence that a few realized that Coy Witmer was being brought to justice.

Witmer tried to muster a leering expression at the curious citizenry, as he sat tall and stared out over his busted nose. He could feel their judgments tossed at him with the contempt and derision he deserved.

They pulled up in front of the jail. As Luke dismounted, Bones had already opened the door and was greeting him with a friendly expression. "Good to see you, Luke. Seems you've brought me a present."

"Howdy, Bones. Yep, he was a wily critter, but my Comanche friend helped me capture him."

"Dang, but you do have a way with them Comanche savages." Bones strode over to Witmer's horse and with Luke's help began to ease the outlaw out of the saddle. "Well, let's get this human buffalo chip parked in the hoosegow."

"Holy smoke, Bones. What did you do to the back of your head?"

Bones's shoulders slumped a tad. "Got blindsided by the butt end of a Henry rifle."

"Blindsided?"

"Don't ask so many questions."

Luke shrugged as they shoved a reluctant Witmer along into the jail. Once the prisoner was out of sight, the small crowd of bystanders broke up.

Witmer didn't resist, as he was roughly ushered into a cell.

"Sit on the bed, Witmer." Bones was making it clear who was in charge. The deputy was looking to save face after not having dealt with the outlaw a few weeks back when he'd stirred up trouble in the saloon.

The outlaw sat on the straw mattress. Its cover likely hadn't been changed in months, so it stank to high heaven. "Damn place stinks!" he snarled. The odor was strong enough to penetrate his busted nose.

Luke stood behind the deputy to be sure Witmer was secured in the jail. The odor was bad enough that he half covered his nose and mouth with his bandana. "He's right about that, Bones. You likely can't smell it over that chaw you're working on."

Bones shot Luke a glance of umbrage, then turned back to the prisoner. "You won't be here long enough for the smell to matter none, Witmer." The deputy attached one end of the manacles to Witmer's good arm and the other to one of the iron rods that comprised the door to the cell.

"I gotta pee."

"You can reach the bucket. Don't let me stop you."

The proud excuse for a human who'd thus far killed thirty-five human beings tried to turn himself from the two lawmen in a show of modesty as he answered nature's call.

Bones looked at Luke and gave a sort of grin. "He don't want no one to see how small his weeny is."

"I've got to get to the post office and send a telegram to Captain McMurray. I'll leave you to do the paperwork, Bones, then I'm heading home."

"You go ahead, Luke. I'll tend to the man's horse, too."

"His cayuse has a Circle H brand on it. Might want to let them know we recovered their stolen horse."

By this time, Witmer had finished his business. His beady eyes followed Luke out the door.

SIXTEEN
NUMBER 36?

LUKE STOOD at the window watching the postmaster write out his message to Captain McMurray. He was pleased to have this duty out of the way. Soon enough, he'd be riding back to Elisa and the ranch.

Back at the Alice jail, Bones sat at his creaky old desk painstakingly writing a report for transfer of the prisoner to his care.

"Deputy! It stinks bad in here. Can you at least dump this bucket?"

Bones looked up from his writing. His natural urge was to ignore Witmer's plea. He thought long and hard on it. Finally, he spat into the spittoon, put down his pen, and headed over to the cell. He fumbled a bit with the keys, but eventually unlocked the cell door as he kept a wary eye on his prisoner. "Push the damned thing over here with yer foot, Witmer."

Witmer began to push the bucket, then of a sudden kicked it, sending pee all over Bones's boots.

"Dammit! What the..."

Witmer grabbed the deputy's revolver with his still healing hand and delivered a crushing blow with the gun butt on the deputy's head.

Bones sank to his knees and slowly crumpled into the pool of pee on the floor. He was out cold.

The prisoner quickly found the key to the manacles and freed himself. He glanced out the front window of the jail. His horse was still saddled at the hitching rail. He stepped over Hollingsworth's unconscious body and strolled easy-like to the gun rack. He selected a nice Winchester and grabbed a handful of bullets.

Bones had begun to come to. "What you doin'?"

Witmer aimed and squeezed the trigger. A flash of light blasted from the muzzle of the Colt and a bullet found its way into the deputy's forehead. Gunsmoke hung in the air. The report was still echoing in the outlaw's ears, as he grabbed the rifle and headed out the front door. A fugitive once again, he was quickly mounted and galloping out of town. He figured to put Alice, Texas behind him as fast as possible.

He sped by the post office just as Luke was about to hand his message to the postmaster.

Luke couldn't believe what he'd just seen out of the corner of his eye. It took perhaps three big strides, and he was on the front walkway and firing shots at the fleeing desperado. Witmer was already well out of range.

Frustrated, Luke stepped back into the general store that housed the post office.

"You still want to send this message?" The postmaster had to ask.

Luke shook his head. "Just tear it up. I've got to see to the deputy."

The gunshot had attracted a couple of folks to the jail, and they looked none too happy.

Luke walked into the jail and right away saw Bones lying on the cell floor in a growing pool of blood. "Couldn't hold the man for ten minutes," Luke muttered.

Luke reemerged from the jail.

The mayor appeared. "What we going to do for a sheriff?"

They were the first words from his mouth. The mayor didn't even have enough respect to ask about Bones. He was a short corpulent man wearing a vest that didn't quite button. "I'm the mayor, and I need to know."

Luke gave the self-important man a cold hard glare. He wanted to tear the cigar from the mayor's mouth and cram it where the sun didn't shine. He took a deep breath. "Looks like you have a problem, Mr. Mayor. Good luck." He normally would have patiently endured, but this stuck in his craw. "I've got an escaped killer to pursue."

The mayor's mouth gaped.

Luke mounted the big Appaloosa and headed out in the direction Witmer had escaped. As he approached the town limits, he pulled up. After the initial shock of seeing Bones lying dead as a doornail on the jailhouse floor, he'd noticed the empty spot in the normally full gun rack in the jail. A lot of ammunition had been missing, too. His prey was now armed with a decent rifle and was likely more incentivized than ever to bag himself a Texas Ranger. Maybe it was time to take a break and get a fresh perspective on this manhunt. He'd captured Witmer once, so he was confident he could do it again. Neither was he especially interested in being bush-whacked again. Luke decided to telegram Captain McMurray after all and let the Texas Ranger know the status of Luke's pursuit.

Witmer rightly calculated that no one would be following him out of town. He pulled up near a mesquite tree a couple of miles out of Alice to give his well-lathered mount a breather. He drew the old pocket watch from his vest pocket, pulled out his knife, and carved another groove on the casing. He muttered to himself, "Here's another one for you, Pa." There were now thirty-six killings memorialized on the watch.

He gazed out from whence he'd come. He was right. No one was following. The Texas Ranger was smart enough not to give chase. He flexed his hand a bit. It was healing quite nicely. He'd soon be able to work with reasonable effectiveness the Winchester rifle he'd stolen.

The desperado especially wondered whether Luke might try to track him, but he'd already reckoned the Ranger was disinclined to follow him by himself and risk an ambush. With the Comanche chief gone, he figured the lawman to be far more vulnerable. Witmer found himself relishing the thought of an unhindered ambush, the opportunity to blow the Texas Ranger's brains out.

Witmer had a decision to make. Where would he go? He wanted to lay low for a few days. He thought back fondly to his sexual romping with Cora and Anne back in Laredo but decided he'd head eastward. He'd already gone through Laredo a couple of times and surely didn't want to press his luck by being too predictable.

He knew there was a growing town near Corpus Christi, a place called Nuecestown. Had he recalled that he'd effectively be in Luke Dunn's backyard, he might have chosen a different destination. Ignorance wasn't necessarily bliss. On the other hand, his stay could be brief once he discovered that there was no saloon.

The task at hand was to skirt Alice wide to the north and follow the north bank of the Nueces River to the ferry at Nuecestown.

Unbeknownst to the fugitive outlaw, Luke had decided to head back to Heaven's Gate for a few days. He really did need to take a fresh look at his mission. There'd simply been too many near misses. If McMurray would authorize it, Luke was giving serious consideration to recruiting a couple of reliable men to help in the pursuit and capture. He was maintaining an easy pace, and it gave him time to think. Twister didn't seem to mind, as the big Appaloosa seemed to sense that they were heading home.

Ironically, he was traveling eastward about a mile south and a couple of hours behind Witmer. Luke looked out to his right and spotted a familiar live oak motte. With the sun bearing down, he decided to take a break in the shade of the trees and resume his journey in the late afternoon.

He pulled up to the clump of trees and was immediately struck by the numerous hoofprints. Looking up at the branches, his practiced eye saw bark freshly rubbed from the tops of a couple of limbs in at least three places. He couldn't be absolutely sure, but it had the telltale markings of a necktie party. He spotted a hat nearby, but there was nothing special about it. Whatever had occurred hadn't happened very long ago. No more than a couple of days and not more than a week before he'd happened on the spot. He rein-tied Twister to a low-hanging live oak branch, sat under its shade, leaned back, tipped his hat over his eyes, and took what turned out to be a not-so-brief nap.

Luke uncharacteristically cursed under his breath, as he felt the Appaloosa's drooling tongue on his face and awakened to see long shadows cast by a sun that was creeping ever-closer to disappearing beneath the horizon fashioned by the rolling grasslands to the west. He patted Twisters snout and worked himself upright. Hard ground did him no favors these days. He flexed a bit to loosen his muscles before mounting up. He was in familiar territory. Looking up at the darkening sky to the east, he could see that a half-moon would be providing a little light. It'd be enough that he could easily ride through the night and arrive at Heaven's Gate first thing in the morning. He relished the thought of surprising Elisa.

★☆

There was a newfound confidence in the way he sat his saddle as Witmer rode easy-like into Nuecestown. It was getting on toward dusk, and he'd been riding all day.

The town was already losing some of its economic luster as ferry traffic across the Nueces River had begun to dwindle. It had gained some notoriety about ten years back, as it was one of the primary sites involved in the famous Good Friday raid by Mexican bandits. The bandits had kidnapped some local folks, stolen merchandise, and managed to kill a couple of citizens. The bandits were run off by a posse that included Luke Dunn's cousins and was headed by Pat Whelen and Texas Ranger Red John Dunn. Many bandits were later killed. The town managed to endure.

The population had swelled to more than 150 folks by 1885. There was even some talk of running a railroad through the town, though a growing rumor had it that Nuecestown would be bypassed. That would ultimately seal its fate, a death knell as it were. Meanwhile, the town enjoyed the economic splendor engendered by a meat-packing plant, cotton gin, general store, smithy shop, and the ferry. Deputy Bill Meaney still holed up on occasion at the jail, but he'd received a telegram from the mayor in Alice about replacing Bones Hollingsworth. The murdered deputy back in Alice had barely been tucked away in his grave when the message had gone out.

Pastor Horace Rucker, a retired Army colonel and friend of Luke, had decided to move his little church closer to Corpus Christi, and the delightful Victorian-style boarding house that Bernice and Agatha had run was pretty much getting run down. The sweet old ladies had passed within days of each other, and their deaths took a lot of the life if not gossip from the little town. The stagecoach inn still functioned along with the general store and the smithy shop. A schoolhouse had been built, and that was still delivering education to ranchers in the area. It was a sturdy building and one of the largest in the region. The school was likely to endure well beyond its useful purpose. The cemetery held a lot of local history, as it featured graves spaced over a broad swath of rolling hillside.

Witmer looked around and felt just an inkling of the town's softening vitality already seeping into his own evil bones. He could feel his renewed belief in himself being sucked from him by the atmosphere so was of a mind to just keep on riding. But the stagecoach inn beckoned, as he trotted by. He decided he might hang his hat at the inn for a few hours until he decided whether to continue on to Corpus Christi.

The saddle creaked nearly as much as Witmer's knees as he dismounted after several hours in the saddle. He hitched his horse, took a scan of the street to his left and right, and strode on through the front door. The inn was empty of travelers. It had been designed as a way station for stagecoaches, so wasn't set up like a saloon with a bar and tables jammed together. It was designed to meet the needs of folks passing through Nuecestown on their way to some other destination. Three old tables dominated one side of a fair-sized room. Four cane-backed chairs were spaced at each table. The other side of the room featured a counter displaying various necessaries that travelers might need or not depending on their druthers. The place was clean enough such that folks passing through would find it fairly comfortable. It didn't give off the obnoxious aromas of sweat, booze, cigar smoke, pee, and occasional horse droppings that might be found in a saloon. The outlaw had his choice of tables. He figured to grab a small bite to eat and think on next steps before likely heading out.

The proprietor watched Witmer with an appraising eye. Something about the stranger wasn't right. Bull Samuels had a sense of these things. "Can I help you, mister?" Maybe Witmer's busted nose gave off a hint or so of its owner's undesirability.

"You have something to eat for a hungry traveler?"

Dinner hour had passed, so the limited menu was even

more limited. "Got some fried chicken, taters, and cornbread if that suits you."

The outlaw mulled that over for a few seconds. He finally nodded. "That ought to do just fine, if you don't mind?"

"Coming right up." The proprietor took another suspicious glance at Witmer and then called over his shoulder. "Hey Martha, whip up a plate of that dinner special." He turned back to his guest. "You want a drink? I've got beer and water."

"Water sounds just fine."

"Might I ask where you're headed?" asked Samuels.

"Well, you might tell me how far I am from Corpus Christi."

"Shoot, friend. Corpus is about a dozen miles up the road."

"You happen to know where a traveler might hole up for a night. I'm thinking I'd prefer heading to Corpus in the morning." Witmer was feeling fairly comfortable, as the proprietor hadn't gotten nosey, at least not yet.

"The boarding house is closed, and we don't have a hotel. We have a storage room in the back where you might be comfortable. It's feeling like we might see some rain, so staying dry would probably suit you."

Witmer conjured up a crooked smile. About this time, Martha waltzed in with dinner and set it down before him. The fugitive took a whiff through his mostly aroma-blocked nose. "Smells mighty tasty."

Martha cast a jaundiced eye on him. "You ain't tasted it yet."

The outlaw took a couple of bites of chicken before sinking his teeth into the cornbread. "My but this is great cornbread. Y'all make it here?" Witmer figured to try to be cordial. It made no sense to stir anything up unnecessarily.

Martha smiled at the compliment. "We have a friend up the road a piece who bakes it for us. Elisa Dunn is famous around these parts for her cooking, especially cornbread."

"Dunn, you say?" Witmer's ears perked up big time. For a

moment, his expression was like a mountain lion when prey simply drops in his paws. He hoped Samuels hadn't seen his reaction.

"Oh yes. Her husband is a famous Texas Ranger, though he mostly ranches these days."

The desperado nearly choked on his mouthful of potatoes. "Um...he sounds like someone I'd like to meet. I'm impressed with these fine men who keep law and order on what is still mostly rough country." Witmer was starting to salivate over the prospect of being so close to Heaven's Gate Ranch. It hadn't been that long ago that he'd ridden past its gateway and seriously considered a deadly visit.

"Martha, why don't you get on back to the kitchen." Samuels was beginning to do the mathematics of Witmer's appearance plus his strange reaction to the revelation about the Texas Ranger. "When you're done chowing down, you can put your bedroll in the store room. Just head on through that door over there." He nodded to the outlaw and headed back to the kitchen. He lowered his voice as he sidled up to Martha. "Keep an eye on things...I'm going to stroll on up to Deputy Meaney's office. Something doesn't seem quite right with this stranger." He noted that Witmer was still enjoying his dinner as he headed out the back door.

"You wouldn't be looking to make trouble, would you?" Witmer had quickly slipped out the front door like an attacking serpent and stood not twenty feet from the proprietor.

"Just going to answer nature's call, mister. That's not a problem, is it?"

Witmer took his hand from the Colt half-hanging from his holster. "Guess I must be tired. I didn't mean to be so jumpy. Don't let me stand between you and a good piss." The outlaw turned and headed back inside.

Samuels decided that any communicating with Meaney would have to wait.

The outlaw decided it was now likely a safe bet that Samuels wouldn't do anything untoward. He figured to take the proprietor up on the offer of a place to rest up for the night. He didn't want to seem overly curious about the Texas Ranger so decided to wait until morning to get directions to the ranch. He was beginning to feel pretty good about himself for having made the decision to spend the night in Nuecestown. No telling what opportunities might be afforded an outlaw visiting the hometown of the man he most wanted to kill.

As he downed the last of his dinner, a stagecoach pulled up. Witmer looked up to see a smallish man in a tweed suit enter the inn. He turned out to be the only passenger.

The man walked over to the ticket window. "Are you Mr. Samuels?"

Samuels glanced at Witmer before ambling over to the window. "How can I help you, traveler?"

"I was wondering whether you might care to make these books available to folks who pass through here. My Cowboy Tales have been selling quite well."

Witmer's ears perked up. "Say...did you say Cowboy Tales?"

The traveler seemed momentarily disconcerted, as there was just a hint of threat in Witmer's voice. "Yes. My name is Elroy Stuart, and I write the tales. Made a few folks famous."

Witmer held in his temper. "Did you write about Coy Witmer?"

"Oh, yes, sir. He's one of the baddest gents to roam the west."

"Well, little man...Mr. Elroy Stuart...you better learn to spell Mr. Witmer's name correctly."

"Why...I thought it was correct. How should you know I misspelled it?"

Witmer glowered and stood to his full height. He towered over the traveler. "Because my name is Coy Witmer. There's no 'h' in Witmer. If you don't want to be number thirty-seven, you be sure to make it right."

The man recoiled in horror, and Samuels stood helplessly by as the drama unfolded.

"I'll be sure to correct the oversight, Mr. Witmer. You can be certain of that. My deepest apologies." The traveler seemed about to burst into tears.

Witmer shook his head in mock dismay. "Go on your way, Mr. Stuart. If I find any more copies with my name spelled wrong, I'll come looking for you." With that, he nudged the frightened traveler out the door. He turned to Samuels. "I'll be about ready for that sleeping spot you offered." He paused. "Don't be getting any crazy ideas."

Silver moonbeams reached down onto the ribbon of road tracking the south bank of the Nueces River. Luke let the Appaloosa stallion take his own pace, an easy almost gentle stride. The night was about as peaceful as they come with the landscape awash in starlight and that ever-present moonlight. The only sounds were cricket chirps and an occasional frog croak. Now and then a critter would scamper across the road, but none seemed to bother horse or rider.

It was still in the wee hours of the morning when Nueces-town came into sight. Twister sensed that they were getting close to home. It was as though the horse had sent some sort of signal to Luke, as he of a sudden became more alert to his surroundings.

The Texas Ranger rode slowly down the main street. Passing the stagecoach inn, Luke took notice of the single horse grazing on a long tether from the corral post. He thought it was unusual enough to warrant a closer look. Luke eased the Appaloosa to his left and slowly rode on past the horse. He did a double take, as the Circle H brand came into view. Upon closer inspection in the moonlight, the horse began to look more familiar.

Luke remained mounted as he looked around, but saw nothing else unusual. He wasn't sure that the possibility of Coy Witmer being close by was luck or a curse.

He decided not to tarry long at the corral, so turned Twister back up the road toward the jail. Bill Meaney had built a small house next door that he and Clara enjoyed when they weren't in Corpus Christi. In the dim light, Luke could see wisps of smoke rising from the fireplace, a good signal that Meaney was at home.

Luke hitched the Appaloosa in front of Meaney's house, dismounted, and gently knocked on the front door.

There was a rustling and growling from inside.

Luke knocked again…a little firmer this time.

The latch slid, and the door creaked open just a little. A pair of sleepy eyes squinted at Luke. "Who the hell is…Luke? Dang! What're you doing here at this hour?" He opened the door fully. "Come on in."

"Good to see you, too, Bill. Sorry to barge in so late, but I thought you might want to know that you've got a fugitive staying the night up at the stagecoach inn."

"I've got a what?"

"Coy Witmer."

"You serious?" Meaney flashed an incredulous look. "I just looked at his wanted flyer the other day. Killed nearly thirty men."

"If my count is right, it's more like thirty-six. He murdered Bones Hollingsworth back in Alice to escape the jail."

"Holy beejeezus, Luke. They just offered me the deputy job in Alice. I had no idea Witmer had killed Bones!"

"I thought he'd finally meet his fate, when I captured him and stuck him in the Alice jail. He tricked old Bones somehow."

"You say he's at the stagecoach inn?"

"I haven't seen him, but the stolen horse he was riding is tied up at the corral. You up for some investigating?"

"Sure. Let me get tidied up a bit, let Clara know I'm stepping out, and get my gun."

Luke tried to be patient. Seemed as though Meaney was taking forever.

The deputy finally emerged looking a tad sheepish. "Sorry Luke. Clara is…well…sorry." Meaney's blush told it all.

"Dang, Bill. Time is of the essence here."

Unbeknownst to Luke who was concentrated on the deputy's delay, Witmer had arisen early. He'd overheard Bull Samuels telling Martha that he was convinced they had a fugitive from justice under their roof and she dared not tell him that Luke lived up the road at Heaven's Gate Ranch. The outlaw had saddled up and begun a cautious ride up the main street. He quietly passed the silhouetted form of a tall man standing in front of the deputy's house. The big Appaloosa confirmed his suspicion as to who the shadowy figure was. Putting two and two together, Witmer calculated that Luke was heading home and must have seen the horse with the Circle H brand.

In his deviant mind, the desperado could think of little that would be more gratifying than to ambush the Texas Ranger on his very own property.

As Witmer rode out of Nuecestown, Luke and Meaney were cautiously walking up to the stagecoach inn. As they approached the corral, Luke stopped abruptly. "Sonofa…!" His voice trailed off. "He's flown the coop, Bill. Just our luck."

"What's all the damn noise?" Samuels called from the doorway to the inn. "Folks are trying to sleep around here."

His eyes began to come into focus, and he realized that he had two lawmen on his doorstep. He shook his head as if to shake off the cobwebs of sleep. "Sorry…y'all need me?"

Luke stepped forward into the light being cast from behind Samuels. "Bull, did you have a guest here last night?"

"Yeah, Captain. I had a funny feeling. Something about the man didn't feel right. I was going to come up and fetch Bill here, but the fella was keeping an eye on me. Didn't want Martha to get hurt." Samuels scratched his head. "Sure got riled up over one of them writer fellas last night. Seems the man got Witmer's name wrong. Thought the man would be shot right there in my inn."

"Well, the man was a wanted murderer named Coy Witmer." Luke gave him an especially serious look. "Did he say anything suspicious?"

"Not him, Luke. But Martha was a chattering up a storm. The man you call Witmer got real interested, when she said she got her cornbread from your wife."

Luke immediately went back to Meaney's house to fetch Twister. Samuels didn't know what to make of his quick departure, until Meaney gave him a rock-hard stare down before following Luke. "Damnit Bull. The man must have figured where Luke lives. You and Martha must have…" His words trailed off as he ran after Luke.

Luke was mounted up by the time Meaney arrived. "Bill, get saddled up and follow me. I'm headed for Heaven's Gate."

"You damn sight be careful Luke Dunn. They say the man likes to bushwhack his victims."

Luke didn't have time to tell Meaney that he'd already sampled that aspect of Witmer's style.

Luke knew better than to throw caution to the winds and charge up the road to the ranch. He prayed that the man wouldn't attack his family like Horatio Thorpe had done a few years back. He glanced at the eastern horizon and spotted the first rays of the sun poking through a gathering cloud cover.

From the look of them beginning to billow into storm clouds, it appeared as though some rain was coming. It could make tracking Witmer more challenging, if it was strong enough to wash away any sign.

At this early hour, there was no traffic on the road toward Heaven's Gate, so it was fairly easy to follow the hoofprints of the outlaw's horse. By now, Luke had also spotted a notch in the cayuse's shoes that the Circle H apparently used to identify their horses were someone to try to burn in a brand on top of theirs.

About ten minutes into his tracking, Meaney caught up with Luke. They were getting close enough to the ranch, that whispering became appropriate…hand signals even better.

Luke pulled up a couple of hundred yards from the gateway entrance to Heaven's Gate and dismounted. "Bill," he whispered. "See how his tracks turn up the lane into the ranch. You can be sure he wants us to follow him." He surveyed the area around them and continued in a whisper. "There's a berm that runs parallel to the entrance lane. It's got a lot of tall grasses pretty much all the way to my barn. Witmer will likely see it as a perfect place to set an ambush. We'll walk on down the road a piece past the berm then get in behind Witmer."

Meaney smacked his lips with a bit of relish. "Sounds like we're gonna bushwhack the bushwhacker."

Luke put his finger to his lips. "Keep your voice down, Bill." He and Meaney led their horses over to a pecan tree alongside the river and hobbled and hitched them so they'd stay put. "Hey, look at this," he whispered. Witmer's horse was secured just a few trees away. Luke smiled. He'd rightly guessed what the fugitive's plan was. He pulled the Winchester from its scabbard. He left the telescopic sight behind, as he wouldn't be needing it just now. He chambered a round. "Did you check your load, Bill?" He kept his voice as low as he could.

They returned to the road and began walking on past

where the berm began. They managed to climb over the fence and began to walk parallel to but several yards behind the earthen berm that Witmer would surely be using to set his ambush. "Looks as though we're about to get a bit of rain," he whispered. He looked at Meaney and smiled. Luke knew he had the advantage of knowing the terrain intimately. Witmer would be relying on an easy target riding up the lane leading to the barn and ranch house.

The rain began with small droplets that bounced easily from the outlaw's hat. He knew the damned Texas Ranger would be along soon, likely fearing for the safety of his family. Witmer's thinking was that fear would make the Ranger careless. A little rain wasn't going to keep him from number 37, the biggest kill of his heinous career.

The rain began to fall a bit heavier. Now and then a shard of lightning followed by the boom of thunder could be seen and heard off to the east. A storm coming in off the Gulf of Mexico could be nasty, but Coy Witmer had no idea as to the storm that was to come.

SEVENTEEN
THUNDER

LUKE RAISED his hand to bring Meaney to a stop. He pointed about thirty yards ahead of them as a bolt of lightning lit up the landscape.

Meaney barely caught the dark image but a few yards off from someone lying along the berm. The flash of a bolt of lightning reflected from the soaking wet brim of the fugitive's hat.

Luke waved his hand low and palm down, as he motioned Meaney to crouch down. As hard as it was raining, the ditch between the berm and the lane would be filling up soon. There was another flash of lightning. Luke counted the time between the lightning and the thunder. He wanted to move just a little closer and needed the noise cover. He motioned the deputy to stay put. "Cover me," he whispered.

Witmer waited patiently with rifle at the ready, despite getting soaked to the skin. He got up from his prone position, as water began to rise around his boots and up his legs. From being well-hidden behind tall clumps of grass, he now stood with his head just above the foliage. He figured he'd still be hard to see. So far as he was concerned, a little discomfort was worth the wait. His passion for vengeance was such that his squinty black eyes easily focused on the trail despite the steady drumbeat of the driving rain. The rain had a hypnotizing effect, and he found his mind wandering to the prospects of celebratory drinking and whoring in Corpus Christi. A crash of thunder brought him back into focusing on the trail before him. Where the hell was the Texas Ranger? Where was Luke Dunn?

Elisa looked out the window at the thunderstorm now pounding its driving rain against the house. She turned to Junior and Sean. "All the stock is in the barn, right?" It was mostly a rhetorical question.

"Made sure of it last night, Mom." Junior was invariably first to answer. He'd been cleaning one of the Colt revolvers and placed it gently on the table. He knew that the horses were just fine.

"Our beeves could sure use a long drink." Sean tended to think on the welfare of the longhorns. "It's been a tad dry lately." He was mastering understatement, as he watched the storm from the dry comfort of the kitchen.

Elisa turned back to the window, marveling at the intricacies of the shards of light snaking their tentacles across the sky. "It's looking like a gully washer, but I see sunlight on the horizon under the clouds. Shame the storm won't be lasting very long."

"I think I'll run out and check on the horses, Mom. Wildfire's likely okay, but I want to be sure." Junior absentmindedly stuffed the now cleaned and loaded gun into his waistband.

Luke was no more than twenty feet behind Coy Witmer. The rain was pouring about as hard as any rain could. He smiled as he peeked through the sheet of water running from his hat brim and carefully sighted the Winchester at the outlaw's back. Rain drops ricocheted from the steel blue barrel. There was another bolt of lightning. Luke counted. Thunder followed. He couldn't hold back a grin. "You move a muscle, Witmer, and you're a dead man." His voice growled between the raindrops.

The fugitive froze. This couldn't be possible.

"Drop the rifle and turn real slow with your hands high."

Witmer did as he was told. His Colt still hung from its soaking-wet holster. The peashooter in his vest was likely getting soggy as well.

"Bill, come finish disarming this sorry excuse for manhood." Luke motioned Meaney to come forward. "Give me an excuse, Witmer. I'd as soon not have you trying to escape from another jail."

Witmer stood stock still. In but a moment, he'd once again turned from hunter to prey. He was still amazed at how he'd been a victim of his own over-confidence. "How?"

Luke couldn't hold back a satisfied grin. "You're on my turf, my land, Witmer. I counted on that."

Meaney by now had cautiously divested Witmer of his weapons and stepped away. "He's about as dumb as a box of rocks, Luke. Typical of his kind."

"Stay clear, Bill." Just about the time Meaney had said 'dumb as a box of rocks,' he managed to take a hesitant step sideways to avoid some deeper water and momentarily placed himself between the two. Witmer saw his opportunity, leaped over the berm, and began to run up the lane. "Bill! Get down, dammit!" Meaney ducked and Luke swung the muzzle of the Winchester in the direction of the fleeing outlaw.

The blast from Luke's Winchester gave off a muffled boom in the rain-laden air. He worked the lever, chambering another round and firing again. He was close enough to hear the sickening sound a bullet makes when it hits a human body.

Witmer felt rather than heard the bullet drive into the back of his left shoulder. He involuntarily coughed out whatever air remained in his lungs as he saw blood, bone, and mashed bullet burst from his chest. It stunned him—nearly dropped him. He gasped for air. His senses told him that it was a kill shot. Blood mixed with rain ran all-too-freely down his chest. He was still running then staggering, and it quickly became clear that it wouldn't be for much longer.

Luke and Meaney had already begun their pursuit. Luke glanced behind at the deputy. "I hit him with that second shot, Bill. Come on!"

Through a fog of rain and semiconsciousness, the outlaw saw the barn looming ahead and someone with a lantern. Meaney had emptied his holster and he'd lost the water-logged Derringer. He hoped whoever it was at the barn had a gun he could grab. If he could only get there, he'd yet make a final stand. He coughed up blood and swiped it away with his forearm.

With the hard rain and final claps of thunder, Junior didn't see or hear the outlaw approaching.

Witmer took a couple of final staggering steps, as blood loss was fast catching up with him. He lowered his shoulder into the back of Junior's legs, sending the lantern flying.

Witmer frantically grappled for Junior's Colt. It was to no avail, as his grasp failed and the revolver began its tumble to the ground. Even his attempt to curse came out as a ghastly death rattle and died on his lips.

By sheer chance, the revolver had thudded on the rain-soaked earth and found its way into Junior's free hand just about the time he hit the ground. The teen found himself looking but a couple of feet away into the cold final death stare of a desperate killer who was breathing his last. He wrapped his finger around the trigger. As Luke and Meaney dashed into the clearing beside the barn, an explosion split the air. Hit between the eyes, the back of Witmer's head blew into pieces.

Luke and Meaney paused. That was no thunderclap.

Junior fought his first inclination to burst into tears but held back, as he saw his dad and Meaney arriving. He suddenly became acutely aware of something hot behind him. The airborne lantern had flown into some straw among sheltered near the side of the barn and shattered. Smoke was rising and flames began to lick at the dampened blades of straw.

Luke leaped over Witmer's body and began stomping on the flames. The gully washer of a rain had been a blessing, as the straw was slow to catch fire. There was just enough smoke wafting into the barn that the horses started carrying on a bit, but it soon became clear that they'd have everything under control before it could turn into a full-fledged conflagration.

Elisa had heard the gunshot in between thunderclaps and run to the window with its view of the barn. She initially thought she was seeing three men dancing, then realized they were stamping out embers and few flames. She grabbed a slicker and headed off to join them. By the time she reached the barn, the situation was under control. "Lucas! Junior! Bill! I heard a gunshot. Are you all right?"

Luke nodded. He was catching his breath and standing with his arm over Junior's shoulder reassuring his son enough to keep him from breaking down. He turned to face him, placed both hands on his shoulders, and looked into his eyes. "You okay, Junior?" He held back his own tears of pride. "You did real well, son."

They were ignoring the last few drops of the storm as the rain eased up. Luke, Junior, and Meaney were soaked to the skin but relieved as to the ultimate outcome. All seemed well at last. Luke used his foot to turn Witmer onto his back. There was a gaping wound in the outlaw's chest, and half of his evil face was gone. The hideous snakelike smile with its jagged scar remained as testament to his wickedness. A relieved Elisa eased over beside Luke. He held her closely, shook his head, and said to no one in particular, "He made one mistake too many. Happens every time."

Meaney glanced at the outlaw's body, then at the family reunion. It was just a shade uncomfortable for him. He turned and headed up the lane. "I'm gonna fetch the horses." The rain had turned into a light drizzle.

Elisa clung to Luke's side, ignored the fact that he was soaking wet, and gave him a thank-God-you're-home hug.

"Dad, look at this." Junior held a bandana over his face, as he reached down and picked Witmer's gold watch from a muddy puddle. He wiped it off on his shirt and glanced at the grooves in its casing. "What do you make of this, Dad?" He handed the watch to Luke.

Luke studied the grooves, then popped the casing open. He studied the engraving. "The watch belonged to Witmer's father. From the number of grooves carved into it, I'd guess it was his sick way of keeping track of his kills." Luke shook his head.

"What will we do with it, Dad?"

"Looks like it's still ticking. If it's all right with Bill, you keep it son as a reminder of how souls go bad." He purposefully handed the watch to Junior.

For his part, Junior palmed the timepiece, rubbed the grooves, and slipped it into his pocket. He nodded to Luke to indicate that he understood the significance.

Luke broke the momentary silent spell. He looked around. "It's over. We'll clean this up later." He double-checked Junior to be certain he was steady. "Let's tend to the horses before we back up to the house and dry out." It was a steadying, cathartic sort of remark that eased the all-enveloping emotional charge that had engulfed the scene. "You too, Bill." Currying the horses would have a calming effect.

The horses were quickly cared for, and the men soon walked arm-in-arm on up to the house. Elisa and the girls had served up coffee and cooked a breakfast of eggs, ham, and biscuits. Luke and Junior quickly changed from their wet clothes, as the aroma of breakfast mixed with odors of wet leather and horses.

Deputy Meaney shook out his hat and wiped away excess water on the gallery as best he could before he walked in the front door. "Y'all got any breakfast left?" He forced a damp smile.

Elisa handed him one of Luke's old shirts and a pair of trousers Junior had worn out. "Dry out before you eat, Bill... and get out of those boots." He didn't need his arm twisted.

When Meaney reemerged to join them, he looked to be dressed for some sort of comedy act. The sleeves of the over-sized shirt were rolled up, the shoulder seams fell nearly to his elbows, and the trousers were above his ankles. But he was dry. He pulled up a chair at the table. "So, what's new?"

There was a pregnant silence before Luke began to laugh.

"Yer pretty fair for an old man, Luke." Meaney laughed.

With everyone laughing, no one was paying attention to Junior. His laughter had turned to tears. He half whispered, "I killed him. I killed a human being." It was a confession of the soul.

Luke was first to notice. He stood up—a move that brought silence to the room. He locked eyes with his son. "You didn't kill him, son. It was my bullet that brought him down. He was already dead when you shot him."

"How...How could you know?"

"I could see it plain as day." He saw that Junior wasn't fully convinced.

"Your dad's right, Junior. He's seen it plenty before. Coy Witmer was dead just about the time he got to you."

"You never get used to killing, son. Every life, no matter how evil, is nevertheless a life. Witmer could have surrendered peaceably. He knew he was destined for the gallows, so he chose to run." Luke sensed that Junior was beginning to come around. "Likely been the toughest part of my job, son. Squeezing the trigger is a last resort. Just about any man on the honest side of the law can likely tell you the same. It never feels good."

Elisa poured more coffee. It was time to lighten the conversation. It wouldn't do to dwell on the outlaw's fate. "Junior has something to talk with you about, Lucas."

Junior flashed a questioning look at his mother before it struck him as to what she meant. "Er...yeah. Dad, I've been working with that young stallion. He's saddle broke now. Named him Wildfire."

Meaney smiled at what he figured was to come.

Luke took another swig of coffee. When someone puts a name on a horse or any animal for that matter, ownership is a given. He waited in rapt anticipation for the expected question.

Junior cleared his throat. "Dad, I want to keep Wildfire for my own. I visited cousin Mike and he set a value, so I'm willing to work to pay for him."

Luke put on his business face. "What sort of price did Mike suggest?"

"Two hundred dollars."

Luke stroked his mustache. "Sounds fair. He's a fine piece of horseflesh." He looked over at Elisa and then back at Junior. "You'd have to work a long time to earn that sort of money."

Elisa smiled and nodded to Junior.

Luke, Junior looked down a bit sheepishly. "I'll be getting most of the money, Dad."

That got Luke's attention. "How'd you come up with that sort of money?"

Junior sighed and his eyes rolled skyward. "Reward."

Now, both Luke's and Meaney's curiosity was aroused.

"Helped capture some rustlers. One of them had a price on his head. Deputy Hollingsworth gave me a share, and Mike gave me his share."

"Rustlers?" Luke had missed most of what Junior had said.

"I was on my way to Mike's to get a value on Wildfire, when I discovered a break in our fence where several head of cattle had been run through. I followed the tracks to the other side of Mike's ranch to another fence break. I rode to Mike's, and we got the deputy to put a posse together. I helped lead them to the rustlers. They had about a dozen head of beeves, a couple with our brand."

"They let you go after rustlers?"

"No, Dad. I had to stay back while they arrested them."

Luke breathed a sigh of relief. "So, you retrieved the cattle and earned a reward. What happened to the rustlers?"

Junior frowned and hung his head despairingly. He and Mike hadn't shared this with his mother. "Posse hung them. Deputy couldn't stop them."

Elisa looked aghast. "Junior! You..."

"Sorry, Mom. Mike thought it best."

Luke was more concerned with the visual image of a lynching. "Sorry you had to see that, son." Luke thought on what life realities Junior had faced in the past couple of months: helping transport a dead Texas Ranger, chasing rustlers, seeing a lynching, and putting a bullet into a human being. It was a lot for a fifteen-year-old boy...enough to turn him into a man right quickly. "How much reward money are you due?"

"One hundred fifty dollars."

Luke nodded. End of conversation.

By this time, they'd finished breakfast and dried out enough to return to the here and now of what passed for a normal life. "That was a right fine breakfast, Lisa." Luke got up and took a look out the window. "Sun's come out. Come on, Bill...Junior...let's go clean up the mess down at the barn."

They threw Witmer over the saddle of one of the older Heaven's Gate nags. They'd see to the return of the stolen horse to the Circle H ranch. As Meaney rode off with Witmer's body in tow, Luke turned to Junior. "Let's go take a look at this stallion...Wildfire you call him."

Junior followed Luke into the barn and stood beside his father as they looked into Wildfire's stall.

"Great looking cayuse there, son." He stroked his mustache thoughtfully.

Junior had long ago picked up on what it meant when his father stroked his mustache. "He's grown on me, Dad."

"Tell you what. I don't want to take all your reward money. I'll sell him for a hundred dollars."

Junior instantly put out his hand. "Done."

And they shook on it.

EIGHTEEN
OPPORTUNITY

EDWARD THORPE STEPPED to the platform amid clouds of hissing steam that added to the stifling humidity of the San Antonio afternoon. He dabbed a bit of perspiration from his brow. It was a given that a man in a fancy suit with polished boots and a walking cane didn't sweat...he perspired. His walk up the platform took him past the second and third passenger coaches emblazoned in large gold letters with GH&SA, the Galveston, Harrisburg, and San Antonio Railroad. The GH&SA had been purchased by the Southern Pacific a couple of years earlier and had netted Thorpe a tidy sum as an equity shareholder. With barely a day's rest, he'd disembarked from one of his ships at Galveston and grabbed the first scheduled train to San Antonio.

Following a whirlwind business tour in Europe, Thorpe had decided it was high time he visited his old friend Luke Dunn. Time had blazed by. Better than twenty years had passed, since the Texas Ranger had rid the world of Thorpe's father, Horatio.

Horatio Thorpe had been a scion of the agrarian plantation culture of eastern Texas, ultimately building a vast business empire that included a major shipping operation trading with

Europe and even the Far East. With money came power, greed, and, in Thorpe's case, bizarre behaviors. The elder Thorpe ran a string of brothels that stretched across Texas and established an elicit trading operation that robbed from Indian agencies and Army forts. With power came obsessions, and food became one as he ate himself into obesity. Already a tall man, it didn't take Horatio long to expand his girth fast enough to bust the buttons from his stylish vests. He eschewed guns owing to an incident with a disgruntled fellow officer while he was an adjutant in the Mexican American War. But the obsession that would prove his ultimate downfall, the one that would get his head blown off by Luke Dunn, was with the Laredo whore Scarlett Rose. Dunn was Scarlett's guardian angel and thus had been a thorn in the elder Thorpe's side. He sent more than one hired gun to kill the Texas Ranger. Bad enough that Luke had brought down Thorpe's government theft scam, but he had eliminated every killer Thorpe had sent including the man's youngest son Gascon.

It might have been easy to assume that Edward Thorpe would hold deep resentments against Luke, even seek some sort of revenge. In a twist of fate, Thorpe had been estranged from his father. He resented Horatio's disrespect of his mother, his ill treatment of the slaves on Magnolia Plantation, and his grossly immoral obsessions. When his mother passed away and his father put Magnolia up for sale, Thorpe began to make moves to rectify or redeem his father's legacy. He purchased Magnolia and began freeing slaves in the midst of the great conflagration southerners called the War of Northern Aggression. Upon Luke's killing of Horatio, Thorpe fully inherited his father's business empire. He'd spent the intervening two decades building it into an even larger, more diverse enterprise.

The stagecoach awaited him at the end of the train platform as he had arranged. He could hear the screech and grind of the train behind him, as it slowly pulled from the station. The train from San Antonio to Corpus Christi was as yet an uncertain proposition due to track repairs, so the stagecoach had been arranged as a stopgap. It would take a couple of extra days, but was deemed more reliable for now.

Thorpe was on a mission, and it was long overdue.

Jesús Santos took in his image in the full-length mirror. He admired what a mean-looking sonofabitch he'd become. From his colorful, bead-decorated, wide-brimmed sombrero to the intricately fashioned silver of the rowels on his spurs, he exuded death…in a fashionable sort of way.

The bandit cinched the buckle of his gun belt featuring its black leather holsters. Leather straps hung down from the fancy conchos decorating the holster shafts. He slipped a blackened-steel Colt Frontier into each and tied down the straps securing the holsters to his legs.

His dark eyes took another admiring look in the mirror. The black silken shirt and black leather trousers with their outer seams decorated with silver conchos adorned with leather fringe combined to make precisely the statement of evil that he sought. Santos smiled as he turned the ends of his black almost-handlebar mustache, so they were displayed for utmost effect with the tips turned up ever-so-slightly.

His sources in Nuevo Laredo had told him about a Texas Ranger turned rancher who owned a successful spread out near Corpus Christi. He learned that the man was named Dunn, and his sources further suggested that the man had made some hefty bank deposits. The question for Santos was how to tap into the Ranger's wealth. It took him a while to come up with a scheme, even to the point of investing time near Luke's ranch.

He recalled his encounter with Coy Witmer back in Nuevo Laredo and had learned that the Texas Ranger on his trail was indeed Luke Dunn. Moreover, word had traveled quickly that Luke had stopped Witmer permanently from getting any further kills. There'd be no more dime novels about Coy Witmer, and the Texas Ranger was certainly not someone to be trifled with.

The late afternoon sun cast its long shadows from the portico of the Longhorn Saloon. Corpus Christi had grown to more than 4,200 residents despite the War of Northern Aggression, and the Longhorn Saloon had spurred plenty of competition. Its increasingly decrepit appearance seemed to attract an ever-less-desirable clientele and that in turn was reflected in the corpulent, well-used whores who frequented its special facilities. It had seen far better days back when the Corpus Christi sheriffs kept trail-hardened cowboys out of trouble and challenged drunks and card cheats. Santos's dark form striding through the swinging doors actually represented an upgrade to the premises.

With but two other customers, Santos had his choice of tables. He took one toward the rear, sitting as was his custom with his back to the wall. The chair creaked. He wasn't a big man, but the chairs were old and tended to groan their protest when virtually anyone sat on them. He nodded to the barkeep who immediately grabbed a glass and a bottle. He wasn't about to offend a steady customer.

Santos had no sooner poured himself a drink, when two well-armed Mexicans strode in. From the dust on their well-worn boots, it appeared they'd been on the trail a while. Both wore single bandoliers and each had a pistol hanging loosely from a holster and another stuffed in their belt. Their sombreros were not so ornate as Santos's, and they didn't compare in terms of exuding a degree of vileness and evil. The men nodded toward Santos and joined him.

Santos smiled broadly. *"Hola, ha pasado mucho tiempo."* Seems this was a reunion of sorts, as they hadn't seen each other for some time.

The two merely returned his smile.

"*¿Quieres una bebida?*" Santos sought to be a hospitable host.

They nodded. "*Cerveza.*"

Santos motioned to the barkeep. "*Dos cervezas, aquí.*"

The barkeep placed a beer before each of what were obviously bandits, and the mugs were emptied before he could get back to the bar.

"*¡Dos más, ahora gringo!*"

Not wanting to see any trouble start, the barkeep shrugged off the insult and hustled two more beers to the table.

Santos smiled at the barkeeper's response. "Thank you Sam." The sprinkling in of a touch of English caught the two bandits off guard. They obviously hadn't spent much time in Texas with its tendencies toward multiple languages from English to Spanish to Mestizo and even occasional German and French.

Franco, the larger of the two bandits, raised his eyebrows. "*¿Tú hablas inglés?*"

"*Puede ser necesario.*" Indeed, it was necessary to any viable existence north of the Rio Grande.

The bandits looked at each other. "*No hablamos inglés.*"

Santos observed their discomfort. Knowing English gave him a bit of an edge and that translated into control. He already held the ace card by virtue of a reputation for murder and mayhem that extended well into Mexico. His fashionable accoutrements had the peasants calling him El Bandido de Lujo, the fancy bandit or Lujado for short. There was nothing especially fancy as concerned his modus operandi. He was a cold-blooded killer. As was typical of the breed, he preferred ambush to face-to-face confrontations. Santos always seemed to be well-fixed so far as money, as many of his victims were wealthy folk from whom he was pleased to relieve them of their fortunes as best he could.

"*¿Qué tienes planeado?*" Franco wasn't into pleasantries.

Santos sipped from his whiskey, as he took a long apprising look at the two men. He hoped he hadn't made a mistake in bringing them up from Monterrey. A cousin had recommended them. *"Nosotros vamos a robar ganado."* He'd already begun to have doubts about the two. Whether they'd be up for cattle rustling would give him a better measure of their worth.

The two looked at each other and then suspiciously at Santos. Franco shook his head. *"No...no...no robar ganado."*

"Qué lástima. Es mucho dinero." Santos shrugged. *"Vuelvan a Monterrey. Vaya con Dios, amigos."* He was employing an age-old strategy of taking the opportunity away by inviting them to return to Monterrey.

The bandits had come a long way on the promise of making a lot of money. They hadn't figured to have to work so hard for it. Santos's reputation as a gunman had led them to believe they might be robbing a bank or a train, a quick piece of work that didn't entail driving stolen cattle along dusty and often treacherous territory. They looked questioningly at each other. After all, they were already here. They'd departed Monterrey with boasts of quick riches. It wouldn't do to return empty-handed. They'd be laughing stocks. Franco stared deeply into Santos's eyes. *"¿Me prometes mucho dinero?"*

"Sí, pero debes trabajar." Indeed, they'd have to be willing to work for it.

The bandits nodded reluctantly.

"Bien." Santos thrust his glass of whiskey forward to touch the beer mugs, and the three men forged their verbal agreement such as it was. *"Salimos de aquí al amanecer."* They'd leave at sunrise. *"Mientras, tanto cerveza y mujeres."* Beer and women would be more to the bandits' liking in the meantime. The lusty whores of the Longhorn might not be the comeliest, but for two men preparing to rustle cattle they'd do.

Santos smiled broadly, twisting the tip of his mustache in a decidedly evil manner. He punctuated it with a dark sort of laugh.

Luke propped his legs up on the newly installed railing that ran along the gallery of the house. His faded jeans and cracked old leather boots offered stark contrast to the new white paint.

"Don't go scratching up the paint with your spurs, Lucas." Elisa brought two cups of coffee with her, gave one to Luke, and gently sat beside him. She smiled demurely. "You sure have a way of compensating for being away. If we could still have children, I'd surely be pregnant after last night."

Luke grinned wryly. "You certain you can't?"

Her eyes widened. "Lucas Dunn, don't you go even suggesting the possibility."

"Lisa darling, I've been thinking." He stroked his mustache slowly as if measuring his words.

Elisa had long ago learned the wisdom that came of her husband stroking that fiery-red mustache...even though it now had flecks of gray. She locked onto his eyes with anticipation.

Luke turned his head, took a long sip of coffee, and looked off into the distance. "How would you feel about a new house?"

Elisa involuntarily spit out the coffee she'd just sipped.

His jaw dropped. "Don't you like the idea?"

He couldn't know that she'd been thinking the very same thing. "No...no...I love the idea. But where?"

"Don't see us giving up Heaven's Gate. I'm thinking we'd build it up on yonder hill." He pointed off to his right at a knoll that might have been a couple of feet higher elevation than their present house. "I'm even thinking of an indoor water pump." He smiled broadly at that and then laughed. "I heard of some Englishman named Crapper working on improving something called a flush toilet." Luke thought it ironic in his experience that an Englishman would worry about human waste. "We don't have them in America just yet, but I figure to design a space for one. Imagine an indoor toilet, Lisa."

She'd lost most of what he'd said after suggesting a new house. "Picket fence?"

Luke nodded. "Whatever you'd like, sweetheart." He was still thinking on the indoor plumbing.

Elisa cuddled up closely with him on the bench.

The door opened, and Junior and Sean stepped out with determination in their strides.

"Where y'all headed?"

They were caught off guard, not having realized that their mom and dad were sitting on the gallery.

Junior paused in mid-stride. "Gonna check for strays."

"You going to herd them or shoot them?" Luke had taken note of the arsenal his sons were packing. He smiled but was serious. His sons carrying Colts and Winchesters was not taken lightly.

Junior sighed. "Figure to find some strays, Dad, but we've heard there's a big buck along our southern line...maybe twelve points or more."

Luke smiled broadly. He didn't need to tell them to be careful. "I'm already tasting the venison, boys."

The boys paused. Junior winked at his father. "We'll do the best we can, Dad. Bye Mom."

★★

"*¡Buenos días, amigos!*" Santos greeted his hired guns with his usual smile.

The two looked him over. They had dressed to find and herd cattle. Santos in his fancy duds looked as though he was ready to prowl the brothels of Corpus Christi.

His only wardrobe difference from the previous evening was a light-colored shirt. He didn't figure to wear black in the heat and humidity of late summer. More surprising, he had three vaqueros with him. It became abundantly clear that he had no intention of herding cattle. "*¿Estás listo?*"

The bandits nodded. "*Si, Señor Santos.*" They were figuring that this might go better than they'd expected. Who knows what other surprises might be on Santos's mind.

"*Pues…¡vámonos!*"

The six men were soon heading westward from Corpus Christi.

It wasn't long before they encountered a barbed wire fence. Santos was up to the task. "*Mira este, hombres.*" He drew a pair of fence cutters from his saddlebag and promptly cut a wide gap in the fence. He pointed to the gap and laughed. "*Entra por favor.*" He was clearly enjoying this adventure.

Nearly an hour later, Santos led the men to the crest of a low rise on the prairie. He gestured toward a dozen or so beeves gathered in the shade of a motte of live oak. "*Mira amigos. ¡Hay ganado!*" He motioned the vaqueros to get to work while he and his hired guns kept watch.

Franco and his friend shrugged. He didn't figure that a dozen scrawny longhorns would bring them the riches they had been led to expect. Santos had surprised them with the vaqueros, so the Mexican obviously had something else in mind. The two were determined to be patient.

Santos kept his eyes on the horizon as though expecting someone or something. Patience was not his strength, but this would be an exception. He might have to come back and rustle more cattle, but he'd eventually lure the Dunns to him. Surely, this day's venture would contribute to the outcome he was seeking. Riling up trouble was second nature to him.

The stagecoach was hardly a comfortable way to travel so far as Edward Thorpe was concerned. He got to thinking that it might have made sense to wait until track repairs were made such that he could have traveled smoothly and efficiently to Corpus Christi.

He'd been thinking for several months on his proposition for Luke, so a few more days weren't going to make any particular difference. He had several hundred people handling his business affairs these days, so he felt confident that he wouldn't be missed. His wife knew what he was up to but had demurred on traveling to Corpus, preferring instead to remain at the totally renovated Magnolia Plantation with their four children. Thorpe had made up his mind to relax, and relaxation was something that mostly eluded him.

Junior and Sean wound their way through meandering dry creek beds and tall grasses as they made their way toward the southernmost boundary of Heaven's Gate. The arroyos made for slow travel, especially as they didn't exactly represent the shortest distance between two points. Then again, if they were to find strays it would likely be in the brush and grasses near the ever-rarer waterholes.

"You really think we needed to bring so much firepower, Junior?"

Junior smiled. "You've waited this long to ask?"

"Figured you had something in mind besides rounding up strays or shooting some prize buck."

"I needed reinforcements."

"Reinforcements?" Sean's eyes suddenly grew wide with the realization of what his brother was up to. He shook his head as he laughed. "McCully's daughter?"

"Her pa is a tough nut. I've got to get past him to get to her."

"Why don't you go ask?" It struck Sean that Junior had brought the extra guns as cover, to appear tougher and more manly.

"He already shot at me once."

"You think returning fire is going to help?"

Junior rolled his eyes. "Of course not. I got to thinking that he might not be so ornery if I brought reinforcements and made this out to be an unexpected social call of sorts."

"I'm not sure I agree with your thinking, but I expect we've passed the point of no return. Their spread is only an hour ahead of us." Sean shook his head resignedly. "What's her name?"

"Cassie." Her image flashed across Junior's mind, as he mouthed her name.

"Dang, brother, she's only fourteen."

"Well, shucks. Mom was only sixteen, when she and Dad hitched."

There wasn't much Sean could say to that. He'd been looking to do a bit of sparking himself, but hadn't yet found a lass to his liking. "I expect you're right, Junior. I expect you're right."

NINETEEN
BANDIT THREAT

JUNIOR PULLED UP SHORT. "You hear that?"

"Voices...Mexicans?"

"And beeves bawling. Got a bad feeling about this." Junior turned Wildfire toward the sound and began moving cautiously through the grasses. He beckoned to Sean to follow. "Keep your voice down." He paused. "Seems we're down-wind." He smiled with cautious confidence.

Sean was five years older, but had come to respect his brother's sense of these sorts of situations especially after the recent incident with the rustlers up near Alice. Seemed these days they were facing dangers at just about every turn.

Junior slipped from the saddle and motioned his brother to do likewise. They were on a slight rise and could see far enough ahead through the grasses and brush to get a fair picture of what was going on. A lot of dust was being kicked up, and they could now better make out the sounds of vaqueros driving cattle. "Keep low," Junior whispered as he pulled his Winchester from its scabbard.

Too late! "*Levanta tus manos.*" Voices from his rear.

Junior found himself staring into the muzzles of three

rifles. Unthinkingly, he swung his rifle toward Santos, levered a round into the chamber, and fired. He missed Santos but hit one of his bandits who looked down at a hole in his chest, watching blood begin to bubble from it before falling from his horse.

Santos was so surprised at Junior's reaction that his own shot went wildly awry. Chaos momentarily reigned, as the vaqueros rode off upon hearing the shooting and Santos had to make a quick decision as to how to react.

A rage already enveloped Franco as he saw his amigo fall. He leveled his rifle at Sean and coldly squeezed the trigger. "*¡Bastardo!*" he hollered. Once. Twice. Flashes exploded from the muzzle.

Sean doubled over.

Junior saw his brother's grimace but had no time as he swung his rifle toward Franco. Half the bandit's head exploded in a shower of brain and skull.

"*¡Alto! ¡Levanta tus manos!* Raise your hands!" Santos had taken aim and was ready to deliver a kill shot to Sean.

It pained Junior to stop. He would have to swing his rifle too far to hit the Mexican and that would have given Santos the time to deliver a kill shot at Sean. Junior dropped the Winchester and threw up his hands.

"Smart gringo. Very smart." He nodded toward Sean. "He is not badly wounded. No die." He knew better, but wasn't of a mind to let Junior get close.

"What do you want?" Junior was holding back his own rage, trying to remember how his father taught him to keep his cool.

Santos looked around. His vaqueros had deserted and his hired guns were dead. The shooting had gotten out of hand, but he figured he still could execute his plan. He fully appreciated the sheer chance that the two Dunn youngsters had chosen this day to venture out. It was a big country, and luck thus far mostly seemed to be on Santos's side. "This man is your brother, yes?"

Junior nodded, slightly relaxing his knitted eyebrows. It was becoming clear that this Mexican hadn't suddenly showed up in a random incident.

"I hold him here and keep him alive. You get money from your family, and I let him go." A sinister wry grin appeared across Santos's lips. "You bring $10,000. You come back unarmed with money. If I see your father, your brother dies. Tell him Jesús Santos has your brother."

Junior and Sean exchanged looks. The pain in Sean's eyes nearly caused tears in Junior's, but he couldn't show weakness.

"Go...go get the money, Junior," Sean said weakly. He was hurting pretty badly and from where Junior stood, he couldn't be certain the wounds weren't mortal.

"You have until sunrise...then..." Santos made a slicing motion across his throat.

Wildfire was well-lathered as Junior pulled up to the house at Heaven's Gate. "Dad! Dad!"

Luke ran from the barn at the sound of Junior's shouting.

Junior slid from the saddle and ran to Luke. "He's got him!" He was so breathless from the hard ride, that he couldn't get out all he wanted to say.

"Easy...take a breath. What's happened? Where's Sean?"

The youngster took a couple deep breaths. "We ran into rustlers. Turned out to be a trap. We killed two bandits, but Sean got wounded pretty bad. Man named Santos is holding him for money."

"Jesús Santos?"

"Yes...yes...that's his name."

"He says he'll let Sean go if we come unarmed and pay him $10,000."

Luke rubbed his mustache.

"What will we do, Dad?"

"We're going to save your brother. You tend to your horse. Wildfire looks pretty well-lathered, so saddle another." Luke began to head up to the house. "Throw a saddle on Twister while you're in the barn, son."

Junior was dumbstruck at how cool, calm, and collected his father could be.

As he walked up to the house, Luke's brain was racing and stomach churning. He'd have to tell Elisa what he was up to. He barged through the front door.

Elisa was startled as she stood near the kitchen hearth. She almost lost her grip on the soup ladle in her hand. "Lucas! What on earth!?"

"It's Sean...he's in trouble."

She watched him retrieve the Winchester with its telescopic sight. This was serious. "Trouble?"

"Junior and Sean were attacked by some Mexicans. Sean's wounded and being held for ransom. The kidnapper wants $10,000."

"Are you going to get the money?" She knew that was not going to happen but had to ask.

Luke looked at her matter-of-factly as he grabbed a handful of ammunition. He knew she had to ask the question, and she knew his answer without his saying. "Tell Jaime to find Jake Barber, Bill Meaney, Jubal Strong, and anyone else he can round up. Maybe my cousin Nick will join in. We'll be at the southern boundary of the ranch. By the time they arrive, I should have settled this."

Elisa always admired Luke's confidence, but he seemed especially sure of himself at this moment. She headed for Jaime Sanchez's house up the road. As she ran down past the barn, she met Junior emerging with a slightly rested Wildfire and Luke's Appaloosa, Twister. "Is Sean hurt bad?"

Junior couldn't lie. "He's shot up, but I don't think he'll die, Mom."

She paused. "Be sure to do what your dad says." There was no stopping the momentum in the air to save Sean. She gave her youngest son a hug and continued her run for help.

Once Junior reached the house with the horses, Luke climbed down the steps from the gallery and took Twister's reins from Junior. "I've got a big job for you, son. You've got to be my spotter. I'll tell you as we ride what you'll have to do." He looked askance at Wildfire. "Hope that young stallion of yours is rested enough to not slow us down." Luke was a tad annoyed that Junior hadn't saddled another bronc but wasn't going to let that delay them any further.

For his part, Luke wished his sharpshooter friend Clay Bell was still living nearby. As it was, he figured he'd have to make a single long-range shot count. The tough part of this sort of business was locating the target and its physical position far too close to his wounded son.

The stagecoach tossed and jostled along the dirt road as it headed toward Corpus Christi. Thorpe found it a fascinating if not unsettling contrast to the relative comfort of the train. He'd managed to fend off his father's genetic tendency toward obesity, but aging wasn't exactly treating him kindly.

He was of a mind to visit his father's old obsession, the former Laredo whore that had proven the old man's undoing. He was gratified to have heard that she was married, happy, raising a family, and running a haberdashery business with her husband, a former Texas Ranger of some repute.

"It hurts," Sean moaned weakly. "Hurts bad."

Santos sneered. He was not above killing the young man, but figured that he needed to keep him alive at least until the ransom was delivered. The Dunn boy had grown increasingly pale, and his skin ever clammier. The outlaw had mostly stopped the bleeding, but time wasn't on his side. Where was the damned brother with the money?

"Thirsty. I'm thirsty."

Santos wet a rag and put it to Sean's lips. It wouldn't do to waste precious water.

"Why...why you doing this?" Through labored breaths, Sean struggled to get the words out.

Santos smiled evilly. "*Dinero*." One word said it all. Santos didn't give a tinker's damn for the young man's life. It was about the money. He figured to kill both brothers and then escape to Mexico with his loot.

The Mexican began to notice the odors emanating from the bodies of his two dead hired guns. Vultures circled overhead awaiting a feast. Santos was relieved that he didn't have to pay Franco and his partner, and their deaths had saved him from wasting bullets on them. As to the vaqueros, they were long gone. The cattle had already dispersed across the countryside. It was quiet, disturbingly quiet.

Another foul odor wafted toward where he was sitting in the shade of a live oak beside Sean. Soon enough a half dozen javelinas eased up a nearby arroyo toward his position and slightly above him. He cursed his luck. Wasting bullets on the nasty beasts was not an option. He saw little choice. The lead javelina flattened its ears, lowered its head, and began to paw its front hooves in preparation for a charge.

Santos was resigned to fending the smelly beasts off. He aimed his rifle carefully and squeezed off a shot. The beast's snout blew apart, as it screamed before falling over and writhing in pain.

The explosion startled Sean who had by now nearly lost his battle with consciousness.

The remaining javelinas wasted no time mourning their dead companion, as they scattered into the brush.

Now, Santos was stuck with the smells of rotting flesh, human and animal. He dared not move from his position, as the young Dunn boy would be returning and this was the only reasonably shady spot for at least a mile around. It also offered the advantage of being on the crest of a gentle hill that gave him a good view of his surroundings. He confidently scanned the horizon. No movement, no sounds.

Luke pulled up at the sound of the gunshot. He looked over at Junior. "We're getting close." It was obvious.

"When I left, they were under a tree at the top of a gently rise. That old dry creek bed is nearby."

"If he's where I'm thinking, it's going to be tough to get close."

"What about the spotter business?"

Luke handed Junior a telescope from his saddlebag. "My plan is to take him out at long range. We don't want a gun battle with Sean so close."

Junior put the telescope to his eye and scanned across the prairie. Grass and low-lying brush were the primary landscape features. He stopped and focused in on what appeared to be the distant live oak motte. "I think I see it."

"You sure?"

"It's a long way off."

"Time to dismount. We walk from here."

"Is this what a spotter does, Dad?"

Luke turned deadly serious. "When I shoot the target, you've got to tell me whether I hit it. With the recoil of the Winchester, I'll lose sight for a moment." Luke swallowed hard and spoke softly and intensely. "If I miss or don't kill the man, you might be seeing your brother die."

"You won't miss...you can't miss."

"We need to stop talking now. See that slight rise to our left?" Luke pointed. "That should be maybe three or four hundred feet from Santos. If he doesn't spot us, we should be able to set up there." Luke began to hobble the horses. "We'll leave our horses here. Stay low and stay quiet." He slipped off his spurs and stuffed them into his saddlebags while motioning for Junior to do the same.

They began the slow process of moving toward their prey.

Junior pulled out the telescope and began to lift it.

"Put that away!" Luke whispered intently. He feared that the sun would reflect off the lens and give them away. "It's not time."

Junior swallowed and did as he was told.

As they neared the rise Luke had selected, he poked his bare head above the undergrowth. He saw Santos standing and pacing. The bandit was obviously growing impatient. Now, he could see Sean's and the bandit's horses behind the motte. Both mounts were still saddled. Santos was apparently interested in a quick getaway, sort of take the money and run.

While Santos had an issue with javelinas, it's worth reminding that rattlesnakes are quite plentiful in Texas. This day was no exception. Luke found himself suddenly stopping causing Junior to nearly walk right into him. He slowly motioned with his hand to back up. Not one but two snakes were coiled and singing their rhythmic death rattles right in the path father and son were on. There was no way that Luke was going to shoot them, as the gunshot would obviously give them away. The only alternative was to slowly back up and hope the snakes would lose interest.

When he felt they'd achieved enough distance from the danger, Luke shifted their pathway to the left through some brush and continued toward their selected vantage point.

Junior couldn't help but admire how coolly his father had handled the threat.

The sun was beginning to take its toll, as Luke could feel rivulets of sweat trickle down his back and he stopped more than once to wring out the bandana around his neck. They finally reached the spot Luke had chosen. He and Junior made a quick scan for more rattlesnakes, but thus far none had come to investigate the humans trespassing on their turf.

Luke cautiously raised his head above the tall grasses. The motte was perhaps three hundred feet away. He could see the Mexican and the horses clearly. The outlaw had apparently sat back down under the shade of the live oaks. Luke's location was downwind, which meant that their whispers were unlikely to carry to Santos's position. The Texas Ranger looked at the position of the sun and felt it was now safe to look through the telescope. "Junior," he whispered. "Take a gander with the spyglass and tell me what you see." Luke could have done this himself and would have preferred to, but Junior was part of this mission and there were life lessons being taught here.

Jesús Santos was sweating despite the shade. He was growing increasingly impatient to the point of not really caring whether his captive lived or died.

Sean for his part had fallen into a stupor, partly from the shock induced by his wounds and partly from the heat. He was desperately dehydrated, and every minute was bringing him closer to death's doorstep. He'd completely lost his sensibilities.

Santos was growing ever more restless. Where the hell was the damned kid with the money? He by now figured to kill them both and bolt for Mexico.

★★

Junior whispered. "I see him, Dad. Leaning against a tree branch. I don't see Sean."

Given the height of the underbrush, Luke would have to take a standing shot. At such a distance, this was going to truly test his steadiness not to mention marksmanship. It would be the sort of shot that forged legends. "Keep your eye on the target, Junior," he whispered. The air was still. Luke lifted the Winchester to his shoulder and sighted through the telescopic sight. A trickle of sweat ran down his cheek and onto the rifle butt. The crosshairs quickly fell into place on Santos's chest. Luke prayed that the man didn't move. He needed this to be a kill shot. He'd not likely get a second chance.

Luke took a breath to relax, then breathed in, partially exhaled, held his breath, and squeezed the trigger. An explosion...a flash from the muzzle. The sound exploded across the prairie but not nearly so fast as the bullet. The .45-caliber slug plowed into Santos's shoulder and spun him around hard against the branch he'd been leaning on. He screamed upon its impact. The pain had to have been excruciating.

Junior heard the blast but wasn't prepared for the sound of the bullet as it struck human flesh and bone. It was a cross between a thump and a whack. The sound was...well...it was nothing like hitting a coon or squirrel or even a deer. Those were barely noticeable. No, a bullet slamming into human flesh and bone seemed to have a distinct sound...or just maybe it was because he'd already watched one strike a man. Unexpectedly, he actually felt a sort of rush come over him, as adrenaline coursed through his blood.

"Did I get him?" Luke whispered.

Junior shook off the shock of seeing Santos shot. He wouldn't soon forget. "He's hit bad, Dad." Junior watched as Santos staggered to his horse. The outlaw was obviously in terrible pain and intent on getting away. Sean Dunn was the least of his worries. He had to escape before whoever was out there could get off another shot. "He's climbed onto his horse. He's heading away."

Luke realized that whispering was by now fully unnecessary. "Fetch our horses. I'm going to see to Sean." He'd already begun to move toward the motte. "We'll need the canteens."

He so wanted to pursue Santos, but his son's life was far more important. He threw caution to the wind as he bolted toward the motte, praying that Sean would be alive. He didn't even notice the rattlesnake that he stomped on along the way.

About the same time Luke reached the motte, Junior had reached the horses and untied the hobbles. He leaped onto Wildfire and, with Luke's Appaloosa in tow, galloped toward the motte. He was desperate to learn of his brother's fate.

Too late. As Junior drew near, he saw his father slowly stand and remove his hat. Luke never took off his hat. It could only signal one thing.

Luke looked up as Junior pulled up at the motte.

Sean lay still in the shade of the motte. He was pale as a ghost and his chest was still. His lips had begun to turn the blue color of death.

Junior dismounted and fell at his brother's side. "No! No! No!" Tears flowed, as he cradled Sean's head. "This can't happen!" Grief was quickly replaced by anger and a burning desire to pursue Santos. "I'll kill him!" He shook his fist in the direction by which Santos had escaped even as he trembled with his grief.

Junior's words of vengeance awakened Luke from his own shock. "No," he said quietly and forcefully. "There's time for that. We must take Sean home." Luke unhitched Sean's horse from the live oak and began the heartbreaking task of wrapping his son's body in a blanket and hoisting it over the saddle. He couldn't help but take note of the blood splattered around where Santos's horse had stood. The bandit was seriously wounded and might very well die before Luke could ever hope to catch up with him. He turned his attention back to the task at hand.

Junior stood immovable at the spot where his brother had died. He had fallen into a mind-numbing trance.

Luke walked over and put a hand on his son's shoulder. "It wasn't your fault, son."

Junior locked on to his father's eyes. "Why? Why does God let these things happen?"

"It was Sean's time, son. God called him."

"But the pain...why the pain?"

"He's not in pain anymore. The pain is now ours to bear." Luke gently guided Junior toward the horses. "You're going to have to be strong for your mother and sisters." He watched his son mount up, and then climbed into the big Appaloosa's saddle. "Let's go, Junior. Let's take Sean home."

"I feel like I killed him as sure as that Mexican did. You can forgive me, but how do I forgive myself?"

Luke sighed softly. "Tell you a secret, son. It's one my father shared with me. You must learn to forgive to relieve burdens of guilt. And know that a father's love for his children never ends. It can't even be ended by death." Luke sensed Junior's understanding albeit reluctantly. "In time, you'll learn to forgive yourself. Only then will the burden be bearable."

Luke made a final wistful scan of the countryside. Inside he battled his own turmoil. His head was filled with "if-onlys." If only he'd stopped the boys' adventure from the start. If only he'd arrived sooner while Sean might have still been alive. If only Sean hadn't died. He shook his head as if to ward off the haunting. He needed to listen to his own advice to Junior. His son had questioned God, and it was too easy for Luke to fall into the same trap of blaming Him. For all the years he had pursued lawbreakers across the Nueces Strip, he'd long ago learned that everything worked on God's timing. He just wished that this time it hadn't been so personal. Santos would pay, but it wouldn't be revenge. There were no "if-onlys" on the Texas frontier.

Junior rode beside his father with Sean's mount following behind on a long lead. "Are we going after him, Dad?" He finally mustered the strength to ask the question.

"Jaime is pulling together a posse. After we tend to Sean's funeral, we'll chase after Jesús Santos." Luke stroked his mustache. "If Santos is hit badly, it might not matter. He might be dead by now. One way or another, we'll bring him in…dead or alive."

"Can I come?"

Luke knew that risking the loss of another son would be tough for Elisa as well as himself. But Junior was growing up fast and needed closure on his self-blame for Sean's death. He'd already dealt with more death and mayhem than many adults. "Yes." A simple one-word answer firmly put.

They were soon riding up the trail to the ranch house. Luke dreaded what was to come.

Pain…deep throbbing pain. Blood loss was weakening him. He'd already lapsed into occasional hallucinations. The bullet had shredded his shoulder. His arm hung limp and useless at his side. Without medical attention, Jesús Santos was a dead man. "¡Maldito gringo!" he muttered under his breath through clenched teeth. Every jostle of the horse produced shards of pain. He knew who'd shot him. He hoped his son was dead—small compensation for his wound.

Where to go? Corpus Christi? He had no friends there. He'd never make it to Alice either. He headed north and soon rode into Nuecestown. By chance there wasn't a soul on the street, as he rode easy-like through the town. The place was already showing signs of economic hardship given the railroads passing it by. The increasingly decrepit old stagecoach inn beckoned as he was riding past. Any port in a storm would do, and this storm was killing him. He halted and slid from the saddle. Santos staggered to the door and tried the latch. It was broken, and as the door swung open, he fell to his knees.

Bull Samuels looked up from his seat where he'd been doing a bit of whittling. A wounded Mexican was not exactly tops on his list of welcome guests. "Who the hell are you?" He couldn't help but think back to his previous unwelcome guest, Coy Witmer.

"¡Ayúdeme!" Santos collapsed.

"Sonofabitch...yer bleedin' all over my floor!" Samuels rolled the bandit onto his back. He drew back at the sight of Santos's shoulder. "Damn, but yer not dyin' here." He picked up the bandit's feet and dragged him over near a wall where there was better light. "Martha, git me some water."

Martha dutifully brought the water. Her eyes widened and hands went to her mouth upon seeing the streak of blood across the wooden floor along the path Samuels had dragged the man.

The inn proprietor tore open Santos's shirt and began a halfhearted attempt to cleanse the wound. Given that he was dealing with a Mexican, he wasn't exactly gentle about it. The bandit was unconscious, and that was just as well.

"What happened to him, Bull?"

Samuels shook his head. It was pretty obvious that the man had been shot. He sighed. "Shot. Likely he's gonna die. Shoulder's all broke up. Slug went clean through. Been bleedin' a might."

"Should I fetch Bill Meaney?"

"I expect. Not sure it matters none." Samuels dressed the wound as best he could and strapped Santos's arm to his body to stabilize what remained of his shoulder.

Martha headed off to the deputy's office.

★ ★

Luke tied Twister's reins off at the post in front of the house.

Elisa emerged expecting to be greeted with another successful mission. Upon seeing Sean draped over the saddle, she collapsed. For all she'd been through in years past, her mother dying, her father and brother killed by Comanche, another brother prey to a rattlesnake, and her husband gravely wounded, the sight of one of her children brought home dead was far too much.

Luke climbed the gallery stairs, lifted her in his arms, and sat on the bench comforting her as best he could.

Junior stayed in the saddle, tears once again flowing.

Soon Heather and Grace emerged.

Junior dismounted, and the three children joined together and wept.

The rough prairies of Texas could be unforgiving as to the varmints it brought forth, and this was no exception. As the Dunns yielded to sorrow, the sound of hoofbeats could be heard coming up the trail. Jaime had arrived with Jake Barber, Bill Meaney, Jubal Strong, and Nick Dunn riding behind. They pulled up short at the sight that greeted them. Hats were doffed out of respect and all dismounted.

Jaime came forward first, putting his arms around the three Dunn children. There was really nothing to say—no true comfort to be given.

Elisa began to come out of her swoon and pressed herself hard against Luke as great heaving sobs racked her body. "Why, Luke?"

All Luke could do was hold her close.

The other men simply stood and prayed silently. Grief was not such an easy thing to handle even for the toughest of men.

Finally, Luke stood with Elisa beside him. He cleared his throat. "Jaime, would you be so kind as to go into town and fetch a box. I think Dan has one or two." As Jaime hustled off to hitch the buckboard and head into town, Luke turned to Elisa. "Lisa, we can't bring Sean back. He was a fine young man, and I'm sure he fought to hang onto life. I wish we had arrived sooner, but we still may not have been able to save him. His wounds were mortal. It wasn't Junior's fault. The boys were bushwhacked." He knew his words made sense, but they wouldn't heal the emotional wounds already delivered by Sean's death.

Elisa strove to gather her wits. "When Jaime gets back and we bury our son, what will you do?"

"I wounded the man that shot Sean. He's bleeding pretty heavy. I expect we'll be able to track him right easily."

Jaime put a whip to the mules and had the buckboard in Nuecestown in a mere twenty minutes. He didn't waste any time, pulling to a halt right in front of the livery stable.

The smithy happened to be out front tending to a cracked hitching post.

"Señor Dan, we're in need of one of your boxes."

"Dang, Jaime, you're driving that rig like it's a race. What's up?"

Jaime gave the smithy a serious look. "Señor Dunn's son has been killed."

Dan's mouth dropped. "Oh no. Was it an accident?"

"Murdered, murdered by cowards."

"Let me grab a box from out back. I'm heading back to Heaven's Gate with you if you don't mind."

While Dan fetched the coffin, Jaime looked up the street. The wife of the stagecoach inn proprietor seemed distressed. Upon seeing Jaime looking in her direction, she ran over.

"Have you seen Deputy Meaney?"

"Yes, Señora Samuels. He's back at Heaven's Gate with a posse. A Mexican killed Sean Dunn, and they're fixing to chase the killer after the funeral."

Martha's jaw dropped. "We might have him right here in Nuecestown. Bull is tending to a badly wounded Mexican."

A new urgency coursed through Jaime. "Please try to keep him here. I'll let Luke know."

"Oh, I don't think he's going anywhere. He's in terrible shape."

As soon as Dan had the box loaded onto the buckboard, they headed at breakneck speed back to the ranch. Jaime could hardly wait to share the news with Luke.

Jaime had no sooner arrived then he sidled up to Luke and gave him the news from Nuecestown.

Luke was itching to pursue, but had to tend to last rites for his son. Nevertheless, there'd be no time for a burial with a priest and proper service.

Once the box was ready, Sean was laid inside. It just about fit his lanky form. Junior had time to swap out Sean's bullet-riddle shirt for one of his favorite embroidered dancing shirts. Junior couldn't get over how peaceful his brother looked.

The large group of family and friends gathered around the private plot on the hill behind the old homestead cabin. Off behind them was the spot where Luke had buried three Comanche, including Three Toes the chief whom he'd befriended.

Elisa had found black dresses for herself and the girls.

The men? Well, they had no time to get a change of clothing. Besides, they were itching to get the Mexican murderer and string him up.

Heather and Grace were beyond tears by now. They stoically stood beside Junior as Luke did his best to offer appropriate prayers over his son's coffin. Tears only began again, as the box was lowered with its finality into the grave beside the graves of Elisa's parents and brothers.

No parent can ever imagine having to bury a child, and it was all-too-frequent on the Texas frontier. Luke and Elisa had been blessed to have raised ten children up to now without such a loss. That such an event happened was devastating yet entailed a shade of resignation...as though it was to be expected eventually.

With the ceremony ended, Luke turned to Elisa. "Lisa, I've got to take care of this."

She nodded her head. "Lucas, the posse can wait until morning. The children need you here."

Luke thought to protest but held off. He turned to his friends. "Men, thanks for coming. If what Jaime told me is true, Santos isn't going anywhere. He might even be dead, when we get to him. Let's gather at dawn at the Nuecestown jail."

There were general nods of agreement. Despite emotions running high, there was no cause for immediacy, so it made sense to wait until morning when everyone would be fresh and have their wits about them. The emotions surrounding revenge would have been tempered just enough to ensure rational thinking.

Elisa stood at the doorway to Sean's empty room.

Luke slipped behind her. "Junior's saddling us up. We've got to get to Nuecestown."

"Can I come?"

Luke was caught totally off guard. It hadn't crossed his mind. "Um...er...I expect. You'll have to..."

"I'm ready." She slid the Colt Frontier from the folds of her riding skirt.

Luke looked deeply into her eyes and saw the fire that reached deep within her soul. He nodded. "We'll saddle the mare."

Together, they walked down to the barn.

When Junior spied his mother with her determined gait and a gun in her hand, he quickly went into the barn to saddle her horse. He was nothing if not a bright young man.

Once mounted, they wasted no time heading up the trail from Heaven's Gate and galloping down the road to Nueces-town. It wasn't long before they'd joined up with the men gathered at the jail.

TWENTY
COMEUPPANCE

"HELL, MARTHA, HE'S BEGINNIN' to come to." Samuels had hoped through the night that the Mexican would breathe his last.

Santos blinked in the dimly lit bowels of the inn. The wool blanket under him did little to cushion him from hard oak floors. After a night flat on his back, he'd have been hurting even without the pain of his shattered shoulder. Samuels attempt to stabilize it simply had added to the man's misery. The Mexican struggled to bring his surroundings into focus, but soon yielded to the dizziness and set his head back on the blanket. He turned just enough to make out the bandages soaked through with his blood. He closed his eyes.

Samuels was torn. He had plenty of prejudice against Mexicans, but he felt obligated to make the apparently dying human as comfortable as possible. Now, the possibility of the man's death didn't seem so imminent despite loss of a lot of blood. He turned to Martha. "Did you find Bill?"

Martha kept her voice just above a whisper. "No. I did tell Jaime Sanchez. He said Bill was at the Dunn's ranch for a funeral. He promised to tell him."

Samuels was losing his hearing but understood enough to

be satisfied. The words acted like some sort of adrenaline rush to Santos. Hearing the Dunn name sent conflicting waves of dread and anger shooting through him. He found the strength to open his eyes and tried to sit up.

Samuels held his breath, watching the wounded man's attempt and exhaled with relief as Santos fell back with a desperate groan.

"*¡Ayúdeme! ¡Por el amor de Dios!*" Santos was trying his very best to arise. He'd become overwhelmed with his vulnerability, especially with the prospect of the very Texas Ranger whom he was extorting coming after him. Had he known that his hostage had died and he'd be arrested for murder as well, he'd likely have been even more desperate. "*Y agua por favor.*"

Samuels and his wife exchanged glances. The innkeeper sensed something especially evil at work.

Martha began to shake with nervousness.

"What's with you, Martha?"

"Jaime said some Mexican killed the Dunn's son Sean and that Luke had wounded the man. This could be him, Bull."

Upon overhearing their conversation, Santos made a super-human effort to sit up…and finally succeeded. It nearly made him pass out. He saw a pistol on a table perhaps ten feet away. If only he could get to his feet. "*¡Hijo de puta, gringo! ¡Te mataré!*" Sonofabitch indeed!

The threat was too much for the innkeeper. Samuels stepped back. "Let's go find Deputy Meaney." He pulled his wife out the front door, and they headed up the street. A twinge of guilt ran through him that he didn't have the courage to put the Mexican out of his misery. It would have saved the trouble of any trial and formal execution plus there might be a reward. It wouldn't have taken all that much given Santos's condition.

Meaney had just arrived back in town and was standing in front of the jail with some other men from Sean's funeral, as Samuels ran up with wife in tow.

"Santos is awake, Bill!" shouted the innkeeper. "He's awake!"

Meaney looked at him with anger beginning to well up. He struggled to hold it in check. The murder of his friend's son weighed heavily. He glanced up the street as Luke rode up belatedly then turned back to the innkeeper. "You left the man alone! You couldn't put him back to sleep, Bull? Damn!" He looked up the street toward the stagecoach inn. "That the man's horse? Damned if it's still got a rifle showing plain as day!"

Luke grimly slid from the Appaloosa's saddle and hitched him at the post. He took in the exchange between Samuels and Meaney. "Everyone calm down." He waited for silence. "What's going on, Bill?"

"Bones here says the man he figures is Santos is in the inn."

"He's hurt real bad, Mr. Dunn." Martha couldn't contain herself and looked to defend herself and her husband leaving the bandit alone.

Meaney shook his head. "Can he stand?"

"Doubt it, deputy. He lost a lot of blood…shoulder is shattered."

Luke's gaze cut through Bull Samuels like a glass shard. There was an uncharacteristic tinge of venom in the look he laid on the innkeeper.

"He…he's inside the inn, Mr. Dunn. I'm sorry."

Luke wasn't convinced that Santos couldn't defend himself. Men as evil as Santos invariably found the strength for one last effort, be it escape or killing or fighting off inevitable death.

"Did you see that?" Junior pointed at the stagecoach inn. "I saw a face in the window."

Everyone looked up the street at the inn. Mutterings of recognition swept through the gathering. It was crystal clear that Santos would be putting up a fight.

Luke waved everyone to be quiet. He sought to collect

himself. He knew emotion must not rule his thinking. He softened his gaze at Samuels. "You needn't be sorry, Bull. You're only doing what you're able to do." Luke scanned the area around the inn. Silence. Not a soul moved around the outside of the decrepit building. "Jubal, Jake...go around to the left. Bill, you, and Nick head around to the right behind the inn. Bull, find yourself some cover. Lisa and Junior stay here out of any line of fire." He ignored the protests sweeping their faces. "I'm going straight up to that front door and say hello." He forced a grin. "Cover me."

Back inside the stagecoach inn, Santos had struggled but managed to a decidedly unsteady standing position. The pain was excruciating, but he was determined. He took a couple of halting steps toward the nearby table. He almost fainted but finally managed to reach it. His hand moved shakily toward the pistol that lay on the rutted table surface. He pinched between his eyes as though to check the dizziness that wanted to swallow him. The bandit checked that the pistol was loaded and stuffed it into his waistband. A bottle of whiskey close at hand caught his eye, and in a heartbeat, he'd fortified himself with a long swallow. He was barely able to focus, but his eyes found the window. Still in a pain-induced daze, he stood at the window in plain sight. He hoped and perversely prayed that his horse still stood outside. He had no idea that Junior had seen him.

Santos took a deep breath and paused to gather his wits such as they were. The effect of booze, loss of blood, and lack of sleep clouded his already muddled thinking. He staggered to the door and eased it open a crack. He cautiously peeked outside. His horse was indeed right where he'd left it, but the sight up the main street at the jail was not what he wanted to see. He found himself in a serious predicament to say the least.

He ducked back into the inn. The sudden movement brought on another spell of dizziness. He readjusted his eyes and scanned the room. There was a side exit, but that was his only other option. He slid the latch on the front door, assured himself that it was locked, and staggered to the side door. He gently eased the creaky old door open to find himself looking at a fence surrounding a corral with a couple of horses. There were no saddles in view. Mounting a saddled horse while in his condition would be very challenging. Hoisting himself up to ride bareback next to impossible.

As Luke approached the front door of the inn, he heard the telltale squeak of a door off to his right swinging open near the corral. Coupled with the whinnying and dull thud of hooves in the dirt along with what was obviously a groan of a pained human, it was a dead giveaway that Santos was desperately trying to escape.

The horses' whinnies were followed by a growing cloud of dust and plenty of muffled cursing, as Santos struggled to climb aboard one of the unsettled cayuses. Somehow, the bandit succeeded in mounting. He was desperate and wasted no time charging through the corral gate. Upon sighting Luke, he drove his heels hard into the sides of his mount and charged directly at the Texas Ranger.

Surprised at the wounded man's unexpected aggression, Luke brought up his Colt and leveled it at the oncoming horse and rider. The other members of the posse dared not shoot for fear of hitting one of the Dunns or each other in a crossfire.

A wild-eyed Santos began shooting in Luke's general direction as he rode directly at his intended victim. Through gritted teeth, he hissed, "¡Te mataré!" He barely gripped the horse's mane in his snarling teeth as his hatred and now obsessive goal of killing Luke Dunn drove him on like the madman he'd become.

Elisa had found her way to the corral and fell backward with surprise into Junior as Santos galloped past.

Luke stood his ground...waited...aimed...and fired once... twice. His first shot drilled a slug through the horse's head and began what seemed like a slow-motion tumble that threw Santos over its head and nearly at Luke's feet. Luke's second bullet had torn a chunk from Santos's ear in mid-flight.

The Mexican bandit landed hard on his already near-useless shoulder. He let out a horrible scream from the intense pain and fought the urge to pass out. Somehow, he found the strength and presence to maintain his grip on the pistol and raise it to shoot again at Luke. Blood—the horse's and Santos's —had sprayed seemingly everywhere. He struggled desperately to find the strength to pull back the trigger of the heavy gun. He sought to aim through eyes veiled with his own blood.

A single blast exploded in the heavy Nuecestown air and a slug found its way through the Mexican bandit's head, spewing brain, blood, and bone into the sky. Elisa Dunn had not forgotten how to shoot.

Santos writhed convulsively in the dusty street in front of Luke as though his body didn't yet know that he was dead.

Luke glanced down at Santos and then at the now dead horse the killer had been riding. He wasn't paying attention as yet to Elisa or Junior.

Junior had just gotten up from having been bowled over by his mother and watched as she walked calmly and silently over to Santos and fired the remaining rounds of her Colt into Santos's by now inert body. One...two...three...four...five. The body jerked convulsively with each bullet. Every shot fired was payment for murdering her son. The acrid odor of gun smoke surrounded the scene.

Everyone was stunned. They'd never seen a woman behave in such a manner. Then...silence.

"Mom?" Junior's whisper was the first sound. He looked down at Santos. Death...violent death...had claimed another evil soul. The feelings that had consumed Junior back when he'd witnessed Santos being shot by his father were absent. He was now witness to a peculiarly unsatisfying but oh-so-necessary form of justice—hard, tough justice. His mother had delivered it again and again...with each bullet blasted from the muzzle of the Colt.

Elisa nodded to Junior, looked down at Santos, and then up at the sky. "It is finished," issued forth from her lips in an emotionally strained tone. It was said like an amen to a prayer. She turned, let the tears flow, and silently embraced Luke who had slipped up beside her. The Colt slid from her hand, its thud in the dirt a punctuation mark to a harsh judgment.

Bill Meaney strove to break the silence. "Mrs. Dunn, that was fine shooting," he said dryly. There were nods, hat wringing, nervous feet shuffling, and lots of murmurs of agreement.

"Let's go back to Heaven's Gate, Lucas." Elisa had already closed the chapter on this book. She picked up the gun and stared at it through misty eyes. Another evil human had been sent to the devil's abode, and that was the end for Jesús Santos. The price for his death had been far too high.

Jaime nodded to Luke. "I'll take care of this, Señor Dunn." Likely as not, he needn't have said a word.

Luke and Elisa walked gently arm in arm back to their horses with Junior following close behind. The young boy glanced back once, twice with jaw agape, as though trying to bring the ethereal scene back into some semblance of reality. What had just happened? What had his parents just done? He stood in the rawness of the moment beside his horse before mounting and following his mother and father. He never looked back again.

Meaney watched with a heavy heart as the Dunns rode off.

He stood beside Jaime, then turned to him and a couple of onlookers. "Let's give them some peace, men. They haven't had a chance to grieve." He looked down at the dead Mexican and the horse beside him bleeding out on Nuecestown's main street. "Give me a hand cleaning this up."

Thus, Jesús Santos became another page in outlaw history buried anonymously under the brown grasses of the Nuecestown Cemetery. If anyone was compassionate enough to plant a cross over his moldering bones, it likely wouldn't even have had his name on it.

Luke and Junior led the horses to the barn. They curried, fed, and watered them gently, as much to salve their own psyches as bring comfort to the horses. There was no hurry. Neither wanted to disturb Elisa. First thing upon dismounting, she'd walked up the hill to the little family plot to pray over Sean's all-too-fresh grave. As she stood, she slowly emptied the six shell casings from the Colt and tossed them ever-so-gently, one-by-one on the soil that covered his coffin. They could as well have been flower petals.

Luke remained quiet as he and Junior tended the horses. He finally paused and stood back staring at Junior.

"What's wrong, Dad?"

The Texas Ranger shook his head. "Dang, but you've grown a bit, son. If you had a mustache and a bit more muscle, folks would likely mistake you for me."

Junior smiled broadly.

"Funny how time flies. Suddenly your children are all grown up." Luke was recognizing a new chapter in the Dunn saga.

"Hadn't noticed, Dad. Have to admit to letting out a notch on my belt."

Luke smiled at that and patted his own still reasonably

trim belly. "Might yet need another notch myself, son. Your mom cooks right well." He turned back to stroking the Appaloosa's nose.

Upon finishing with the horses, Luke sent Junior on to the house to share as gently as possible Santos's demise with Heather and Grace. Their other children would find out soon enough. He sighed thoughtfully and quietly strode over beside Elisa. As he removed his hat, he saw the casings. They were as fitting a tribute to the son they'd lost as could be imagined. He slipped his arm around her shoulders and softly offered his own prayer for Sean's soul—that he'd rest in peace and the family would live on.

Elisa leaned into him. There were no more tears to be shed. She took a deep breath and a final look at the grave. This burial had been different. She'd buried her parents and young brother here, but burying her son was a far different matter.

Luke admired her strength in the moment. For all his toughness as a lawman and frontier rancher, he had a vulnerable side that only she could know. It wasn't supposed to be manly to cry, and yet Luke Dunn was all the more a man for having been able to offer tears over his son.

Elisa smiled up at him and squeezed his hand. "Get washed up, Lucas. I've got a dinner to cook." It was indeed Texas in 1885. They'd been blessed with ten children. To have lost one even as a twenty-year-old meant that they had beaten the odds of the frontier. Elisa had experienced her share of the loss and near loss of loved ones, but when the loss is of a child born of your own loins it's all the more difficult to endure. But endure she would, they would.

Edward Thorpe had high hopes of reaching Corpus Christi before nightfall. He was intent on seeking out Scarlett, the former prostitute that had been one of the driving obsessions of his father. His sources had told him that she'd married a reformed bank robber and former Texas Ranger named Walker Carson, and they ran a successful haberdashery in Corpus. He'd also heard that they had a daughter and son, the daughter apparently the product of a rape by a local sheriff. That she had been able to put her past behind her and find a promising future was what intrigued and drove Thorpe for what he had in mind. He'd read Charles Dickens's A Christmas Carol many years ago and now featured himself a youthful reincarnation of the reformed old miser Ebenezer Scrooge. He'd accommodated any sins of his family's past and was committed to sharing his wealth.

He'd grown used to the swaying and jostling of the coach so was pretty much able to relax, watch the scenery unfolding as they sped past, and reflect further on how he might implement his largesse.

As the stagecoach lurched on, Thorpe did take notice of a lone traveler walking the road toward Corpus Christi. He was nondescript save for what appeared to be a military-style hat. The man carried a modest-sized pack on his back. He didn't think all that much of it, gave passing thought to offering the traveler a ride, but thought better of it and continued on. Thorpe was never one to court unknown outcomes. After all, the man could be a thug up to no good.

Randall O'Connell heard the carriage approach, didn't look up as it passed by, and then watched as it faded into the distance. He wondered that he hadn't been offered a lift. These Texans seemed a strange lot, mostly friendly but less so out on the frontier. As he reached the crest of a rise in the road, he caught a glimpse of Corpus Christi in the distance. He was bone tired and thirsty. No surprise that he craved a long swig of Irish whiskey, if he could find some.

He walked with an odd gait, one that revealed a certain military bearing but compromised by age and possibly old wounds.

His had been a long trek. After disembarking in New Orleans, he'd found a train to take him to San Antonio. Encountering the same rail line breakdown as Thorpe, he'd obtained a rather aged mule and managed to get past Nueces-town before the beast gave out. He thus found himself walking the final few miles.

O'Connell had a score of sorts to settle or he'd likely have given up on his travels long before this. It could be said that his singular purpose was what kept him alive and enduring the blisters surely forming on his feet. Still, he thought, a bit of whiskey would be nice.

Luke and Elisa sat on the bench on the gallery of the ranch house, as young Heather and Grace cleaned up from the dinner. The day had taken an emotional toll, yet they appeared outwardly at least to have put the tragedy and violence behind them. Even as civilization was conquering the Texas frontier, folks still couldn't afford to dwell for long on the challenges that crossed their paths be they ever-so-troubling. Laying Jesús Santos to rest in a potter's grave in the Nuecestown cemetery had been deemed a fitting and certainly humbling end for the Mexican bandit.

Elisa sought peace in the innermost reaches of her soul as she laid her head against Luke's chest. She sought to be as close as possible to him, to feel protected by him.

Luke sensed her need. "The rain got the creeks running again."

She knew what he was thinking, and she needed it... desperately. She needed to absorb his strength deep within her to refortify herself to better face the future. "What do you have in mind, Mr. Texas Ranger?"

"Later. After Junior and the girls go to bed."

Elisa looked at the sky spread from horizon to horizon. "There's going to be plenty of stars tonight...and another full moon." Lolling in the cooling current of the water hole with Luke would be a remedy of sorts, though it touched her physical needs rather than far deeper emotional yearnings.

As the late afternoon sun continued on its path toward delivering another spectacular sunset, Thorpe couldn't help but marvel at the growth of the city. Corpus Christi had grown to more than 4,000 residents and was thriving economically. The stagecoach pulled up in front of the St. James Hotel. The driver jumped down and opened the door, but his passenger was in no great hurry. Thorpe sat for a moment reflecting and listening to the sounds of the living city. "Go ahead and take my bags in, George. I'll be along in a minute."

While the driver tended to his luggage, Thorpe finally emerged from the stagecoach. He glanced up and down the street before climbing the stairs onto the boardwalk along the front of the St. James and walking on in. This wasn't the pulsating mass of life that was New York City or Paris or London. It was on a much smaller scale, of course, but it bustled in its own way, nevertheless. He wore a self-assured smile, as he entered the hotel and strode up to the desk. "Thorpe, Edward Thorpe. I believe you have a room ready for me."

The bespectacled young man at the counter looked up politely, then jumped to an awkward sort of attention. He was well aware of his guest's importance. "Ah yes, Mr. Thorpe. If you'd be so kind as to sign in, the bellman will take your luggage to your suite."

Thorpe paused as he thought for a moment on how civilized the desk clerk sounded. But for the melodiousness of his Texas twang and homespun clothes, the clerk might just as well have been behind the check-in desk in a larger city back east. He signed in and followed the bellman past a boot black to a stairway and upstairs to his suite. The room was spacious and the front window afforded a wide view of the street below. He turned to the bellman. "Young man, might I impose upon you to deliver a message?"

"Of course, sir."

Thorpe pulled an envelope from his jacket breast pocket. "Please deliver this to the proprietor of the Cacti & Boots haberdashery."

The bellman took the envelope. "Yes, sir. Pleased to, sir."

He tipped the bellman and escorted him to the door of the room before setting about to unpacking.

The Longhorn Saloon had continued its slow demise. It had certainly seen better days. The odors of sweat, booze, blood, and piss were forever embedded in the wood floors and combined with cigar smoke to penetrate the walls and ceiling. It was fair to say that a customer could eat a meal and never taste the food owing to the lingering stench that overwhelmed olfactory senses.

Before entering, O'Connell detoured to the side of the saloon and pulled an old coat from his bag. It was of a faded royal blue color with brass buttons, frayed red piping, sagging rows of gold braids across the chest, and festooned with a few campaign medals. He slipped it on and stretched the fabric with his hands in an attempt to smooth out the wrinkles. He buffed the visor of his hat with his sleeve. Its tall conical shape covered in black fur and featuring a badge with angelic harp topped by Albert's crown. The colorful red tassel lent itself to the military embellishments typical of thirty years ago. O'Connell had worn it in the Crimean War at Balaclava, was quite proud of it, was determined to wear it even here in Texas.

O'Connell eased himself on in through the front door. Upon first entering, he crinkled up his nose just a bit as if to better accommodate the atmosphere. He found an empty table off to the side opposite the bar. There, he was hidden from view by the bodies of men and a couple of scantily clad women milling about. He placed his bag on the floor alongside his chair.

He'd been seated and observing the crowd but a few moments, when a middle-aged, slightly overweight woman with huge breasts sashayed up to his table. "My name's Irma. Y'all wanna drink?"

He mustered his best Irish brogue. "Aye, do ya got a bit o' Irish whiskey?"

The woman gave him a strange look and took in his military tunic. "Oh my, yer not from 'round these parts, are ya?" She leaned in such that her ample chest was nearly brushing his nose. "We likely have yer whiskey." She batted her eyes. "One glass or two?"

O'Connell might not have been a gentleman of high social order, but he had his limits. He smiled, revealing a mouth virtually devoid of teeth. "One glass, lass."

Disappointed, she began to turn away.

"And where can a lad find a room for the night?"

She was quick, almost eager to respond. "Ya can sleep in my room upstairs. Five dollars and another five if ya share the bed with me."

"I'll think on it, lass. Bring the whiskey." He was beginning to consider any port in a storm, though this vessel was a bit pricey given its wear and tear.

Soon enough, Irma returned with a bottle and a glass. She showed him the label on the bottle. Her thumb covered whatever word was imprinted over the word whiskey. She poured some whiskey into the glass and sat opposite O'Connell, placing the bottle such that he couldn't make out the label.

O'Connell shot her a suspicious look and took the sip of whiskey he so craved. "Phhht!" He spit it out. He gave an angry look, reached across the table, and spun the bottle such that the label faced him. "Damn. This here's Scots' swill!" His raised voice got the attention of a couple of customers at close by tables. They looked up with startled expressions before burying themselves back in whatever they were doing.

"Din't know there was any difference." Irma played innocent.

O'Connell stood. He hadn't journeyed this far to be treated in such a way. He reached down for his bag, peered inside, and drew out a flapped holster with a belt. He strapped it on, brushing the flap up just enough to reveal a recent-issue Enfield revolver. He gave Irma a deferential look and moved toward the door.

"Wait...I might be able to find yer Irish whiskey, mister."

O'Connell paused, turned, and gave her a don't-be-messing-with-me look.

"Come foller me." She grabbed his hand and led him toward the stairway in the back of the room.

The Irishman was actually rather mesmerized, as he followed her swaying butt up the stairs.

She inserted a key in a door and pulled him into a stuffy but plushly decorated room. She walked over to an old oaken cabinet and unlocked it with another key. What she drew from her private stock caused O'Connell's eyebrows to nearly rise off the top of his head. This was indeed Irish whiskey. Irma produced two glasses and proceeded to pour a bit of the smooth beverage into each. "Here's to yer health, mister..."

"O'Connell...me name is Randall O'Connell, late of Her Majesty's 8th King's Royal Irish Hussars."

"Hus what?"

"Cavalry, madam."

Irma poured another round. Nary another word was spoken. Soon enough the bottle was empty, clothes had come off, and a naked Irma was fully satisfying herself with the Irishman.

It didn't take long for either to satisfy their lusts. As they lay back on her bed, O'Connell turned to her. "I be looking for what you call a Texas Ranger. A man named Dunn. You know of him?"

They weren't exactly romantic words, but then Irma had long ago come to expect no more or no less. "There are lots of Dunns around these parts."

"I'm looking for Luke Dunn."

"Yeah. I know of him."

"Does he live in Corpus Christi?"

"Naw. He has a ranch west of town. Lots of cattle an' horses."

"Big man, is he?" O'Connell wanted to be certain she was talking about the man he was asking about.

"Taller than most." She rolled on her side to face him, her ponderous breasts coming together in a way that made O'Connell happy that none of his appendages were between them. "You know him?"

"Aye."

"I can git another bottle."

The Irishman wasn't that desperate. "That's all right, lass. I be needing some sleep."

Irma's face revealed her disappointment, but such was her fate.

"Tell ya what. I need to get a message to Mr. Dunn. Perhaps you could help me in the morning."

Irma saw possible financial gain. She wasn't about to let a good bottle of whiskey go to waste. "I can help ya there." She paused. "It'll cost ya."

O'Connell smiled. "Not a problem, lass." He slipped his Enfield under the pillow and was soon sound asleep.

TWENTY-ONE
GIFTS

"YES, Miss Scarlett, ma'am. A finely dressed gentleman over at the St. James asked me to deliver this envelope to you and Mr. Carson." The bellman stood hat in hand and shuffled his feet anxiously.

Scarlett took the proffered envelope and gave the young man a tip for his trouble.

"Scarlett. Who's there?"

"The bellman from the St. James has delivered an envelope from a man he described as finely dressed." She turned to the bellman. "You can go."

"Sorry, ma'am." The young man continued to shuffle his feet nervously. "The gentleman said to wait for your response."

Carson walked over beside Scarlett and peered over her shoulder. "Nice stationary, sweetheart. I wonder who it might be from?"

She grabbed a letter opener from a nearby desk and slit open the envelope flap. She unfolded the contents so her husband could see. "Why, it's from Edward Thorpe. He's inviting us to lunch at the St. James tomorrow." She gave a curious look at Carson. "I wonder what this is about, Walker? We haven't seen him since forever ago."

Carson nodded. "Must be important to bring him all the way to Corpus Christi. Look at the cities named on the letterhead."

Indeed, the cities made for an impressive list. He'd clearly built a rather far-flung international business empire. "I expect we should accept his invitation, love."

"I'm as curious as you." Carson nodded as he recollected Scarlett's tale of what she'd endured as victim of Thorpe's father's obsession.

"You can tell Mr. Thorpe that we'll be pleased to accept his invitation."

The relieved bellman nodded and scampered back to the hotel.

The moon was larger than usual, magnified in the rippling heat waves that emanated from the surrounding prairie. It was bright enough to all but wash out any light cast by the stars. In any case, the path to the swimming hole at the creek was easy to follow. Luke led the way with a firm grip on Elisa's hand to be sure there were no mishaps along the way. The path was well worn, having seen many a load of wash carried to and from the creek not to mention at least one captured Comanche. They soon reached the swimming hole and it didn't disappoint. The recent rain had filled the spot to overflowing, and the sparkling clear waters caught the moonbeams as they spilled over rocks on their meandering journey to the Nueces River.

They sat quietly taking in the incandescence of the swimming hole and glow shed on the scene by the vast sky with its endless bounty of stars.

Luke's hands stroked Elisa's face and followed the cascade of her long golden locks to her breasts.

She turned her lips upward to meet his and enjoyed the surge of arousal coursing through her being. She pulled away and stood before him, slowly disrobing...very very slowly.

It took all of Luke's willpower to hold back from taking her then and there.

"Let's swim." She beckoned him to the swimming hole and began her tentative steps into its tepidly cool waters.

Luke watched her as she entered the water. He was ever caught up with what an incredibly lucky man he was to have a wife of such beauty and love and with an incredibly sexy slim body despite or perhaps because of bearing ten wonderful children. As he stripped off his own clothes, he saw her admiring look at his own quite obvious arousal. He entered the water and wasted no time pulling her wet body closely to him. The heat of passion was far too hot to hold back.

She opened herself to him, absorbing his manhood within her. They sank back into the waters with but head and shoulders visible to the world. Intense passions hidden from sight heated the waters below. "Lucas...oh, Lucas..." Her words were lost in the erotic flames kindled within every inch of her body.

Luke's lips explored her body firing both their passions and heightening his own explosive climax.

They parted and sank back into the soothing waters as their ardor abated for the moment.

Elisa was first to return to the blankets on their perch above the swimming hole. She could feel Luke's eyes following her and slowed so as not to disappoint him. Moving seductively, she wrapped her blouse loosely around her shoulders and poured two glasses of wine. She sat and looked back toward him. Save for the ugly scar on his side from a near-fatal bullet, he was a perfect specimen of manhood. Rippling muscles at age fifty were an extra benefit she never failed to fully appreciate. She thought on her own scar, the one that ran from her breastbone to just short of her genitals and was now nearly invisible. She'd long ago pushed the memory of Horatio Thorpe's razor-sharp knife from her subconscious as he'd first cut then attempted to rape her. The husband whose body and tender loving ways she always so craved had saved her that day.

Luke wasn't far behind in climbing from the swimming hole, as he picked up his shirt and wrapped it around his waist before sitting beside her. He took the wine she offered. "Lisa, here's to the joys of our now and our future. May God ever bless us." He gently touched his glass to hers, the telltale clink of crystal shattering the stillness of the night. In fact, the evening was so quiet, it seemed that they could hear the twinkling of the stars.

They found their way to satisfying still smoldering passions a couple of more times before getting dressed and heading back to the ranch house. Blue, their beloved dog, was the sole observer of their quiet climb up the stairs to the comfort of their bed. Elisa winked playfully at the lovable beast, as she savored the warm effect of just a bit too much wine and surely enough sex. Blue was oblivious and seemed to understand, as he nestled into his blanket near the door.

Elisa and Luke collapsed in their bed and were quickly overtaken with sleep. For her part, she was ever so grateful for the love of her man and his deep appreciation of all she was. He was her North Star by which she navigated life.

For Luke, it would be easy to say such feelings were mutual. After tough beginnings battling the British in Ireland, he'd come to America and found his place in the world and in life. Elisa served to multiply that appreciation many times over.

The shaft of sunlight through the window split O'Connell's head in two like an axe stroke. The Irish whiskey, and surely it was Irish whiskey, had for a few moments taken away the pains of the years. He blinked and covered his eyes with his hand. He looked about him. There, but six inches from his face, was a bounteous cleavage like no other. He reflexively recoiled, but not enough to disturb Irma. His head throbbed, though didn't hurt enough to be affected by the whore's soft snoring.

O'Connell pushed the blanket away and realized that he was naked from the waist down. From the look of things, Irma apparently had her way with him, though he could remember none of it. The corners of his mouth actually turned up in bemusement at the thought that he could have been smothered to death by her gargantuan breasts.

He swung his legs to the floor and felt for the Enfield pistol under the pillow. It was there.

He grabbed his pants from the floor and began to slip them on.

"Goin' somewhere, Mr. Hussar?"

The words sent an involuntary chill up his spine. His headache was bad enough. Another round of whatever this woman wanted simply wasn't in his constitution. "Perhaps a bite of breakfast, milady?" He put a kindly emphasis on the last word of his offer. It was a decidedly Irish twist that he punctuated by turning briefly to her and executing a sweeping bow from his waist.

"Happy to buy breakfast, Miss Irma." He turned such that his back remained to her. He rolled his eyes. O'Connell couldn't bring himself to look at her—not yet anyway. He took a deep breath and finally turned toward her. He ignored her come-hither expression. "Might you see to delivering a message for me. I have an invitation for that Mr. Dunn whom you mentioned."

By now, she had slipped close behind the Irishman and

reached her hand around to stroke his privates. "I can deliver anything, Mr. Hussar," she said playfully.

He stepped away abruptly and pulled up his pants. "Let's go eat."

Luke sat thoughtfully, as he chowed down ravenously on the eggs and ham Elisa had whipped up. They were both unusually hungry.

Junior, Grace, and Heather sat around the table trying to figure the expressions being exchanged by their parents. Such things happened now and again, but it nevertheless tended to bewilder them just a tad.

"That was incredible shooting yesterday, sweetheart." Luke overlooked the fact that she'd killed Santos with her first shot. The next five had been for Sean.

"Yeah, Mom. I could only watch from the dust of the street." He, of course, alluded to her having inadvertently knocked him down. "You should have seen her shooting, Gracie. It put us to shame."

Luke couldn't hold back a grin. While the purpose behind the shooting was grim, his wife's marksmanship—at least for the first shot—was indeed amazing. Subsequent firing into a dead body had hardly been a test of marksmanship. "Your mother has experience with these sorts of things, especially under pressure. If y'all haven't already figured it out, you can learn a whole lot from her." There was little choice but to overlook the macabre nature of their celebration. It was very much an antidote for sadness over the loss of Sean.

Elisa blushed at Luke's expressed admiration, as she sat to enjoy her breakfast. She took a deep breath. "Do you think our lives might settle into something resembling normal?" It was an open question, not directed at anyone in particular.

Heather was normally the quietest but couldn't resist.

"There's never anything normal about our family." She couldn't hold back a giggle.

Luke stroked his mustache. "We can begin with getting our vaqueros together and looking to check on the west acreage."

Everyone laughed at his seriousness.

The table at the St. James was set perfectly and lunch had been pre-ordered to be served at Edward Thorpe's signal. He sat quietly awaiting the arrival of his guests. He heard the church bells begin to sound the Noon hour.

Scarlett and Walker strolled into the dining room as if on cue.

Thorpe arose to greet them, giving Scarlett a slight bow and brief kiss on her hand before shaking Carson's hand. "Please, do take a seat."

They quietly sat across from the business tycoon.

"I'm so very pleased that you accepted my invitation. I'm sure you are crazy with curiosity at what might have brought me to Corpus Christi and invited you to join me for a fine midday meal."

Scarlett cocked her head. The beauty that had obsessed Thorpe's father still lingered about her, especially as the long red waves of her hair cascaded over her smooth alabaster shoulders. Walker Carson was certainly a very fortunate man.

"We were surprised, Mr. Thorpe. And are indeed curious." Scarlett leaned slightly toward Thorpe, inadvertently thrusting a gentle swell above her bodice at their host.

Thorpe tried to ignore the natural sensuousness that exuded from Scarlett. Had he been his father, Carson would be a dead man. He shook off the thoughts. "My father was a disgrace to humanity. No one can argue that. Nothing of the temporal world can compensate for his evil, much less the agony that he caused you." He looked directly at Scarlett.

She nodded and looked over at Carson who half-smiled uncomfortably.

"What are you getting at, Mr. Thorpe?" Carson had become a student of business and its dealings and had a sense that Thorpe was preparing to offer something.

"I've had my representatives study your business, and I've been impressed with what you both have accomplished. I'm still more impressed with how you put the past behind you. You are blessed for that, and in my humble observation, Texas Ranger Luke Dunn's influence, his redemptive considerations, if you will, helped you both." Thorpe signaled the server to begin bringing the meal.

"My sources tell me that if you had the resources, you would like to expand your Cacti & Boots haberdashery. Is that true?"

Scarlett was about to take her first bite of salad but dropped her fork. "Oh, excuse me. How clumsy."

Carson smiled. "Yes, we are looking to expand to other cities."

Thorpe smiled. "What I'm about to offer is out of my admiration for both of you and in no way as atonement for my father's transgressions." He chewed thoughtfully then swallowed a piece of steak. He stared intently at the couple before him. "I am prepared to gift you with a sum of money to enable your business expansion to up to ten stores. I want no equity, no stake. The gift would be free and clear and only to be used for business purposes. It would make me very happy to do this."

Scarlett's and Carson's jaws dropped. For all the struggles she and he had endured, this was an incredible gift. "You want no stake in this?"

Scarlett looked at Carson. "Walker, what do you think?"

Carson's brain had gone into overdrive at the prospect before them. "Mr. Thorpe, we deeply appreciate your generous offer."

Scarlett looked at him dumbfounded, wondering what he was about to do but stayed silent.

Carson cleared his throat. "We accept your offer on one condition."

Thorpe looked at Carson with momentary incredulity. "Yes?"

"You absolutely must be an equity partner. We cannot accept your offer any other way. It would seem unpatriotic, even un-American, and certainly un-Texan to do this any other way."

Thorpe nodded. He'd heard what he'd hoped for. "A third?"

Scarlett offered up a broad smile. "You have a deal, Edward Thorpe."

The business arrangement seemed far sweeter than the pecan pie they enjoyed for dessert.

"Don't sass me, boy. Jus' take the damned note to Mr. Dunn." Irma wasn't going to truck being disrespected by a child, much less one of such dire straits as young Bucky. "You respect yer elders." Whore or not, she was at a pecking order above the halfwit boy. "Here be half now. Other half when ya git back."

The boy ran off to deliver O'Connell's note to Luke.

Irma breathed in the crisp morning air and paused before entering the Longhorn. She figured that Mr. Hussar was up and finishing breakfast and she'd be having to walk past him. She quivered with pleasure just a bit as she recalled having her way with the Irishman last night. She knew he'd been too far gone with the booze to have been an enthusiastic lover, but it had been a fine investment of her precious stock of Irish whiskey. With any luck, she'd coax him into another round of pleasuring.

"Irma, where ya been, lass?" O'Connell didn't miss much,

and the saloon was pretty much empty but for the barkeep and him sitting at a table finishing the last remnants of breakfast.

"Sent Bucky to deliver yer note. You owe me two bits."

O'Connell smiled deviously. "I'll take it in trade, wench." He punctuated his retort with a laugh. He'd easily transitioned from calling her lass to the earthier sobriquet of wench once the idea of whoring entered his consciousness.

"Ya might git lucky."

"You have more of that fine whiskey?"

Irma winked. "Maybe," she replied coyly.

★★

The rider pulled up in front of the Dunn's ranch house. He'd taken his sweet time. No point lathering up a good horse, especially a borrowed one. He dismounted and was about to climb the stairs to the gallery, when Elisa emerged.

"Welcome to Heaven's Gate Ranch. May I help you?"

"I have a message for Mr. Dunn, ma'am."

"Well, I'm Mrs. Dunn. I'll be pleased to accept it. He's out checking on our beeves."

The messenger handed Elisa a fancy envelope. It was obviously some sort of invitation.

"Hang on. I'll get you something."

"That's all right, Mrs. Dunn. I've been well paid." He was honest if not a tad addle-brained.

From the appearance of the envelope, Elisa didn't doubt it. "Your name's John, isn't it?"

"Yes, ma'am."

"Well, wait a moment anyway." She went back into the house and reemerged with a napkin wrapped around a piece of warm cornbread.

"Thanks kindly, Mrs. Dunn." John was about to be on his way, when he paused. "Oh, I near forgot, ma'am. I'm supposed to wait for an answer." He looked down sheepishly. "Sorry, ma'am."

Elisa sighed disconcertedly and turned her attention to the envelope. The message was addressed to Luke. He might not return for another couple of hours. If it was so important, and it surely did look important, he might want to know sooner than later. She broke the seal and slipped the message from the envelope. The letterhead was impressive. Edward Thorpe had apparently not forgotten them and had done quite well in his far-flung business enterprises. The note was cordial and invited Luke to meet him for dinner that evening at the St. James Hotel. A postscript invited Luke to "bring your lovely wife, if convenient."

There was no point in having the messenger hanging around while she searched for Luke. "You can tell Mr. Thorpe that we accept his invitation."

"Thank you, ma'am." John turned and put spurs to his horse as though needing a quick getaway.

Elisa smiled and turned to go back inside. "Gracie?"

"Yes, Mom?"

"You and Heather look after things for a bit. I need to go find your father."

A short while later, Elisa was mounted on her favorite mare and setting out westward to roughly where she expected she'd find Luke. As she rode, she wondered what could Edward Thorpe possibly have in mind? The last time she'd seen Thorpe's father, the repulsive creature had bound her spread-eagled, cut her with his knife and was attempting to rape her when Luke blew his brains to smithereens with a well-aimed slug from the Sharps rifle. What had brought the son here? She knew he was not like his father by any measure. What indeed could he have in mind?

She'd been riding perhaps a half hour when she saw Luke off in the distance waving a lasso as he focused on persuading a reluctant longhorn yearling to join a small herd. Heaven's

Gate had grown to encompass thousands of acres added to the original homestead, so she'd been quite fortunate. Finding her husband on the ranch was generally not unlike finding a needle in a haystack, so she was pleased at having found him so quickly. His back was to her as she rode up. "Lucas," she called out! "Lucas!"

At her call, Luke pulled Twister up to a sudden stop. His lasso stopped in mid-flight and landed far short of the yearling that was the intended target. He gathered his wits a moment before turning his head to the familiar source. "Lisa? What brings you out here?" He genuinely wondered at what could cause her to make a very rare venture out onto the range.

"We've got an invitation." She was making sure there was no question that it was for both of them.

By now, Luke had gathered his rope, dug his heels into Twister, and begun riding over to her. "An invitation to what, sweetheart?" He drew up beside her and, given his height and the size of the Appaloosa, awkwardly leaned in for a kiss.

"An old friend has invited us to dinner at the St. James in Corpus this evening."

"An old friend? This evening?"

Elisa smiled. "Why yes. You remember Edward Thorpe?"

"Well, come on. I've got to get cleaned up. Time's a wasting. We can talk on the way back to the house. Did he say what brought him here? This evening you say?"

Elisa looked with a smile of mock exasperation at the barrage of questions. "It was just an invitation, Lucas. Nothing about why." She lightly touched her spurs to the mare's sides and galloped off ahead of him.

Not to miss a clear challenge, Luke gave just enough head to the big Appaloosa to stay up with her. The little mare was no match for Twister, but Luke wasn't going to make a race of it. Then, too, he didn't mind watching Elisa's posterior bouncing ahead of him.

The mule had decided to play stubborn a couple of times on the way from Corpus Christi, but Bucky had persisted to the point of dismounting and half-dragging the beast up the trail into Heaven's Gate.

He'd just managed to reach the hitching post in front of the house when Luke and Elisa rode up. "Mr. Dunn?" he called out.

"I'm Luke Dunn. May I help you?"

"I have a message for you, sir." Bucky passed the note to Luke.

Luke took the note and opened the folded piece of paper. He turned to Elisa. "Seems to be a day for invitations."

"Who's it from, Lucas?"

"Corporal Randall O'Connell of Queen Victoria's 8th King's Royal Irish Hussars to be precise. Seems he wants to meet with me."

"Someone you knew in Ireland?"

"We knew each other back in Kildare." As he spoke, Luke handed Bucky a coin and sent the poor lad with the stubborn mule on his way. "Tell Mr. O'Connell I'll come see him."

"What of Mr. Thorpe's invitation?"

"I'll see O'Connell first. You can visit with Scarlett and Walker while I take care of whatever O'Connell is concerned with. He's likely come a long way to see me, and I don't want to put him off." He helped Elisa dismount. "You freshen up while I see to our horses. I'll be up shortly."

Elisa shook her head resignedly. Luke had made up his mind.

Corporal O'Connell straightened his tunic. He's managed to dust off his boots sufficiently to bring back just a bit of shine.

He checked the position of his cap in the mirror as he strapped belt with the gun and saber around his waist. He made certain the Enfield was loaded.

"Do ya think my beard needs a trim?"

Irma had been watching his meticulous preparations. "The whiskers are just fine, Mr. Hussar." She gave him a once over, then moved close. She pressed her ample chest into him and grabbed his crotch. "When you're done with yer meetin', I'll be ready."

He wasn't quite so repelled by the prospect. After all, there was that fine Irish whiskey in the equation. Meanwhile, it was business before pleasure. He pulled away and headed toward the door. "I'll be back, lass."

He'd switched back from wench to lass. She noticed and held hopes of another evening of lust.

Luke parked the buckboard in front of Cacti & Boots haberdashery. He helped Elisa down from the seat, admiring how she had so quickly transformed from riding a horse to fetch him at Heaven's Gate to God's answer to femininity in her pale blue brocaded dress with matching parasol and her hair done up such that it showed off her long golden curls. He was indeed a very lucky man.

She alighted gently with her hand nestled in his. "Thank you, Lucas." She so admired the way her husband could fill out the gray suit. The white shirt and black string tie gave him a decidedly gentlemanly appearance. He set it all off with black boots and a black leather gun belt and holster that housed his Colt Frontier. A stranger might admire his obvious strength and confidence, but it was unlikely they could fully appreciate what a dedicated, tough, and very successful lawman and rancher he was. He was legendary by any measure.

"I'll tend to this business with O'Connell, sweetheart. I expect to be back in plenty of time for our rendezvous with Edward Thorpe." He escorted her to the door, peeked in to offer brief greetings to Scarlett and Walker, and walked up the street to the Longhorn Saloon.

As he approached the saloon and scanned the area around him, he couldn't help but note how the place had gone to seed. It needed far more than a fresh coat of paint and new signage. He began to smell the pungent aroma of the Longhorn as he came ever closer. He straightened his jacket before taking his first stride inside. The sour aromas within hit him as though he'd run into a wall. A quick scan led his eyes to focus on Randall O'Connell sitting at a table near the rear and decked out in a threadbare version of the uniform of the 8th King's Royal Irish Hussars. But for he and O'Connell, the saloon had but a half dozen customers.

The man that O'Connell watched enter the Longhorn was nothing like he expected. The last vision he'd had of Luke Dunn was a bloodied, sweaty, rebel warrior outfitted in tartan and kilt and carrying a claymore with its blade barely holding an edge. Before him now, was a tall, well-dressed, quite civilized-looking apparition. Only Luke's black leather holster with its blue metal Colt revolver gave any hint as to the lawman image. O'Connell hesitated, then stood and moved beside his table upon seeing Luke enter. His body pretty much hid the half-emptied bottle of Irish whiskey he'd stolen from Irma and had been using to build his confidence.

Luke walked over and extended his hand in greeting. "Randall O'Connell, this is a surprise. Welcome to Corpus Christi."

O'Connell motioned Luke to an empty seat. "Please do join me, your lordship."

Lordship? Luke thought it a rather strange greeting. He had already given O'Connell a once over as he'd approached the table and noted the Enfield revolver nestled in its holster on the Irishman's right hip. "Been a long time, Randall." Luke sat opposite the Irishman.

"Care for a bit o' whiskey, your lordship?"

"Thanks, Randall, but my wife and I have a dinner engagement this evening, so I must pass on your offer. I see you've acquired a bottle of fine Irish whiskey. Don't hesitate to enjoy it."

"I've heard tales of your adventures, your lordship. A Texas Ranger or something?"

"Yes, I've been a lawman since just about the time I arrived in Texas." Luke tried to lock on to O'Connell's eyes, but the man kept looking away. "Why do you keep referring to me as your lordship, Randall? Back in Kildare, you had other names for me."

O'Connell finally smiled, revealing his near toothless mouth. "Guess that was so. Can't say that some of us took well to your fightin' with the rebels that firebrand John Mitchel stirred up. The redcoats took out their anger on us half loyalists, when they couldn't find you. Then one day, you disappeared. No one had a clue or at least would tell where you'd gone. Figured ya must've come into money and escaped." O'Connell's smile disappeared. "The damned Brits pinched me to go to the Crimea in '54 with the Light Brigade. I managed to survive the charge at Balaclava, but me leg's never been quite the same. Been doing odd jobs around Dublin ever since. Married once, but she died."

"Sorry to hear that, Randall." Luke didn't much appreciate that O'Connell kept his right hand within easy reach of the Enfield. "I must admit it had begun to get hot for my friends and me. The redcoats were tracking us down one by one, and I knew it was only a matter of time before they'd find me." He laid a penetrating stare on O'Connell. "Seemed that some lads were saving their skins by telling them where we were hiding."

"Well, I wasn't tellin'm nothing, even took some strokes by

the lash. But I kept my lips tight, your lordship. Ya can be sure of that."

"I'm certain you did, Randall. In any case, I found a small boat, crossed to Liverpool, and caught a ship to America. It landed in New Orleans, but I have family in southern Texas so headed here first chance. With my fighting experience, I hired on with a local sheriff and later signed up with the Texas Rangers to keep peace on the Texas frontier. Along the way, I met a young lass, we married, built a cattle ranch, and have grown our family."

A tear welled up in O'Connell's eye. "Damn it, Lucas Dunn. All these years I been trying to find where you'd gone. I came here with anger in my heart. I saw you as the cause of my life's misery, and I came here to kill you for it. Now, damn it, I can't do any such thing. I'm angry with myself that I didn't leave Ireland when you did." Now, he fell into actually sobbing.

Luke was at a loss for just what to do. He wasn't going to insult this man with money regardless of his intentions. He steadfastly believed in the old adage, "give a man a fish and you feed him for a day, give him a fishing pole and you feed him for life." He sat back and stroked his mustache. "What sort of work did you do in Dublin, Randall? Oh, and stop calling me lordship. Luke works just fine." Luke breathed a sigh of relief that it seemed that this situation was not going to entail gunplay.

"Odd jobs, lord...er...Luke. Collier, barkeeper, farmer... jobs like that. Not much steady."

"Randall, would you accept my help?"

"Help? What sort of help?"

"Are you willing to work? Willing to work steady and learn a trade?"

"You have something in mind?" O'Connell had stopped his tears and wiped his now ruddy face of them. Luke had his attention.

"I can't make up for what difficulties life laid before you, Randall O'Connell. However, I may be able to offer you opportunity here in Texas." Luke pulled out some cash. "You be here tomorrow morning. Get yourself some new clothes."

"I'm not a charity case, Luke."

"Didn't say you were, Randall. This is a loan. You can pay me back later. There's a haberdashery up the street. Go there and get yourself outfitted like a proper businessman. Get a bath and shave." Luke strove to be reassuring.

"Why are you doing this? After all, I came here to kill you."

"Randall, my life as a lawman wasn't always about capturing and even at times killing lawbreakers. I stand by what I call the twin pillars of peacekeeping: justice and redemption. I expect I've always tried to find redeeming value in folks."

O'Connell's eyes widened. "You think I'm redeemable?"

Luke just smiled. "Aren't you?" He stood. "Be here in the morning and be ready."

O'Connell stood and shook Luke's hand. "Maybe calling you lordship wasn't so far off, Luke Dunn."

Luke strode out the front door of the Longhorn. The meeting with Randall O'Connell had gone easy...perhaps, too easy. His lawman's gut feel told him that the man didn't totally add up. It shouldn't have taken the Irishman better than two decades to learn his whereabouts. An uneasy feeling was warranted. An itinerant soldier come all that way intending to kill him and then folding like a cheap bedroll simply didn't add up. He wished he had time to do a bit of investigating.

The Hussar lifted the whiskey bottle and downed the last of its spirits to fortify his own. He'd watched Luke leave. Envy now touched the chords of revenge that has brought him to this godforsaken place to confront the man he believed had ruined his life. Was he to take charity from the man he'd hated for so long?

✯✯

Edward Thorpe's last meeting with Luke two decades back had involved breaking up a land fraud scheme as the War of Northern Aggression wound down. The Luke Dunn he recalled wore a loose-fitting blue cotton shirt with a broad-brimmed tan hat and packed a Colt revolver on each hip. The Texas Ranger badge pinned to his shirt couldn't be missed, as his underlying muscular chest thrust it at any who might deign to look. And thrust it he did, as his sense of justice was ever strong. But what struck him the most was Luke's devotion to his family and the Heaven's Gate Ranch. Indeed, Luke had thriving livestock and land holdings as proof of ranching success as well as the many children that came with a strong family bond. He fully admired Luke's unwavering devotion to Elisa. He even wondered whether Luke would accept his proposal. It might be disruptive after all.

He was lost in these musings as Luke and Elisa entered the dining room. Thorpe was immediately struck less by how well-dressed they were than by how well they'd aged. But for a few flecks of gray in Luke's mustache and around his temples, he might have been judged to be ten years younger. And Elisa? Such a beauty. He stood and walked toward them.

"Edward Thorpe, how good to see you." Elisa did a slight curtsy as she extended her hand.

Thorpe took it with gentlemanly courtesy and planted a light kiss, then looked at Luke with mock cautiousness.

Luke smiled. "Fear not, Edward. I promise not to crush your hand this time." They shook hands and had a good laugh.

"Please come and join me." Thorpe led them to his table.

Luke and Elisa hadn't dined at the St. James in years and found themselves impressed with the fine table settings. Silken napkins and silver flatware flanked fine china plates accompanied by crystal goblets. Civilization seemed to have been quite kind to Corpus Christi.

After a few minutes of small talk to catch up on the intervening years, Thorpe motioned to a server. "I hope you like steak." He said it coupled with a wry grin, as though having fun with his own brand of ironic humor. What cattleman would not enjoy steak?

They were roughly halfway through their meal, when Thorpe paused and put his knife and fork down. He looked from Luke to Elisa and back to Luke. He took a last chew and swallow and cleared his throat. "I'm not going to bore you with how I admire you both or how much I appreciate you bringing my perverted father to justice. Let me get right to the main reason I invited you to join me for dinner this evening."

Luke paused and then casually brought another mouthful of steak to his mouth. He gave a this-is-the-moment glance to Elisa, and she returned his look. "What do you have in mind, Edward?"

Thorpe directed his attention to Luke but didn't fail to glance at Elisa every now and then. He well knew that she'd be part of any decision making. "I must believe you are aware that Richard King passed away back in April."

Luke and Elisa nodded. "Huge ranch, Edward. They say it's better than a million acres. I think his wife Henrietta is running it, but her youngest daughter Alice married a pretty sharp young man named Robert Kleberg. I expect he'll be running it from the shadows until Henrietta passes."

Thorpe wasn't surprised as to Luke's awareness of the King Ranch. After all, it was just a few miles south of Heaven's Gate and there had to be plenty of gossip about goings-on at the nearby ranching behemoth. "As I've mentioned in our earlier conversation, I have rather extensive international business holdings. Perhaps, I'm yielding to a bit of nostalgia, but I miss the days of the Magnolia Plantation. I don't miss the slaves, of course, but the agricultural production was substantial. I want to build a large ranching operation, and I know next-to-nothing about the business. I need someone I can trust to run such an enterprise."

Now, it was Luke's turn to put down his knife and fork and pause from the meal. He leaned back as though more fully taking in the scene unfolding before him. He adjusted his tie.

Elisa simply gave a look of mock surprise. Her women's intuition had figured that Thorpe would have some sort of proposition up his sleeve.

Luke remained calm. "What do you have in mind?"

"I would have you be equity owners as I acquire ranch holdings from around your Nueces Strip. I don't pretend or aspire to ever matching up with the King Ranch, but I'd sure like to build a respectable ranch...maybe a third to half the size of the King operation."

Luke and Elisa exchanged glances. This was going to take some serious consideration.

Randall O'Connell opened his eyes. Who was he fooling? He was never cut out to be a success at anything. He'd even failed thus far at his primary mission of revenge on the sonofabitch who ran off and left him at the mercy of Queen Victoria's red-coated enforcers.

He sat on the edge of the bed.

Irma walked in. "You ready, Mr. Hussar?" Her negligee hung loosely around her, as she walked to the liquor cabinet.

"It's not there, lass."

"You bastard. You drank the whole bottle without me?!"

"Twas a business meeting, lass."

She peered into the cabinet. "Don't you 'lass' me, you two-timing, thieving sonofabitch. Where's the money I stowed in here? I may not be in my prime, but I'm better than that." With that, she pulled a Derringer, aimed point-blank at O'Connell, and fired.

The quick flash and puff of smoke was promptly followed by his yell of pain as the bullet grazed his neck. Anger welled within. "I didn't take no damned money!" The Enfield found its way from under his pillow, an explosion echoed in the tiny room, and one of its bullets plowed through Irma's prodigious chest and into her already-broken heart.

"What've ya done? My God, you've killed me!" She gasped and spit blood. Her Rubenesque body half fell, half slid to the floor.

O'Connell stood shakily. His first feeling was of shock tinged with a touch of remorse. What had he done? He hadn't shot to kill in a long time, and not out of anger back then. There was nothing that damnable Luke Dunn could offer him that would matter now. He'd now become a killer, a murderer, a wanted man. And he was a foreigner to boot.

A bang at the door broke him from his stupor. "Who's there?"

"Bucky. What's happened?" The voice penetrated the door. The halfwit kid, Irma's friend, would show up at such an inopportune time.

O'Connell opened the door. As Bucky stepped in, he pistol-whipped him across the back of his head. The poor kid had barely seen Irma prostrate on the floor in a pool of blood. Bucky fell like a sack of potatoes with the coins from the whore's liquor cabinet spilling about him on the floor.

The Irishman grabbed his bag, made sure the money from Luke was in his pocket, and headed for the stairs. He bowled over two men that were on their way up to investigate the gunshots and soon enough found himself breathlessly standing on the boardwalk across the front of the Longhorn. They'd be coming after him. He headed up the street toward the stable. He'd need a horse, a fast one.

Nestled as they were in the St. James dining room, Thorpe, Luke, and Elisa were oblivious to the goings on blocks away. Thorpe had spent about an hour explaining his proposition to Luke and Elisa. "That's my proposal, folks. It's up to you. I wouldn't take it as an insult, if you sought some expert advice before you decide. It is a big decision."

Elisa watched Luke quietly stroking his mustache then seized the moment herself. "I think your proposal has a lot of merit, Edward. It's certainly worth seriously considering." She reached over and squeezed Luke's hand. "What do you think, Lucas?"

"One thing you have right for sure, Edward, is that Texas is all about land. The more we have, the more influence is ours to exercise. You can bet that Henrietta King is listened to in Austin. A million or so acres will do that." Luke had stopped his mustache stroking. "I'm not into power and outsized influence, Edward, though I'm inclined to accept your offer. If you don't mind, Elisa and I would like to consider it for a couple of days."

Thorpe smiled friendly-like. He couldn't help but admire these folks. He understood and appreciated that they didn't leap at his offer. "Part of the reason I'm offering this to you is that you're not some power-crazed businessman or politician, Luke. I need someone with both feet solidly planted on the ground and their head not too big for their hat."

Luke and Elisa both smiled at Thorpe's closing "Texanism" about the hat.

"I'll be here until Friday. I do hope you might decide by then, though you can take as long as you like. I'll be sure to let you know where to reach me." He picked up his knife and fork. "I expect we should finish this wonderful steak before it gets much cooler. Me flapping my lips too long can do that." He chuckled a bit as he sliced into the meat. He found himself easily getting into Texas humor. He recalled how his mother could deliver some of the funniest observations of people.

Luke flinched at the ever-so-faint sound of a gunshot off in the distance. He took a bite of steak. Corpus Christi had a capable sheriff in Jim Bob Whitely.

With dinner over, Thorpe bade farewell to Luke and Elisa, escorting them to their buckboard.

"Just a minute, Edward." Luke had caught sight of the sheriff in his peripheral vision. While Thorpe helped Elisa up into the buckboard seat, Luke hailed the sheriff. "Say, Jim Bob...what was the shooting about?"

Whitely acknowledged Luke with a nod and strolled on over behind the buckboard. He kept his voice low out of respect for Elisa. "One of those whores from the Longhorn got herself shot and killed. There's been more shootin' at the livery."

Questions quickly came to Luke's mind. "Was it self-defense? Any clue as to who shot her?"

"Can't take off your lawman hat, can you, Luke Dunn?" Whitely chuckled. "From what the two fellas that got bowled over on the stairway had to say, it was a man in some sort of uniform brandishing a gun they'd not seen before. They said the man looked to be wounded, so that would account for the whore's Derringer having been fired." The sheriff paused as though in thought. "Oh, and they said the shooter had a foreign accent."

Luke began to get the feeling that he knew whom they were talking about. "I spoke with someone matching your description earlier today. His name is Randall O'Connell. I lent him some money to get himself presentable. I'd hoped to help him find work." Luke looked off ruefully. He was decidedly uncomfortable with misjudging folks. "Any idea where he was headed?"

"The boy at the livery said he bought a horse. He shot at the poor fellow but missed. Guess that was the shot you heard.

The boy says the man was headed up the road toward Nueces-town. That would likely take him past your ranch. The boy said this fella you call O'Connell was pretty panicky. I'm figuring to tail after him."

Luke wished he'd brought the Appaloosa with him. He sighed, as his hand went to his mustache. "Hmmm. Sounds like I'd best be careful heading home. I think it would be best for Elisa to stay here tonight with Scarlett and Walker. No point placing her in danger."

Whitely looked quizzically at Luke. "If I were you, I'd hole up here for the night, too." Then he rolled his eyes ever-so-slightly. "But then, I'm not a famous Texas Ranger." He punctuated it with an easy laugh.

"Might bring you a present for your humble jail, Jim Bob." Luke nodded and turned back to Elisa and Thorpe.

"Lisa, sweetheart, that gunshot I heard earlier was fired by someone I know. He carries a grudge against me. I've got to tend to it. This fellow is headed toward Nuecestown and will surely be looking for me. I'm thinking you should spend the night here with the Carsons."

Elisa glanced deviously at Thorpe and Whitely as if to say, "watch this." She turned back to Luke with a determined smile. "I think we outnumber him."

What was Luke to say? He looked over at Thorpe, who shrugged. "We'll get you a decision on the ranch venture shortly, Edward." Luke flipped the reins and clucked at the horses. The buckboard lurched forward as he pointed the rig toward home.

O'Connell had headed westward away from Corpus Christi along the road to Nuecestown. He had no idea where he was headed, just that he needed to escape. He had to put distance between himself and his crime. His neck ached where Irma's bullet from her nasty Derringer had creased the muscle, but the handkerchief he'd swiped from her dresser staunched any bleeding. He dreaded the thought that Luke Dunn would show up in the morning, and he'd not be there as promised. It had all gone so wrong. He should've simply killed the Ranger, when he had the chance. At least, if he were eventually caught and executed, he'd have completed what he'd set out to do. Dunn's escape from Ireland had in his view caused him too much life pain and hardship to let Luke off without paying a penalty.

It wasn't long before he came upon the gateway to Heaven's Gate and reined in his mount. He thought back to the instructions he'd heard Irma give to Bucky and realized that this must be Luke's ranch. It occurred to him that if Luke was detained in a meeting in Corpus Christi, he'd be arriving home late. The Irishman figured he just might lie in wait for his return. A shot or two from the Enfield pistol at close enough range should get the job done. Ambush, bushwhack, call it what you will, he'd at least accomplish what he'd left Ireland to do.

He turned his horse up the trail leading into Heaven's Gate, keeping his eyes on the lookout for a good spot from which to bag his prey. Night had settled, but there was still a mostly full moon and plenty of stars to guide his way. He figured to have plenty of time to set an ambush.

TWENTY-TWO
ENDINGS

THE BUCKBOARD CLATTERED and jostled up the rutted and well-worn road from Corpus Christi. "You're pretty bold, Mrs. Dunn."

"Thought you admired my spunk, Mr. Dunn."

"Aye, that I do." His hands were too busy with the reins to adequately stroke his mustache as he tended to do when considering situations, but Elisa could see that he was churning over a plan in his head. "This O'Connell fellow has a grudge for me. I thought I'd calmed him down by giving him hope for his future, but it seems that circumstances intervened to snatch that away. Assuming he connects me with Heaven's Gate and given his desperation, I figure he may lie in ambush." He felt it best not to share his concern with Elisa over her decision to not stay back in Corpus Christi. In fact, he knew it was generally best to let her have her way.

"What do you have in mind, Lucas?"

"If he's setting an ambush, it'd likely be as we approach the ranch. Clouds are picking up and ought to be dimming the moonlight." She could almost feel the inner machinations of Luke's brain as he mulled over a strategy. "The horses know the way to the barn without me driving them. I'm thinking that we climb out maybe a quarter mile from the Heaven's Gate entrance. That's about when we'll encounter the first cover that someone might bushwhack from. We walk in by that back path that our boys used to sneak down to fish on the river. If I've guessed right, O'Connell will drill the empty buckboard full of holes best he can with that Enfield of his."

Elisa looked at him with admiration but had a lingering question. "How do you figure we're going to capture him?"

Luke delivered a look that said it was obvious. "We'll only be a hundred and fifty feet or so off the main entry trail. I've got a fair notion as to where he may set his trap." With that, he pulled the Winchester from its cover behind the seat. "I've got something in mind."

As they came nearer the Heaven's Gate entrance, he pulled up and helped Elisa step down. He gathered some blankets and rope from behind the buckboard seat and created an amorphous lump in the seat that might be mistaken in the dark for a driver and passenger. He stood back and looked over at Elisa. "If he empties his gun into the blankets, he should be right easy to capture."

"Nice work, Mr. Texas Ranger." She smiled admiringly. "What if he reloads?"

Luke winked. He gave one of the horses a slight touch on its rump and the team headed up the road. "Reloads? He should hope not," he whispered.

As he and Elisa turned up the path that paralleled the entrance trail, he was pleased to see the team turn at the Heaven's Gate entrance as expected. So far, his plan was working. If there was to be any ambush, this would flush it out.

Junior made certain the girls were settled in before he parked himself on the gallery to enjoy the night air. He thought back to the night before, when he'd heard his mother and father carrying on in whispers as they returned from wherever they'd been.

He had Cassie McCully on his mind. The whole affair with Santos and the tragedy of his brother's death had temporarily put sparking a girl out of his consciousness. She stirred something within his 15-year-old body that he hadn't quite figured out. Her raven locks cascading in curls onto her shoulders was an image that was ever-imprinted on his mind ever since seeing her at church one Sunday. Cassie's bright blue eyes sealed the deal so far as Lucas Dunn Jr. was concerned. She'd smiled at him. He'd been captured in the snare she'd set.

Junior figured to stay up until his folks arrived home from Corpus Christi. By his reckoning, he shouldn't have that long to wait. They weren't exactly night-owls these days. Blue curled up beside the bench, keeping him company and now and then Junior would scratch him behind his ears and stroke his back. He was one very satisfied dog.

Junior took in the stars and watched clouds moving in. They'd soon cover the moon. Now and then, there'd be a noise from the barn, the chirp of crickets, or a bullfrog's croak but nothing unusual.

It was about midnight, when Blue sat up and stared down the trail. Something had grabbed his attention. "You hear something, Blue?" Whatever it was, it wasn't the sound of a buckboard. Must have been something about the Lacy breed that they were hyper-sensitive to sounds. Blue had been trained to stay quiet when he went on alert. He looked up expectantly at Junior as if expecting a command to investigate.

O'Connell sat his horse nervously. He kept having to dry off the grip of the Enfield, as his palms sweated profusely even in the cool night air. He focused intently on the trail, straining his eyes to see in the ever-dimming night. With heat, humidity, and nerves, pretty much everything got damp.

At last, he heard considerable noise coming up the trail. There was no mistaking that it was a wagon of some sort. He wiped his brow and dried his hands once more. By now for all the brow and rifle wiping, his bandana could have used a wringing out.

As the shadowy image of the buckboard drove into view, O'Connell couldn't make out any well-defined shape of a driver. But someone was in the seat driving the rig, and it had to be Dunn. The clouds had done their job of darkening the landscape. He had no choice but to seize his advantage of surprise. He couldn't wait.

The Hussar corporal sat tall, then leaned forward and dug his spurs into his mount. The steed vaulted forward and headed at breakneck speed toward the buckboard. At first, it was all O'Connell could do to stay in the saddle. He steadied himself on the galloping horse, aimed as best he could, and fired off as many rounds as he could into form on the front seat of the wagon as he sped by. The shots echoed in the night. He was certain he'd hit whoever was in the buckboard seat. The shots sent the horses into a gallop up the trail toward the barn. O'Connell brought his now-lathered and heavy-breathing horse to a halt and turned back to chase down the buckboard. He had to know whether he'd been successful in killing Luke Dunn.

Luke stood perhaps a hundred feet from the Irishman. He'd followed him through the scope of the Winchester. No beads of sweat formed on his brow. He was coolly steadying the rifle. Elisa stood behind him awaiting the explosion that was sure to come. Luke fixed the crosshairs of the scope on target, exhaled a bit, held his breath, and squeezed the trigger. There was a bright muzzle flash and an explosion rocked the air.

★★

Junior had bolted from the gallery at the sounds of O'Connell's gunfire. He ran to the barn, had Wildfire saddled in record time, and was headed toward where he figured the sound of the shooting had come. Blue followed on Wildfire's heels. Junior nearly galloped headlong into the buckboard but was able to turn and rein in the panicking team. He quickly realized that there was no driver, just a bullet-riddled lump of blankets.

He was able to look back up the trail to see what had spooked the rig, a rider giving chase. In that instant, he heard the report of Luke's Winchester and saw the mounted man blown from his saddle. Junior realized he'd left the house unarmed. A helpless feeling swept over him at the oversight. A wave of vulnerability seemed to crash about his psyche. Who was the rider?

The shot that hit O'Connell came from Junior's right, and he had no idea who had fired it. He brought Wildfire to a halt, jumped from the saddle to finish calming the buckboard horses, and peered out into the night. "Who goes?"

"Junior?" Luke yelled back.

As the teen looked away from where the mortally wounded O'Connell was struggling to get on his feet, the clouds began to clear, and he could just barely make out his father and mother nearby. "That you, Dad?"

"We're coming in. Watch yourself. The man is armed."

At that, Junior remounted Wildfire and cautiously approached the spot where the man had fallen. He heard the telltale sound as O'Connell pulled back the hammer of his Enfield. Somehow, the dying Hussar had managed to retrieve it and risen to his knees. He squeezed the trigger. Nothing. He'd failed to reload after the attack. A Hussar, especially a mortally wounded one, with an empty gun, was a sorry example of any military code.

Junior had ridden to within a mere ten feet of the dying man and dismounted while keeping an eye on the attacking stranger.

O'Connell threw the revolver at Junior in a last gasp effort.

The teen ducked and hugged Texas dust as the weapon sailed on past.

Luke and Elisa arrived on the scene none too soon.

By now, O'Connell had fallen on his face. Throwing the Enfield at Junior had sapped the last of his energy. He was obviously in excruciating pain, more so as his revenge-fed anger subsided. He twisted as best he could to face the approaching Texas Ranger. "Damn you, Lucas Dunn! Damn you!" His breathing had already become labored as his lungs filled with blood.

"Randall O'Connell, what have you done?" It was a rhetorical question of course. Luke shook his head ruefully at what might have been. There was little he could do but watch the man die. The wreck of a man lay in the dust in the bloodied remnants of the uniform of Queen Victoria's 8th King's Royal Irish Hussars. Such an ignominious end.

O'Connell tried to speak but no words came forth. He tried to rise but fell back onto the road. He closed his eyes as pain racked his body, opened them suddenly, jerked involuntarily as he choked on his own blood, and breathed his last as the Dunns looked on.

"Who was he, Dad?"

Luke sighed. "An Irish countryman named Randall O'Connell. He made some bad choices, son. He was consumed by a misplaced hatred for me. It drove his life...imprisoned him. Never forget that feasting on hate makes for a very sparse meal." Luke placed his hand on Junior's shoulder. Elisa came up alongside. They stood silently for a few moments, before Luke shook himself loose from a seeming trance. "Let's get him in the buckboard. We can take him to Corpus in the morning. Jim Bob will be looking for him. We can send a message back to Ireland, though I doubt he has any immediate next-of-kin." With that, they hauled O'Connell's body up into the wagon bed, and all headed to the ranch house.

The boat would be leaving Corpus Christi at a bit after one o'clock. Traveling up the coast to Galveston by boat seemed far preferable to another rough stagecoach ride. Thorpe hadn't heard from his Texas Ranger friend as yet. He'd whiled away the time working out the details of his arrangement with the Carsons. He knew Luke had stopped briefly in town early that morning, apparently on business with the sheriff, but the Texas Ranger had left quickly as though to avoid contact. Clearly, Luke and Elisa had not reached a decision as yet.

He slipped on down to the hotel dining room for a late breakfast.

"Good morning Mr. Thorpe. We're offering bacon and eggs this morning with a side of cornbread." The young waitress paused. "You're a friend of Mr. Dunn, aren't you?"

Thorpe looked up and nodded. "Yes."

"Well, you might be interested in knowing that he enjoyed breakfast here right early this morning. He said he'd delivered a special package to the sheriff." The young girl apparently was feeling talkative, and Thorpe was now a captive audience. "Well sir, there was a bit of a dustup. Seems the editor of one of those novels…I think it was Cowboy Tales…approached Mr. Dunn as he was about to enjoy a bite of bacon."

She had Thorpe's rapt attention. He nodded. "Go on."

"Well, he introduced himself as Elroy Stuart. He was the one that wrote about that Coy Witmer outlaw fella. Well, he asked Mr. Dunn if he could interview him and do a story he planned to call 'Luke Dunn: Nueces Legend.'" The girl paused for a moment. "You won't believe what happened next. I was standing over there at the kitchen door and saw the whole thing."

Thorpe's eyes pleaded for her to continue. "And?"

"It was so unlike Mr. Dunn. I've heard he's such a peaceful man except when he's hunting down Injuns and outlaws. Well, he grew red in his face and rose up from his seat. He towered over poor Mr. Stuart. It was as though the words 'Nueces legend' had lit a fire in Mr. Dunn. He laid out Mr. Stuart with one punch then dusted himself off, picked Mr. Stuart up by the collar, and threw him out the front door of the hotel. Then he came back into the dining room right calm-like, smiled at me like a sort of apology, and finished his breakfast."

"Did he say anything?"

"Oh, he did say he and his wife were sending you a message."

"Thank you, young lady. The bacon and eggs with cornbread will do just fine." He smiled reflectively, and wished he'd come to breakfast earlier.

From what Thorpe later heard in local gossip, apparently Luke had the better of an encounter with the man who'd murdered the prostitute. It never ceased to amaze him how Luke Dunn was consistently successful in delivering justice in this still very wild country. It made Thorpe all the more determined to want to partner with him. A man of Luke's head smarts, strong character, and enduring strength seemed next to impossible to find. As to those smarts, he'd heard it said that Luke was no empty hat, Thorpe had seen nothing to disprove that.

He'd already decided to pull together his ranch enterprise proposition with or without Luke and Elisa. Land was the main currency that drove the Texas economy, especially as it fed livestock, crops, banks, and politics. While he eschewed his father's evil ways, he'd at least inherited the man's business savvy. The difference was that the younger Thorpe was focused on legitimate endeavors. Food and whores would never be distractions to Edward Thorpe.

He rightly sensed better than to pressure Luke and Elisa into any decision. A man who'd so often ridden alone on the vast range of the Nueces Strip wasn't likely to be pushed. To have been so committed to delivering justice to the frontier yet find the time to build a ranch and raise a family...well, it wasn't a one-man job. Thorpe rightly understood that he'd never get Luke without Elisa. She was surely the driving force that kept their entire enterprise running.

He still had a couple of hours before he'd have to get himself down to the pier to catch the ferry out to the schooner that was making the run to Galveston. He rather looked forward to the trip and the fresh sea air, especially as the schooner was one of the smaller boats in his fleet of trading vessels. While his far-flung international business interests involved shipping products on waterways around the world, he found himself taking satisfaction in turning to raising cattle, horses, sheep, and more. His youth at Magnolia Plantation had taught him the cotton and tobacco business, but he was less interested in that these days. He had an in-bred prejudice against those crops owing in part to the memories of his father's moral dysfunction, not to mention the huge effort it had taken to divest it of slave labor and turn it into a profitable business. He thought it wonderfully ironic that the men who managed Magnolia Plantation interests these days were descendants of the slaves who'd served under his father's whip and carnal obsessions.

Jaime Sanchez had returned from a pre-dawn supply trip to Nuecestown. He pulled up the buckboard at the barn and had just jumped down when he spotted Luke ambling down from the ranch house. "Señor Dunn, I have a message for you." He pulled a crinkled shop-worn envelope from his hip pocket. "It's been in Nuecestown for a few weeks."

Luke took it and began unfolding it. "Who was hanging onto it?"

Jaime shrugged. "It was under Deputy Meaney's desk at the jail. Guess somebody finally got around to cleaning the place and found the envelope."

Luke straightened it out and could barely make out the official Indian agency address on it. "Seems it's from the government agency up in the Indian Territory." The address looked as though a child had painstakingly written Luke's name on it. Of a sudden, it occurred to Luke just whom the writer of that childlike script might be. He looked at Jaime for a moment before tearing open the envelope. The message was brief but clearly produced by a hand unfamiliar to writing. Luke smiled. "It's from One Arrow."

Jaime thought back to past visits from Chief Three Toes and his protégé and now a chief, One Arrow. He recalled how the Comanches had become close friends with Luke. He also recalled the not-so-friendly encounters that led to Luke's relationships with the Comanche, and the memory sent a bit of a chill up his spine. It was but twenty-five years back that several Comanche with evil intentions had met their end at Heaven's Gate. "What does he say, Señor Dunn?"

Luke smiled. "He calls me Ghost-Who-Rides. I tried to get him to call me Luke." He chuckled as he began to read the message aloud. Just then, Junior appeared from the barn. Luke hesitated and motioned his son over, as memories flooded into his head.

Ghost-Who-Rides.

One Arrow well. Blue Eyes have two child. Lone Arrow own 8 horses. 3 wives. No buffalo. White men pay to rest cattle. Miss you Luke.

One Arrow.

Luke saw the humor the chief was sending by holding off to the end to call him Luke rather than Ghost-Who-Rides.

Junior sidled on over. "Who is that from, Dad?"

Luke realized that Junior had never met the Comanche chief. "A Penateka Comanche friend, Junior. He helped me hunt down Coy Witmer, but headed back home unaware that the outlaw had escaped. Maybe you'll meet One Arrow one day. He is a very wise Comanche."

"Did he take scalps?"

"I'm afraid so. But I don't think he does anymore." Luke grinned. "He sought to learn the ways of the White man. Curious about our God, too. His adopted father was a very brave Comanche chief named Three Toes. We met as enemies and became friends. Your mom killed some of his warriors and so did I." Luke fondled the letter, looked off sort of dreamily on to the prairie before them, and handed it to Junior.

"How'd you become friends with this Comanche—Three Toes—after killing his warriors?"

Luke smiled a bit sheepishly at the memory. "Snuck up on Three Toes while he thought he was tracking me and captured him. Go figure. He respected that and the fact that I'd respectfully treated the bodies of the warriors your mom and I killed."

"You captured a Comanche chief?"

Luke looked at Junior with mild amusement. "You think I couldn't? It was a far rougher frontier twenty- years ago, and I was just a tad younger...and sneakier."

Junior shook his head in amazement. "One of the kids in Nuecestown said you were a legend, Dad. Do you think you're a legend?"

A hint of a blush crept across Luke's cheeks. "Only if you think so." He thought on having cold-cocked the dime-store novelist that morning for calling him a legend.

Junior's mouth gaped slightly in amazement and admiration. "You never said..."

Jaime stepped up. "Señor Junior, I think your friend in town is right." He smiled broadly and went to work finishing unhitching the mules, then looked back at Junior. "I think *su padre* might say to follow the footsteps of those who brung you. You do well to follow in his footsteps."

Luke grinned bashfully, as he nodded agreement with Jaime. "He's right, Junior. Come on, let's see what grub your mom has fixed." And they walked on up to the ranch house.

The family talked a bit about the letter from One Arrow and plans for the new ranch house as they enjoyed an extra bountiful early lunch.

Elisa leaned toward Luke while looking at the three teens seated with them. "Lucas Dunn, I have a surprise for us." The look in her eyes was a giveaway.

Luke gave her an incredulous look. "Are you?"

She nodded. A true pioneer mother with another bun in the oven.

Heather and Grace became all atwitter while Junior's jaw dropped.

"But..." Luke was obviously thinking how Elisa was no longer a young woman.

Elisa laughed. "Don't forget what God did for Abraham."

Luke nodded. "Well, I must say, that lends a new perspective on Edward Thorpe's proposal. What do you think, Lisa?" Luke leaned back as they finished breakfast. He was trying not to push hard for an answer. After all, there was still the surprise of her announcement. He took in the fragile beauty of her face as she wrestled with an answer. He rather liked it, when she debated with herself. She'd get sort of a placidly serious expression. He figured it was akin to the way he stroked his mustache when deep in thought.

She thought back to their tryst a couple of nights back at the swimming hole, then the meeting with Thorpe, and finally the shootout with O'Connell. Her man was her rock. "I'll support whatever you decide, Lucas."

Luke drew the envelope with Thorpe's proposal from his pocket. He scratched out the address and return address and wrote Thorpe's name in neat letters in the space above the crossed-out address. "Junior, please deliver this to Mr. Thorpe in Corpus Christi."

Elisa looked incredulously at Luke. "What's the message inside say, Lucas?"

"Tells him our decision."

She was amazed that he'd already made a decision even before waiting for her answer. He knew her that well. "And our decision is?"

Four pairs of eyes looked inquisitively at Luke. "I've got to tend to some strays. Junior, deliver that message sooner than later. You must catch him before he departs." Luke promptly got up, grabbed his gun belt and rifle, and headed to the barn smiling all the way.

He left four gaping mouths in his wake.

"Mr. Thorpe?" Junior rode up just as Thorpe was finishing seeing to his luggage being loaded on a cart for the trip to the ferry.

"I'm Lucas Dunn, Junior. I've got a message for you from my father."

"Pleased to meet you, Lucas." Thorpe accepted the message. He offered an amused look, as he appreciated Luke's efficient reuse of his envelope. "Do you know your folks' decision?"

"No sir, Mr. Thorpe."

Edward Thorpe opened the envelope and read Luke's and Elisa's message. He smiled, folded the note, and stuffed it into a pocket. "Thank your father for me, young man. Please tell him that I look forward to seeing him again right soon."

Junior gave a look as though hoping Thorpe would tell him his folks' decision, but that was not to be.

"It's close to midday, and I must be going or I'd invite you to lunch." Thorpe fished a gold coin from his pocket. "I know your father wouldn't approve of me tipping you, so please let me pay for you to have lunch up at the St. James. Tell them I sent you, and they'll treat you well." He shook Junior's hand, turned, and followed his hired cart to the pier.

Junior didn't know what to make of the exchange. Had his father accepted Thorpe's offer or not? He had no idea. As he watched Thorpe depart, he caught movement in his peripheral vision. His jaw dropped. There was Cassie McCully with her parents. All thought of his folks' business decision left his head about as fast as a deer fleeing a mountain lion. He looked down at the coin in the palm of his hand and then back up in Cassie's direction. He thought he saw her smile toward him. The money from Thorpe could easily pay for a meal for four at the St. James. He even forgot that his belly was full from the early meal at Heaven's Gate. Such was love.

On slightly shaky knees, Junior walked awkwardly toward the McCully family. It was all he could do to not trip over himself. He glanced furtively about and was relieved that her pesky brother Robert was nowhere to be seen.

He was about halfway to where the McCully family had gathered just a little way down from the St. James Hotel, when Grant McCully looked up and spotted him approaching. Junior's heart sank to his stomach.

McCully smiled and waved him on over.

The unexpected welcome did little to settle Junior's nerves.

As he drew near, he mustered the courage to speak up. "Howdy, Mr. and Mrs. McCully...Miss Cassie. How are y'all?"

Now Cassie was doing all she could to contain a winsomely broad smile. She looked down, blushed just a tad, and shyly batted her crystal-blue eyes.

"Just fine, thanks. Being it's Sunday, we've come to Corpus to attend church." McCully looked at Junior and then over at the now fully blushing Cassie. "Sorry to hear of the loss of your brother, Lucas." He added a sympathetic nod and smile.

"Thank you, Mr. McCully."

"Say, it's near time for services to start. The church is just around the corner. Would you care to join us?" McCully motioned for Junior to join them, as they began to turn toward the church.

"Thank you, sir. I'd be pleased." His pounding heart by now felt as though it would burst from his chest. His stomach growled just a bit, but he'd muster whatever it took to contain his growing appetite and impatience to be with Cassie. Junior stepped in close behind Cassie but not before giving Mrs. McCully a hand ascending the steps in front of the church. He looked up as if to offer a thank you to the Man upstairs. It wasn't as though Junior was deeply religious, as he'd attended Sunday services occasionally at his Uncle John Dunn's home more as a matter of family obligation. However, an invitation like this one tended to bring him around to thinking seriously as to belief in a higher power.

McCully glanced at Cassie and then winked at Junior. "We'd be right pleased to have you join us for a bite to eat after the service, Lucas."

Junior had suddenly found himself at the heavenly gates. "Thank you, sir. I'd sure be pleased to, if Miss Cassie doesn't mind." He hoped and prayed the morning's message wouldn't be overly long.

Junior fell in with the McCully family. He nodded in Cassie's direction and awkwardly offered his arm. "Do you like to go plinking, Miss Cassie?" The seemingly clueless expression on her face caused a wave of embarrassment to sweep over Junior. It was heightened by seeing Mr. McCully's head shake with just a touch of incredulity and then turn to a knowing smile.

Cassie's laugh relaxed everyone. "I can shoot, if that's what you're asking, Mr. Dunn." Her laugh turned to a smile that said she liked him. "And I can cook a bit."

Junior nearly stumbled. The rest of his day looked as though it would be a dream come real.

Luke sat back in the bench with his crossed legs resting on the gallery railing. He was thinking back to the recent conversation with Junior and Jaime about apparently having attained legendary status. He stroked his mustache as he gazed into the distant skies of the vast prairies before him.

"What's on your mind, Lucas?" Elisa slid onto the bench beside him. "I heard Junior mumble something this morning about you being some sort of legend." She smiled demurely.

"Now, stop that sort of talk, Lisa." The telltale blush had begun to return to Luke's cheeks. "I'm nobody's legend. The Texas Rangering things I did all these years were only my humble efforts to set the world as right as one man could. Nothing legendary there."

"Well, Mr. Ranger, you're my legend." She laid her head dreamily against his shoulder.

"Love you, Lisa."

TWENTY-THREE
NEW BEGINNINGS

FOUR MORE YEARS raced by in the lives of the Dunn family. Luke Dunn had arguably been the greatest Texas Ranger of all time...a true legend if ever one lived. He was the measure of famed Rangers like Jack Coffee Hays, Ben McCulloch, Rip Ford, and Leander McNelly but with the added dimension of a flourishing home life. He was the prototypical Texas Ranger, as courage, determination, dedication, respect, and integrity radiated from his very pores. His notoriety was not without the sorts of risks that often led him to become the hunted as well as the hunter. He had delivered true frontier justice, accomplishing what many brave folks would have quailed at. Yet bravery, grit, and a tough hide belied the vulnerable lover within who sired eleven children with his beloved Elisa. His physical scars bore testimony to his endurance and resolve. The blood of his Irish forebears ran strong in his veins. Luke never truly retired. He and Elisa took up Edward Thorpe's offer to manage a ranching empire of some 150,000 acres west of Nuecestown. It paled compared to the King Ranch to the south with its nearly million acres, but was impressive nonetheless.

For youngest son, Lucas Jr., it meant that responsibility for running the family ranch Heaven's Gate increasingly fell into his inexperienced but eager-to-learn hands. It took the boy some time to totally grasp the prodigious tasks of ranching, even with—or despite—his mother and father using it as operational headquarters for Edward Thorpe's vast spread.

Ranching responsibilities effectively placed Junior's blossoming love life on hold, much to the chagrin of his beloved Cassie. There was more to it than that, a certain wanderlust, a yearning deep within the young man to not so much as follow in his famous father's footsteps as carve out his very own bona fides independent of his father's achievements. He bore his father's sense of justice and compassion, but thus far had lacked the opportunity to exercise that birthright.

Junior learned all the skills that went with ranching, but his heart was not fully in it. Riding out at the crack of dawn to search for cattle or mend fences on the vast reaches of Heaven's Gate failed to excite him. And there was that one section of the ranch that he could never quite accommodate, that invariably left a sadness deep within his soul that he wouldn't or couldn't shake off. He'd never truly forgiven himself for the impetuosity that had led to his brother's death.

Lucas Dunn Jr. was getting nigh unto twenty years old, when the reality of his true heart confronted him. It occurred on one unusually hot evening in Corpus Christi, as he strode up the street past the Longhorn Saloon on his way to a nearby stable to fetch his horse. He'd completed the sale of a couple of hundred head of prime beef and was anxious to get back to Heaven's Gate before it got too late.

Notable to the times, men journeying from outlying ranches always carried their guns. Junior was no exception. He packed a brand-spanking-new Model 1890 Remington single-action revolver loaded with six .44-40 caliber bullets. He'd barely had a chance to practice with the new piece, but he loved its balance and heft. He carried it in a holster slightly below waist high. Junior was left-handed, so the Remington hung comfortably in a custom-made but under-stated holster of dark brown leather on his left hip. On his right, he sported the ubiquitous Texas toothpick or Bowie knife in a fringed buckskin sheath. Given the heavy humid air, Junior's shirt hung loosely, even carelessly from his tall muscular frame. His tousled red hair and steely-blue eyes told of a young man of purpose and strength, mature beyond his years. But this particular evening, he had visions of returning to Heaven's Gate in time to dive into the cooling waters of the creek that ran past the ranch house and eventually emptied into the Nueces River.

His stride was interrupted by a raggedly dressed body thrown from the front door of the saloon and directly into his path. He quickly ascertained that it was some grizzled old-timer reeking of liquor and pretty much skin and bones. Whoever or whatever this apparition of withered manhood was now lay helplessly on his back with vacant eyes and toothless mouth agape.

What emerged from the Longhorn in the next moment stunned Junior by virtue of the man's prodigious size and evil facial expression.

"You've got til tomorrow, you spineless sonofabitch." The big man snarled and fired two shots into the ground close to the helpless old man. They were far too close to Junior's intended path for comfort.

Junior stopped and gave the big man a hard look—a pene-tratingly hard look. A weak man would have quickly paled beneath such a gaze.

The big man paused and then sneered. He knew his aim had been askew...though uncomfortably close to this unex-pected passerby. "What the hell you lookin' at, mistah? I didn't shoot ya...yet." A dribble of tobacco juice slithered down his chin.

A chill ran through Junior. He looked down at the now sniveling creature groveling in the Corpus Christi dust. A sense of injustice coursed through his bones, yet he strove to hold his temper. His father had taught him how cooler heads invariably prevailed. "What's this man done to deserve such treatment?" It was a reasonable, steady, and coolly spoken question. His icy gaze demanded an answer.

"Ain't none of yer bizness, cowpoke. Move on to yer damned cows." He snarled out the command, punctuating it with a wave of his hand. He used his forearm to swipe away the tobacco dribble from his chin.

Junior, nonplussed by the bully's threats, shook his head as though lamenting the situation. "Doesn't rightly seem like a fair fight, pardner."

The big man hesitated. He blinked. Any sort of confrontation was fully unexpected. It seemed that no one with good sense ever challenged him. "He ain't paid his rent in a year. He ain't no man deservin' consideration." His huffed up his chest to seem more imposing. From his position up on the saloon boardwalk coupled with enough booze to cloud his thinking, he hadn't yet realized that he was actually facing a physically bigger man in Junior. "My name's Booger Nyland, an' I take no truck with folk meddlin' in my bizness. You have a problem with that, cowpoke?"

"No call for beating up on a man half your size and twice your age, pardner."

He looked Junior over, as he sought to size him up. "So, yer gonna protect his sorry ass?" The bully's hat and shirt were soaking wet with sweat mostly from throwing the old man out from the Longhorn. Grime streaked his stubble-bearded cheeks, and he smelled of liquor.

Luke was sizing up Nyland as well. Big for certain. The man's gloveless right hand that hovered over a serviceable gun was pale. It'd likely rarely seen sunlight, but rather enjoyed the sheltering protection of a glove. By that clue, Junior judged the man as no gunfighter. A mean bully yes—gunfighter no. "I suggest that you help this elderly gentleman to his feet and tend to the cuts and bruises you've laid on him, pardner." Junior maintained his steely-eyed gaze on Nyland.

The bully then grinned ear to ear, as he snorted out the challenge. "I ain't yer pard." The words delivered directly at Junior reeked of enough an aroma of booze to have caused a weaker man to keel over.

Junior shook his head ever-so-slightly. His jaw was set for a moment; then he smiled broadly. "Maybe...just maybe mind you...your hearing is going bad."

The bully's jaw dropped. "Why you..."

Nyland's hand moved swiftly to the butt of his revolver. He'd barely begun to slip it from its holster, when he realized that he was staring into the business end of Junior's Remington. The muzzle was but a half dozen feet away, pretty much point-blank range. His eyes opened wide. He hadn't even cleared leather. His gaze followed the line of the blued steel barrel to some location roughly between his own eyes. The man released his grip on his own revolver, letting it slide gently back into the holster. He raised both hands to shoulder level with fingers spread wide.

The bully forced a nervous smile. "Er...let me see if I can help this poor fellow." He stepped down from the wooden sidewalk and only then realized that Junior towered over him. "I...I'm sorry, mistuh. So sorry." He kneeled to help the old man.

Junior felt an involuntary shudder course through him, as he realized that he'd been within a split second of blowing the bully's brains out.

About this time, Sheriff Jim Bob Whitely came strolling by. "What's goin' on, Mr. Dunn?"

"This kind gentleman was about to help this elderly man who'd tripped and fallen, Sheriff. Seems all's well. I was just happening up the street to fetch my horse and head back to Nuecestown."

Whitely saw that all guns were safely nestled in their

holsters. He nodded knowingly at Junior. "It does seem that all is well. Say hello to your father for me, Junior."

As Whitely strode away, Junior turned to the bully. "I expect you'll bully this man no further, Mr. Nyland. If he owes you a debt...well...there are legal ways to deal with such things. Violence solves nothing."

Nyland nodded. He'd been bested by a far younger man and couldn't deny that he'd made perfect sense. Times were changing. "Yessir, Mr. Dunn. You'll hear no more trouble from me." He gently sat the drunken old man on the edge of the sidewalk and began tending to his wounds. He sighed resignedly. "As to you, Mr. Smith. I'll give you another thirty days to pay what you owe, or I'll be going to the law."

Junior nodded to the now becalmed bully, offered a satisfied smile, and continued his walk up toward the stable. It was implied that there'd be no further trouble. Inside, Junior was realizing that he'd actually enjoyed the feeling of having protected the victim and faced down the big man. He felt a sense of having delivered justice and found himself coming to terms with what his father must have felt during all those years as a Texas Ranger. He couldn't help but hang on to a lingering feeling of nearly killing someone, but he hadn't. He'd shown restraint. That was important. The entire experience felt right good. Maybe that Nyland fellow was redeemable. Junior's destiny seemingly awaited.

The cooling waters of the creek soothed the farthest reaches of Junior's body. The ranch house had been dark when he'd returned from Corpus save for a dimly lit lantern hanging on the gallery post. He'd stabled Wildfire and made a beeline for the creek. Far as he could tell, no one was around. He disrobed, stacking his clothes on a rock with the revolver within easy reach on top.

As he lolled in the creek, he marveled at the heavenly blanket of stars that spread across the sky. The moon hung on the horizon like a great white ball. Crickets chirped, a coyote let the world know it was around, and now and again an owl hooted. Junior figured to enjoy a quick relaxing dip, gather his things, and turn in. He closed his eyes to better enjoy the soothing waters.

The stillness was broken by the snapping of a twig and the sound of a few loose stones rolling down the path to the creek. He started. Being buck naked, Junior was about as vulnerable as could be possible. His clothes and that all-important Remington revolver sat on top of his pants roughly ten feet away on top of the rock. Might as well have been a mile away, as his body worked against the swirling waters. The gun was barely visible in the starlight. He began to move toward the rock as fast as the swirling waters permitted.

"Lucas Dunn, Junior, don't you move a muscle."

"Cassie?" Junior's jaw dropped.

She'd been waiting in the gathering darkness for his return from Corpus Christi and was already reveling in the predicament that had been presented to her. "Don't move." She looked him over from head to the waterline just below his navel. She felt a blush coming on but held it back.

"What...what are you doing here?"

"It's time, Lucas."

"Time?" He was clueless.

"Why are you men so thickheaded?" She went over, picked up the Remington, and sat herself down on the rock beside his clothes. She hefted the revolver a bit.

Junior cocked his head a bit and looked at her inquisitively. He didn't even feign any embarrassment, as he placed his hands on his hips. He'd begun to sense what she was referring to. "Careful with that gun."

Cassie waved the gun around, sweeping an arc across the horizon. "You know, I'm a pretty fair shot." The gun barrel picked up the moonlight and reflected it across her face. She bore a devious if not purposeful smile. Finally, she couldn't hold back. Her eyes weren't blind to the glistening well-muscled man before her. If only he weren't so goldarned handsome. "Damn it, Lucas Dunn, do you ever think of me?"

Junior's hands dropped from his hips and his jaw fell agape. "All the time, Cassie…all the time."

"You have a strange way of showing it."

Junior took a halting step toward her.

She waved the gun toward him.

He became aware that, as the water hole grew more shallow, he was about two steps away from revealing far more of himself than he was prepared to.

"Er…you keep your distance, Lucas." Now, she was unable to hold back the blush. She shook her head to bring her thinking back into focus. "It's time."

Suddenly, Junior realized what she was talking about. "Toss me my pants and turn around, Cassie McCully." She did, and he strode over and slipped them on. Soaked to the bone as he was, they at least afforded some degree of modesty. He ignored the shirt and boots.

"Are you decent?"

Junior laughed. "Never"

Cassie turned to him. "Well?" Her crystal-blue eyes locked on him. She shook her strawberry blond locks and flipped them back from her face. There was a certain provocativeness to her expression, a come-hither aura that couldn't fail to penetrate Junior's seeming cluelessness.

Junior grew serious. He knew very well what this was about. She'd been waiting nearly four years, and her patience had understandably worn thin. He leveled a gaze on her that penetrated her earthly skin like an arrow. Cupid's mind you. He saw her body tremble, and he gently but firmly grasped her arm. He took the revolver from her hand and placed it on the rock. He wiped a tear from the corner of her eye. Junior let out a soft but resolute sigh. "I love you, Cassie." He swallowed hard. "Will you marry me?"

Cassie's eyes grew wide. He did get it. Men might not be so thickheaded after all. "Yes...yes, Lucas. I will marry you."

The deep lingering kiss that followed was so impassioned...so very impassioned. Cassie trembled in Junior's embrace as the rippling muscles of his arms fully enveloped her.

Junior pulled away slightly and gently brought his fingers up under chin. He tilted her face up toward his as though better to see her eyes reflecting the stars. "I expect we should get married sooner than later, sweetheart." The words fell from his lips so smoothly as to surprise himself.

Cassie found herself totally flustered. There'd been far too many laters. The time for waiting was long past. Still, she hadn't expected this to be so easy. He'd rarely called her sweetheart, and that alone was enough to cause her to blush again. She then became aware that her hands were lustfully caressing his muscular bare chest and arms as if her fingers had a mind of their own. "I like sooner, Lucas," she cooed. Her lips parted and met his. Another deep kiss.

Junior took a deep breath and eased himself back from her. He picked up his shirt and slipped on his boots. He gave a little cough. "I...I think I'm done dipping in the creek."

"But the stars...the moon..."

He again gazed lovingly into her eyes. It was incredibly tough to pull himself away. "I definitely agree with sooner, Cassie." He led the way back up the path to the house.

As they crested the path, Junior saw his father setting on the gallery taking in the stars. He walked up. "Hi, Dad. Um... you're the first to hear. We're getting married."

Cassie blushed demurely.

Luke scanned the two. He smiled as he saw that Junior's clothes were wet and Cassie's were dry. "Well, congratulations. Shall I awaken your mother with the news?"

Junior didn't miss a beat. "I think it best that Cassie get on home. I figured to escort her."

"Seems the right thing to do for your future bride, son. See you bright and early." He turned his gaze to Cassie. "Congratulations, young lady. We're pleased to have you join our family." Luke nodded toward the horses.

Junior took the hint, and the couple mounted up and were soon out of sight.

Luke looked longingly after them. If he'd had to do everything over again, life could hardly have turned out any better. Justice...redemption...grit...love...it had all been good toward making Luke whom he was. Elisa was right, as she most always was. His grit and determination in successfully delivering justice and redemption across the rough hills and prairies of South Texas had enabled him to forge a life of significance. Through it all, he'd found love, ranched, and raised a family. He'd become a beacon, a light that leads the way. His was not a candle to be snuffed out, but a lantern that would burn far longer than a long time.

Luke adjusted his hat, stood slowly, and eased on over to the door. He paused and looked up over his shoulder, taking in the majesty of the twinkling stars blanketing the night sky. He stroked his mustache. "Legend?" he whispered. "Hrumph," he half-snorted. Luke shrugged resignedly, then ever-so-slowly shook his head and stepped inside. Elroy Stuart's ill-fated dime-store novel aside, Luke Dunn truly was a Nueces legend.

EPILOGUE

THE TEXAS NUECES Strip of the 1890s was still mostly a vast prairie of tall grasses and loamy sands that stretched as far as the eye could see and then some. Nueces is a Spanish word for nuts and refers to the many pecan trees found along the Nueces River. The grasses on the Strip often grew high enough to reach a horse's withers. The Nueces Strip, called "Wild Horse Desert" by some, reached south from the lazily flowing Nueces River all the way to the meandering Rio Grande along Texas' southern border. Its eastern extremity enjoyed the sea breezes wafting in off the Gulf of Mexico from Corpus Christi all the way to Brownsville. Nestled in hills at its northern extreme was the little town of Uvalde near Fort Inge. The semi-arid rolling terrain of Laredo with its nearby Fort McIntosh was generally regarded as the main outpost of the western Nueces Strip. It afforded an easy crossing of the Rio Grande. Corpus Christi founder Colonel Henry Kinney had the foresight to build a road from Corpus to Laredo and another to San Antonio. The roads were rough but serviceable except when soaked by rain. Notably in 1892, Corpus Christi unveiled a water system that would endure salt in the water, drought, a ruptured dam, and water rationing.

The Nueces Strip could be inhospitable six ways to Sunday. The similarities between natural and human dangers were often striking. Wild beasts competed with humans for territory, yet could often be said to have similar habits. Imagine the intense yellow eyes and coiled muscles of a mountain lion stalking a fawn. Patience. A light breeze stirs the thick fur along his back. The moment of attack must be exactly right. Only an infinitesimal twitch of the tip of his tail reveals the sinewy muscular tension in the beast. He dares not indulge a blink of eyes or lick of tongue. The fawn looks about innocently unaware. A leap, a snarl, and the mountain lion is fed. In its vast silence, the Nueces Strip spills the guts of reality and then sucks it all in.

Inhospitable and uninviting in many ways, the Nueces Strip nevertheless drew settlers like moths to a light bulb. Mottes or small clusters of live oak or mesquite offered occasional shade relief on the sunbaked prairies. The often-dry creek beds and arroyos eventually filled with rainwater or snowmelt and emptied into Nueces Bay and...farther to the east...Corpus Christi Bay. Flash flooding was an ongoing fear. Summers? Well, they tended to be hot and humid. Weather was pretty much whatever you wanted, if you waited long enough.

The plentiful and accessible longhorn could be called the "low-hanging-fruit" of the regional economy. They were a hardy breed that could withstand the South Texas heat, fend off disease-carrying pests, and carry just enough meat on their bones to make them reasonably profitable to raise. Originally imported from the Iberian Peninsula by early Spanish priests, the longhorns eventually escaped the mostly failing missionaries, proliferated, and roamed wild and free across the prairies. Millions of the beasts soon covered Texas and especially the excellent grazing lands of the Nueces Strip. They competed with the wild mustangs that had descended from horses also introduced by the Spaniards. Of course, there were the indigenous buffalo to the north—millions of those beasts as well. They were a staple of the Indian way of life. If you liked meat, and self-respecting folk did, the Texas prairies provided plenty of feed for all.

Despite the roughness of the frontier, the predations of savages and bandits, and the detritus of wars, the factor that would ultimately win Texas would be the family; the larger the better as children struggled to grow up in the face of all manner of lurking dangers. Families established the ranches and farms popping up not only throughout the eastern portions of the Nueces Strip but across Texas as a whole. The territory east of the 98th meridian that sliced through the very heart of Texas was fast becoming an economic juggernaut, and the Strip was no exception. Its economy was based on growing cotton and raising cattle and horses. Cotton was bundled and hauled to port for transport to markets in Louisiana and points east. While some cattle were shipped eastward by train, Corpus Christi would eventually become a hub for the beef industry.

To the west of the aforementioned 98th meridian had been the Comancheria. Tribes were pushed ever westward, as they were overcome by a deadly cocktail of violence, socioeconomic forces, and disease. Indigenous tribes of Comanche, Kiowa, Apache, and Ute rode ever-less-free across this vast region that extended into New Mexico and north into the Texas Panhandle.

The far reaches of the mostly untamed prairies of the strip beckoned to principled men like our protagonist Texas Ranger Captain Luke Dunn. The tall grasses and brush of the Nueces Strip were surely high enough to hide a growing population of lawbreakers. All this served to keep early Texans on this wild and often lawless frontier ever vigilant. It was easy to make the case for calling up companies of Texas Rangers to patrol the Nueces Strip, as lawbreakers took it upon themselves to go where the military found it politically undesirable. On the other hand, the legislators in the state capital in Austin were often unable to pull together the financial means to fund the necessary companies of Rangers.

What of the ultimate outcome of *Nueces Legend*? Texas Ranger Luke Dunn retired? Do lawmen ever truly retire? They sure don't fade into any contrived sunset. Luke Dunn has spent most of his adult years bringing outlaws to justice on the rough and tumble vastness of the Texas Nueces Strip. He fought savage Indians and rogue soldiers. He rode into danger, stopped bullets, and survived. With Elisa, the love of his life, he built Heaven's Gate Ranch and helped raise nine children. If we define a legendary person as extremely inspirational, famous, or notorious person, Texas Ranger Luke Dunn filled the role. As his days wound down, what of his legendary legacy?

Will Junior marry Cassie McCully? Can he carve a life from the Nueces Strip, as drought and a rough economy take their toll? Does Luke Dunn Jr. have the mental acuity, the raw courage, the skills that might lead him to take up his father's legacy?

The incredible durability of the western novel seems owed largely to the mystique that's wired into our DNA. It's at least partly because westerns dish up thrills, action, and adventure in a way that entertains while tapping directly into America's pioneer myths. Westerns have also been quite good at reflecting the times in which they were made. There's truly no other genre that reflects their era as well as the determination, courage, morality, and adventure in which they are set. Westerns are effectively a magnifying glass on America's heritage; the intersection of savagery and civilization. They trace our nation's shifting self-image from economic booms to crashes, morality to depravity, faith to hopelessness, but are invariably rooted in rugged individualism. The western is a classic trope of the triumph of good over evil.

Back in 1932, my poet/novelist cousin, Mary Maude Dunn

Wright (pseud. Lilith Lorraine), posed a question when writing the preface to Perilous Trail of Texas, the biography of her Texas Ranger and rancher father John "Red John" Dunn. The preface to the book asks: "Not in the spirit of judging their actions by artificial standards which in their day had no existence, but by asking ourselves if we were in their places, should we have acquitted ourselves as well, and by putting to ourselves the still more potent question: how well have we kept the birthright that thy have given us, how well have we safeguarded the liberties that they purchased through untold privations, how courageously are we meeting the problems that confront us today; in short when we stand before the tribunal of remote posterity, to whom shall the laurel be awarded...?" Y'all might think on that.

The old west represents the brave pioneering spirit of settlers that met the challenges and transcended mere survival to enable America to achieve exceptional growth. The settlement of the American west is replete with tales of leveraging freedom for individual achievement. I hope you'll agree that reliving our past—even through history-based fiction—often has the effect of pointing the way to an ever-brighter future. Might we be up to it?

ACKNOWLEDGMENTS

Authoring books simply doesn't happen in a vacuum. The author provides the creative talent and crafts the stories, but there's so much more that demands acknowledgment. There's lots of folks and places that contribute to my authoring endeavors. This seventh Tumbleweed Saga: Nueces Legend: The Final Mission takes place in 1885, roughly twenty years after the sixth Saga. The epic exploits of the legendary Texas Ranger Captain Luke Dunn have been at the core of this series of stories of the taming of the Nueces Strip. Dunn symbolizes the lawman image, the pursuer of law and order in the person of a hero, protector, knight-errant sort of character. But there's much more to him. He embodies grit, tenacity, rugged individualism, and bravery nuanced with a masculine vulnerability and a search for redeeming values. Luke can befriend a savage Comanche chief yet embody the vulnerability to hold the love of a beautiful frontier woman. Luke Dunn epitomizes the freedom of America's western frontier and represents a final bastion of honor in America. Hopefully, readers will find this final contribution to the Sagas an adventure worthy of their time and emotional involvement. Fear not, as Nueces Legend does sew up the politically delicate loose ends from my award-winning sixth Tumbleweed Saga, Nueces Truth: Texans Face War's Realities.

I've been blessed with many friends and family who have supported my writings. My wife Carolyn's reviews and encouragement were a huge help along with very important tech support from our sons Mike and Matt. Other supporters have included Cara Miller, Jim May, Ernie Angell, Chris Haug, and my dear cousins Johnny Dunn, Jim & Cindy Holmgreen, Mary Kureska, Joseph Meaney, and Eddie and Nancy Thornton. Many more friends have contributed support at some level to the creation and publication of Nueces Legend: The Final Mission be it encouragement or advice.

Naturally, I am major grateful to the great folks at Wolfpack Publishing. The team they bring to publishing is first rate from promotion to editing, cover design, and the myriad tasks that lead to successful book sales.

It's only right to acknowledge my ancestors who were actual settlers of the south Texas frontier. In addition to inspiring me, they provided a quite helpful true-to-life framework as to the life and times on the Texas Nueces Strip. It was appropriate to weave them into the tapestry of the Tumbleweed Sagas. Matthew Dunn (1815-1855) was the first brother to arrive in 1845, serving as a sutler to General Zachary Taylor and managed Corpus Christi founder Colonel Kinney's fighting cocks. Peter Dunn (1807-1890) immigrated from Ireland in 1850 and established a blacksmith shop in Corpus Christi; John Dunn (1803-1889) ranched and grew thousands of acres of cotton that he did in fact haul to Matamoros during the war; Lawrence Dunn (1837-1864) fought and died with Captain Ware's Confederate cavalry; and my great-great-grandfather Nicholas Dunn (1835-1912) was a rancher, drover, livestock speculator, and Comanche fighter of some repute. My cousin John Beamond "Red John" Dunn (1851-1940) served as a Texas Ranger in the 1880s, subsequently joined a "vigilance committee," was a farmer and merchant, and curated a museum of military weapons displayed to this day in the Corpus Christi Museum of Science & History. Then, there was John Hillard Dunn (1883-1958) whose personal narrative about his family and his own adventures drove my pursuit of my Texas family and inspired my own writings. Such real-life characters coupled with actual events have served to reinforce the historical setting for the Tumbleweed Sagas.

Most of my authoring has occurred in my office as decorated to channel my inner Texan, but my creative juices have often been inspired and imagination stoked in cafés and coffee houses across America. My favorites were Hester's Café & Coffee Bar in Corpus Christi, TX; Nueces Café in Robstown, TX; Java Ranch Espresso Bar & Café in Fredericksburg, TX; PAX Coffee & Goods in Kerrville, TX; Ragged Edge Coffee House and Bantam Coffee Roasters in Gettysburg, PA; 1889 Coffee House in Helena, MT; Dunn Brothers Coffee in Rapid City, SD; Postmasters Coffee & Bakery and Brio Coffeehouse in Waynesboro, PA; Birdie's Café and American Ice Co Café in Westminster, MD; Deja Brew Coffee House, New Oxford, PA and Deja Brew at Miney Branch, Carroll Valley, PA; Baltimore Coffee & Tea Co., Frederick Coffee Company & Café, and Dublin Roasters in Frederick, MD: Qualle Café and Grounded Coffee & Bakery, Cherokee, NC; Palace Café, Amarillo, TX; and Unto Others Café, Lamar, CO. I must admit to also frequenting a few Dunkin Donuts and Starbucks around our fine nation. The décors and easy listening music in these fine establishments combined with savory cups of coffee tended to set me in the right creative frame of mind.

Last but far from least, I am especially thankful for the many folks who have read and enjoyed my books.

I do believe it's important to acknowledge how the old west represents the brave pioneering spirit of settlers that met the challenges and transcended mere survival to enable America to achieve exceptional growth. The settlement of the American west is replete with tales of leveraging freedom for individual achievement. I hope you'll agree that reliving our past—even through history-based fiction—often has the effect of pointing the way to an ever-brighter future. Might we be up to it? I hope that the inspiration I've drawn from my having walked the very earth my characters have trodden coupled with my extensive historical research will enable readers to fully experience the grit, adventure, and passion of my characters while sensing aromas of gunsmoke, trail dust, saddle leather, and bluebonnets.

Thanks to all of you.

A LOOK AT BOOK EIGHT
LONE STAR VIGILANTE

The Nueces Strip is no place for a young Texas Ranger to earn his stripes.

Lucas Dunn, Jr. has spent his life in the shadow of a legend—but now the badge is his, and the frontier wastes no time testing his mettle. Lawbreakers still run thick through the brush country, but one ghost stands out: a lone vigilante bushwhacking from the shadows with an 1895 Winchester and a score to settle.

The bodies pile up. The clues don't. And Junior's only lead is a name whispered on dying lips. Family ties twist the trail, and the deeper he rides, the darker the truth becomes. Around every bend wait desperate killers, ruthless rustlers, and powerful men with blood on their hands. Every step toward justice feels like a step closer to a bullet.

With a fast gun, a loyal few at his side, and his father's grit running through his veins, Junior fights to bring order to a land that knows nothing but chaos.

Lone Star Vigilante is a tale of law, vengeance, and legacy in the untamed borderlands of South Texas. Saddle up and ride into the fire.

AVAILABLE JUNE 2025

ABOUT THE AUTHOR

 Award-winning author Mark Greathouse's love for the Western genre draws upon his deep family roots and love of the outdoors, honed from teen years spent hiking the Appalachian Trail and family travels across America's frontier. He hopes his work reveals his passion for America's western history.

A member of Western Writers of America and the Wild West History Association, Mark also contributes articles on the history of America's west to Western-themed magazines. He was recognized as a 2024 Finalist in the Western genre by the American Literary Book Awards for his sixth Tumbleweed Saga, *Nueces Truth: Texans Face War's Realities*.

Mark began writing full time after a successful career as a business executive and later as an entrepreneurial investor and advisor. His service as president of several business and community nonprofits led to their extraordinary growth. He holds a BA in English and MBA in marketing.

Mark also donates time and books annually to support wounded military warriors. He was a Boy Scout leader (Eagle Scout) and served on a local school board earlier in life.